Black Noir

Black Noir

Mystery, Crime and
Suspense Stories by African-
American Writers

Edited by
Otto Penzler

PEGASUS BOOKS
NEW YORK

Pegasus Books LLC
80 Broad Street, 5th Floor
New York, NY 10004

Collection copyright © 2009 by Otto Penzler

First Pegasus Books edition 2009

Introduction copyright © 2009 by Otto Penzler

"Corollary" copyright © 1948 by Hughes Allison. First published in
Ellery Queen's Mystery Magazine, July 1948.
"The Canasta Club" copyright © 2000 by Eleanor Taylor Bland. First
published in *The World's Finest Mystery and Crime Stories,* 2000.
"Oprah's Song" copyright © 2009 by Robert Greer
"The First Rule Is" copyright © 2009 by Gar Anthony Haywood
"Strictly Business" copyright © 1942 by Chester Himes. Reprinted by
permission of Da Capo/Thunder's Mouth, a member of
Perseus Book Group.
"Old Boys, Old Girls" copyright © 2005 by Edward P. Jones. First published
in *The New Yorker,* May 3, 2005.
"Black Dog" copyright © 1997 by Walter Mosley. Reprinted by permission of
W. W. Norton & Company, Inc. First published in *Always Outnumbered,
Always Outgunned,* 1997.
"On Saturday the Siren Sounds at Noon" copyright © 1943; renewed in 1969
by Ann Petry. Reprinted by permission of Rossell & Volkening as agents
for the author. First published in *The Crisis,* December 1943.
"House of Tears" copyright © 2006 by Gary Phillips; revised in 2008.
First published in *Murdaland #1,* September 2006; revised version first
published in this volume.
"I'll Be Doggone" copyright © 1998 by Paula L. Woods. First published in
Mary Higgins Clark Mystery Magazine, Summer 1998.

Library of Congress Cataloging-in-Publication Data is available.

Hardcover ISBN: 978-1-60598-039-3
Trade Paperback ISBN: 978-1-60598-057-7

10 9 8 7 8 6 5 4 3 2 1

Interior design by Maria Fernandez

Printed in the United States of America
Distributed by W. W. Norton & Company, Inc.

For Michael Malone
A true southern gentleman and a true friend

Contents

Introduction

Otto Penzler

Mystery fiction written by black authors is, not surprisingly, often very different from work in that broadly defined genre written by white writers. The early novels and short stories, in particular, tended to show the detective in a reasonably insular community, trying to solve crimes with black victims and committed, in all likelihood, by black villains. There was little reliance on the outside (mainly white) world to administer justice.

A nation's government, in order for detective stories to flourish, needs to be a relatively democratic one. Under dictatorial and repressive regimes, it is the police themselves who are regarded by much of the citizenry as villainous, not as the source of relief from fear and injustice. The police, or their closely allied counterparts, militia, are in the employ of governments that use them to suppress the freedom of the men and women under their control. To speak out against emperors, czars, dictators, or monarchs means a swift trip to prison or the gallows, and it is the police who arrest the dissidents and bring them to their fate. As the enemy, then, it

is hardly likely that fiction would be created in which these figures would serve as the righteous heroes who would protect
society from murderers, robbers, and other criminals.

For mystery fiction to attain any degree of popularity, the culture in which it could be created requires the same elements upon
which all forms of literary entertainment depend. A country has
to be fairly prosperous, allowing a significant portion of the pop-
ulation to have leisure time. Edgar Allan Poe's invention of the
first genuine detective story, "The Murders in the Rue Morgue,"
in 1841, approximately coincided with the start of the industrial
revolution, beginning the process of changing America from a
largely agrarian society to a manufacturing one. Gone for many
thousands of people were the endless hours required to run a
subsistence-level farm, replaced by increased income and the
commensurate free time that allowed for the pursuit of relaxation
and entertainment. As schools and literacy increased, so did the
number of books and magazines that fed a newly created demand.
England, a mighty colonial power, had been increasing the
national wealth for many years, much of it trickling down to its
populace. After France recovered from the excesses of its revolution, the French, too, enjoyed relative political freedom and a
robust economy.

Sadly, little of this newly found social and political freedom
affected the majority of Africans. On the continent of their
homeland, there was virtually no tradition of the written word.
As millions of Africans were uprooted to becomes slaves in
America, the Caribbean, and many other parts of the world, there
was little opportunity to learn to read or write; the very concept
of creating literature was absurd in the context of the lives they
lived. Even after British and American slaves were freed, their lack
of educational opportunities, in confluence with an absence of a

literary history, were not conducive to an establishment of any meaningful body of work.

As the twentieth century approached, society, slowly and reluctantly, began to shift in small ways as modest numbers of blacks entered such mainstream elements of the culture as academia, law, medicine, science, and the arts. Fiction by black writers, often but not exclusively, produced for magazines run by and for blacks, became more abundant. It tended to portray life in black communities that were theoretically part of America but in fact were separated from white America. Stories were frequently set in the black ghettoes or the black middle class section of a city, often in dialect that was clearly designed to appeal to core black readers. While many of these stories featured blacks as the victims of institutionalized racism, a large number of stories and novels by black writers of the time were highly sentimental romances—just as were those written by white writers.

Fiction is a mirror of society. While individual works may be filtered through the prejudices and limitations of their authors, the entire oeuvre of a given period of time, compared or contrasted with a different time, will accurately illustrate changes of attitude and practice. The black American experience following World War I reflected a greater level of integration into the rest of society, particularly in the north. The economic growth of the first three decades of the twentieth century affected Americans of all socioeconomic levels. The rich got richer while the poor got less poor. Mandatory schooling improved literacy rates, so more people, black and white, were able to read and write, so they did. Fiction magazines flooded newsstands, millions being sold every month, and, while no type of fiction was ignored, none was more eagerly consumed than detective stories, notably in the pulps, most of which were written by white writers, about white characters, and read by white readers.

There were exceptions, of course. W. Adolphe Roberts, a black Caribbean author, wrote three mystery novels, beginning with *The Haunting Hand* in 1926, and some adventure fiction that bumped against the edges of the genre. Rudolph Fisher wrote an important Harlem renaissance detective novel, *The Conjure Man Dies,* in 1932, and one of the most significant figures in the development of the black crime and mystery story, Chester Himes, wrote his first story in 1933, beginning a career that would span more than four decades.

The years following World War II marked the continuation of the absorption of black Americans into a more integrated society, a process dramatically accelerated during the civil rights movement that began in earnest during the 1960s.

While many novels and short stories by black Americans had been published during the twentieth century, very few were detective novels. Many blacks saw the police as adversaries whose job it was to maintain the social status quo by beating them into submission. Therefore, just as nondemocratic societies failed to produce detective fiction, so did the black community, though a high percentage of the fiction created by these authors contained elements of crime fiction. Alcoholism, drug addiction, and violence, with black characters both as the perpetrators and as the victims, were frequently found in the works of Richard Wright, James Baldwin, Clarence Cooper Jr., and others, but it has not been until the past twenty years or so that there has been a regular flow of detective stories by black writers.

Although not the first, certainly the opener of the way was Walter Mosley. The debut of Easy Rawlins in *Devil in a Blue Dress* (1990) marked the beginning of the crossover era in which white readers didn't need to feel virtuously liberal for reading a black mystery writer; they could read it for the pure pleasure of reading an excellent novel about fascinating, original characters, bringing to the experience the same incentive they had had for years when reading books by white writers with white characters: entertainment. The books in the Rawlins series have gone on to enjoy tremendous success, both critically and with frequent appearances on the best-seller list. Mosley has indicated his intention to abandon the character, but his other work has also found a large readership, especially his mystery and crime fiction. After Mosley, readers discovered the work of such black writers as Barbara Neeley, Hugh Holton, Gar Anthony Haywood (whose first novels actually preceded those by Mosley), Paula L. Woods, Robert Greer, Gary Phillips, Eleanor Taylor Bland, and the British writer Mike Phillips, among others.

Many of the books and stories by contemporary black writers continue to examine the black experience in a society in which it remains a minority, focusing on the ways in which it is different and separate from its fellow citizens. In this collection, for instance, Rudolph Fisher's "John Archer's Nose" and Robert Greer's "Oprah's Song" could never be made into a film with white actors. Others have little or no relation to race. The thieves in Gary Phillips's story "House of Tears" could just as easily be white and the story would be unchanged. The police in Paula L. Woods's story "I'll Be Doggone" could be Latin or Indian, black or white, and it wouldn't make a bit of difference. There is much to be said for a tale that emphasizes and highlights the colorful differences between one group and another. There is an equally valid point to telling a story in which differences between people vanish, or at least have little significance. Ultimately, what should matter is whether the story is a good one. On the pages that follow, you will find stories that transcend race and genre to fulfill their primary purpose—to inform and entertain.

EDWARD PAUL JONES (1951–) was raised in Washington, D.C., and educated at Holy Cross in Massachusetts and then received an M.F.A. from the University of Virginia. After teaching creative writing, he took a job as a proofreader and rewriter at *Tax Notes*, a publication devoted to changes in tax laws. It was during this time that he began writing short fiction, which was eventually collected in his first book, *Lost in the City*, which was short-listed for the National Book Award and won the Pen/Hemingway Award but failed to sell more than 5,000 copies.

He then spent twelve years researching and writing *The Known World* (2003), a novel set in pre–Civil War Virginia that focused on the free blacks who owned slaves. It was also nominated for a National Book Award and won both the Pulitzer Prize and the 2005 International IMPAC Dublin Literary Award. The following year, he was given a MacArthur Fellowship. In 2006, Jones published his third book, *All Aunt Hagar's Children*, another short story collection about African-American working-class people in Washington.

Jones prefers a simple life, living conservatively as he remembers when he couldn't find a job after graduating college. He was on his way to live with his sister in Brooklyn, New York, when he learned that his first story had been bought by *Essence* magazine.

"Old Boys, Old Girls" was first published in the May 3, 2004, issue of *The New Yorker*; it was chosen for both *Best American Short Stories* and *Best American Mystery Stories 2005*.

Old Boys, Old Girls

Edward P. Jones

They caught him after he had killed the
second man. The law would never connect him to the first
murder. So the victim—a stocky fellow Caesar Matthews shot in
a Northeast alley only two blocks from the home of the guy's parents, a man who died over a woman who was actually in love with
a third man—was destined to lie in his grave without anyone officially paying for what had happened to him. It was almost as if,
at least on the books the law kept, Caesar had got away with a
free killing.

Seven months after he stabbed the second man—a twenty-
two-year-old with prematurely gray hair who had ventured out of
Southeast for only the sixth time in his life—Caesar was tried for
murder in the second degree. During much of the trial, he
remembered the name only of the first dead man—Percy, or
"Golden Boy," Weymouth—and not the second, Antwoine Stoddard, to whom everyone kept referring during the proceedings.
The world had done things to Caesar since he'd left his father's

house for good at sixteen, nearly fourteen years ago, but he had done far more to himself.

So at trial, with the weight of all the harm done to him and because he had hidden for months in one shit hole after another, he was not always himself and thought many times that he was actually there for killing Golden Boy, the first dead man. He was not insane, but he was three doors from it, which was how an old girlfriend, Yvonne Miller, would now and again playfully refer to his behavior. Who the fuck is this Antwoine bitch? Caesar sometimes thought during the trial. And where is Percy? It was only when the judge sentenced him to seven years in Lorton, D.C.'s prison in Virginia, that matters became somewhat clear again, and in those last moments before they took him away he saw Antwoine spread out on the ground outside the Prime Property night club, blood spurting out of his chest like oil from a bountiful well. Caesar remembered it all: sitting on the sidewalk, the liquor spinning his brain, his friends begging him to run, the club's music flooding out of the open door and going *thumpety-thump-thump* against his head. He sat a few feet from Antwoine, and would have killed again for a cigarette. "That's you, baby, so very near insanity it can touch you," said Yvonne, who believed in unhappiness and who thought happiness was the greatest trick God had invented. Yvonne Miller would be waiting for Caesar at the end of the line.

He came to Lorton with a ready-made reputation, since Multrey Wilson and Tony Cathedral—first-degree murderers both, and destined to die there—knew him from his Northwest and Northeast days. They were about as big as you could get in Lorton at that time (the guards called Lorton the House of Multrey and Cathedral), and they let everyone know that Caesar was good

4

people, "a protected body," with no danger of having his biscuits or his butt taken.

A little less than a week after Caesar arrived, Cathedral asked him how he liked his cellmate. Caesar had never been to prison but had spent five days in the D.C. jail, not counting the time there before and during the trial. They were side by side at dinner, and neither man looked at the other. Multrey sat across from them. Cathedral was done eating in three minutes, but Caesar always took a long time to eat. His mother had raised him to chew his food thoroughly. "You wanna be a old man livin on oatmeal?" "I love oatmeal, Mama." "Tell me that when you have to eat it every day till you die."

"He all right, I guess," Caesar said of his cellmate, with whom he had shared fewer than a thousand words. Caesar's mother had died before she saw what her son became.

"You got the bunk you want, the right bed?" Multrey said. He was sitting beside one of his two "women," the one he had turned out most recently. "She" was picking at her food, something Multrey had already warned her about. The woman had a family—a wife and three children—but they would not visit. Caesar would never have visitors, either.

"It's all right." Caesar had taken the top bunk, as the cellmate had already made the bottom his home. A miniature plastic panda from his youngest child dangled on a string hung from one of the metal bedposts. "Bottom, top, it's all the same ship."

Cathedral leaned into him, picking chicken out of his teeth with an inch-long fingernail sharpened to a point. "Listen, man, even if you like the top bunk, you fuck him up for the bottom just cause you gotta let him know who rules. You let him know that you will stab him through his motherfuckin heart and then turn around and eat your supper, cludin the dessert." Cathedral straightened up. "Caes, you gon be here a few days, so you can't let nobody fuck with your humanity."

He went back to the cell and told Pancho Morrison that he wanted the bottom bunk, couldn't sleep well at the top.

"Too bad," Pancho said. He was lying down, reading a book published by the Jehovah's Witnesses. He wasn't a Witness, but he was curious.

Caesar grabbed the book and flung it at the bars, and the bulk of it slid through an inch or so and dropped to the floor. He kicked Pancho in the side, and before he could pull his leg back for a second kick Pancho took the foot in both hands, twisted it, and threw him against the wall. Then Pancho was up, and they fought for nearly an hour before two guards, who had been watching the whole time, came in and beat them about the head. "Show's over! Show's over!" one kept saying.

They attended to themselves in silence in the cell, and with the same silence they flung themselves at each other the next day after dinner. They were virtually the same size, and though Caesar came to battle with more muscle, Pancho had more heart. Cathedral had told Caesar that morning that Pancho had lived on practically nothing but heroin for the three years before Lorton, so whatever fighting dog was in him could be pounded out in little or no time. It took three days. Pancho was the father of five children, and each time he swung he did so with the memory of all five and what he had done to them over those three addicted years. He wanted to return to them and try to make amends, and he realized on the morning of the third day that he would not be able to do that if Caesar killed him. So fourteen minutes into the fight he sank to the floor after Caesar hammered him in the gut. And though he could have got up he stayed there, silent and still. The two guards laughed. The daughter who had given Pancho the panda was nine years old and had been raised by her mother as a Catholic.

That night, before the place went dark, Caesar lay on the bottom bunk and looked over at pictures of Pancho's children, which Pancho had taped on the opposite wall. He knew he would have to decide if he wanted Pancho just to move the photographs or to put them away altogether. All the children had toothy smiles. The two youngest stood, in separate pictures, outdoors in their First Communion clothes. Caesar himself had been a father for two years. A girl he had met at an F Street club in Northwest had told him he was the father of her son, and for a time he had believed her. Then the boy started growing big ears that Caesar thought didn't belong to anyone in his family, and so after he had slapped the girl a few times a week before the child's second birthday she confessed that the child belonged to "my first love." "Your first love is always with you," she said, sounding forever like a television addict who had never read a book. As Caesar prepared to leave, she asked him, "You want back all the toys and things you gave him?" The child, as if used to their fighting, had slept through this last encounter on the couch, part of a living-room suite that they were paying for on time. Caesar said nothing more and didn't think about his 18k.-gold cigarette lighter until he was eight blocks away. The girl pawned the thing and got enough to pay off the furniture bill.

Caesar and Pancho worked in the laundry, and Caesar could look across the noisy room with all the lint swirling about and see Pancho sorting dirty pieces into bins. Then he would push uniform bins to the left and everything else to the right. Pancho had been doing that for three years. The job he got after he left Lorton was as a gofer at construction sites. No laundry in the outside world wanted him. Over the next two weeks, as Caesar watched

Pancho at his job, his back always to him, he considered what he should do next. He wasn't into fucking men, so that was out. He still had not decided what he wanted done about the photographs on the cell wall. One day at the end of those two weeks, Caesar saw the light above Pancho's head flickering and Pancho raised his head and looked for a long time at it, as if thinking that the answer to all his problems lay in fixing that one light. Caesar decided then to let the pictures remain on the wall.

Three years later, they let Pancho go. The two men had mostly stayed at a distance from each other, but toward the end they had been talking, sharing plans about a life beyond Lorton. The relationship had reached the point where Caesar was saddened to see the children's photographs come off the wall. Pancho pulled off the last taped picture and the wall was suddenly empty in a most forlorn way. Caesar knew the names of all the children. Pancho gave him a rabbit's foot that one of his children had given him. It was the way among all those men that when a good-luck piece had run out of juice it was given away with the hope that new ownership would renew its strength. The rabbit's foot had lost its electricity months before Pancho's release. Caesar's only good-fortune piece was a key chain made in Peru; it had been sweet for a bank robber in the next cell for nearly two years until that man's daughter, walking home from third grade, was abducted and killed.

One day after Pancho left, they brought in a thief and three-time rapist of elderly women. He nodded to Caesar and told him that he was Watson Rainey and went about making a home for himself in the cell, finally plugging in a tiny lamp with a green shade which he placed on the metal shelf jutting from the wall. Then he climbed onto the top bunk he had made up and lay down. His name was all the wordplay he had given Caesar, who had been smoking on the bottom bunk throughout Rainey's efforts to make a nest. Caesar waited ten minutes and then stood and pulled the lamp's cord out of the wall socket and grabbed Rainey with one hand and threw him to the floor. He crushed the lamp into Rainey's face. He choked him with the cord. "You come into my house and show me no respect!" Caesar shouted. The only sound Rainey could manage was a gurgling that bubbled up from his mangled mouth. There were no witnesses except for an old man across the way, who would occasionally glance over at the two when he wasn't reading his Bible. It was over and done with in four minutes. When Rainey came to, he found everything he owned piled in the corner, soggy with piss. And Caesar was again on the top bunk.

They would live in that cell together until Caesar was released, four years later. Rainey tried never to be in the house during waking hours; if he was there when Caesar came in, he would leave. Rainey's name spoken by him that first day were all the words that would ever pass between the two men.

A week or so after Rainey got there, Caesar bought from Multrey a calendar that was three years old. It was large and had no markings of any sort, as pristine as the day it was made. "You know this one ain't the year we in right now," Multrey said as one of his women took a quarter from Caesar and dropped it in her purse. Caesar said, "It'll do." Multrey prized the calendar for one thing: its top half had a photograph of a naked woman of indeterminate race sitting on a stool, her legs wide open, her pussy aimed dead at whoever was standing right in front of her. It had been Multrey's good-luck piece, but the luck was dead. Multrey remembered what the calendar had done for him and he told his woman to give Caesar his money back, lest any new good-fortune piece turn sour on him.

The calendar's bottom half had the days of the year. That day, the first Monday in June, Caesar drew in the box that was January 1st a line that went from the upper left-hand corner down to the bottom right-hand corner. The next day, a June Tuesday, he made a line in the January 2nd box that also ran in the same direction. And so it went. When the calendar had all such lines in all the boxes, it was the next June. Then Caesar, in that January 1st box, made a line that formed an X with the first line. And so it was for another year. The third year saw horizontal marks that sliced the boxes in half. The fourth year had vertical lines down the centers of the boxes.

This was the only calendar Caesar had in Lorton. That very first Monday, he taped the calendar over the area where the pictures of Pancho's children had been. There was still a good deal of empty space left, but he didn't do anything about it, and Rainey knew he couldn't do anything, either.

The calendar did right by Caesar until near the end of his fifth year in Lorton, when he began to feel that its juice was drying up. But he kept it there to mark off the days and, too, the naked woman never closed her legs to him.

In that fifth year, someone murdered Multrey as he showered. The killers—it had to be more than one for a man like Multrey—were never found. The Multrey woman who picked at her food had felt herself caring for a recent arrival who was five years younger than her, a part-time deacon who had killed a Southwest bartender for calling the deacon's wife "a woman without one fuckin brain cell." The story of that killing—the bartender was dropped head first from the roof of a ten-story building—became legend, and in Lorton men referred to the dead bartender as "the Flat-Head Insulter" and the killer became known as "the Righteous Desulter."

The Desulter, wanting Multrey's lady, had hired people to butcher him. It had always been the duty of the lady who hated food to watch out for Multrey as he showered, but she had stepped away that day, just as she had been instructed to by the Desulter.

In another time, Cathedral and Caesar would have had enough of everything—from muscle to influence—to demand that someone give up the killers, but the prison was filling up with younger men who did not care what those two had been once upon a time. Also, Cathedral had already had two visits from the man he had killed in Northwest. Each time, the man had first stood before the bars of Cathedral's cell. Then he held one of the bars and opened the door inward, like some wooden door on a person's house. The dead man standing there would have been sufficient to unwrap anyone, but matters were compounded when Cathedral saw a door that for years had slid sideways now open in an impossible fashion. The man stood silent before Cathedral, and when he left he shut the door gently, as if there were sleeping children in the cell. So Cathedral didn't have a full mind, and Multrey was never avenged.

There was an armed-robbery man in the place, a tattooer with homemade inks and needles. He made a good living painting on both muscled and frail bodies the names of children; the Devil in full regalia with a pitchfork dripping with blood; the words "Mother" or "Mother Forever" surrounded by red roses and angels who looked sad, because when it came to drawing happy angels the tattoo man had no skills. One pickpocket had had a picture of his father tattooed in the middle of his chest; above the father's head, in medieval lettering, were the words "Rotting in Hell," with the letter "H" done in fiery yellow and red. The tattoo guy had told Caesar that he had skin worthy of "a painter's best canvas," that he could give Caesar a tattoo "God would envy." Caesar had always told him no, but then he awoke one snowy night in March of his sixth year and realized that it was his mother's birthday. He did not know what day of the week it was, but the voice that talked to him had the authority of a million loving mothers. He had long ago forgotten his own birthday, had not even bothered to ask someone in prison records to look it up.

There had never been anyone or anything he wanted commemorated on his body. Maybe it would have been Carol, his first girlfriend twenty years ago, before the retarded girl entered their lives. He had played with the notion of having the name of the boy he thought was his put over his heart, but the lie had come to light before that could happen. And before the boy there had been Yvonne, with whom he had lived for an extraordinary time in Northeast. He would have put Yvonne's name over his heart, but she went off to work one day and never came back. He looked for her for three months, and then just assumed that she had been killed somewhere and dumped in a place only animals knew about. Yvonne was indeed dead, and she would be waiting for him at the end of the line, though she did not know that was what she was doing. "You can always trust unhappiness," Yvonne had once said, sitting in the dark on the couch, her cigarette burned down to the filter. "His face never changes. But happiness is slick, can't be trusted. It has a thousand faces, Caes, all of them just ready to reform into unhappiness once it has you in its clutches."

So Caesar had the words "Mother Forever" tattooed on his left bicep. Knowing that more letters meant a higher payment of cigarettes or money or candy, the tattoo fellow had dissuaded him from having just plain "Mother." "How many hours you think she spent in labor?" he asked Caesar. "Just to give you life." The job took five hours over two days, during a snowstorm. Caesar said no to angels, knowing the man's ability with happy ones, and had the words done in blue letters encased in red roses. The man worked from the words printed on a piece of paper that Caesar had given him, because he was also a bad speller.

The snow stopped on the third day and, strangely, it took only another three days for the two feet of mess to melt, for with the end of the storm came a heat wave. The tattoo man, a good friend of the Righteous Desulter, would tell Caesar in late April that what happened to him was his own fault, that he had not taken care of himself as he had been instructed to do. "And the heat ain't helped you neither." On the night of March 31st, five days after the tattoo had been put on, Caesar woke in the night with a pounding in his left arm. He couldn't return to sleep so he sat on the edge of his bunk until morning, when he saw that the "e"s in "Mother Forever" had blistered, as if someone had taken a match to them.

He went to the tattoo man, who first told him not to worry, then patted the "e"s with peroxide that he warmed in a spoon with a match. Within two days, the "e"s seemed to just melt away, each dissolving into an ugly pile at the base of the tattoo. After a week, the diseased "e"s began spreading their work to the other letters and Caesar couldn't move his arm without pain. He went to the infirmary. They gave him aspirin and Band-Aided the tattoo. He was back the next day, the day the doctor was there.

He spent four days in D.C. General Hospital, his first trip back to Washington since a court appearance more than three years before. His entire body was paralyzed for two days, and one nurse confided to him the day he left that he had been near death. In the end, after the infection had done its work, there was not much left of the tattoo except an "o" and an "r," which were so deformed they could never pass for English, and a few roses that looked more like red mud. When he returned to prison, the tattoo man offered to give back the cigarettes and the money, but Caesar never gave him an answer, leading the man to think that he should watch his back. What happened to Caesar's tattoo and to Caesar was bad advertising, and soon the fellow had no customers at all.

Something had died in the arm and the shoulder, and Caesar was never again able to raise the arm more than thirty-five degrees. He had no enemies, but still he told no one about his debilitation. For the next few months he tried to stay out of everyone's way, knowing that he was far more vulnerable than he had been before the tattoo. Alone in the cell, with no one watching across the way, he exercised the arm, but by November he knew at last he would not be the same again. He tried to bully Rainey Watson as much as he could to continue the façade that he was still who he had been. And he tried to spend more time with Cathedral.

But the man Cathedral had killed had become a far more constant visitor. The dead man, a young bachelor who had been Cathedral's next-door neighbor, never spoke. He just opened Cathedral's cell door inward and went about doing things as if the cell were a family home—straightening wall pictures that only Cathedral could see, turning down the gas on the stove, testing the shower water to make sure that it was not too hot, tucking children into bed. Cathedral watched silently.

Caesar went to Cathedral's cell one day in mid-December, six months before they freed him. He found his friend sitting on the bottom bunk, his hands clamped over his knees. He was still outside the cell when Cathedral said, "Caes, you tell me why God would be so stupid to create mosquitoes. I mean, what good are the damn things? What's their function?" Caesar laughed, thinking it was a joke, and he had started to offer something when

Cathedral looked over at him with a devastatingly serious gaze and said, "What we need is a new God. Somebody who knows what the fuck he's doing." Cathedral was not smiling. He returned to staring at the wall across from him. "What's with creatin bats? I mean, yes, they eat insects, but why create those insects to begin with? You see what I mean? Creatin a problem and then havin to create somethin to take care of the problem. And then comin up with somethin for that second problem. Man oh man!" Caesar slowly began moving away from Cathedral's cell. He had seen this many times before. It could not be cured even by great love. It sometimes pulled down a loved one. "And roaches. Every human bein in the world would have the sense not to create roaches. What's their function, Caes? I tell you, we need a new God, and I'm ready to cast my vote right now. Roaches and rats and chinches. God was out of his fuckin mind that week. Six wasted days, cept for the human part and some of the animals. And then partyin on the seventh day like he done us a big favor. The nerve of that motherfucker. And all your pigeons and squirrels. Don't forget them. I mean really."

In late January, they took Cathedral somewhere and then brought him back after a week. He returned to his campaign for a new God in February. A ritual began that would continue until Caesar left: determine that Cathedral was a menace to himself, take him away, bring him back, then take him away when he started campaigning again for another God.

There was now nothing for Caesar to do except try to coast to the end on a reputation that was far less than it had been in his first years at Lorton. He could only hope that he had built up enough good will among men who had better reputations and arms that worked a hundred per cent.

In early April, he received a large manila envelope from his attorney. The lawyer's letter was brief. "I did not tell them where you are," he wrote. "They may have learned from someone that I was your attorney. Take care." There were two separate letters in sealed envelopes from his brother and sister, each addressed to "My Brother Caesar." Dead people come back alive, Caesar thought many times before he finally read the letters, after almost a week. He expected an announcement about the death of his father, but he was hardly mentioned. Caesar's younger brother went on for five pages with a history of what had happened to the family since Caesar had left their lives. He ended by saying, "Maybe I should have been a better brother." There were three pictures as well, one of his brother and his bride on their wedding day, and one showing Caesar's sister, her husband, and their two children, a girl of four or so and a boy of about two. The third picture had the girl sitting on a couch beside the boy, who was in Caesar's father's lap, looking with interest off to the left, as if whatever was there were more important than having his picture taken. Caesar looked at the image of his father—a man on the verge of becoming old. His sister's letter had even less in it than the lawyer's: "Write to me, or call me collect, whatever is best for you, dear one. Call even if you are on the other side of the world. For every step you take to get to me, I will walk a mile toward you."

He had an enormous yearning at first, but after two weeks he tore everything up and threw it all away. He would be glad he had done this as he stumbled, hurt and confused, out of his sister's car less than half a year later. The girl and the boy would be in the back seat, the girl wearing a red dress and black shoes, and the boy in blue pants and a T-shirt with a cartoon figure on the front. The boy would have fallen asleep, but the girl would say, "Nighty-night, Uncle," which she had been calling him all that evening.

An ex-offenders' group, the Light at the End of the Tunnel, helped him to get a room and a job washing dishes and busing tables at a restaurant on F Street. The room was in a three-story building in the middle of the 900 block of N Street, Northwest, a building that, in the days when white people lived there, had had two apartments of eight rooms or so on each floor. Now the first-floor apartments were uninhabitable and had been pad-locked for years. On the two other floors, each large apartment had been divided into five rented rooms, which went for twenty to thirty dollars a week, depending on the size and the view. Caesar's was small, twenty dollars, and had half the space of his cell at Lorton. The word that came to him for the butchered, once luxurious apartments was "warren." The roomers in each of the cut-up apartments shared two bathrooms and one nice-sized kitchen, which was a pathetic place because of its dinginess and its fifty-watt bulb, and because many of the appliances were old or undependable or both. Caesar's narrow room was at the front, facing N Street. On his side of the hall were two other rooms, the one next to his housing a mother and her two children. He would not know until his third week there that along the other hall was Yvonne Miller.

There was one main entry door for each of the complexes. In the big room to the left of the door into Caesar's complex lived a man of sixty or so, a pajama-clad man who was never out of bed in all the time Caesar lived there. He could walk, but Caesar never saw him do it. A woman, who told Caesar one day that she was "a home health-care aide," was always in the man's room, cooking, cleaning, or watching television with him. His was the only room with its own kitchen setup in a small alcove—a stove, icebox, and sink. His door was always open, and he never seemed to sleep. A green safe, three feet high, squatted beside the bed. "I am a moneylender," the man said the second day Caesar was there. He had come in and walked past the room, and the man had told the aide to have "that young lion" come back. "I am Simon and I lend money," the man said as Caesar stood in the doorway. "I will be your best friend, but not for free. Tell your friends."

He worked as many hours as they would allow him at the restaurant, Chowing Down. The remainder of the time, he went to movies until the shows closed and then sat in Franklin Park, at Fourteenth and K, in good weather and bad. He was there until sleep beckoned, sometimes as late as two in the morning. No one bothered him. He had killed two men, and the world, especially the bad part of it, sensed that and left him alone. He knew no one, and he wanted no one to know him. The friends he had had before Lorton seemed to have been swept off the face of the earth. On the penultimate day of his time at Lorton, he had awoken terrified and thought that if they gave him a choice he might well stay. He might find a life and a career at Lorton.

He had sex only with his right hand, and that was not very often. He began to believe, in his first days out of prison, that men and women were now speaking a new language, and that he would never learn it. His lack of confidence extended even to whores, and this was a man who had been with more women than he had fingers and toes. He began to think that a whore had the power to crush a man's soul. "What kinda language you speakin, honey? Talk English if you want some." He was thirty-seven when he got free.

He came in from the park at two-forty-five one morning and went quickly by Simon's door, but the moneylender called him back. Caesar stood in the doorway. He had been in the warren for less than two months. The aide was cooking, standing with her back to Caesar in a crisp green uniform and sensible black shoes. She was stirring first one pot on the stove and then another. People on the color television were laughing.

"Been out on the town, I see," Simon began. "Hope you got enough poontang to last you till next time." "I gotta be goin," Caesar said. He had begun to think that he might be able to kill the man and find a way to get into the safe. The question was whether he should kill the aide as well. "Don't blow off your friends that way," Simon said. Then, for some reason, he started telling Caesar about their neighbors in that complex. That was how Caesar first learned about an "Yvonny," whom he had yet to see. He would not know that she was the Yvonne he had known long ago until the second time he passed her in the hall. "Now, our sweet Yvonny, she ain't nothin but an old girl." Old girls were whores, young or old, who had been battered so much by the world that they had only the faintest wisp of life left; not many of them had hearts of gold. "But you could probably have her for free," Simon said, and he pointed to Caesar's right, where Yvonne's room was. There was always a small lump under the covers beside Simon in the bed, and Caesar suspected that it was a gun. That was a problem, but he might be able to leap to the bed and kill the man with one blow of a club before he could pull it out. What would the aide do? "I've had her myself," Simon said, "so I can only recommend it in a pinch." "Later, man," Caesar said, and he stepped away. The usual way to his room was to the right as soon as he entered the main door, but that morning he walked straight ahead and within a few feet was passing Yvonne's door. It was slightly ajar, and he heard music from a radio. The aide might even be willing to help him rob the moneylender if he could talk to her alone beforehand. He might not know the language men and women were speaking now, but the language of money had not changed.

It was a cousin who told his brother where to find him. That cousin, Nora Maywell, was the manager of a nearby bank, at Twelfth and F Streets, and she first saw Caesar as he bused tables at Chowing Down, where she had gone with colleagues for lunch. She came in day after day to make certain that he was indeed Caesar, for she had not seen him in more than twenty years. But there was no mistaking the man, who looked like her uncle. Caesar was five years older than Nora. She had gone through much of her childhood hoping that she would grow up to marry him. Had he paid much attention to her in all those years before he disappeared, he still would not have recognized her—she was older, to be sure, but life had been extraordinarily kind to Nora and she was now a queen compared with the dirt-poor peasant she had once been.

Caesar's brother came in three weeks after Nora first saw him. The brother, Alonzo, ate alone, paid his bill, then went over to Caesar and smiled. "It's good to see you," he said. Caesar simply nodded and walked away with the tub of dirty dishes. The brother stood shaking for a few moments, then turned and made his unsteady way out the door. He was a corporate attorney, making nine times what his father, at fifty-seven, was making, and he came back for many days. On the eighth day, he went to Caesar, who was busing in a far corner of the restaurant. It was now early September and Caesar had been out of prison for three months and five days. "I will keep coming until you speak to me," the brother said. Caesar looked at him for a long time. The lunch hours were ending, so the manager would have no reason to shout at him. Only two days before, he had seen Yvonne in the hall for the second time. It had been afternoon and the dead light bulb in the hall had been replaced since the first time he had passed her. He recognized her, but everything in her eyes and body told him that she did not know him. That would never change. And, because he knew who she was, he nodded to his brother and within minutes they were out the door and around the corner to the alley. Caesar lit a cigarette right away. The brother's gray suit had cost $1,865.98. Caesar's apron was filthy. It was his seventh cigarette of the afternoon. When it wasn't in his mouth, the cigarette was at his side, and as he raised it up and down to his mouth, inhaled, and flicked ashes, his hand never shook.

"Do you know how much I want to put my arms around you?" Alonzo said.

"I think we should put an end to all this shit right now so we can get on with our lives," Caesar said. "I don't wanna see you or anyone else in your family from now until the day I die. You should understand that, Mister, so you can do somethin else with your time. You a customer, so I won't do what I would do to somebody who ain't a customer."

The brother said, "I'll admit to whatever I may have done to you. I will, Caesar. I will." In fact, his brother had never done anything to him, and neither had his sister. The war had always been between Caesar and their father, but Caesar, over time, had come to see his siblings as the father's allies. "But come to see me and Joanie, one time only, and if you don't want to see us again then we'll accept that. I'll never come into your restaurant again."

There was still more of the cigarette, but Caesar looked at it and then dropped it to the ground and stepped on it. He looked at his cheap watch. Men in prison would have killed for what was left of that smoke. "I gotta be goin, Mister."

"We are family, Caesar. If you don't want to see Joanie and me for your sake, for our sakes, then do it for Mama."

"My mama's dead, and she been dead for a lotta years." He walked toward the street.

"I know she's dead! I know she's dead! I just put flowers on her grave on Sunday. And on three Sundays before that. And five weeks before that. I know my mother's dead."

Caesar stopped. It was one thing for him to throw out a quick statement about a dead mother, as he had done many times over the years. A man could say the words so often that they became just another meaningless part of his makeup. The pain was no longer there as it had been those first times he had spoken them, when his mother was still new to her grave. The words were one thing, but a grave was a different matter, a different fact. The grave was out there, to be seen and touched, and a man, a son, could go to that spot of earth and remember all over again how much she had loved him, how she had stood in her apron in the doorway of a clean and beautiful home and welcomed him back from school. He could go to the grave and read her name and die a bit, because it would feel as if she had left him only last week.

Caesar turned around. "You and your people must leave me alone, Mister."

"Then we will," the brother said. "We will leave you alone. Come to one dinner. A Sunday dinner. Fried chicken. The works. Then we'll never bother you again. No one but Joanie and our families. No one else." Those last words were to assure Caesar that he would not have to see their father.

Caesar wanted another cigarette, but the meeting had already gone on long enough.

Yvonne had not said anything that second time, when he said "Hello." She had simply nodded and walked around him in the hall. The third time they were also passing in the hall, and he spoke again, and she stepped to the side to pass and then turned and asked if he had any smokes she could borrow.

He said he had some in his room, and she told him to go get them and pointed to her room.

Her room was a third larger than his. It had an icebox, a bed, a dresser with a mirror over it, a small table next to the bed, a chair just beside the door, and not much else. The bed made a T with the one window, which faced the windowless wall of the apartment building next door. The beautiful blue-and-yellow curtains at the window should have been somewhere else, in a place that could appreciate them.

He had no expectations. He wanted nothing. It was just good to see a person from a special time in his life, and it was even better that he had loved her once and she had loved him. He stood in the doorway with the cigarettes.

Dressed in a faded purple robe, she was looking in the icebox when he returned. She closed the icebox door and looked at him. He walked over, and she took the unopened pack of cigarettes from his outstretched hand. He stood there.

"Well, sit the fuck down before you make the place look poor." He sat in the chair by the door, and she sat on the bed and lit the first cigarette. She was sideways to him. It was only after the fifth drag on the cigarette that she spoke. "If you think you gonna get some pussy, you are sorely mistaken. I ain't givin out shit. Free can kill you."

"I don't want nothin."

" 'I don't want nothin. I don't want nothin.' " She dropped ashes into an empty tomato-soup can on the table by the bed. "Mister, we all want somethin, and the sooner people like you stand up and stop the bullshit, then the world can start bein a better place. It's the bullshitters who keep the world from bein a better place." Together, they had rented a little house in Northeast and had been planning to have a child once they had been there two years. The night he came home and found her sitting in the dark and talking about never trusting happiness, they had been there a year and a half. Two months later, she was gone. For the next three months, as he looked for her, he stayed there and continued to make it the kind of place that a woman would want to come home to. "My own mother was the first bullshitter I knew," she continued. "That's how I know it don't work. People should stand up and say, 'I wish you were dead,' or 'I want your pussy,' or 'I want all the money in your pocket.' When we stop lyin, the world will start bein heaven." He had been a thief and a robber and a drug pusher before he met her, and he went back to all that after the three months, not because he was heartbroken, though he was, but because it was such an easy thing to do. He was smart enough to know that he could not blame Yvonne, and he never did. The murders of Percy "Golden Boy" Weymouth and Antwoine Stoddard were still years away.

He stayed that day for more than an hour, until she told him that she had now paid for the cigarettes. Over the next two weeks, as he got closer to the dinner with his brother and sister, he would take her cigarettes and food and tell her from the start that they were free. He was never to know how she paid the rent. By the fourth day of bringing her things, she began to believe that he wanted nothing. He always sat in the chair by the door. Her words never changed, and it never mattered to him. The only thanks he got was the advice that the world should stop being a bullshitter.

On the day of the dinner, he found that the days of sitting with Yvonne had given him a strength he had not had when he had said yes to his brother. He had Alonzo pick him up in front of Chowing Down, because he felt that if they knew where he lived they would find a way to stay in his life.

At his sister's house, just off Sixteenth Street, Northwest, in an area of well-to-do black people some called the Gold Coast, they welcomed him, Joanie keeping her arms around him for more than a minute, crying. Then they offered him a glass of wine. He had not touched alcohol since before prison. They sat him on a dark-green couch in the living room, which was the size of ten prison cells. Before he had taken three sips of the wine, he felt good enough not to care that the girl and the boy, his sister's children, wanted to be in his lap. They were the first children he had been around in more than ten years. The girl had been calling him Uncle since he entered the house.

Throughout dinner, which was served by his sister's maid, and during the rest of the evening, he said as little as possible to the adults—his sister and brother and their spouses—but concentrated on the kids, because he thought he knew their hearts. The grownups did not pepper him with questions and were just grateful that he was there. Toward the end of the meal, he had a fourth glass of wine, and that was when he told his niece that she looked like his mother and the girl blushed, because she knew how beautiful her grandmother had been.

At the end, as Caesar stood in the doorway preparing to leave, his brother said that he had made this a wonderful year. His brother's eyes teared up and he wanted to hug Caesar, but Caesar, without smiling, simply extended his hand. The last thing his brother said to him was "Even if you go away not wanting to see us again, know that Daddy loves you. It is the one giant truth in the world. He's a different man, Caesar. I think he loves you more than us because he never knew what happened to you. That may be why he never remarried." The issue of what Caesar had been doing for twenty-one years never came up.

—⁓—

His sister, with her children in the back seat, drove him home. In front of his building, he and Joanie said goodbye and she kissed his cheek and, as an afterthought, he, a new uncle and with the wine saying, *Now, that wasn't so bad,* reached back to give a playful tug on the children's feet, but the sleeping boy was too far away and the girl, laughing, wiggled out of his reach. He said to his niece, "Good night, young lady," and she said no, that she was not a lady but a little girl. Again, he reached unsuccessfully for her feet. When he turned back, his sister had a look of such horror and disgust that he felt he had been stabbed. He knew right away what she was thinking, that he was out to cop a feel on a child. He managed a goodbye and got out of the car. "Call me," she said before he closed the car door, but the words lacked the feeling of all the previous ones of the evening. He said nothing. Had he spoken the wrong language, as well as done the wrong thing? Did child molesters call little girls "ladies"? He knew he would never call his sister. Yes, he had been right to tear up the pictures and letters when he was in Lorton.

He shut his eyes until the car was no more. He felt a pained rumbling throughout his system and, without thinking, he staggered away from his building toward Tenth Street. He could hear music coming from an apartment on his side of N Street. He had taught his sister how to ride a bike, how to get over her fear of falling and hurting herself. Now, in her eyes, he was no more than an animal capable of hurting a child. They killed men in prison for being that kind of monster. Whatever avuncular love for the children had begun growing in just those few hours now seeped away. He leaned over into the grass at the side of the apartment building and vomited. He wiped his mouth with the back of his hand. "I'll fall, Caesar," his sister had said in her first weeks of learning how to ride a bicycle. "Why would I let that happen?"

He ignored the aide when she told him that the moneylender wanted to talk to him. He went straight ahead, toward Yvonne's room, though he had no intention of seeing her. Her door was open enough for him to see a good part of the room, but he simply turned toward his own room. His shadow, cast by her light behind him, was thin and went along the floor and up the wall, and it was seeing the shadow that made him turn around. After noting that the bathroom next to her room was empty, he called softly to her from the doorway and then called three times more before he gave the door a gentle push with his finger. The door had not opened all the way when he saw her half on the bed and half off. Drunk, he thought. He went to her, intending to put her full on the bed. But death can twist the body in a way life never does, and that was what it had done to hers. He knew death. Her face was pressed into the bed, at a crooked angle that would have been uncomfortable for any living person. One leg was bunched under her, and the other was extended behind her, but both seemed not part of her body, awkwardly on their own, as if someone could just pick them up and walk away.

He whispered her name. He sat down beside her, ignoring the vomit that spilled out of her mouth and over the side of the bed. He moved her head so that it rested on one side. He thought at first that someone had done this to her, but he saw money on the dresser and felt the quiet throughout the room that signaled the end of it all, and he knew that the victim and the perpetrator were one and the same. He screwed the top on the empty whiskey bottle near her extended leg.

He placed her body on the bed and covered her with a sheet and a blanket. Someone would find her in the morning. He stood at the door, preparing to turn out the light and leave, thinking this was how the world would find her. He had once known her as a clean woman who would not steal so much as a needle. A woman with a well-kept house. She had been loved. But that was not what they would see in the morning.

He set about putting a few things back in place, hanging up clothes that were lying over the chair and on the bed, straightening the lampshade, picking up newspapers and everything else on the floor. But, when he was done, it did not seem enough.

He went to his room and tore up two shirts to make dust rags. He started in a corner at the foot of her bed, at a table where she kept her brush and comb and makeup and other lady things. When he had dusted the table and everything on it, he put an order to what was there, just as if she would be using them in the morning.

Then he began dusting and cleaning clockwise around the room, and by midnight he was not even half done and the shirts were dirty with all the work, and he went back to his room for two more. By three, he was cutting up his pants for rags. After he had cleaned and dusted the room, he put an order to it all, as he had done with the things on the table—the dishes and food in mouseproof cannisters on the table beside the icebox, the two framed posters of mountains on the wall that were tilting to the left, the five photographs of unknown children on the bureau. When that work was done, he took a pail and a mop from her closet. Mice had made a bed in the mop, and he had to brush them off and away. He filled the pail with water from the bathroom and soap powder from under the table beside the icebox. After the floor had been mopped, he stood in the doorway as it dried and listened to the mice in the walls, listened to them scurrying in the closet.

At about four, the room was done and Yvonne lay covered in her unmade bed. He went to the door, ready to leave, and was once more unable to move. The whole world was silent except the mice in the walls.

He knelt at the bed and touched Yvonne's shoulder. On a Tuesday morning, a school day, he had come upon his father kneeling at his bed, Caesar's mother growing cold in that bed. His father was crying, and when Caesar went to him his father crushed Caesar to him and took the boy's breath away. It was Caesar's brother who had said they should call someone, but their father said, "No, no, just one minute more, just one more minute," as if in that next minute God would reconsider and send his wife back. And Caesar had said, "Yes, just one minute more." *The one giant truth . . . ,* his brother had said.

Caesar changed the bed clothing and undressed Yvonne. He got one of her large pots and filled it with warm water from the bathroom and poured into the water cologne of his own that he never used and bath-oil beads he found in a battered container in a corner beside her dresser. The beads refused to dissolve, and he had to crush them in his hands. He bathed her, cleaned out her mouth. He got a green dress from the closet, and underwear and stockings from the dresser, put them on her, and pinned a rusty cameo on the dress over her heart. He combed and brushed her hair, put barrettes in it after he sweetened it with the rest of the cologne, and laid her head in the center of the pillow now covered with one of his clean cases. He gave her no shoes and he did not cover her up, just left her on top of the made-up bed. The room with the dead woman was as clean and as beautiful as Caesar could manage at that time in his life. It was after six in the morning, and the world was lighting up and the birds had begun to chirp. Caesar shut off the ceiling light and turned out the lamp, held on to the chain switch as he listened to the beginnings of a new day.

He opened the window that he had cleaned hours before, and

right away a breeze came through. He put a hand to the wind, enjoying the coolness, and one thing came to him: he was not a young man anymore.

He sat on his bed smoking one cigarette after another. Before finding Yvonne dead, he had thought he would go and live in Baltimore and hook up with a vicious crew he had known a long time ago. Wasn't that what child molesters did? Now, the only thing he knew about the rest of his life was that he did not want to wash dishes and bus tables anymore. At about nine-thirty, he put just about all he owned and the two bags of trash from Yvonne's room in the bin in the kitchen. He knocked at the door of the woman in the room next to his. Her son opened the door, and Caesar asked for his mother. He gave her the hundred and forty-seven dollars he had found in Yvonne's room, along with his radio and tiny black-and white television. He told her to look in on Yvonne before long and then said he would see her later, which was perhaps the softest lie of his adult life.

On his way out of the warren of rooms, Simon called to him. "You comin back soon, young lion?" he asked. Caesar nodded. "Well, why don't you bring me back a bottle of rum? Woke up with a taste for it this mornin." Caesar nodded. "Was that you in there with Yvonny last night?" Simon said as he got the money from atop the safe beside his bed. "Quite a party, huh?" Caesar said nothing. Simon gave the money to the aide, and she handed Caesar ten dollars and a quarter. "Right down to the penny," Simon said. "Give you a tip when you get back." "I won't be long," Caesar said. Simon must have realized that was a lie, because before Caesar went out the door he said, in as sweet a voice as he was capable of, "I'll be waitin."

———

He came out into the day. He did not know what he was going to do, aside from finding some legit way to pay for Yvonne's funeral. The D.C. government people would take her away, but he knew where he could find and claim her before they put her in potter's field. He put the bills in his pocket and looked down at the quarter in the palm of his hand. It was a rather old one, 1967, but shiny enough. Life had been kind to it. He went carefully down the steps in front of the building and stood on the sidewalk. The world was going about its business, and it came to him, as it might to a man who had been momentarily knocked senseless after a punch to the face, that he was of that world. To the left was Ninth Street and all the rest of N Street, Immaculate Conception Catholic Church at Eighth, the bank at the corner of Seventh. He flipped the coin. To his right was Tenth Street, and down Tenth were stores and the house where Abraham Lincoln had died and all the white people's precious monuments. Up Tenth and a block to Eleventh and Q Streets was once a High's store where, when Caesar was a boy, a pint of cherry-vanilla ice cream cost twenty-five cents, and farther down Tenth was French Street, with a two-story house with his mother's doilies and a foot-long porcelain black puppy just inside the front door. A puppy his mother had bought for his father in the third year of their marriage. A puppy that for thirty-five years had been patiently waiting each working day for Caesar's father to return from work. *The one giant truth . . . Just one minute more.* He caught the quarter and slapped it on the back of his hand. He had already decided that George Washington's profile would mean going toward Tenth Street, and that was what he did once he uncovered the coin.

At the corner of Tenth and N, he stopped and considered the quarter again. Down Tenth was Lincoln's death house. Up Tenth was the house where he had been a boy, and where the puppy was waiting for his father. A girl at the corner was messing with her bicycle, putting playing cards in the spokes, checking the tires. She watched Caesar as he flipped the quarter. He missed it and the coin fell to the ground, and he decided that that one would not count. The girl had once seen her aunt juggle six coins, first warming up with the flip of a single one and advancing to the juggling of three before finishing with six. It had been quite a show. The aunt had shown the six pieces to the girl—they had all been old and heavy one-dollar silver coins, huge monster things, which nobody made anymore. The girl thought she might now see a reprise of that event. Caesar flipped the quarter. The girl's heart paused. The man's heart paused. The coin reached its apex and then it fell.

Paula L. Woods (1953–) was born and raised in Los Angeles, receiving an M.A. in public health from UCLA. She and her husband began a book packaging and marketing company. Her first book was the distinguished anthology *Spooks, Spies and Private Eyes: Black Mystery, Crime, and Suspense Fiction of the 20th Century* (1995), the first collection devoted exclusively to the work of African-American crime writers.

In 1999, her series character, Charlotte Justice, made her debut in *Inner City Blues*, which was nominated for an Edgar Allan Poe Award, and an Anthony Award, and won the Macavity and the Black Caucus of the American Library Association Best First Novel Award. The Los Angeles homicide detective has also starred in *Stormy Weather* (2001), *Dirty Laundry* (2003), and *Strange Bedfellows* (2006), all of which have appeared on the best-seller list of the *Los Angeles Times*. In addition to being a member of the Mystery Writers of America, Sisters in Crime, and the International Crime Writers Association, she is a member of the National Book Critics Circle and reviews regularly for the *Los Angeles Times* and the *Washington Post*. She has also written and edited such nonfiction works as the best-selling *I, Too, Sing America: The African-American Book of Days* (with Felix H. Liddell) and *Merry Christmas Baby: A Christmas and Kwanzaa Treasury*.

"I'll Be Doggone" was first published in the Summer 1998 issue of *Mary Higgins Clark Mystery Magazine*.

I'll Be Doggone

Paula L. Woods

Back when I was twelve, overweight, and dying for a boy, *any* boy, to notice me, my Grandmama Cile would warn, *Girl, you lie down with dogs, you gonna get up with fleas.*

Tonight as I watch the fat, gray-muzzled canine sprawled at the foot of my bed, snoring like he was lord of the manor, I wonder if this was what my grandmother had in mind.

When I first saw the tan and white boxer a little over eight years ago, he was squirming in the custody of Officer Marie Hessburg, an LAPD uniform. He had issued a call to nine one one from his common as white thread, post-war tract house on Eighth Avenue, not more than two miles from South Bureau Homicide, where I worked at the time. Or more precisely, a Mrs. Redmond had called at two in the morning because the puppy had been sitting at a neighbor's front door and later on their St. Augustine grass, howling and whimpering like he'd lost his last friend.

The poor thing had. For beyond the front porch of the house

where he sat waiting for the patrol car, beyond the torn screen door he'd wiggled through, beyond the living room cluttered with toys, a plaid dog futon, and a hospital bed, there in the long, blood-spattered hallway lay the dead bodies of a little girl at one end and her mother at the other, their blood soaking into the thick, white, new-smelling carpeting.

I don't know how the dog felt about the woman, but I was certain the girl belonged to him in only the way children can. A T-shirt billowing like a sail around the child's thin frame was all the evidence I needed. It was a T-shirt you can have made at any large copy shop, the ones with the Xerox-transfer photos emblazoned on the front. The child and the puppy captured under a Christmas tree, her smile wider that she was and the dog no more that a little lump of caramel-colored fur in her lap. BEAUTY AND BEAST, XMAS 1989, I read through the torn and blood-darkened fabric. Hard to believe how happy the child and how tiny the dog were just four months ago.

Danny Bansuela, my partner at the time, had arrived ahead of me and was crouching over the mother's body at the far end of the hall, deep in conversation with Tom Moran, the coroner's investigator called out on the case. Danny look up, nodded, his face devoid of it usual good-natured cheer.

"We got an ID yet?" I asked him.

"Driver's license in her wallet says she's Chantal Walker. The little girl's her daughter, Linda."

Moran was removing the thermometer from the incision he'd made in the woman's side. "Ninety-two point three," he announced. He stood up, looked at the woman's rigid features, and calculated, his face a frown beneath his new, so-real-you'd-never-know Hair Club for Men purchase. "I'd say they've been dead about four hours. Looks like the killer came in, surprised

Mrs. Walker in her bedroom, struggled with and then stabbed her. The commotion probably woke up the child and when she came down the hall, he did her, too."

"But outside of the dog's, there ain't no footprints in the hallway," Danny noted. "What was he—a ninja or something?"

I moved to the other end of the hallway. "The child was stabbed in the stomach," I said, already knowing the answer I sought in the grisly scene at my feet. "So she saw her assailant?"

Moran nodded. Danny angled his dark, glassy eyes my way: "Without a doubt."

The room began to feel a little close. Even though I'd worked homicide for five years at that point, I always had problems dealing with a scene when there's a kid involved. For me, it packed an extra wallop because my own child was murdered years ago, but it gets next to every cop I know. I could tell it was working on Danny's head, too. He had a daughter about this girl's age.

I tried to busy my mind. "Any evidence of forced entry?"

Danny shook his head. "The door and windows are all secured, although there are some muddy footprints coming from the back door into the kitchen."

"Is there a Mr. Walker to be notified?" I asked.

Danny stepped over the woman's body, and rolled down the hall to me, his thick thighs making soft, percussive sounds inside his wool pants. "According to the neighbor who made the call, the husband and wife separated a few months ago. She says he's been back a dozen times since then, fighting with the wife."

"About what?"

"Seemed they raised pit bulls and boxers. Mrs. Redmond says they were always arguing about the dogs."

"You're kidding me."

Danny waved a hand at the walls. "Check it out."

A dozen of those photo collage frames held pictures of a man, the woman and occasionally the child posing with boxers and pit bulls of all colors and sizes. The little girl, just a toddler in the earliest pictures, seemed to get smaller and more frail as the pictures progressed down the hall. Although she looked unhappy in the pictures, the woman was undeniably striking—late twenties to early thirties, a full three inches taller than my five-five, her skin that lovely cola color I liked much better than my sickly almond-shell tone. And the man—well, he looked like one of the dogs he bred: compact, morose, tight-jawed with small, wide-set eyes that looked like they belonged on a pit bull.

Or a cold-blooded killer.

I put on some latex gloves and removed one of the photos from the frame. "Where did they raise these dogs?"

Danny jerked his head toward the back yard. "Back there, but they're gone now. Mrs. Redmond said the husband and two other guys came and got them earlier this evening."

I'd bet dimes to donuts it was about four hours earlier.

Ben Matsumura, a trace evidence specialist from the Special Investigation Division—the LAPD's crime lab—was busy collecting fibers from the child's clothing. I tiptoed around him and made my way through the postage stamp of a kitchen, past the bottle of Tanqueray, carton of orange juice, and empty glasses on the table, and down the back steps. I passed two other lab rats—Ygnacio Zamora, a senior photographer, and Herman Wozniak, a latent print specialist—who were busy taking photos and lifting prints from the white linoleum floor and the things on the table.

Most of the squarish back yard was taken up by wire kennels for I guessed at least thirty dogs from the pungent evidence in those cages. There was a bigger pen against the garage and back

wall, a little too wide for a dog run, with a shelf running around
the exposed sides. A few dead soldiers, mostly Schlitz Malt Liquor
bottles, lay atop it.

The puppy had somehow slipped through a gap in the fence and
run into the back yard. He sniffed the cages, looking into them like
he had lost something, then turned and half-cocked his leg.

Officer Hessburg ran up behind him. "I've called the Department of Animal Regulation to come and pick him up," she
panted.

The puppy looked like an escapee from San Quentin, hiding in
the forest of my legs. I reached down to pet him; he backed away,
wary. "Come here, Beast," I coaxed. "Is that your name. . . Beast?
Come on over to Auntie Detective Justice."

Hessburg repressed a smile. "*Auntie* Detective? That's a new
one on me, Charlotte."

I kept my voice in singsong pitch: "Whatever works, Officer
Hessburg."

Soon Beast started wiggling his little stump and doing an elab-
orate approach/avoidance routine that eventually put him within
grabbing distance. Once I had him by the collar, he started
sniffing and trying to lick my face, happy the way only something
that young and full of life can be.

I found a leash near one of the pens, attached it to his collar,
and handed him back to Hessburg. There was blood on his face
and coat. I thought of his young mistress inside, so still, and wondered if he had licked her face, too, trying to wake her up.

Walker would have needed at least two trucks to transport as
many dogs as I estimated had been there. Did he load up the
trucks, his wife arguing with him the whole time? Maybe he sent
his friends away, then slipped in the back door, tracking mud on
her nice linoleum floor. Did she make him take off his shoes

before giving him a drink? Maybe the gin only fueled his rage until it exploded, red-hot and brutal, in that snow white hallway.

Juanita Redmond certainly considered Walker capable of that, and a lot worse. She stood in a long, dark-colored robe, arms crossed over her chest. A self-appointed, flannel-clad judge and jury of Milton Walker.

"Milton was there about eight, fussing with Chantal as usual. And to think he killed her, and that poor little girl!"

"We don't know that for a fact, ma'am," I pointed out. "What time did Mr. Walker leave?"

"A little after ten. I remember cause the Channel 5 news had just started when the last truck pulled away." The corners of her mouth pulled down in disgust. "I'm so glad those nasty things are gone. Didn't do nothing but stink up the neighborhood and bring down my property values! Attracting a bunch of young hoodlums at all hours, drinking their forties and betting on those poor animals."

I had already figured that was what the pen was all about. "You know dog fighting is illegal, Mrs. Redmond. You could have called the police or Animal Regulation."

"Milton Walker ran with a rough crowd. I'll be doggone if I was going to get shot in a drive-by for complaining about what they were doing over there. Chantal didn't like it, and look where it got her!"

"I guess you wouldn't be interested in taking the little girl's dog?"

Juanita Redmond, her robe drawn up around her, pronounced her sentence on the puppy: "No way on God's green earth! I'm on a fixed income. Dog like that would eat me out of house and home!"

The neighbor on the other side, Victor Cuthbert, substantiated Mrs. Redmond's account of the evening and sentiments about the entire Walker clan. Thirty-seven or -eight, a dead ringer for Billy

Dee Williams in *Lady Sings the Blues* but with peroxide-tinged red hair and a bodybuilder's chiseled torso, I could tell Cuthbert fancied himself a ladies' man. In fact, it seemed I had caught him on his way to a late-night creep—an after-shower humidity lingered in the air of the small house, mixed with a flowery cologne and the smell of disinfectant. And although he was in a bit of a hurry—"her husband works the graveyard shift," he winked—he was only too glad to stop and add a few more nails to Milton Walker's coffin.

"Chantal was pissed off about him taking those dogs." Cuthbert flexed his fingers back and forth into a fist, and dropped them in his lap.

"Why was that?"

"Those dogs were worth a lot of money!" Fingers exploded on Cuthbert's strong hands. "Three of the bitches were in heat, four more were pregnant, and there were at least three males Milton was making big bucks off of in stud fees and in the ring."

"How much money?"

Cuthbert's fingers couldn't count that high, and hid in his lap again. "I don't make it a habit of getting up in other folks's business, but Milton was making grand theft dough. A lot better than either one of them was doing working at the post office."

"Which station would that be?"

"World Way Center, out near the airport."

There was a knock at the door. Cuthbert limped over to answer it. It was Officer Hessburg. "They're here for the dog," she said.

As if on cue, Beast emerged from behind her legs, growling and straining at his leash. Cuthbert backed away from the door. "Get that runt away from me!"

"What do you want me to tell them, Detective?" Hessburg asked.

"I guess you're not interested in keeping the dog?" I asked Cuthbert.

"Hell, no!" he said. "I don't even like dogs! Besides, Chantal said that one's got a heart murmur."

The bristling hairs on Beast's back told me the feeling was mutual. And yet, for all his bravado, the blood-spattered puppy looked so forlorn. The runt of his litter, the last member of his human family, an orphan two times over.

I took his leash and held him away from Cuthbert and my clothes. "Tell them I'm going to keep him for a few days," I told Hessburg.

Beast began to strain against the leash, and jump for my knees. "Let's you and I go see Uncle Criminalist Matsumura and get you cleaned up, okay? I bet you he's got some extra special wipes in his case for little doggies like you."

On my way downtown to the morgue, I decided to stop and get the dog checked out. I knew from my pet-owning friends that the Westside Animal Medical Center was the only choice. One of those high-tech, glass and steel buildings, it looked like the Cedars Sinai of veterinary hospitals—big, reliable, expensive.

Despite the early morning hour, a curly-headed vet on duty named Dr. Cignelli saw us right away. "He does have what sounds like a low-gradient pulmonic stenosis," she said. "We can do an echocardiogram to check the extent of the damage if you like, but I wouldn't worry about it—many boxers with minor heart problems like this live to a ripe old age."

"I'm more concerned about how the murder of his owners will affect him," I said.

She squatted down on Beast's level, massaged him under the chin, and spoke to me via a soothing voice aimed at him. "Well, doggies are very sensitive animals. Did this little fella see the murder?"

"I'm afraid so."

"Was it a domestic homicide or a stranger?" He licked her face. "Yes, yes, you're a brave doggie," she assured him as she picked him up.

"Not sure yet. Would there be a difference in the way he responded?"

Dr. Cignelli set Beast down on a metal table, and began to gently examine him. "This isn't an exact science, but we do know dogs are pack animals," she said in a normal voice. "In any pack, there's always an alpha leader, the top dog. In a human household, that's usually the man of the house. If the alpha leader snarls at another member of the pack, especially an alpha female—who doesn't count for much in the canine scheme of things—the dog is not going to be inclined to challenge his leader."

"What if the alpha leader kills the alpha female?"

"No one knows for sure, but some canine behavioral scientists suggest the dog would be unlikely to take sides, unless the alpha leader hurt someone especially close to the dog, like a child."

"There was a child involved."

Dr. Cignelli's blue eyes narrowed in my direction. "Then I'd look for bite marks on your suspect. Dogs will attack if provoked, even a calm breed like the boxer. And it would be highly unusual for a dog not to defend a child, even a little fella like this."

"And how would the dog behave if he saw the killer again?"

"Aggressiveness combined with fearful avoidance would be my guess. But as I said before, we're not talking an exact science here, no matter what you see on the talk shows."

I sat in the windowless office of Wilmer Foster, the postmaster at

World Way Postal Center. A walking advertisement for the U.S. Postal Service, Foster wore half a dozen postage stamp pins on his burgundy vest, and had even given me one I had admired—a LOVE stamp with a dog on it.

That was before I gave him the bad news about Chantal Walker.

"She was one of my best supervisors." Foster sat fingering a pin, the creases and crevices of his face rigid with shock. "A great motivator of people, but Chantal wasn't afraid to get tough when she had to. Got Eddie Montoya out of here last week, which took some guts, as big a fool as that man was."

"What happened?"

"Eddie was stealing Social Security checks. Had been for several months, until Chantal set up a sting with some undercover postal inspectors."

Foster's face came to life. "Eddie swore he was going to get even with her. Do you think. . ."

"Did Mr. Montoya make bail?"

"I'm not sure," he said, turning to extract a file from the mound on his desk, "but I can make a call and find out."

While Foster was on the phone, I went to find Chantal Walker's estranged husband to do the next-of-kin notification.

Milton Walker was shocked at the news of his wife and daughter's deaths, and did not hesitate to show it. *The ones who make the biggest fuss are usually the most guilty,* my Grandmama Cile always says, a philosophy I remembered as I considered the thick-necked, grieving little man. "I'm sure it's doubly tough on you since you two argued last night," I said.

Walker's head came up and his ears practically twitched. "According to who?"

"There were some complaints," I said, keeping my face nonjudgmental.

"You're talking about Mrs. Redmond and than damned Victor Cuthbert, aren't you? They should keep their noses to themselves! Both of them were constantly meddling in our business, the whole time Chantal and I were together."

Walker pushed a big bin of mail to a loading dock, paused to wipe his face with a bandaged hand.

"How did you hurt yourself?" I asked.

"Cut myself on one of the pens last night," he said, and hid his hand.

I was reminded of Dr. Cignelli's words and Matsumura carefully wiping Beast's bloody face and paws a few hours ago. I was glad the SID trace evidence specialist was able to collect some of those blood samples for analysis at the lab.

"Dog breeding must be a pretty lucrative business," I said.

"That's right. Stud fees were getting up to four, five hundred dollars for some of my pits and those pregnant boxer bitches . . . that's a technical term . . . were AKC-registered, going to bring in between two and three thousand, depending on the size of their litters.

"What about the dog fighting?"

He looked at me sideways. "I never was involved in that!"

"I saw the pen, Mr. Walker, and I've talked to the neighbors, so you can drop the act!" I warned, my voice harsh. I could press him on the dog fighting charge—it was a felony—but I had bigger fish to fry. "Is that what you and Chantal argued about?"

I noticed one of Walker's female co-workers leaning against a pole, eavesdropping while pretending to read a copy of *Newsweek* magazine. I remembered I hadn't gotten my current issue, and hoped that wasn't it.

"Linda had a heart condition. Been sick most of her life. That's why the money from the dogs came in handy, even though Chantal hated the mess. The doctors at Children's Hospital tried to treat Linda medically, but she was just getting worse. They called us in last Friday to say they were going to have to operate."

Walker took in a few shaky breaths before he could go on. "Dr. Sharim said it was better for her parents to donate blood than rely on the blood bank, but when I got over to the hospital yesterday, they said I couldn't."

Walker seemed to be in his early thirties, buffed, and very healthy. And while he didn't appear to have any infectious diseases, I asked anyway. You never know.

"No, it wasn't that," he said. Walker glared at his eavesdropping co-worker, who hurried away. Then he stalked back to get another bin of mail, stopped, turned, and pointed in my face. "Now I've only got a high school diploma, but even I know that Linda should have had my blood type, B positive, not her mother's. O positive is what they call a universal donor, can mix with anybody's blood—B positive plus O positive should equal B positive, not another O. I learned that much from the blood drives at work."

He walked over to the vending machines, shoved some quarters into it for coffee. "When I confronted Chantal about it last night, she got all up in my face yammering about how I just had to live with it since the fish was caught in my net!" Walker's jaw tightened, his eyes narrowed as if for a fight. "And that wasn't even it! I love . . . loved that little girl with all my heart, and I was gonna do right by her." His jaw quivered, his eyes filling with tears. "But I *wasn't* gonna let my wife lay up with that dog and let him make the money off of the sweat *I* put into those animals. If they thought that, they had another think coming."

"Who are you talking about?"

"Ask *him* what his blood type is! That slick little sonofa—excuse my mouth, ma'am—weasel! Up in my face being 'neighborly,' and the whole time he was doing a back door Jody number on me."

"That must have made you mad," I said.

"You're doggone right about that!"

"Mad enough to kill her?"

Milton Walker started backing up, realizing probably for the first time he was pointing the finger at himself. "Naw . . . naw . . . it wasn't like that." His short fingers flicked the tears aside furiously. "I loved that little girl like there was no tomorrow. Much as I hated her mother, I would have moved mountains for my baby."

"So why did you take the dogs?"

"Chantal said she was tired of taking care of them and Linda, too. Said they were too much work. So after I got me a house rented and the pens built, me and a couple of buddies went over there last night to pick them up."

"Why go over there at all, especially after what you learned at the hospital? Weren't you just asking for trouble?"

"I'd already rented the trucks and all . . . plus I wanted to get the animals away from that woman as quick as possible. If she wasn't going to take care of them, how was I going to keep the money flowing for my baby's medical care? Health insurance doesn't cover everything."

That cinched it for me. Out of curiosity, I asked if he stayed after they'd finished loading up the dogs.

"Only a minute," he replied. "I wanted to peek in on Linda, but Chantal said my feet were too muddy to track onto her new carpeting. But I knew what the score was. She comes to the back door in one of those Frederick's of Hollywood numbers she used to wear for me. I could smell the gin in her juice glass. I saw the other glass on the table. *He* was there."

The postmaster walked up behind Walker, shrugged, and shook his head. "Thanks, Mr. Foster."

"What's going on?" Walker asked.

"You want to come out to my car with me, sir?"

He began to get belligerent. "Why, you gonna arrest me?"

"Well, we would like you to give us a blood sample later, but there's something I want you to take a look at first."

Beast was curled up asleep on his plaid bed in the back seat of my department-issued Ford. When Walker saw the puppy, his eyes began to mist over again. "Linda loved that little dog."

When Beast saw his former master, his stump began to vibrate and he jumped up on the window, trying to lick Walker through the crack I'd left in the window.

"He's gonna need his ears clipped soon," he said wistfully, "if he's gonna keep that classic boxer look."

"Do you want to take him?" I asked.

Walker had already opened my car door and was rubbing Beast under the chin. "I couldn't. It would be too hard to see him every day, knowing . . . Why don't you keep him, Detective?"

I tentatively wiggled my fingers in Beast's direction. The puppy started licking and nipping them. "I haven't had a dog since high school."

Walker watched the two of us, a ghost of a smile flickering on his face. "Well, I think you do now."

After he submitted to the blood test downtown, Walker agreed to meet Danny Bansuela and me at the house on Eighth Avenue that evening. We probably wouldn't get the results back from the blood test for couple of days, but I was hoping to get this case wrapped up and to the deputy DA before then.

Danny and I sat waiting in my car, while a black-and-white

containing Officer Hessburg and her partner was positioned across the street. Beast—who'd spent the day sleeping, eating from the twenty-five-dollar ceramic dish I'd been suckered into buying at the vet's, or relieving himself on the newspapers I had spread under my desk—was galloping on the grass in front of the house and christening every shrub he could find.

Danny had checked Walker's alibi with the friends who helped him move the dogs. "If you're right, Charlotte, I'm going to nominate this case for *Top Cops*," he joked, slapping the papers in my palm.

"You're just jealous because you don't get to clean up puppy poop," I laughed in return.

We got out of the car as Walker pulled up. I leashed the dog while Hessburg and her partner split up, the male officer covering the rear entrance to the house, Hessburg staying with us. Walker took Beast's leash and led us up the walkway.

We rang the bell, hands on our guns. Victor Cuthbert opened the door, and seemed surprised to see us.

"Mr. Cuthbert, can we come in?" I asked.

"Sure, but I was on my way out."

Cuthbert was wearing cutoffs over an expensive sweatshirt. "What is it this time, Victor—a date to pump iron?" I asked. I noticed a four-by-four bandage on his ankle. "How'd you get the injury?"

"Nicked myself."

Danny raised an eyebrow. "Shaving your legs, Victor?" he asked.

Walker, who had been standing behind us, surged forward. "You killed them, you . . ."

"Don't come trying to throw the blame off on me!" Cuthbert growled from behind Hessburg's back.

Walker let Beast off his leash. The little boxer raised his hackles, and proceeded to add his own whining growl to the ruckus.

"Tell him to keep that dog away from me!" Cuthbert shouted at me. "I told you I'm afraid of dogs."

"You're lying!" Walker shouted. "Chantal told me last night you wanted her to keep the dogs so you could breed them yourself."

"I didn't want *that* one!" Cuthbert sneered. "He wouldn't have brought in a dime with that bad heart!"

I slapped Cuthbert in the chest with the papers. "Victor Cuthbert, this warrant authorizes us to search the premises for items related to the murders or Chantal Walker and Linda Walker, and to obtain a blood sample from you."

While I was serving him with the papers, Danny reached down and snatched the bandage from Cuthbert's ankle. Underneath it were two swollen puncture wounds. "Well, looky here," he smiled. "You were right, Charlotte."

Beast stood back in his hind legs, I think even now, with a bit of pride. *Yeah, I did that,* he seemed to say.

Our suspicions confirmed, my partner stood panting in front of Cuthbert like he wanted to take a bite out of his other leg, but had to turn his attention to Milton Walker, who seemed hell-bent on the same mission.

"I didn't intend to kill the kid," Cuthbert said to whoever cared to listen. "But she knew I was in the house with her mother while you were outside. She heard us arguing about the dogs afterward. Somehow she got out of that damn hospital bed and came down the hall to see what was the matter. What choice did I have?"

Danny and Hessburg were having more than a little trouble restraining Walker; the cuffs were just about, but not quite, on the furious father's struggling wrists.

"Partner, why don't I step outside for a minute with Officer Hessburg," I said slowly. "You've got this situation under control, don't you?"

Danny glanced at me for a moment then nodded, his eyes shining fire, his mouth a grim line. "I think I can handle this one alone."

I knelt down to pet the little hero, who had retreated to a spot behind Walker, his back still up, his teeth bared. "Come on, Beast. Auntie Detective has a nice treat in her car for you. You've been such a good, brave dog."

Officer Hessburg had been joined by her partner outside. They positioned themselves outside the front door. Beast and I were standing under a spreading elm tree while he enjoyed a peanut butter biscuit when the guys from SID pulled up in their van. There was a crash inside the house. Hessburg and I looked at each other. I counted to three before making a move for the door. It was a slow five before Danny finally opened it.

"You won't have to stick him for the sample," he told the guys from SID as he ushered out the unrestrained Milton Walker. "Mr. Cuthbert is already bleeding."

HUGHES ALLISON (1908–1974) was born in Greenville, South Carolina, his father a superintendent of the North Carolina Mutual Life Insurance Co., which was at one time the world's oldest and largest black business, and his mother a school teacher. In 1919, the family moved to Newark, N.J., where his father again worked for an insurance company and his mother became executive director of a branch of the YMCA. Allison attended Upsala College in East Orange, N.J., and soon began an active writing career, ghost writing a half dozen novels of little consequence. His first short story was published in *Challenge* magazine in 1935, after which he wrote radio plays.

In 1937, his first play, *The Trial of Dr. Beck,* became the first Federal Theatre production to be brought from outside New York City to Broadway, and the only play written by an African-American to be produced by the Federal Theatre on Broadway. It also marked the first stage appearance of the future stage, movie, radio, and television star, William Bendix. Allison went on to write for the National Service Bureau, the New Jersey Writers' Project, and the New Jersey WPA Information Service Bureau. His 1941 play, *Midnight Over Newark,* so powerfully illustrated the lack of black doctors and nurses in Newark's City Hospital that the policy was altered.

"Corollary" was first published in the July 1948 issue of *Ellery Queen's Mystery Magazine;* it was the first story by a black writer to appear in that magazine and appears to be the only detective story Allison ever wrote.

Corollary

Hughes Allison

Joe Hill should have been assigned to the
case three months before its bolder principals accidentally tangled
with a radio patrol car and were arrested that Wednesday
morning in Oldhaven. But neither Inspector Duffy nor Chief
Richard Belden had ordered Joe assigned to the case in the beginning. By that Wednesday it was late. Already a pernicious web—
fashioned out of mutilation, terror, and indecision—had begun
to coil itself around four unsuspecting persons: a pair of stupid,
elderly grandparents; an alert but inexperienced child; and a sin-
cere, though too-exacting, schoolteacher.

It was late Wednesday afternoon, a few hours after the arrests
had been announced in the public press, that Joe was finally summoned to the Chief's third-floor office.

Belden, seated behind his desk, was in high humor. "Huh!"
he growled. "One guess! What's in the cell block?"

Joe grinned. "The cure for a three months' headache."

"Right! But they're punks," Belden declared. "I've had a

55

good look at 'em. And only one thing the papers have said in the last three months really fits."

"What's that, Chief?" Joe asked.

"Their handle—'the Bandit Quintet.' "

"The Chief means," Inspector Duffy explained, "we've caught ourselves five yellow jerks with a yen to sing."

Joe said, "With or without persuasion?"

"Without," Duffy replied. "And plenty loud, in a good key, for as long as we want."

Belden said, "I've been a cop for a long time. So I've seen lots of talkers. I don't pretend to know what makes 'em do it. But I do know how to handle 'em. Treat 'em easy, take your time, let 'em spout—and comb every bit of what comes out for leads."

"That's the play all the way," Duffy agreed.

"Not a single one of this Quintet gang seems to have a previous record," the Chief said. "That may be why our stools failed to produce. But just the same. Dig—easy and gently—for crook connections. Lots of cases are still wide-open. Joe, you draw the chauffeur. Says his name is Albert Johnson. Claims he's a powerful church-going fellow. Still, he—watch him, huh?"

"I'll watch him," Joe promised.

Duffy said, "How about the men to work with Hill, Chief?"

One of the telephones on Belden's desk jangled.

"Give him boys with Middle Ward experience," Belden said. Picking up the phone, he growled, "Yes?"

In an aside to Joe, Duffy said, "Make it Shaw from Homicide, Carlton from the Bandit Squad—"

Chuckling at the phone, Belden told it, "Sure. Put *him* on."

"—Swenson from Auto—" Duffy continued.

"Ah! Mr. Prosecutor!" Belden exclaimed at the phone.

"—and Goldberg from Identification," Duffy concluded, matching the grin on Belden's face.

"We're happy as kids about it!" Belden told the phone. "Right this minute Detective Hill's on his way to the cell block for a session with their chauffeur."

Joe looked at Duffy.

"Take a peep at all five of 'em," the Inspector told him. "Skip the murders for the time being. Just touch your man for the overall number of stickups. Then come back here."

Joe had seen the same kind of scared, repentant men before. They were in separate cells. Four were pale-faced nonentities who stared at him as he slowly walked past their barred cages, out of solemn eyes that begged for pity. The fifth man—the chauffeur—was exactly like his confederates. Except that his skin was black.

Stepping close to the bars, Joe said, "I'm Detective Hill."

A trace of surprise showed through the worry, shame, and fear etched in the ebony face.

"I knowed," the chauffeur said, "a few of our folks in Oldhaven was cops. But I thought they was all just street cops."

Joe said, "They tell me you're in a little trouble, Johnson."

The man nodded. "Th' Chief—he come to see me. I said I'd talk."

"Chief Belden's not a bad fellow to talk to."

"I seen you now. So—Well, our people is always so far behind. I was just trying to—to catch up a little bit."

"No regular work?"

"I had been chauffeuring for a rich woman—named Mrs. Stevens. But th' job—it was running out. And I met them other four."

Joe smiled encouragingly. "Yes. The others."

"You see—it was like this," the chauffeur said. "Mrs. Stevens—she's a very old lady. She got sick. Before she let 'em take her to th' hospital, she said to me, 'Albert, you've been with me such a short time; I didn't make the same provisions for you. Because you're still young and healthy.' Well, that made me—"

Joe interrupted. "Ever pull a holdup all by yourself?"

"Naw, sir! Only with them other four."

"How many jobs did you do?"

"We done—lemme figure. Yeah. Twenty. And I just driv th' car. That's all I done. Ever!"

Backing away from the bars, Joe said, "Johnson, we'll talk again—in a little while. Huh?"

A talker, it would be a long time before the chauffeur's confessional jag wore off. Joe left the cell block.

When he reentered the office, the Chief was still on the phone with the Prosecutor. But joy had vanished. Belden was in a rage, shouting, "Yes, I said th' punks would talk! But they've been on a three-month stickup spree. So how'n hell can we feel 'em for leads if we rush 'em off to that alley-house office you run?"

As the Chief paused, Duffy told Joe, "That Prosecutor's loaded with a tom-cat's nerve. He's pushing us to arraign these five bums—like we'd jugged 'em for loitering!"

"Huh!" Belden yelled at the phone. "I don't have the men to do it that quick. You said *Monday* morning first. Now you switch it to *Saturday* morning—so they'll be in court *by* Monday!"

"He's crazy!" Duffy said.

"You're crazy!" Belden said. "But I'll do it! Now get th' hell off my line!" He jammed the phone in its cradle with a bang.

"Try to be nice to some people!" Duffy said. "Try it!"

"Lowell will do anything to be Governor!" Belden said. "He's after headlines. No skin off *his* political beak if *we* mess it up."

Duffy said, "Well, we just got to try and deliver—"

"You listen!" Belden interrupted. "I want the last scrap of information pumped out of that mob. By Saturday morning too! See?"

Duffy said, "Yes, sir."

"You'll proceed from the first to the last stickup. And—"

"In *that* order?" Duffy asked, interrupting.

"Huh! We're only the police!" Belden said. "Will a spread in Sunday's papers land us in the Governor's mansion?"

Duffy said, "Oh! *Lowell* wants it that way."

"Huh! So no sleep for the men you put on it till it's all tied and wrapped up. Understand?"

Homicide's Shaw, Bandit's Carlton, Auto's Swenson, and Identification's Goldberg—the men Inspector Duffy had named to work with Joe in connection with processing the Quintet chauffeur for arraignment—were agreed that meeting the Prosecutor's deadline was one thing, it was another thing, they said, not to miss an important lead in the insane race to beat the exacting hands of the Prosecutor's arbitrary watch. Something would go wrong.

Four other crews—each a duplicate in unit composition—stood with Joe and his particular colleagues and listened grimly to Duffy's procedural instructions.

"Yes, you gotta finish this job by Saturday morning," the Inspector said. "And if you think you can skip being thorough, think some more. See? Comb every word these punks speak, run down every name, every place they mention. For leads. Lots of cases are still wide-open. At all times," he continued, "keep our five guests separated. Be informal, gentle, sympathetic. They'll cooperate. First, let 'em spill their guts. Then ease 'em into handing you the date and location of their first robbery. Clear that with me, so that all of you will be certain about that point.

Same procedure with murder. Next, get the overall number of jobs they did together. Then work forward. Get the relevant, material details of each successive crime: holdup and/or robbery-murder. End with the last stickup. See?"

The processing began at seven o'clock Wednesday night.

The chauffeur insisted upon addressing himself only to Joe, who had to carry the interview. But there were no pointed questions during this stage of the game. Johnson just rambled, naming personalities, places, continuity, and chronology. Goldberg jotted down the man's more pertinent statements. At 11 P.M. Joe went to Duffy, told him the culprit's recollection of the first robbery's date and location.

"He still maintains," Joe added, "there were twenty jobs in all."

"Those three points—date, location, total jobs—check."

"Five murders. They occurred during the sixth, eighth, tenth, fifteenth, and eighteenth robberies."

"That checks. What about the car?" Duffy said.

"Just one. Belonged to his employer, Mrs. Stevens. She's in Wildwood Hospital—an incurable, he says."

"I'll check on her."

Joe said, "Before each job he'd steal a set of license plates and substitute them for the set registered in the Stevens name."

"Swenson from Auto will check that. After each job the boys looked for him down in the Middle Ward. How come they missed him?"

"When Mrs. Stevens had to go to the hospital, she told him he could use a room in her apartment."

"He'd hole up there after a job. What about his dough?"

"He says he put most of it in the Oldhaven Merchants' Bank."

"An original stash for holdup money. Check the bank first thing in the morning. Where'd he spend the rest?"

"Says he gave some to his church."

"Forget it. Where else?"

"Girls. Goldberg has their names. He'd pick 'em up in the Mattox Hotel, a place run by a woman named Big Rose."

"Goldberg is Identification. I'll have him check the women for records and send Shaw to check the hotel. That's a Middle Ward dump, Joe. Too bad we couldn't spare you when this case first got going. Ten to one, you'd have done what the other boys' faces didn't let them do—pick up Johnson's trail. Maybe you'd have run into him there—at the Mattox—before all the killings started."

Joe said, "Water over the dam now."

"Yeah. I'm going to have Carlton round up witnesses. Need 'em for lineups. You check his room in the Stevens place. Take a squad car. Collect his clothes."

When Joe returned to Headquarters, after a look at the Stevens apartment, he had the chauffeur identify the particular garments he had worn during the commission of each crime; each piece of apparel was then labeled with a date, time notation, and a stated location. Next, Joe turned his attention to a long stream of witnesses who viewed the Bandit Quintet in intermittent lineups. He visited the bank, made notes on deposits and withdrawals.

Late Thursday afternoon, during a joint conference with the five processing detective contingents, the Inspector said, "Speed it up! Get 'em out there where the action occurred. Let 'em show you how they did it—in front of a camera. Tomorrow—that's Friday—and not a second later than 4 P.M., we got to let the stenographers start taking down their formal statements. Move!"

Sleep had been a stranger to Joe on Wednesday night. Sleep and Joe remained strangers Thursday night. He kept himself going with cigarettes, sandwiches, and lots of black coffee. Friday afternoon, at ten minutes to four, he marched up to Duffy.

"We have the details and the photographed 'reenactments' of Johnson's part in nineteen successive crimes," Joe announced.

"Well?" Duffy said, frowning.

."We didn't have time to run him through job number twenty."

Duffy grinned. "Okay. The cake's yours."

"Huh?"

"The Prosecutor's really after the details on the five killings. He'll schedule the easiest and juiciest murder for quick trial, so he can grab lots of headlines. Couple of crews had to cram, skip—to get in the murders. They're three and four jobs short, Joe."

"Then I don't get the dunce cap."

"Naw. You and your boys just trot Johnson through the nineteen jobs and he'll sing the whole tune to that last stickup by ear. The Prosecutor ain't worrying about what *we* miss. It's nearly four o'clock. Get going, Joe."

Each processing detective crew herded its own Quintet culprit up to the fourth floor of Headquarters and into an enormous, open, desk-strewn, rectangular room whose facilities were officially the property of the rank and file members of the Homicide Squad. Four of the Quintet were placed, separately, in the big rectangle's corners. Joe, his crew, and a stenographer gave Johnson a chair near a cluster of battered desks in the very middle of the room. He began making his formal statement Friday at precisely 4 P.M.

It was a slow, tedious task: boring, unexciting. They started with the first crime. Deleting extraneous matter as they went along, they retained as best they could the essential, relevant facts which were material to Johnson's own acts and words, and such other acts and words as occurred or were spoken in his presence.

When an original copy and a stack of carbons were typed, Gold-berg read the contents aloud to the chauffeur. Johnson read it aloud, then signed the confession. Joe and his colleagues provided witnessing signatures. A notary's seal was affixed to the docu-ment. And the procedure began again in connection with crime number two.

It went on and on. The detectives and culprits alike drank coffee, chewed sandwiches, lit one cigarette from another, and wistfully toyed with the idea of climbing in a bed.

Inspector Duffy roared, "Chief Belden's at home. He just phoned me. He's been in constant contact with Prosecutor Lowell. They'll be arriving here at Headquarters in a little while. Speed it up! How far off is Saturday morning?"

Gradually, the glare from the room's blazing lights turned the working men's haggard eyes into dull rubies. Their heads ached. Joe and his crew finished with Johnson's nineteenth statement.

When Homicide's Shaw said it was already Saturday morning, Joe glanced at his wristwatch. It was 1 A.M.

Bandit's Carlton said, "I'm dead on my feet."

"These boys," Shaw said, "just didn't mix with other crooks. They ain't handed us a single lead yet. Whiz this last one along."

Carlton said, "Joe, take a squint at that Wednesday's 'squeal sheet.' Go by that—and get this job over with!"

Glancing at a piece of paper, Joe said, "Give us the facts on your last job, Johnson."

Johnson said, "Tuesday night, I stole a set of license plates. Then I went in a phone booth and called the poolroom where them other boys was at. We got a job set for next day."

"Go on," Joe said.

"I went straight home," Johnson said, "and got in bed. Next

morning—Wednesday—I got up at eight o'clock. I was by myself. I never took nobody to my room—'cause ol' Mrs. Stevens trusted me. Once, her lawyer—Mr. Colbax Todd—writ a 'portant paper for her. She told me what was in it, axted me to put my name on it. So she musta trusted me. And I—"

Joe interrupted. Irrelevancies were creeping in. "You got up at 8 A.M."

Johnson said, "That paper never took care of me—lak it did them others. So I let them other boys talk me into—"

Joe interrupted again. "You got up at eight o'clock!"

"All that," Johnson said, "was before Mrs. Stevens went to th' hospital."

Shaw said, "What did you do Wednesday after eight?"

"I fixed a meal," Johnson said, "and et it. I was nervous. So I went and got th' car and driv to th' Middle Ward."

"Take time out there to talk to anybody?" Joe asked.

"I seen Prophet Hamid. He was right in front of his temple on Nickle Street. I knowed him. So when he called me, I stopped th' car. He axed me would I go and git an ol' man by th' name of Tom Turner. And I said yes. I went."

Joe said, "Anybody go with you? Where does Turner live?"

"I was by myself. He live on Dawkins Place. I don't know th' number. I just knows th' house. I driv there. Ol' man Turner was just coming out his front door. I driv him to th' Prophet's temple. I never got out. I driv to Oldhaven Park and done what I always done in there—switched license plates on th' car."

"Go on," Joe said.

"Then I driv to Commerce Square. A loan shop we was going to rob was there. I parked a block off. Them four other boys walked past and went in th' loan shop. They run out, jumped in th' car, and I started it. A block off we run into a radio car with two cops in it. They was awful mad at us for hitting 'em. They found out we was robbers. So they 'rested all five of us."

Joe said, "It was 11 A.M. Just who is Tom Turner?"

"An ol' man what used to go to th' church where I goes at."

Shaw said, "What about Prophet Hamid?"

"Him?" Johnson said. "Everybody down in th' Middle Ward knows *him*. I seen him 'round lots."

"In the Mattox—for instance?" Shaw asked. "With Big Rose?"

"Yeah. He make lak he know what you thinking 'bout. I give him plenty chances to tell me my mind. He's just a lot of big mouf."

Shaw said, "This wraps it up, boys. I'll call Duffy." He did.

Duffy said, "You fellows all through?"

" 'Cept for one thing," Johnson said.

"Yeah?" Duffy said. "What's that?"

"I b'lieves," Johnson replied, "I deserves a break—'cause I just ain't what you can call *bad*. Before I met up with them four other boys, I had never been in no real trouble. Mrs. Stevens—she took very sick. She said to me, 'Albert, you'll need another job. Use the car to look for one if you like.' So I—"

Interrupting, Duffy said, "She didn't mean for you to use her car in twenty stickups and five murders."

"I never done th' killings," the chauffeur said. "I just driv th' car. For them other boys. Before that I had a good record. Axt my pastor, Reverend G. J. Ball. Axt Mrs. Stevens."

Duffy said, "She's comatose."

"She's *what?*" Johnson said.

"In a coma. Unconscious," Duffy explained.

"Oh," Johnson said. "But Detective Hill—he know th' real thing what made me rob folks. And I think he should help git me a break."

Duffy said, "First, give him a break. Sign this last statement."

"Okay. Sure! Didn't I sign them other statements?"

At 2 A.M. Joe got in an elevator. When he stepped out on the first floor, Chief Belden was waiting to go up.

"The arraignment is set for 1 P.M., Monday," Belden said. "You look busted up."

Joe was a big man: six feet one inch in height, with two hundred pounds of solid muscle appropriately strung along an excellently developed frame. Ordinarily, his eyes were a shade of brown in complete consonance with the chestnut hue of his skin. But now his eyes were bloodshot, his face a mat of unshaven black bristles, and his huge physique literally drooped.

He said, "I *feel* busted up too."

"I know," Belden said. "You needn't come in till noon, Monday."

Wearily, Joe stumbled out to the sidewalk in front of Headquarters just as several cars pulled up to the curb. Prosecutor Elwood Lowell and some of his assistants got out. A taxicab rounded a corner. Joe signaled its driver.

He got in the cab. "The Wallace Thurman Houses—Unit Four—on the far side of the Middle Ward."

Pulling away from the curb, the taxi driver said, "What'd they have you down to Headquarters for, huh, buddy?"

Tired, on edge, Joe snatched a gold-plated shield out of his pocket. Sticking it over the driver's shoulder and under the man's nose, he said, "Cop! Central Bureau. See? I'm in a hurry."

The tiny three-room apartment on the fourth floor of the model housing development where Joe maintained bachelor quarters was a welcome sight. Joe took one look at himself in the bathroom mirror. Then he stumbled into the bedroom and collapsed across the bed without removing anything except his hat.

———

The telephone awakened him. Rolling over, he picked up the jan-
gling instrument and heard Chief Belden's voice say: "Lad, Joe,
my boy! This is a helluva crime, and I should be eternally incarcerated for committing it. But you've got to come back to Headquarters. Right away."

"Huh?" Joe grunted. "What time is it?"

"Four A.M.," Belden replied. "I know you just left here. But
listen: an old-fashioned school teacher, named Middlesexton,
brought a little colored kid down here just now. The kid says she
don't trust white cops. Her teacher backs her up about that. If it
wasn't for that teacher—wait'll you see her—we'd take the box."

Joe said, "Box?"

"Yes. The kid's got something in a box."

"There're ten other Negro cops in Oldhaven," Joe said.

"Yeah! In uniform." Belden said. "You know they can't—get th'
hell down here, Detective Hill!"

"Yes, sir," Joe said, adding, "as soon as I put on my hat!"

Luck brought a cab for Joe in ten minutes. At fifteen minutes
to five Saturday morning he entered Chief Belden's office where
he found the Chief, a freshly shaven Inspector Duffy, Prosecutor
Elwood Lowell, and two other people. One was a gray-haired
little old lady, dressed in a style years and years out of date, whose
chalk-white countenance was a combination of grim sternness
and prim stubbornness. The other was a very small black girl. She
was shabbily clothed, but clean. Her eyes were big, round, packed
with frank suspicion, and jammed with naked fear. With trembling hands she clutched a package about five inches long, three
inches wide, two inches deep—wrapped in white paper, tied with
a green string.

The Chief was seated behind his desk. Duffy and the Prosecutor occupied chairs near Belden. Their faces seemed unusually pink. The child and the little old lady sat side by side in straight-back chairs against one of the room's walls. The little old lady favored Joe's rumpled clothes, bearded face, and red eyes with one glance. She reacted unfavorably.

Looking at the little old lady, the child said, "He's colored. But is he a real policeman? He don't wear clothes lak none."

"He *doesn't* wear clothes *like one,* June," the old lady replied.

"Yes, ma'am," the child said. *"Doesn't—like—one."*

The little old lady fixed Chief Belden with a stern stare. "Is this the person we've been waiting for?"

Belden gulped, sputtering, "Er—madam—he—"

"Miss Middlesexton, please."

"Yes, ma'am," Belden said. "Miss Middlesexton."

Duffy said, "This person—as Miss Middlesexton calls Detective Hill—has been continuously at work since Wednesday afternoon. He hasn't had time to bathe, shave, or put on clean clothing."

The Inspector had addressed the Chief who regained enough composure to say, "Detective Hill, ma'am, is a graduate of a most reputable university where he was a high-ranking student and an ace athlete. He won—and I do mean *won*—a post in our Department when he was twenty-two years old. He spent seven and a half years in uniform before we had the good sense to upgrade him to plainclothes status. For more than a year now he's been a member of my own personal organization, the Central Bureau."

"And we think," Duffy added, "he's a nicely balanced piece of physical and mental machinery."

"June," Miss Middlesexton told the child, "I'm satisfied that this man is an authentic officer. You may tell him your story."

Belden said, "Ma'am, let's hear a word from you first."

"Thank you," Miss Middlesexton said. "June, whose last name is Jones, is a second-grade pupil of mine at Public School Twenty. Early Friday morning she came to my desk and asked me to escort her to a policeman, adding that he must be colored. Unfortunately, Chief Belden, some Middle Ward children are afraid of—"

Belden said hastily, "Please continue, ma'am."

"I didn't care to become involved in a trifling matter," Miss Middlesexton said. "I demanded that June tell me why she needed a policeman."

"She wouldn't talk?" Belden said.

Miss Middlesexton nodded. "I know now I was too exacting. At one o'clock this morning June rang my doorbell at 54 Wilson Avenue."

Belden interrupted. "Where does June live?"

The child said, "Sixty-eight Dawkins Place. Top floor. Rear."

Belden leaned forward. "Miss Middlesexton, June is a mere child. Dawkins Place and Wilson Avenue are five miles apart. How'd she know where you live? How'd she get there?"

"Once a semester for the past thirty years," Miss Middlesexton explained, "I entertain my school charges in my home. Of course, on those occasions, I escort them there. June attended the last party a month ago. I presume she—"

Looking at Joe, June interrupted. "I walked to where she lives at."

Miss Middlesexton said, "June showed me the contents of the box—" The little old lady swallowed hard, her pale face turning gray.

Belden smiled at June. "Let's see what's in your box. Hmmn?"

The child looked at Joe.

"Chief Belden," he said, "is a nice man. Cross my heart!"

The child got out of her chair and sat on the floor. She untied her package's green string, stripped off its white paper, holding the underside up so Joe could see it.

Wearily, he sat down on the floor beside the child. "Letters apparently cut out of newspapers," he said, "are pasted here, saying, 'Talk only to the Lord's True Messenger.' "

Duffy got out of his chair. "It's an ordinary matchbox," he said. "Slide it open, kid."

As enormous tears welled up in her eyes, the child said, "Pa Tom never come home Wednesday night. Nor Thursday night. Nor before I slipped off from Ma Grace, and—and—"

Miss Middlesexton said, "I understand June's parents were killed some time ago in an automobile accident. She lives with an elderly pair of grandparents. Her maternal grandparents."

Duffy said, "Come on, kid. Open the box."

The child said, "There was another box—before this one. Me and Ma Grace found it Thursday morning laying on th' floor in th' hall—jes' outside th' door. Ma Grace acted real scared. 'Chile,' she told me, 'don't you talk to nobody 'bout this!' When I come back from school, Ma Grace was laying on her bed, crying, moaning, and praying to God to tell her what to do. Friday morning I found this here box. Pa Tom—he was still gone. So I never tole Ma Grace I had done found it. Miss Middlesexton—she's white. But I trusts her. So I axted her to help me."

Joe said, "Pa Tom. Tom. Dawkins Place."

"He my grandpa," the child said. "And that's where I lives at."

Miss Middlesexton said, "Her grandparents are Thomas and Grace Turner."

Belden picked up one of the telephones on his desk. "Rush this," he said. "Steer a prowl to 68 Dawkins Place, top floor, rear flat. Investigate the absence of Thomas Turner."

Miss Middlesexton said, "June, you must—must open it now."

"Yes, ma'am," the child said. Then she slid the box open.

Inspector Duffy said, "Good God!"

"What is it?" Belden said.

Joe said, "A finger. It's black. A piece of cotton is stuck on the spot where it was cut off from—"

He stopped talking because the child had burst into loud hysterical sobs. His weariness seemed to evaporate. Anger rose up inside of him, heating his brain, stimulating it, making bits of images and word pictures rush through his mind. He stayed right where he was—on the floor—and took the screaming little girl in his arms, cradling her, rocking with her from side to side.

He was only half aware that Miss Middlesexton had seated herself beside him to help soothe the child with a woman's voice and hand. He hardly noticed the routine fashion with which Belden and Duffy and Prosecutor Elwood Lowell were handling the telephones on the Chief's desk—summoning Homicide Squad Lieutenant O'Hara, photographers, fingerprint technicians, an Assistant Police Surgeon, Prosecutor's Investigators. Joe gave practically all his attention to the assembly of image and word fragments so that he could examine the result for a clue to what he knew would be missing.

He heard Belden saying, "Joe! Joe! Snap out of it!"

"Yes, sir." He looked at his wristwatch. It said 5:45 A.M.

"This is your case, Joe," Belden said. "Looks like a nasty one."

Duffy said, "Joe needs rest."

One of the telephones on the Chief's desk jangled. When Belden replaced the instrument, he said, "Prowl car boys reporting on the trip to Dawkins Place. They found another box outside the Turners' hall door. They broke into the flat and found Grace Turner—she was very old—a D-O-A."

"D-O-A?" Miss Middlesexton said. "What does that mean?"

Duffy glanced at the child whom Joe was still cradling in his arms. She had quieted down. "Do it mean," she said, "that Ma Grace done been scared so—she's dead?"

"D-O-A," Duffy told Miss Middlesexton, "means dead on arrival."

"Frightened into her grave!" the little old lady exclaimed. "Can't you *do* something?"

Joe said, "I think I'm onto what it's about, ma'am. I want June to answer a few questions. What work do your grandparents do, June?"

"They worked," the child replied, "a long time ago. But not now. Because of th' Gov'ment checks and my state check."

"Do you mean," Joe said, "that your grandparents get old age pension checks, and that you—"

June interrupted. "Yes, sir. And I'm what they call a 'State Child'—'cause my parents is dead. Th' state—it gives Pa Tom and Ma Grace money for my keep."

Belden said, "That kind of money isn't big enough for a motive—"

Joe interrupted. "June, where'd your grandparents *used* to work?"

"Pa Tom—he driv th' carriage. Ma Grace—she done th' cooking. It was for a rich lady. Then she got a automobile. And she give up her big estate. And Pa Tom and Ma Grace—they was too old to do much more work. So then my father and mother—they chauffeured and cooked for—"

"Now this is it!" Joe said. "What was the rich lady's name?"

"I don't rightly know her name," the child replied. "Pa Tom and Ma Grace—they got mad at th' lady. Because she said they was too old to work. And Pa Tom wanted th' rich lady to keep th' carriage. But she got th' car. That was how my mother and father was killed—in the car one day, going somewhere. And Pa Tom—

he said he never wanted to hear that rich lady's name called in front of his ears."

Joe said, "Where do you go to church, June?"

"I still goes to Reverend G. J. Ball's church. Pa Tom and Ma Grace—they quit going there. Only old people can go where they go. Reverend Ball—he used to come to th' house to axt Pa Tom and Ma Grace to come back to his church. But Pa Tom—he said that all his life he'd been going to Reverend Ball's kind of church and that his kind of church weren't doing our people no good. Reverend Ball—he said no cult was going to help our people either."

"I wonder," Joe said, "if Prosecutor Lowell will telephone a lawyer for us. If the Prosecutor does it, we'll save time."

"Anything," Lowell said. "What's the lawyer's name?"

Duffy said, "Have you got something, Joe?"

"I'll know after the Prosecutor makes that phone call," Joe replied. "His name now. It's in our files. But maybe I can remember it. Bard? Hodge? No. Rod? Doesn't fit."

"You'd better use the files," Belden said.

"I've got it," Joe said. "The name's Colbax Todd."

"Todd?" Prosecutor Lowell said. "What's Colbax Todd got to do with this?"

Joe said, "Ask him if he has a Mrs. Stevens as a client. Ask him if he recently drew up a will for her in which Thomas and Grace Turner appear among the beneficiaries. If so, for what amount?"

Lowell said, "I'll make the call. But I know Todd will insist he has to consult his client before he can give—"

Duffy interrupted. "She's comatose in Wildwood Hospital. Or was. By now, she may be dead."

"Oh!" Lowell said. "Then Todd may—I'll phone him."

"Maybe this'll add up!" Belden exclaimed, motioning Lowell to a phone on his desk.

When Lowell put down the instrument, he said, "Todd's client died about five hours ago. She left the Turners an outright bequest of fifty thousand dollars."

"Okay, Joe," Belden said. "You've got the motive. Now what?"

Joe said, "Can we stage a couple of raids? Simultaneously? And right away?"

"I told you," Belden said, "this was your case. We raid. Now!"

Joe, Belden, and Duffy, riding in the first car of a stream of police vehicles, left Headquarters at 6:45 A.M. The last shades of night were bowing out of the sky and the city was fast discarding sleep for another day of toil and turmoil. The cars kept their sirens silent.

"I've been watching you, Joe," Chief Belden said. "I think this thing's made you mad."

Joe didn't say anything.

The police caravan swung into the section of Oldhaven known as the Middle Ward. It was not at all unlike any other Negro community in any other northern Big City. Most of it was slum area.

Duffy said, "We're on Nickle Street now. So we're almost there."

"The other raiding party, according to you, Joe," Belden said, "is more likely to find Turner than we are."

Duffy said, "As soon as we break in at our end, I'll cover the phones and call Lieutenant O'Hara at the other end of the job."

The car stopped. Belden said, "This place was once a store."

The front of the building before which they stopped had been renovated so that it resembled a combination of sectarian structures: a church, a mosque, a miniature cathedral.

Duffy said, "Give the guys a couple of seconds to get set."

"Pretty early," Belden said. "The door's probably locked."

"There's a bell," Joe said.

"Think he'll try and start something, Joe?" Belden said.

Joe replied, "I hope he does!"

"You keep your head," Belden advised. "No matter how mad you—"

Duffy said, "This is it. Let's go."

Joe rang the bell. A woman opened the door, grasped who the visitors were, and started to back away.

"Just take it easy, sister," Duffy told her. "How many phones in this place?"

"One," the woman said. "It's in the office."

"Where's Hamid?" Belden asked her.

"In the office," the woman replied.

Belden said, "No noise. Get going. Take us there."

The woman led them through a small, dark auditorium. She opened a door. Pushing her inside, they closed the door behind them. A man sat at a desk on which a telephone rested. Belden said, "Are you Prophet Hamid?"

The man stood up. He was short and very slim. The hair on his head was long, kinky, and reddish. Some of it made a sharp, straight line just under his nose and a Vandyke on his chin. His skin was a freckled saddle-yellow. He wore a black cutaway coat with satin lapels, a clerical collar, striped pants, and shiny black shoes with pointed toes. He looked like a dressed-up bantam rooster.

"May I use your phone?" Duffy said, taking over the instrument so that the man had to step away from the desk.

"You're up early this morning," Belden told the man.

The man said, "We always have an early service on Saturdays."

"That used to be," Belden said. "But no more."

"What do you mean?" the man said. "Just who are you?"

Joe said, "The police."

"You can't come in here like this!" the man exclaimed. "This is a holy place. I'm a holy man!"

"Shut up!" Belden told him.

For a while nobody said anything. The only sound in the room was the hard breathing of the woman. Then there was a knock on the door and Duffy said, "Come in!"

A detective opened the door. "We've combed the place," he said. "Upstairs. In the cellar. We didn't find him."

Belden nodded, waved the detective out of the room, and looked at Duffy. "Phone Lieutenant O'Hara. See what he found."

After Duffy put back the phone, he said, "Joe was right, Chief. O'Hara found Turner, three fingers missing, stashed in the Mattox Hotel. The woman who runs the place—Big Rose—is talking."

Belden said, "Okay, Hamid. Now *you* talk."

"The lot of you!" Hamid said. "Get out of here!"

Joe walked over to Hamid and slapped his face.

Belden said, "For your own sake, Hamid—talk."

Standing close to Hamid, Joe said, "How long have Thomas and Grace Turner been members of your cult?"

"Don't crowd me!" Hamid said.

"Not long enough, huh?" Joe said. "Not long enough for you to work your real racket on them."

"Just how does he do it, Joe?" Duffy asked.

"As soon as old people, like the Turners, fall under the spell of his mumbo-jumbo," Joe said, "he demands the last pieces of property they have in the world—their insurance policies. He uses his temple as a front. By persuasion, by force, by tricks, by any means he can think of, Hamid makes the old people change the beneficiaries originally named in their policies so that when they die the money is bequeathed to his temple. The old people will usually sign any paper he hands them. Occasionally, he has them borrow money on their policies. Frequently, he makes them surrender the policies for their cash value. And *he* pockets the money."

"Hamid," Duffy said, "we've been questioning one of the Quintet Bandits. I mean Albert Johnson. We know that Johnson told you that a wealthy woman, Mrs. Stevens, had named Thomas and Grace Turner in her will. We also know that Johnson told you that Mrs. Stevens was dying. You take it from there, Joe."

"There's a clincher—a big payoff—to Hamid's racket," Joe said. "He cuts the whole hog. He knows his own people— Negroes. He draws his cult membership from the most ignorant, the most superstitious, the most stupid of them. He knows they regard all public institutions—including law-enforcement agencies and the courts—as hostile to their interests. So he inveigles his ancient cultists into signing an agreement giving all they own to his temple."

Duffy said, "Hmmn-huh. When he learned that the Turners were beneficiaries in the Stevens will and Mrs. Stevens was dying, he moved fast."

Moving still closer to Hamid, Joe said, "He got his hands on old man Turner, got Big Rose to stash the man in the Mattox Hotel. But Turner held out. Time was short. Hamid cut off the old man's fingers, one by one. He sent the fingers to Grace Turner to terrorize her into coming to him to beg for mercy."

"Move away from me!" Hamid screamed at Joe.

Joe's right shoulder moved suddenly. His right fist smashed hard against Hamid's mouth. Hamid went down on the floor, mouthing profanity and blood.

Belden said, "Easy, Joe. Easy, boy. Don't lose your head."

Duffy said, "Want to talk now, Hamid? Before Detective Hill really goes to work on you? The Chief may try and stop Hill but I won't!"

Belden said, "Hamid, Mrs. Stevens is dead. Bet you didn't know."

Duffy said, "And guess what? The County Prosecutor is going into the courts to have Tom Turner declared incompetent. The Turners' grandchild will get the Stevens dough."

"She wouldn't have got it," Hamid said, "if the old man had signed!"

"The terrorizing you gave Grace Turner," Belden said, "killed her."

Duffy laughed. "Prosecutor Lowell says we can't make a murder rap stick to you, Hamid. But we insist that he have you indicted for murder. Not long ago he asked us—the police—to do the impossible. We did it. Now we want him to do it. After all, no matter how you did it, you murdered Grace Turner. We want you, Hamid—for murder."

"Tell me just one thing," Hamid said. "Johnson—that chauffeur—didn't know. He said he thought it would be about a thousand dollars. But just how much did that Mrs. Stevens leave the Turners?"

Belden said, "Huh! This is funny. This is going to give this rat a bigger thrill than the chair. Tell him, Joe."

Joe said, "Fifty thousand dollars."

ROBERT O. GREER JR. (1944–) was born in Columbus, Ohio, and grew up in Gary, Indiana. He earned his B.A. at Miami University (Ohio) in 1965, then earned numerous degrees in dentistry, medicine, and pathology from Howard University and Boston University, as well as an M.F.A. in Creative Writing from Boston and an Honorary Doctorate of Humane Letters from Miami. He is a professor of pathology, dentistry, medicine, and surgery at the University of Colorado Health Sciences Center. He has written three textbooks and more than a hundred scientific and medical articles. He founded the *High Plains Literary Review* in 1986 and continues to work as its editor-in-chief. A resident of Denver for over 30 years, he also owns a ranch near Steamboat Springs, Colorado, where he raises cattle.

Although he has written several medical thrillers, he is best known for the mystery novels and stories about CJ Floyd, a tough, often curmudgeonly, cheroot-smoking African-American bail bondsman and occasional bounty hunter. The highly respected and much-loved CJ has many similarities to his creator: they both collect license plates and memorabilia of the American West, and share a love for and expertise in jazz. There are seven novels about Floyd, beginning with *The Devils' Hatband* in 1996, and all feature some elements of Greer's life, such as when CJ opens a shop specializing in Western antiques in *The Fourth Perspective* (2006).

"Oprah's Song," which features CJ Floyd, has never before been published.

Oprah's Song

Robert Greer

"Wasn't expectin' that."

"What?"

"The laughin', the clappin'. People stompin' their heels. Do folks always do that at a hangin'?"

"They did for Jimmy. Now let's get the fuck outa here."

Petee Nuñez, Rocky Mountain Puerto Rican transplant, skinny as a rail, his face acne-scarred from chin to brow, tapped the accelerator, and the gunmetal-gray Cadillac he was driving slipped beyond the battered, graffiti-scrawled stage door of the Bohemian Club, past a yellow caution light, onto Champa Street and into the neon Denver night. All the while, the man at his side, Rulon Jakes, continued smiling.

"Shit, we thought he was play-actin', hangin' there like that, tongue bulgin' outa his mouth like a over-roasted weenie, arms flappin', gaspin' for air. Figured it was just a new part of his act."

Everard Townes, all five foot three of him, scratched at a wiry tuft of gray hair sprouting from the middle of his balding crown. CJ Floyd, the much larger man interrogating him, studied the little man's face, trying to decide whether Townes was lying. Still uncertain, CJ slipped a crushed pack of cheroots out of his vest pocket, tapped out the last one, and lit up.

Eyeing Townes again, CJ smiled as he took a long draw on his cheroot. He wasn't being paid $2,500 to smoke or to watch Everard Townes, an aging street hustler, disgruntled former postal worker, and dishonorably discharged soldier, look for wiggle room. He was being paid to find out who had killed Jimmy P. Kane. "'P' for Paul, like in the Bible," Jimmy had always liked to say about his middle name, as if he were some kind of reincarnated holy man instead of a thirty-five-year-old, down-on-his-luck college dropout and former steel-mill worker who was now trying his hand at being a comedian. Scrutinizing Townes's body language, CJ said, "What did you tell Denver's finest?"

"Same thing I'm tellin' you. Course I was less wordy. Gotta be with cops. They'll use what you say against you." Townes smiled. "Course you ain't never done time, CJ, so you don't actually know what I mean. But trust me. They do. Anyway, the cops are callin' Jimmy's death an accident."

CJ responded with an arched eyebrow and a cold, incisive stare. He'd done time. Two years of it. But not the kind Townes was talking about. Time spent not behind bars but in the swampy estuaries and insect-riddled jungles of Vietnam, where he'd spent two navy tours as a machine gunner aboard a 55-foot Swift boat patrolling the twisted waterways of the Mekong River Delta. Now, almost thirty years later, whenever it turned muggy and hot and the night crackled with insects on the wing, his two killing-field tours of duty still clouded his thinking. He'd done the kind of time Everard Townes could never fathom. The kind that stole your youth and crushed your dreams. Tossing aside his half-smoked cheroot, CJ ground the butt beneath the toe of his boot and into the oil-stained concrete floor of the dilapidated machine shop they were standing in, then flashed Townes a *gotcha* kind of smile. "Tell me about Jimmy's act and this *Oprah* thing he was part of," CJ said, leaning back against a workbench.

"Nothin' to tell that I ain't said before, or ain't appeared in the newspaper or on TV. Jimmy had worked his way up to bein' one of ten finalists for a show Oprah was doin' called 'America's Best Amateur Comedians.' Shit, surprised you ain't heard about it. Been in the news for months. Oprah's gonna spotlight three up-and-comin' amateurs. Bring 'em on her show like she did for America's top twenty comic pros about a year ago and, like always, since the girl sits at the right hand of God, deliver somebody a glass of instant fame. And instant cash! Show your mug on the tube, chit-chat with her for a minute or two, and shit, you're mother fuckin' set for life."

"Jimmy's act was that good?"

Everard grinned proudly. "Damn sure was. Helped him polish it up myself. If you spent a little more time hangin' instead of playin' Five Points horseman, CJ, you'd know that."

CJ frowned. Denver's still predominantly black Five Points neighborhood, where he'd spent most of his life, was filled with what his uncle Ike, the man who had raised him and ultimately started him in the bail bond business, had always described as six kinds of people: hustlers, helpers, high ditties, homemakers, whores, and horsemen. As an inquisitive six-year-old CJ had once asked Ike to explain what kind of person he'd eventually turn out to be. Ike had winked and said, "A horseman, what else?"

It wasn't until CJ was nineteen years old and three days away from shipping out for his first tour of duty in Vietnam that his uncle had fully explained what a horseman was. He'd taken CJ aside, given him the Bronze Star Ike had earned in Korea to carry with him to Vietnam for good luck, and explained that horsemen were people charged with keeping the bad on earth from bubbling up to outweigh the good.

CJ turned to Everard and said, "Everybody's gotta choose their own path, Everard. I'll concentrate on mine; you worry about yours."

Everard shrugged. "Whatever. As for Jimmy, he was on a road to the big time. Nobody's act was better. Him playin' the part of a half-high philosophizin' sailor with a little now-and-again magic comin' outa his ass. Had the act down pat. Tweakin' all the political angles, highlightin' the friction between men and women, emphasizin' the head-bangin' between the generations, his special takes on religion and race. Had the whole damn thing nibbled down to a science. He'd be part of the time play-actin', part of the time lyin', and part of the time tellin' the truth. And all the while he'd be swaggerin' across the stage spoutin' wisdom and homilies, folk tales and fact, till he had the audience in a fuckin' frenzy."

"Where'd the magic come in?"

Everard broke into a broad, self-satisfied grin. "Put that in myself. Told Jimmy if he wanted to be on *Oprah*, he needed somethin' to set him apart from the pack. Help him shine up the whole damn comedy nugget. Know what I mean? Shit, I had him pullin' life-sized cardboard cutouts and inflatable blowups of politicians right outa his ass. We'd project images of hip-hop stars on the ceiling, then have 'em appear in the audience like a ghost. He had one routine where he even set his toenails on fire, and I'm the one who figured out how he could do all that." Everard's voice suddenly trailed off. "I even set up the fake hangin' thing at the act's end."

Sensing that Everard had just uttered something he wished he could take back, CJ said, "Don't stop now."

Everard continued, his tone less enthusiastic. "At the end of his act, after Jimmy had worked the crowd into a frenzy sayin' he couldn't stand no more hate, hypocrisy, hemp smokin', or whores, he'd pretend to hang himself. The whole thing was staged to look totally real. He'd walk up six wooden stairs, clunkin' his way toward a makeshift gallows, slip a noose around his neck, spit out a string of one-liners aimed at every sacred cow on this earth, and then drop through a trap door. The door was for real and so was the seven-foot drop—and for that matter, so was the noose—but it had a slipknot in it so that when Jimmy fell, it would slip away and he wouldn't get hurt.

"Same time he was fallin', smoke would blanket the stage, and the next thing you know Jimmy'd pop up in the back of the auditorium, behind the audience, a set of angel wings flappin' from his shoulders, a sailor's Dixie cup cocked to one side of his head, a bottle of Jack Daniel's in his right hand, with his left arm wrapped around a half-naked sista. All the while he be talkin' high-octane smack—the kind you heard from Don King in his prime. Tellin' you, CJ, you missed one hell of an act."

"Sounds like I did. The night he died, what went wrong?" said CJ, hoping to gauge whether Everard's emotion was genuine or rehearsed.

Everard's words came out slowly. "The slipknot failed. Son of a bitch turned out to be real. Fucker was supposed to slip away, but it didn't, and the drop snapped Jimmy's neck."

"Could the audience see what happened?"

Everard paused, briefly chewing his lower lip. "That was the second problem we had that night, 'sides the knot. The smokescreen, the one that should've gave Jimmy his cover so he could sneak to the back of the audience—well, it didn't work, and since the gallows wasn't no real gallows, just a four-by-eight platform with a cutout in the front just big enough for Jimmy's body to drop through, the audience saw the whole thing. Even with all the hootin' and the hollerin', people figured somethin' had gone wrong pretty quick. I cut Jimmy down real fast. His feet wasn't no more than a foot or so from the ground. It was just too late."

"Who was responsible for the slipknot?"

When Everard didn't answer, CJ repeated the question.

"Me," he finally said, rocking from side to side, eyes tearing up, his response a near whisper.

CJ studied the pained expression on Everard's face. Townes had been a hustler, a gofer, a petty thief, and a drunk, and CJ suspected that he was probably better than most people at lying, but right then the one-time street hustler's sentiments seemed to be real.

"Guess that's it," said CJ, preparing to leave. "By the way, how much was Jimmy paying you?"

"A hundred and fifty a week and all the cheap whiskey I could drink. Woulda been more if he'd made *Oprah*."

"But he didn't," said CJ, striding toward the door, leaving Townes nodding in agreement.

Rulon Jakes slipped the Glock he always carried into a specially designed oversized right pants pocket, then walked to the sink, a popcorn bowl tucked under one arm, and washed his greasy hands. The room he and Petee Nuñez were sharing smelled strongly of witch hazel and burned Old Maids.

Petee saturated a cotton ball with the pungent elixir that for most of his life had served as a cure-all, methodically wiped down the fingers and cuticles of his left hand, and quizzically eyed Jakes. "How's Floyd fit in?"

"Arletta Dean," said Jakes in a hollow West Texas drawl. "She hired him to find out what happened to Jimmy."

"I thought she and Jimmy broke up."

"They did. But he was still strokin' her. Know it for a fact."

Petee shook his head. "Damn."

"What's love got to do with it?" said Jakes with a nasal snicker. "Always remember, Petee my boy, when it comes to women, it's the length that counts, not the love."

Petee nodded with a grin. "What the hell's Arletta got to gain?"

"That's my worry." Jakes's response was pointed and forceful.

Nuñez shrugged, backing off the subject like a scalded dog. "Think she'll drag in the cops? You know, they're callin' the whole thing a accident."

"You never know with someone like her. She's been a hooker, a marine, and a nurse. When it comes to women like that, you just gotta guess which turd's gonna surface. I'm betting that if we pay her a visit we'll find out soon enough."

"What if she screams to the cops?"

"She won't scream but once."

Petee nodded in agreement and shoved his bottle of witch hazel aside as he reached for the only other object on the tabletop in front of him, an antique pearl-handled four-inch switchblade. Grinning broadly and flashing matching rows of perfectly aligned gold-capped front teeth, he slipped the knife into his shirt pocket, adjusted himself in his seat, and went back to doing his nails.

"Just stay put, girl. CJ'll be here any minute."

CJ's Las Vegas showgirl-sized partner, Flora Jean Benson, stood directly behind a seated, quivering Arletta Dean, her hands firmly clamped on Arletta's shoulders, hoping the other woman wouldn't bolt.

"I knew I shouldn't've hired you and CJ. All that once a marine, always a marine bullshit you fed me the other night's gonna get me killed, Flora Jean. I knew I should've just let the cops handle it."

"Come on, Arletta, you're tougher than that. And don't knock the corps. They transformed you from a streetwalker to a nurse."

"I ain't knockin' nothin', Flora Jean. I just like breathin'."

Flora Jean stepped away from the chair, leaving a space between them that accentuated Flora Jean's six-foot-one-inch height. Very few clients who entered the bail-bonding offices of Floyd & Benson ever stood eye to eye with either owner—and Flora Jean, plain faced, street savvy, self-assured, and always no-nonsense, a former marine intelligence operative who'd done a tour in Desert Storm, liked it that way.

Arletta said, "Findin' out what happened to Jimmy won't work a lick for me if I'm dead."

"You won't be."

"Humph! It's not your ass they're after, Flora Jean. Rulon Jakes plays for keeps. And that little kiss-ass weasel of a lapdog of his, Petee Nuñez—I hear he's killed people before."

"He's not gonna kill . . ."

"You in there, Flora Jean?" CJ called from outside the locked front door. "Who locked the damn door anyway?"

"Hold your horses; I'm comin'." Flora Jean took three long strides across her office, a cramped converted alcove at the front of the turn-of-the-century Victorian building that had served as CJ's office and home on bail bondsman's row since his return from Vietnam. Shaking her head, she flipped the deadbolt and swung the door open.

"What the hell's going on?" CJ's face was knotted into an unflattering frown.

Flora Jean nodded toward where Arletta was seated. "She's been here almost an hour and she's scared to death. Pleaded with me to lock the door."

Arletta looked directly into CJ's eyes as he approached her, her own eyes filled with fear. "It's Rulon Jakes. He called me this morning a little bit before eight. Said he'd heard I had you lookin' into Jimmy's death. He told me accidents happen, especially to people like me, then he laughed and hung up. I'm scared, CJ. I heard that Jakes had that pet monkey of his, Petee Nuñez, cut off a woman's nipples last year because she refused to dance with him at some club. I don't want either of those two animals comin' after me."

Flashing Arletta a look that said *don't worry*, CJ clasped her right hand in his and squeezed it. "Nuñez won't be cutting anybody. Jakes either."

Not completed convinced, Arletta said, "I heard Nuñez did time in Joliet, a prison back in Illinois."

Flora Jean had heard enough. "And CJ and I both did time in a war! Ain't nobody afraid of that little-ass rodent." The muscles above Flora Jean's eyebrows started twitching.

Concerned because things always seemed to go south whenever his and Flora Jean's war gears started churning, CJ said, "Cool your jets, Flora Jean."

"I'll kick that little weasel's ass myself if need be."

CJ didn't respond, aware that Flora Jean meant exactly what she said. The room fell silent until Flora Jean, now a bit calmer, spoke again. "Let's forget about Jakes and that trained seal of his for the moment. Have the cops changed their tune about Jimmy's death?"

"No, they're still callin' it a accident." Arletta paused and stared up blankly at the ceiling. "You know, we weren't engaged no more, me and Jimmy. We were just good friends. Didn't matter, he and I were still on the very same track. And I'm tellin' you, Jimmy's death wasn't no accident. Jimmy wasn't the kind who left things to chance. The man was a perfectionist, even when it came down to tyin' his shoes. Always made sure the knots were perfectly centered over the middle of each shoe's tongue. I seen him practice his comedy routines for hours on end, four mirrors squared up around him to make sure that every move, gesture, smile, and frown was just right. There is no way Jimmy would make a mistake that might get him killed. He would've checked the slipknot on that noose and every other thing that had to do with that fake hangin' ten times to a hundred. On top of that, he and Everard Townes always checked the props together, including the noose one last time before Jimmy ever went on stage." Arletta's eyes welled up with tears.

"Did anyone else have access to the noose besides the two of them?" asked CJ.

"No!"

"Jimmy have any folks he'd rubbed the wrong way?"

Arletta thought for a moment, tears streaming down her cheeks. "Only Jakes and Nuñez."

"Why the bad blood?"

"Don't know, really, but their differences hadn't been brewin' very long. No more than a couple of months. Come to think of it, they started buttin' heads about the same time the whole *Oprah* thing started."

"You're sure?"

Arletta nodded.

Experience had taught CJ that people as fragile as Arletta tended to give unreliable answers, so he decided not to force the issue. But her sudden silence had him wondering if she was telling him something less than the truth about Jimmy's problems with Jake and Nuñez.

"Any other bad blood I should know about?"

Arletta wiped away her tears and thought for a moment. "Not bad blood, really, but there was some local show-business rivalry, that kind of stuff."

"Between?"

"Jimmy and Gwenette Strong." Arletta rolled her eyes. "You know, that siddity, high-yellow bitch from Park Hill."

"I've heard of her." CJ glanced at Flora Jean, making certain she'd noticed Arletta's sudden animation.

Arletta let out a sigh and shook her head. "Wouldn't you know it? Oprah puts out a cattle call for America's best amateur standup comics. The field gets narrowed down to ten, and two of 'em end up bein' from Denver. Now, you know good and well her people ain't pickin' no two acts from the very same city. Just Jimmy's luck. Up against a vamp with connections."

"Gwenette had connections to Oprah?"

Arletta laughed. "No. But she's connected. To Nelson Riles, and ain't no tellin' where he's got ties."

CJ looked surprised. "He's just a city councilman. Never heard he had entertainment contacts."

"He doesn't. But he's got money, and in America cash still hooks you up. Riles was the money behind Gwenette's resort bookings in Vail and Aspen and the cash behind her regional comedy shows. I heard he was even gonna bankroll a comedy CD for her."

CJ stroked his chin. "Was their deal business or pleasure?"

"Damn, CJ. Whatta you think? Riles was punchin' her clock mornin', noon, and night."

"Bet his wife was real happy about that," said Flora Jean.

"What the hell'd she care? She comes from old-time Denver money. The woman can buy herself a new and better Nelson Riles model any ol' day."

"Guess so," said CJ. "Jimmy have any other problems?"

"Like what?"

"Drugs, debts, other women?"

"No, no, and no. Jimmy was as good a man as they make. Straight up, clean living, the whole nine yards. No skeletons in Jimmy's closet. I were you, I'd talk to Councilman Riles and that Gwenette Strong bitch. They're the ones had the most to gain by Jimmy's death."

"I'll do that." CJ glanced at Flora Jean. "Got anything to add?"

"Yeah. Anybody have it in for Jimmy who's any good at tyin' knots?"

"Don't know for sure. Riles might've. He spent four years in the navy. Boasted about it constantly during his last city council campaign."

"Good. We'll ask him about it."

"And when you do, ask him whether that pussy of Gwenette's was worth him killing my Jimmy."

CJ watched a new lake of tears well up in Arletta's eyes. She'd already made up her mind who had killed Jimmy Kane. At a loss for words, he turned his thoughts back to the day his Uncle Ike, the most important man in his life, had died. "Things will get better, Arletta." But he knew the words rang hollow.

Nelson Riles lived in a stately ivy-covered two-story brick Georgian that occupied the entire corner of Seventeenth Avenue and Albion Street. The house, the lot, the fence, the driveway, and the landscape all announced in terms not intended to be subtle, *We have serious money.* The kind of money you married into if you were a man like Nelson Riles. His wife's family had amassed their wealth during the 1930s brokering oil and gas leases on Colorado's Western Slope. By the1940s, they'd become pivotal in Denver politics; during the '50s and '60s they were Denver society top-dog news. The Tillsdale name lost some of its luster in the 1970s when a Princeton-educated grandson killed his college roommate, and the family name dropped a further peg or two during the 1980 energy bust, but not far enough to dissuade Nelson Riles from burrowing in for the long haul.

In his third term as a councilman from Denver's Park Hill, a well-integrated, strongly middle-class district that for years had served as a national model for ethnic diversity, Riles loved to tout his naval service, family values, and Southern Baptist religious roots. He had made a political name for himself as a fierce advocate of bootstrap upward mobility and the Rainbow Coalition ideals while at the same time lining his pockets by skimming a percentage from every inner-city enterprise-zone deal city government inked. His wife shunned politics but remained civically active, spending most of her time overseeing a system of ten city miniparks planted squarely on land that her family had given to Denver during the late 1960s. Riles like to joke, generally after one too many highballs, that when it came to money, he and his wife had complementary financial pedigrees. She had it, and he liked to spend it.

A menacing bank of rain clouds hung over what some in Park Hill liked to call the Riles compound as CJ and Flora Jean made their way up the cobblestone walkway that led to the front door.

"Gonna pour before the day's over," said Flora Jean, glancing skyward.

CJ nodded in agreement. "We need it. Might put a dent in this drought."

"I'm surprised Riles told you to come by his house."

"He didn't. When I called his office I said I was from the state Democratic Party and that I needed to speak with him about something urgent. Some overeager campaign aide who'll probably get the boot tomorrow, if Riles can identify her, told me the councilman had a meeting this evening, but she was sure he'd be home between five and six." Checking his watch, CJ said, "We'll see if she was right."

The woman who answered the door was about forty-five, tall and stately. CJ thought she looked uncompromisingly serious. Her hair was jet-black and lightly streaked with silver, her glasses wire-framed and expensive, and she was wearing exquisite hand-made leather sandals that looked as if they'd been flown in from some tropical paradise for the sole purpose of matching the rich light-cocoa color of her midsummer tan. "Yes?" she said, friendly enough but distinctly assertive.

"CJ Floyd." CJ tapped the brim of his Stetson. "My partner, Flora Jean Benson. We'd like to speak to the councilman, if we may."

"I'm Mrs. Riles. Is he expecting you?" There was a strong hint of authority in Elizabeth Riles's voice.

"No. But this will only take a moment."

"I'm afraid he's getting ready to go to a meeting."

"I see. Maybe if you told him it's about a murder."

"What? I . . ."

"Who is it, Beth?" A man's baritone voice wafted up from just beyond an archway at the far end of the lengthy hallway that stretched out behind Elizabeth Riles. The walls were awash with scores of photographs and paintings.

"Some people to see you," said Elizabeth. Looking baffled, she opened the door to let CJ and Flora Jean in. Flora Jean eyed the gallery of art as Nelson Riles came into view.

"I wasn't expecting anyone."

"They say it's about a murder."

"What?" In his stocking feet, with a conservative navy-blue tie looped around his neck, Riles briskly walked up the hallway, stopping just short of his wife.

CJ aimed his words past Elizabeth Riles and straight at her husband. "We're here about Jimmy Kane."

"Who?"

"He was a comedian."

"A good one," Flora Jean added.

A look of recognition slowly crept across Riles's face. "That guy who hung himself?"

"We don't think so."

Riles bristled. "How does this pertain to me?"

"Gwenette Strong." CJ watched for some kind of reaction from Riles or his wife, but neither of them so much as flinched.

"I'm afraid I'll have to ask you to leave," Riles said, his tone authoritative and insistent.

"I'd like to speak with you at your office," CJ said without budging.

"Sorry." Riles stepped around his wife and motioned for CJ to leave. "Please." When neither CJ nor Flora Jean moved to leave, he slipped a cell phone from his belt. "I'll call the police."

"No need," said CJ, turning toward the door slowly just before a lingering Flora Jean said, "Those are some real nice photos of sailin' ships you got linin' your hallway. Navy'd be my guess. I'm marine stock myself. Any chance that while you were doin' your navy hitch you learned to tie knots?"

A brief look of confusion crossed Nelson Riles's face, a look that was rapidly replaced by one of anger. As Flora Jean and CJ made their way down the cobblestone walkway and out of sight, it slowly faded. But the look of befuddlement plastered on Elizabeth Riles's face remained until CJ and Flora Jean had driven away.

"You ask me, Jimmy killed hisself on a humbug. Ain't no proof he was murdered." The man speaking, all six foot five inches and 260 pounds of him, was Roosevelt Weeks, CJ's lifelong friend and the owner of Rosie's Garage, arguably the finest gas station and auto repair shop in Denver and hands down the top numbers front and bullshit emporium in Five Points. Black, white, rich, poor, blind, crippled, or crazy, if your radiator sprang a leak, if you wanted to lay fifty dollars down on the latest number, or you wanted gas on the cheap, Rosie's was the place to go.

The two friends were seated in Rosie's dimly lit office, its oil-stained walls offering testimony to the twenty-five years of sweat equity Rosie had built up in the place. Hunched over a wobbly card table on rickety wooden stools, they were busy rehashing possible motives for the Jimmy Kane killing as they savored triple-decker ham and turkey sandwiches that had been delivered minutes earlier from Mae's Louisiana Kitchen, the soul-food restaurant owned and operated by Mavis Sundee, the woman who tugged on CJ's love strings.

CJ set aside his sandwich, took a sip of Coke, and stroked his chin thoughtfully. "Jimmy was murdered all right. I just need proof."

"Proof, smoof. If I was you, I'd be more concerned about Petee Nuñez takin' a swipe outa my nuts. If he's in on this, you the one riskin' bein' murdered."

"I can handle Petee. It's his straw boss Rulon Jakes I'm worried about. I can't figure out how he's tied in to all this."

"Somebody's payin' him to distribute muscle. Same as always."

"I figured that. Question is, why and who? I find that out and I put the finger on Jimmy's killer."

"Answer's easy," said Rosie, grinning broadly. "Has to be somebody with somethin' to gain. Money, pussy, prestige, or power."

"You forgot fame," CJ added.

Rosie chomped down on his sandwich, sending a rivulet of honey mustard coursing down his chin. "Like you said earlier, Gwenette Strong."

"Maybe."

Rosie rolled his eyes. "You sure said that with a lot of authority. Don't sound real convinced she's Jimmy's killer."

"I'm not."

"Nelson Riles, then. You said he's the one backin' her."

"I'd peg Riles for the killing before Gwenette. But I'm still not convinced that either one of them killed Jimmy."

"Riles could've switched the knots. Navy trainin' and all. If Flora Jean said he coulda, that's good enough for me."

"And so could Everard Townes. He was the last person to check the knots before Jimmy started his act."

Rosie took a lengthy swig of Coke. "Brings us back to square one."

"Maybe not." The hint of a smile traced its way across CJ's face. "Like you said, knots. Could be the clue."

Looking puzzled, Rosie took another bite of sandwich and set aside the cola he'd been drinking. Before he could say anything, a noise out in the garage startled him. Seconds later, a lean black man with wiry silver hair and a jet-black mustache walked into the room.

"Dining in, I see. How quaint." Wendall Newburn's voice was authoritative, with a pinch of gravel tossed in for good measure.

"How'd you slip in here, Lieutenant?" Rosie asked, agitated that Newburn, a man he and CJ had gone head to head with ever since junior high school on issues that ranged from women to athletics, war, and the law, and one of only a handful of black command-grade homicide detectives on the Denver police force, had gotten the drop on them.

"I didn't. One of those college kids you're always so eager to hire for the summer gave me a free pass." Newburn nodded at CJ and flashed him a toothy grin that read, as usual, *kiss my ass,* before cutting the smile off like a crisp salute.

CJ responded with a dismissive grunt.

"Talkative tonight, aren't we, CJ? No matter. This won't take long." Newburn took a deep breath. "Heard from Nelson Riles tonight. The councilman tells me you're investigating a murder. Strange. I didn't realize our fair city had issued you a badge. Must've missed it in the papers."

CJ sternly eyed his one-time high school track rival and squared up in his seat. "Just trying to make a poor man's dollar, Lieutenant."

"Every dollar I've ever seen looks the same. But then again, I've always had to work for mine. Take my advice, friend. Fade to black. You're screwing with the wrong end of the stick. Keep it up and you're sure to end up with shit on your hands." Newburn looked at Rosie for support. "Collar your friend, Weeks." All he got was a dismissive shrug. When a garage door to one of the service bays suddenly slammed shut, Newburn instinctively eased his right hand onto the butt of his 9-milimeter. Concerned that Rosie and CJ had seen him sweat, he blurted, "Lose interest in the Kane case and stay away from Councilman Riles," before turning to head for the door.

"Have a nice night, Lieutenant, and while you're at it, try not to jump outa your skin the next time you hear something go bump in the night." CJ capped his advice with a self-satisfied grin as Newburn flashed a final icy over-the-shoulder stare and walked out the door.

CJ felt winded as he climbed the last of the thirty wrought-iron steps to the converted four-room apartment above his office. The fire-escape back entrance was faster than working his way through his downstairs office, where he was certain to face several phone messages and more work. Work could wait, he told himself as he slipped a well-worn key into the lock. He'd barely stepped inside when a voice he knew he'd heard before whispered from behind him, "Lose the Kane case, brother." An instant later something coarse snagged his left ear before dropping around his neck. By the time he realized that a rope was crushing his Adam's apple, he could barely breathe. Grabbing the loop with both hands, he struggled to keep the noose from tightening as he kicked, elbowed, and bulldogged his way down the hallway, dragging along his assailant and knocking over two lamps and a bookcase in the process. He'd nearly reached the hallway's dead end when he ran out of air. The taste of blood was the last thing he remembered before passing out.

Twenty minutes later, in response to CJ's barely audible telephone plea for help, Flora Jean sat across the kitchen table from him, pressing a towel filled with crushed ice to his forehead. A bloody, organic aftertaste filled his mouth as he struggled to talk. "Hell if I know who it was," he said, looking up at Flora Jean. "Son of a bitch left me for dead," he added, his voice grinding. "Didn't see him or the rope. Something about the voice was familiar, though."

I've heard it before." Massaging his neck and trying his best to ward off a painful cough, he added, "I know it."

"Two pieces of advice in one day to back off a case. Now this." Flora Jean shook her head. "Maybe we should be listenin'."

"I am," said CJ, choking out his words. "And what I hear is vengeance."

"Yeah, aimed at you!"

"Don't think so. I'm just a secondary target. Nope, somebody wants to get more satisfaction out of this Jimmy Kane thing than can possibly come from choking the shit out of me or appearing on *Oprah*. If fame was all this was about, Gwenette Strong could crank up her Denver act unopposed, wait for a first-class airplane ticket from Oprah, hope to outclass the competition, and ride off into the Hollywood sunset. And if money was the bottom line, Rulon Jakes and that scruffy puppy of his, Nuñez, would have taken their cut by now and disappeared. No, there's something about this whole thing that goes a lot deeper than fame or money." CJ grimaced, choking out his words painfully. "You've said all along that knots are the key to this puzzle. And since the puzzle started with Everard Townes, I think we should retrace our steps and go back and see him."

"Fine by me. When?"

"Right now."

"It's one A.M., CJ! And you're hurt!"

"And it's a brand-new day." CJ suppressed a cough, removed the compress Flora Jean was holding to his head, stood, and nodded for Flora Jean to follow. When she didn't budge, he said, "I'll go by myself."

"You're a stubborn man, CJ Floyd," said Flora Jean, rising from her chair and walking across the room. "And it's gonna cost you."

"It already has," said CJ, rubbing his neck. "It already has."

———

Everard Townes stood at the door of his darkened Five Points bungalow, holding a scotch on the rocks in one hand and a half-smoked cigar in the other. He was dressed in baggy jeans, a soiled T-shirt, and grass-stained tennis shoes. Greeting CJ with a nod and a grin, he said, "What's up?" His voice was well lubricated by alcohol. A bottle of fifty-dollar Chivas Regal sat on an entryway table behind him.

"Not much," said CJ, glancing toward his Bel Air, where Flora Jean sat in the front seat, agitated at being left behind. "Sorry to hit you up this time of night, Everard, but I need to know a little bit more about knots."

Half stupefied and at first unperturbed by the question, Townes said, "I'm your man, been tyin' 'em for years."

"You any good at tying anything besides a slipknot and a hangman?" CJ said in a painful groan.

"You ain't insinuatin' anything, are you, CJ?" said Townes, finally recognizing in his half-drunken state what CJ was driving at. "'Cause if you are . . ."

"No. Just asking a simple question."

"Well, it sounded like an insinuation to me." Townes looked at CJ suspiciously, then slowly, as if he'd just remembered something long tucked away in his brain, said, "You know somethin' else? You sound like a frog. A fuckin' frog with a cold. What's wrong with your voice?"

"Long story. Too long for two A.M."

Townes shrugged and smiled, convinced that half drunk or not he could still outthink CJ. "As for them knots you're askin' about; I can probably tie fifteen or twenty of 'em. Just like I can sing and dance, dig ditches, sort mail, plant begonias, and come in outa the rain. I know where you're headed, CJ, and it's down the wrong road. Shit, there's probably thousands of people in Denver who can tie just as many knots as me and at least a couple of other folks 'sides me down here on the Points who could've done Jimmy in, includin' a city councilman whose name I ain't gonna mention and Jimmy's main competition for that *Oprah* gig, Gwenette Strong."

"Did anybody pay you to set Jimmy up?" CJ said pointedly, unwilling to continue listening to Everard's song and dance.

"You fuckin' crazy?"

"Rulon Jakes maybe?"

"Get the shit outa my house, CJ. You angerin' me."

"OK, I'll leave—for now," said CJ, straining to get the words out. "But you're in this up to your false teeth and Chivas, Everard, and like it or not, I'll be back. My guess is there's somebody else in the circus ring with you. God knows you're not quick enough to play ringmaster yourself."

"Ain't nobody here but me and you, CJ," said Townes, laughing. "Like I said, anybody can learn to tie a knot. Now get the fuck outa here—don't come back, and go find yourself a new voice box." Townes slammed the door and bolted it.

CJ and Flora Jean were halfway back to CJ's apartment, riding in silence, when CJ said in a painful thin-layered groan, "Wonder where Townes is getting the money to support his habit?"

"What?"

"His liquor fix. He'd polished off most of a fifty-dollar bottle of scotch before our visit."

"Expensive tastes."

CJ sat up in his seat. "Got something for you to do first thing in the morning. It just might help us out."

"And that is?"

CJ's words cracked as he spoke. "Find out what ol' Everard's been doing the last year or so to make ends meet besides tying knots for Jimmy Kane."

"Might take me a while."

CJ glanced at his watch. It was almost two-thirty. "Take your time. We've got all day."

Light early-morning drizzle had shrouded bail bondsmen's row in thick fog so that the street's neon signs announcing "Open 24 Hours" and "Bail Bonds Anytime" were barely visible in the soupy mist. Flora Jean had arrived for work early and called in a few markers: one from an eager-to-be-promoted horny cop who'd been trying to get in her pants for years and one from a small-time fence who owed her for getting him a six-month reprieve from jail. Both men were happy to supply information on Everard Townes. She was busy at her computer checking out a third lead from a numbers runner she knew when CJ walked in.

"It's pissin' nails," he said, resurrecting the description his navy riverboat commander had for the Agent Orange–saturated fog that always seemed to dog them on early-morning patrols in Vietnam.

Flora Jean glanced up from the screen. "Haven't heard that in a while."

"Haven't had the right conditions till now." CJ tossed his Stetson onto a nearby table and unbuttoned his uncomfortably tight vest. "How are you doing?"

Flora Jean grinned. "Better than that vest of yours. Next time Mavis asks you if you want seconds, I say pass." Smiling, she added, "Your voice sounds better."

Aware that he was indeed slowly losing the tale of the tailor's tape, he said, "Feels better, but there's still a knot in my throat."

"Got some dope on our boy, Everard Townes."

"Shoot." CJ took a nearby seat.

"Townes did two years of prison time in Canon City."

"I knew that."

"Six months ago he got fired from his job at Big-O Tires."

"Knew that, too."

"Bet you didn't know this." Flora Jean slipped a sheet of paper out of her printer tray, smiled, and handed it to CJ. "Take a gander."

CJ began reading the smudged, undersized print. By the time he reached the beginning of the third paragraph his eyes were saucers. He handed the paper back to Flora Jean, smiling ear to ear. "Guess we know what rock to look under now."

"Sure do, and for a snake."

CJ nodded thoughtfully, slipped a cheroot from deep inside his vest pocket, and lit up. "Time to make a visit to Park Hill."

This time CJ didn't bother to ring Nelson Riles's front doorbell. Instead he walked around to the expansive gated backyard where the councilman's wife had been busy at yard work for most of the half hour he and Flora Jean had watched the house from the cramped front seat of Flora Jean's pickup.

Elizabeth Riles looked taller and more substantial than she had during his previous visit. Sporting a wide-brimmed Panama hat, the four-hundred-dollar real McCoy, baggy gardening pants, a seersucker blouse, and oversized pink Lolita-style sunglasses, she was weeding a bed of red, white, and blue petunias when CJ walked up and doffed his Stetson. "Like to speak with you if I may."

Aware of CJ's approach from the moment he'd swung open the wrought-iron gate, Elizabeth Riles kept working, unperturbed. Towering cottonwoods lined the yard's southern edge, their sixty-year-old limbs creaking as they swayed in the late-morning breeze. A few feet in front of the trees, a seven-foot-high hedgerow paralleled the trunks of the cottonwoods for most of the yard's length. A narrow opening in the center of the hedgerow served to act as a conduit back to the trees. A badly weathered garden rake and a small shovel rested against a trellis framing that opening.

CJ stood at parade rest, fingering the brim of his Stetson. When Elizabeth Riles didn't respond, he cleared his throat, "Excuse me, I'd . . ."

"You'd what?" There was a strong note of irritation in Elizabeth Riles's voice.

"I'd like to speak with you for a moment."

"So you can embarrass my husband some more? He's not here."

"No, and he's not the one I'd like to talk to."

"Me, then?"

"Yes."

"Why?"

"Because I think you can shed some light on a murder."

Elizabeth Riles looked up at CJ, her sunglasses masking her eyes. "Nelson didn't kill anyone."

"I know that."

Elizabeth Riles removed her sunglasses and flashed CJ a look that was at once pensive and quizzical. "Who, then?"

"I'm not sure."

"I don't think I should be talking to you."

"If not me, then the cops."

"Trust me. Neither you nor that lady friend of yours scares me."

"I don't suppose we would. You're a powerful lady."

"Get to the point, Mr. Floyd."

"Did you know your husband was seeing Gwenette Strong?"

"Yesterday's news, Mr. Floyd."

"Did it bother you? Being cheated on, I mean?"

Elizabeth Riles set aside the garden spade she'd been using and removed her gloves. "Nelson's infidelities are pretty much public record. There are big hurts and little hurts in this world, Mr. Floyd. Ms. Strong—well—let's just say she was a little one."

"I see. And Everard Townes? How would you classify him?"

"Who?"

"Everard Townes. The man you either paid to tie the knot that killed Jimmy Kane or paid to look the other way while you tied the knot yourself."

"Are you on drugs, Mr. Floyd? Why would I do that?"

"Because, as politicians in the very highest places have been known to say, *you could.* Townes was a lush, and he'd worked for you before. I have city Park Service records to prove it. Your probably told yourself you could chance it. Then there are the gas receipts, pay stubs, liquor receipts—trust me, they're all available to connect the dots. Dots that tie you to Townes, forward and backward. Townes was just the tool you needed to help you get Gwenette Strong out of the way."

Elizabeth Riles shook her head in protest. "Then why kill Jimmy Kane?"

"To settle a score with Gwenette. To send everyone, including me, the press, and the cops, sniffing down the wrong path. To make people think that Gwenette killed Jimmy in order to clear a path to *Oprah.* And to keep your man. Need any more reasons? From what I hear, Gwenette's the first dark meat the councilman's ever tasted. Must have really stuck in your craw, a blue-book socialite like you, having to take a backseat to a black woman. Your plan would've worked too. It was clever and crafty. Turn up the investigative heat on Jimmy's competition and force your husband back home. But the cops fumbled the ball and called Jimmy's death an accident instead of a murder."

Her cheeks now crimson, Elizabeth Riles remained silent.

"Your error was using Townes. He's a man whose loyalties run very shallow. Especially when he's full of liquor and out to save his rear. Remember the lady who was with me the other day—tall, serious looking, ex-marine—well, she tells me that early this morning, with only the slightest prodding and the threat of a murder charge hanging over his head, Townes sold you out. Told her and a detective named Newburn that Jimmy's death was a long way from an accident. Said he gave you a few knot-tying lessons recently, and you were a very capable student. Of course, the cops will be several hours behind me on this, maybe more. When it comes to murder, they don't like to tread too heavily on a city councilman's wife without a thousand yards of proof. Me, I don't have the same restrictions."

Caught between reaching a decision and taking action, Elizabeth Riles rose from her crouch, jammed her garden spade into the dirt, and shouted, "Rulon!"

Within seconds Rulon Jakes was through the archway in the hedges and racing toward them, his Glock aimed squarely at CJ.

Aware that trying to run would get him shot, CJ stayed put. Jakes was now just a few paces away. "Wondered where you fit in, Jakes. Now I know. Low-grade, slow-thinking muscle." CJ looked at Elizabeth Riles and shook his head. "Townes and Jakes. Two bad choices. You should've just killed Gwenette Strong yourself."

"And be the cops' number one suspect? No way. I'm not real good at playing the pitiful woman scorned, dumb-as-nails society princess." She looked at Jakes. Her eyes issued a silent order.

Jakes smiled and slammed a fist into CJ's midsection. CJ doubled over, gasping for air as a stream of blood tracked its way down the corner of his mouth. Jakes cocked a leg to kick CJ in the head, but Elizabeth Riles screamed, "No! Not here! We need to leave."

"Where to?"

Nervously wringing her hands, she said, "Let me think for a moment." Before she could decide on a course of action, a woman's voice called out from the archway in the hedgerow, "You think long, you think wrong." Riles pivoted to find the barrel of Flora Jean Benson's nickel-plated .45 aimed squarely at his belly. Before he had a chance to sight in on Flora Jean, CJ slammed his head into the small of Jakes's back, sending him and the Glock crashing into the cobblestone walkway. Grunting, Jakes stretched out and clawed for his gun. His hand was only inches from pay dirt when Flora Jean's foot came crushingly down on it.

"Aaaahhhh!" The sound of delicate finger joints splintering filled the air. A second effort triggered an equally bone-numbing crunch. Before Jakes could scream again, Flora Jean had planted her knee firmly against his neck. "Once a marine, always a marine," she whispered softly into Jakes's ear.

Stunned and confused, Elizabeth Riles took two hesitant steps toward the house. "No need," grunted a still-winded CJ, blocking her way. "To run, I mean," he added as a thin rivulet of blood dropped from his chin.

"Who's running? I'm going to make a phone call," Elizabeth Riles countered in a voice reverberating with privilege.

"To your husband?"

"To my lawyer."

For the next month, Denver's two newspapers played a game of Jimmy Kane murder headlines one-upmanship, enticing readers to gorge on the ever-expanding details. Headlines that read: "Councilman's Wife Prime Suspect in Comic's Killing,"

"Parks Heiress Charged with Murder," and "Blue-Book Spouse Alleged Comic-Killer" served as daily fodder.

The latest headline had Rosie Weeks mumbling and scratching his head. "Alleged my ass, who the hell they think they're kidding? That rich bitch did it." Rosie hefted the beer he'd been nursing, looked around a nearly empty Mae's Louisiana Kitchen, and grunted. "Money talks, bullshit walks. The Riles woman did it all right."

CJ eased into his seat, glanced at Mavis Sundee, who was squeezed up next to him, and shook his head. Although he agreed with Rosie, he was at least willing to allow Elizabeth Riles her day in court, if for no other reason than to hear her side of the story. "Innocent until proven guilty, Rosie, remember?"

"And so's that sand jockey from Iraq, Saddam. He didn't kill nobody either. Bullshit. She killed the boy all right. Couldn't stand the fact that her lyin'-ass husband was spendin' his free time hooked up with a sista. Especially one with an inside track to fame."

"You're certain Gwenette Strong was gonna get picked to be on *Oprah*?"

Rosie's eyebrows shot skyward in surprise. "Gonna? You ain't heard? Gwenette got the gig, along with a brother outa Detroit and a couple of L.A. sistas. Heard it on *Entertainment Tonight* just last night. Leave it to Oprah to pick just one man."

"Your chauvinism's showing, Rosie," said Mavis, leaning her head on CJ's shoulder.

Rosie shook his head in protest. "You got a man, Mavis. And for that matter, so's Oprah. The Riles woman didn't. Just a lyin', womanizin' politician. When you come right down to it, what this whole damn Jimmy Kane killin' is all about is havin' a man. I'm just callin' what I see."

"Maybe Elizabeth Riles killed Jimmy for some other reason," said Mavis. "Have you ever considered that?"

"Nope. CJ pegged it from the start. She killed him hopin' to pin it on Gwenette and maybe get her old man to stay at home. Cops screwed her, though, mainly 'cause she couldn't think black. Remember, we got a black killin' here. In Five Points, whether its an act of God, murder, or suicide, whatta the cops care? The victims are all black. Accident works as good as any for a cop."

"What about Jakes and Nuñez? Think they were in on the killing?" asked Mavis, hoping to get another of Rosie's man-on-the-street takes, but CJ spoke up before Rosie had a chance. "Doesn't really matter." There was a vengeful edge to CJ's response that reminded Mavis of the terror-filled nights and despondent days that had consumed him for almost a year following his return from Vietnam. A terrifying edge that still occasionally reared its head after more than thirty years.

"CJ! You're drifting." Mavis draped an arm over CJ's shoulder. "CJ!" she said, wrapping both arms around CJ's neck when he didn't answer.

CJ couldn't hear her. His thoughts had drifted back to the killing fields of Vietnam, triggered by Mavis's question about Nuñez and Jakes and a TV sound bite that he had heard that morning while shaving. It had lasted mere seconds, but that was all the time he had needed to recognize the voice of the man who a month earlier had tried to strangle him. He had walked over to the television to see Petee Nuñez, a reporter's microphone inches from his nose, denying any part in the Jimmy Kane killing.

Suddenly CJ didn't care whether Elizabeth Riles was ever convicted of killing Jimmy Kane, whether Everard Townes served time as her accomplice, or whether Rulon Jakes, currently out on bond, did a split second of jail time. And it certainly didn't matter whether Gwenette Strong ever saw Oprah's pearly gates. What mattered right then, as his head rang with the resurgent sounds of small-arms fire and the shouts of dying men, was that Petee Nuñez had unleashed a monster that had to be fed.

Flora Jean stood beneath the high-arched flaking plaster inset doorway to Petee Nuñez's first-floor corner apartment, watching dusk settle in and smiling at Nuñez, who was wearing a coffee-stained T-shirt and baggy boxer shorts.

"Whatta you want?" asked Nuñez, cupping his testicles, his eyes aimed directly at Flora Jean's compellingly ample chest.

"Nothin'."

"Then why'd you ring my doorbell?"

"To deliver a message."

"A . . ."

Before Nuñez could complete the thought, CJ stepped from around the corner of the building and launched a roundhouse right into Nuñez's belly that sent him to his knees. A follow-up left hook fractured Nuñez's jaw. CJ cocked his arm, eyes red with anger, to deliver a third blow, but Flora Jean grabbed his wrist with both hands. Struggling to keep him from delivering a punch that would have splintered most of the bones in Nuñez's face, she said, "This ain't a war, CJ. You've sent your message."

Grappling with his anger, CJ began to tremble. Realizing he'd made his point, he looked down at the lost cause of a human being lying at his feet. "You're right, Flora Jean. Let's go," he said, turning away from the darkened archway and toward the early-evening light.

ANN LANE PETRY (1908–1997) was born in Old Saybrook, Connecticut, in a largely white, middle-class town. After graduating from Old Saybrook High School in 1929, she received her degree from the Connecticut College of Pharmacy in 1931. She left her career as a pharmacist to move to New York City with her mystery writer husband, deciding to become a writer as well. Her first published story, "Marie of the Cabin Club," was published in the August 19, 1939, issue of the *Afro-American* under the pseudonym Arnold Petry, as she planned to use her own name for more serious work.

In addition to working as a reporter for the *People's Voice* beginning in 1941, she wrote more stories, took up painting, piano playing, and acting while becoming active in civic affairs in Harlem. When her story "On Saturday the Siren Sounds at Noon" was published, Houghton Mifflin encouraged her to write a novel and gave her a grant of $2,400 in 1945. The following year, her first novel, *The Street*, was published and became the first novel by an African American woman to sell a million copies. She published *Country Place* in 1947 and moved back to Old Saybrook with her family, focusing much of her attention on raising her daughter. Her third and final novel, *The Narrows*, was published in 1953.

"On Saturday the Siren Sounds at Noon" was originally published in the December 1943 issue of *The Crisis* magazine.

On Saturday the Siren Sounds at Noon

Ann Petry

At five minutes of twelve on Saturday there was
only a handful of people waiting for the 241st Street train. Most
of them were at the far end of the wooden platform where they
could look down on the street and soak up some of the winter sun
at the same time.

A Negro in faded blue overalls leaned against a post at the upper
end of the station. He was on his way to work in the Bronx. He had
decided to change trains above ground so he could get a breath of
fresh air. In one hand he carried a worn metal lunch box.

As he waited for the train, he shifted his weight from one foot to
the other. He watched the way the sun shone on the metal tracks—
they gleamed as far as he could see in the distance.

The train's worn 'em shiny, he thought idly. Trains run up and
down 'em so many times they're shined up like a spittoon. He
tried to force his thoughts to the weather. Spittoons. Why'd I have
to think about something like that?

He had worked in a hotel barroom once as a porter. It was his

115

job to keep all the brass shining. The doorknobs and the rails around the bar and the spittoons. When he left the job he took one of the spittoons home with him. He used to keep it shined up so that it reflected everything in his room. Sometimes he'd put it on the windowsill and it would reflect in miniature the church across the street.

He'd think about spring—it was on the way. He could feel it in the air. There was a softness that hadn't been there before. Wish the train would hurry up and come, he thought. He turned his back on the tracks to avoid looking at the way they shone. He stared at the posters on the walls of the platform. After a few minutes he turned away impatiently. The pictures were filled with the shine of metal, too. A silver punch bowl in a Coca-Cola ad and brass candlesticks that fairly jumped off a table. A family was sitting around the table. They were eating.

He covered his eyes with his hands. That would shut it out until he got hold of himself. And it did. But he thought he felt something soft clinging to his hands and he started trembling.

Then the siren went off. He jumped nearly a foot when it first sounded. That old air raid alarm, he thought contemptuously— always putting it off on Saturdays. Yet it made him uneasy. He'd always been underground in the subway when it sounded. Or in Harlem where the street noises dulled the sound of its wail.

Why, that thing must be right on top of this station, he thought. It started as a low, weird moan. Then it gained in volume. Then it added a higher screaming note, and a little later a low, louder blast. It was everywhere around him, plucking at him, pounding at his ears. It was inside of him. It was his heart and it was beating faster and harder and faster and harder. He bent forward because it was making a pounding pressure against his chest. It was hitting him in the stomach.

He covered his ears with his hands. The lunch box dangling from one hand nudged against his body. He jumped away from it, his nerves raw, ready to scream. He opened his eyes and saw that it was the lunch box that had prodded him and he let it drop to the wooden floor.

It's almost as though I can smell that sound, he told himself. It's the smell and the sound of death—cops and ambulances and fire trucks—

A shudder ran through him. Fire. It was Monday that he'd gone to work extra early. Lilly Belle was still asleep. He remembered how he'd frowned down at her before he left. Even sleeping she was untidy and bedraggled.

The kids were asleep in the front room. He'd stared at them for a brief moment. He remembered having told Lilly Belle the night before, "Just one more time I come home and find you ain't here and these kids by themselves, and I'll kill you—"

All she'd said was, "I'm goin' to have me some fun—"

Whyn't they shut that thing off, he thought. I'll be deaf. I can't stand it. It's breaking my eardrums. If only there were some folks near here. He looked toward the other end of the platform. He'd walk down that way and stand near those people. That might help a little bit.

The siren pinioned him where he was when he took the first step. He'd straightened up and it hit him all over so that he doubled up again like a jackknife.

The sound throbbed in the air around him. It'll stop pretty soon, he thought. It's got to. But it grew louder. He couldn't see the tracks anymore. When he looked again they were pulsating to the sound and his eardrums were keeping time to the tracks.

"God in Heaven," he moaned, "make it stop." And then in alarm, "I can't even hear my own voice. My voice is gone."

If I could stop thinking about fire—fire—fire. Standing there with the sound of the siren around him, he could see himself coming home on Monday afternoon. It was just about three o'clock. He could see himself come out of the subway and start walking down Lenox Avenue, past the bakery on the corner. He stopped and bought a big bag of oranges from the pushcart on the corner. Eloise, the little one, liked oranges. They were kind of heavy in his arms.

He went in the butcher store near 133rd Street. He got some hamburger to cook for dinner. It seemed to him that the butcher looked at him queerly and he could see himself walking along puzzling about it.

Then he turned into 133rd Street. Funny. Standing here with this noise tearing inside him, he could see himself as clearly as though by some miracle he'd been transformed into another person, the bag of oranges, the packages of meat—the meat was soft, and he could feel it cold through the paper wrapping, and the oranges were hard and knobby. And his lunch box was empty and it was swinging light from his hand.

There he was turning the corner, going down his own street. There were little knots of people talking. They nodded at him. Sarah Lee who ran the beauty shop—funny she'd be out in the street gossiping this time of day. And Mrs. Smith who had the hand laundry. Why, they were all there. He turned and looked back at them. They turned their eyes away from him quickly when he looked at them.

He could see himself approaching the stoop at 219. Cora, the janitress, was leaning against the railing, her fat hips spilling over the top. She was talking to the priest from the church across the way. He felt excitement stir inside him. The priest's hands were bandaged and there was blood on the bandages.

The woman next door was standing on the lower step. She saw him first and she nudged Cora.

"Oh—" Cora stopped talking.

The silence alarmed him. "What's the matter?" he asked.

"There was a fire," Cora said.

He could see himself running up the dark narrow stairs. Even the hall was filled with the smell of dead smoke. The door of his apartment sagged on its hinges. He stepped inside and stood perfectly still, gasping for breath. There was nothing left but charred wood and ashes. The walls were gutted and blackened. That had been the radio, and there was a piece of what had been a chair. He walked into the bedroom. The bed was a twisted mass of metal. The spittoon had melted down. It was a black rim with a shapeless mass under it. Everywhere was the acrid, choking smell of burned wood.

He turned to find Cora watching him.

"The children—" he said, "and Lilly Belle—"

"Lilly Belle's all right," she said coldly. "The kids are at Harlem Hospital. They're all right. Lilly Belle wasn't home."

He could see himself run blindly down the stairs. He ran to the corner and in exciting agony to the Harlem Hospital. All the way to the hospital his feet kept saying, "Wasn't home." "Wasn't home." "Wasn't home."

They let him see the kids at the hospital. They were covered with clean white bandages, lying in narrow white cots.

First time they've ever been really clean, he thought bitterly. A crisp, starched nurse told him that they'd be all right.

"Where's the little one?" he asked. "Where's Eloise?"

The nurse's eyes widened. "Why, she's dead," she stammered.

"Where is she?"

He could see himself leaning over the small body in the morgue. He still had the oranges and the meat and the empty lunch box in his arms. When he went back to the ward, Lilly Belle was there with the kids.

She was dressed in black. Black shoes and stockings and a long black veil that billowed around her when she moved. He was thinking about her black clothes so that he only half heard her as she told him she'd just gone around the corner that morning, and that she'd expected to come right back.

"But I ran into Alice—and when I came back," she licked her lips as though they were suddenly dry.

He could see himself going to work. The next day and all the other days after that. Going to the hospital every day. Living in an apartment across the hall. The neighbors brought in furniture for them. He could hear the neighbors trying to console him.

He could see himself that very morning. He'd slept late because on Saturdays he went to work later than on other days. When he woke up he heard voices. And as he listened they came clear to his ears like a victrola record or the radio.

Cora was talking. "You ain't never been no damn good. And if you don't quit runnin' to that bar with that dressed up monkey and stayin' away from here all day long, I'm goin' to tell that poor fool you're married to where you were when your kid burned up in here." She said it fast as though she wanted to get it out before Lilly Belle could stop her. "You walkin' around in mournin' and everybody but him knows you locked them kids in here that day. They was locked in—"

Lilly Belle said something he couldn't hear. He heard Cora's heavy footsteps cross the kitchen. And then the door slammed.

He got out of bed very quietly. He could see himself as he walked barefooted across the room. The black veil was hanging over a chair. He ran it through his fingers. The soft stuff clung and caught on the rough places on his hands as though it were alive.

Lilly Belle was in the kitchen reading a newspaper. Her dark hands were silhouetted against its pink outside sheets. Her hair wasn't combed and she had her feet stuck in a pair of run-over mules. She barely glanced at him and then went on reading the paper.

He watched himself knot the black veil tightly around her throat. He pulled it harder and harder. Her lean body twitched two or three times and then it was very still. Standing there he could feel again the cold hard knot that formed inside him when he saw that she was dead.

If the siren would only stop. It was vibrating inside him—all the soft tissues in his stomach and in his lungs were moaning and shrieking with agony. The station trembled as the train approached. As it drew nearer and nearer the siren took on a new note—a louder, sharper, sobbing sound. It was talking. "Locked in. They were locked in." "Smoke poisoning. Third degree burns." "Eloise? Why, she's dead." "My son, don't grieve. It will probably change your wife." "You know, they say the priest's hands were all bloody where he tried to break down the door." "My son, my son—"

The train was coasting toward the station. It was coming nearer and nearer. It seemed to be jumping up and down on the track. And as it thundered in, it took up the siren's moan. "They were locked in. They were locked in."

Just as it reached the edge of the platform, he jumped. The wheels ground his body into the gleaming silver of the tracks.

The air was filled with noise—the sound of the train and the wobble of the siren as it died away to a low moan. Even after the train stopped, there was a thin echo of the siren in the air.

CHARLES WADDELL CHESNUTT (1858–1932) was born in Cleveland, Ohio, the son of "free persons of color" who had moved north from Fayetteville, North Carolina. The family returned to Fayetteville after the Civil War, but Chesnutt and his new wife moved to New York City in 1878 in order for him to pursue a literary career; after six months, he moved back to Cleveland, where he passed the bar exam and established a successful legal stenography business.

He soon became a professional writer, his first short story, "The Goophered Grapevine," being published by *The Atlantic Monthly* in 1887, and he became a prolific short fiction writer. His first published book was a story collection, *The Conjure Woman* (1899), quickly followed by *The Wife of His Youth and Other Stories of the Color Line* (1899). The same year saw the publication of his biography, *Frederick Douglass*, as well as the novel *The Passing of Grandison*. In 1900, the novel *The House Behind the Cedars* saw print, and *The Marrow of Tradition* came out the next year. Poor sales of his books turned him away from a literary life, and in 1901 he became a social and political activist, serving on the General Committee of the NAACP.

"The Sheriff's Children" was first published in the November 7, 1889, issue of the *New York Independent*; it was collected in *The Wife of His Youth and Other Stories of the Color Line* (Boston: Houghton Mifflin, 1899).

The Sheriff's Children

Charles W. Chesnutt

*(The first pages of this story describe the village of Troy,
county seat of Branson County, North Carolina.)*

A murder was a rare event in Branson County. Every
well-informed citizen could tell the number of homicides committed in the county for fifty years back, and whether the slayer
in any given instance had escaped, either by flight or acquittal,
or had suffered the penalty of the law. So when it became known
in Troy early one Friday morning in summer, about ten years
after the war, that old Captain Walker, who had served in
Mexico under Scott and had left an arm on the field of Gettys-
burg, had been foully murdered during the night, there was
intense excitement in the village. Business was practically suspended, and the citizens gathered in little groups to discuss the
murder and speculate upon the identity of the murderer. It transpired from testimony at the coroner's inquest held during the
morning, that a strange mulatto had been met going away from
Troy early Friday morning by a farmer on his way to town.
Other circumstances seemed to connect the stranger with the
crime. The sheriff organized a posse to search for him, and early

in the evening, when most of the citizens of Troy were at supper, the suspected man was brought in and lodged in the county jail.

By the following morning the news of the capture had spread to the farthest limits of the county. A much larger number of people than usual came to town that Saturday—bearded men in straw hats and blue homespun shirts, and butternut trousers of great amplitude of material and vagueness of outline; women in homespun frocks and slat-bonnets, with faces as expressionless as the dreary sandhills which gave them a meager sustenance.

The murder was almost the sole topic of conversation. A steady stream of curious observers visited the house of mourning and gazed upon the rugged face of the old veteran, now stiff and cold in death; and more than one eye dropped a tear at the remembrance of the cheery smile, and the joke—sometimes superannuated, generally feeble, but always good-natured—with which the captain had been wont to greet his acquaintances. There was a growing sentiment of anger among these stern men toward the murderer who had thus cut down their friend, and a strong feeling that ordinary justice was too slight a punishment for such a crime.

Toward noon there was an informal gathering of citizens in Dan Tyson's store.

"I hear it 'lowed that Square Kyahtah's too sick ter hol' co'te this evenin','" said one, "an' that the purlim'nary hearin' 'll haf ter go over 'tel nex' week." A look of disappointment went round the crowd.

"Hit's the durndes', meanes' murder ever committed in this caounty," said another, with moody emphasis.

"I s'pose the nigger 'lowed the Cap'n had some greenbacks," observed a third speaker.

"The Cap'n," said another, with an air of superior information, "has left two bairls of Confedrit money, which he 'spected'd be good some day er nuther."

This statement gave rise to a discussion of the speculative value of Confederate money; but in a little while the conversation returned to the murder.

"Hangin' air too good fer the murderer," said one; "he oughter be burnt, stider bein' hung."

There was an impressive pause at this point, during which a jug of moonlight whiskey went the round of the crowd.

"Well," said a round-shouldered farmer who, in spite of his peaceable expression and faded gray eye, was known to have been one of the most daring followers of a rebel guerrilla chieftain, "what air ye gwine ter do about it? Ef you fellers air gwine ter set down an' let a wuthless nigger kill the bes' white man in Branson, an' not say nuthin' ner do nuthin', *I'll* move outen the caounty."

This speech gave tone and direction to the rest of the conversation. Whether the fear of losing the round-shouldered farmer operated to bring about the result or not is immaterial to this narrative; but at all events the crowd decided to lynch the Negro. They agreed that this was the least that could be done to avenge the death of their murdered friend, and that it was a becoming way in which to honor his memory. They had some vague notions of the majesty of the law and the rights of the citizen, but in the passion of the moment these sunk into oblivion; a white man had been killed by a Negro.

"The Cap'n was an ole sodger," said one of his friends solemnly. "He'll sleep better when he knows that a co'te-martial has be'n hilt an' jestice done."

By agreement the lynchers were to meet at Tyson's store at five o'clock in the afternoon and proceed thence to the jail, which was situated down the Lumberton Dirt Road (as the old turnpike antedating the plank-road was called) about half a mile south of the court house. When the preliminaries of the lynching had been arranged and a committee appointed to manage the affair, the crowd dispersed, some to go to their dinners and some to secure recruits for the lynching party.

It was twenty minutes to five o'clock when an excited Negro, panting and perspiring, rushed up to the back door of Sheriff Campbell's dwelling, which stood at a little distance from the jail and somewhat farther than the latter building from the court-house. A turbaned colored woman came to the door in response to the Negro's knock.

"Hoddy, Sis' Nance."

"Hoddy, Brer Sam."

"Is de shurff in?" inquired the Negro.

"Yas, Brer Sam, he's eatin' his dinner," was the answer.

"Will yer ax 'im ter step ter de do' a minute, Sis' Nance?"

The woman went into the dining room, and a moment later the sheriff came to the door. He was a tall, muscular man, of a ruddier complexion than is usual among Southerners. A pair of keen, deep-set gray eyes looked out from under bushy eyebrows, and about his mouth was a masterful expression, which a full beard, once sandy in color but now profusely sprinkled with gray, could not entirely conceal. The day was hot; the sheriff had discarded his coat and vest, and had his white shirt open at the throat.

"What do you want, Sam?" he inquired of the Negro, who stood hat in hand, wiping the moisture from his face with a ragged shirt-sleeve.

"Shurff, dey gwine ter hang de pris'ner w'at lock' up in de jail. Dey're comin' dis a-way now. I wuz layin' down on a sack er corn down at de sto', behine a pile er flour-bairls, w'en I hearn Doc' Cain en Kunnel Wright talkin' erbout it. I slip' outen de back do', en run here as fas' as I could. I hearn you say down ter de sto' once't dat you wouldn't let nobody take a pris'ner 'way fum you widout walkin' over yo' dead body, en I thought I'd let you know 'fo' dey come, so yer could pertec' de pris'ner."

The sheriff listened calmly, but his face grew firmer, and a determined gleam lit up his gray eyes. His frame grew more erect, and he unconsciously assumed the attitude of a soldier who momentarily expects to meet the enemy face to face.

"Much obliged, Sam," he answered. "I'll protect the prisoner. Who's coming?"

"I dunno who-all *is* comin'," replied the Negro. "Dere's Mistah McSwayne, en Doc' Cain, en Maje' McDonal', and Kunnel Wright en a heap er yuthers. I wuz so skeered I done furgot mo' d'n half un em. I spec' dey mus' be mos' here by dis time, so I'll git outen de way, fer I don't want nobody fer ter think I wuz mix' up in dis business." The Negro glanced nervously down the road toward the town, and made a movement as if to go away.

"Won't you have some dinner first?" asked the sheriff.

The Negro looked longingly in at the open door, and sniffed the appetizing odor of boiled pork and collards.

"I ain't got no time fer ter tarry, Shurff," he said, "but Sis' Nance mought gin me sump'n I could kyar in my han' en eat on de way."

A moment later Nancy brought him a huge sandwich of split cornpone, with a thick slice of fat bacon inserted between the halves, and a couple of baked yams. The Negro hastily replaced his ragged hat on his head, dropped the yams in the pocket of his capacious trousers and, taking the sandwich in his hand, hurried across the road and disappeared in the woods beyond.

The sheriff reentered the house, and put on his coat and hat. He then took down a double-barreled shotgun and loaded it with buckshot. Filling the chambers of a revolver with fresh cartridges, he slipped it into the pocket of the sack-coat which he wore.

A comely young woman in a calico dress watched these proceedings with anxious surprise.

"Where are you going, Father?" she asked. She had not heard the conversation with the Negro.

"I am goin' over to the jail," responded the sheriff. "There's a mob comin' this way to lynch the nigger we've got locked up. But they won't do it," he added, with emphasis.

"Oh, Father, don't go!" pleaded the girl, clinging to his arm. "They'll shoot you if you don't give him up."

"You never mind me, Polly," said her father reassuringly, as he gently unclasped her hands from his arm. "I'll take care of myself and the prisoner, too. There ain't a man in Branson County that would shoot me. Besides, I have faced fire too often to be scared away from my duty. You keep close in the house," he continued, "and if anyone disturbs you just use the old horse-pistol in the top bureau drawer. It's a little old-fashioned, but it did good work a few years ago."

The young girl shuddered at this sanguinary allusion, but made no further objection to her father's departure.

The sheriff of Branson was a man far above the average of the community in wealth, education, and social position. His had been one of the few families in the county that before the war had owned large estates and numerous slaves. He had graduated at the State University at Chapel Hill, and had kept up some acquaintance with current literature and advanced thought. He had traveled some in his youth, and was looked up to in the county as an authority on all subjects connected with the outer world. At first an ardent supporter of the Union, he had opposed the secession movement in his native state as long as opposition availed to stem

the tide of public opinion. Yielding at last to the force of circumstances, he had entered the Confederate service rather late in the
war and served with distinction through several campaigns, rising
in time to the rank of colonel. After the war he had taken the oath
of allegiance, and had been chosen by the people as the most
available candidate for the office of sheriff, to which he had been
elected without opposition. He had filled the office for several
terms and was universally popular with his constituents.

Colonel or Sheriff Campbell, as he was indifferently called, as
the military or civil title happened to be most important in the
opinion of the person addressing him, had a high sense of the
responsibility attached to his office. He had sworn to do his duty
faithfully, and he knew what his duty was as sheriff perhaps more
clearly than he had apprehended, it in other passages of his life, it
was therefore with no uncertainty in regard to his course that he
prepared his weapons and went over to the jail. He had no fears
for Polly's safety.

The sheriff had just locked the heavy front door of the jail
behind him when a half dozen horsemen, followed by a crowd of
men on foot, came round a bend in the road and drew near the
jail. They halted in front of the picket fence that surrounded the
building, while several of the committee of arrangements rode on
a few rods farther to the sheriff's house. One of them dismounted
and rapped on the door with his riding whip.

"Is the sheriff at home?" he inquired.

"No, he has just gone out," replied Polly, who had come to
the door.

"We want the jail keys," he continued.

"They are not here," said Polly. "The sheriff has them himself."
Then she added, with assumed indifference, "He is at the jail now."

The man turned away, and Polly went into the front room,

from which she peered anxiously between the slats of the green blinds of a window that looked toward the jail. Meanwhile the messenger returned to his companions and announced his discovery. It looked as though the sheriff had learned of their design and was preparing to resist it.

One of them stepped forward and rapped on the jail door.

"Well, what is it?" said the sheriff, from within.

"We want to talk to you, Sheriff," replied the spokesman.

There was a little wicket in the door; this the sheriff opened, and answered through it.

"All right, boys, talk away. You are all strangers to me, and I don't know what business you can have." The sheriff did not think it necessary to recognize anybody in particular on such an occasion; the question of identity sometimes comes up in the investigation of these extrajudicial executions.

"We're a committee of citizens and we want to get into the jail."

"What for? It ain't much trouble to get into jail. Most people want to keep out."

The mob was in no humor to appreciate a joke, and the sheriff's witticism fell dead upon an unresponsive audience.

"We want to have a talk with the nigger that killed Cap'n Walker."

"You can talk to that nigger in the courthouse, when he's brought out for trial. Court will be in session here next week. I know what you fellows want, but you can't get my prisoner today. Do you want to take the bread out of a poor man's mouth? I get seventy-five cents a day for keeping this prisoner, and he's the only one in jail. I can't have my family suffer just to please you fellows."

One or two young men in the crowd laughed at the idea of Sheriff Campbell's suffering for want of seventy-five cents a day; but they were frowned into silence by those who stood near them.

"Ef yer don't let us in," cried a voice, "we'll bus' the do' open."

"Bust away," answered the sheriff, raising his voice so that all could hear. "But I give you fair warning. The first man that tries it will be filled with buckshot. I'm sheriff of this county; I know my duty, and I mean to do it."

"What's the use of kicking, Sheriff?" argued one of the leaders of the mob. "The nigger is sure to hang anyhow; he richly deserves it; and we've got to do something to teach the niggers their places or white people won't be able to live in the county."

"There's no use talking, boys," responded the sheriff. "I'm a white man outside, but in this jail I'm sheriff; and if this nigger's to be hung in this county, I propose to do the hanging. So you fellows might as well right-about-face, and march back to Troy. You've had a pleasant trip, and the exercise will be good for you. You know *me*. I've got powder and ball, and I've faced fire before now, with nothing between me and the enemy, and I don't mean to surrender this jail while I'm able to shoot." Having thus announced his determination, the sheriff closed and fastened the wicket and looked around for the best position from which to defend the building.

The crowd drew off a little, and the leaders conversed together in low tones.

The Branson County jail was a small, two-story brick building, strongly constructed, with no attempt at architectural ornamentation. Each story was divided into two large cells by a passage running from front to rear. A grated iron door gave entrance from the passage to each of the four cells. The jail seldom had many prisoners in it, and the lower windows had been boarded up. When the sheriff had closed the wicket, he ascended the steep wooden stairs to the upper floor. There was no window at the front of the upper passage, and the most available position from which to watch the movements of the crowd below was the front window of the cell occupied by the solitary prisoner.

The sheriff unlocked the door and entered the cell. The prisoner was crouched in a corner, his yellow face, blanched with terror, looking ghastly in the semidarkness of the room. A cold perspiration had gathered on his forehead, and his teeth were chattering with affright.

"For God's sake, Sheriff," he murmured hoarsely, "don't let 'em lynch me; I didn't kill the old man."

The sheriff glanced at the cowering wretch with a look of mingled contempt and loathing.

"Get up," he said sharply. "You will probably be hung sooner or later, but it shall not be today if I can help it. I'll unlock your fetters, and if I can't hold the jail you'll have to make the best fight you can. If I'm shot, I'll consider my responsibility at an end."

There were iron fetters on the prisoner's ankles, and handcuffs on his wrists. These the sheriff unlocked, and they fell clanking to the floor.

"Keep back from the window," said the sheriff. "They might shoot if they saw you."

The sheriff drew toward the window a pine bench which formed a part of the scanty furniture of the cell, and laid his revolver upon it. Then he took his gun in hand, and took his stand at the side of the window where he could with least exposure of himself watch the movements of the crowd below.

The lynchers had not anticipated any determined resistance. Of course they had looked for a formal protest, and perhaps a sufficient show of opposition to excuse the sheriff in the eye of any stickler for legal formalities. They had not however come prepared to fight a battle, and no one of them seemed willing to lead an attack upon the jail. The leaders of the party conferred together with a good deal of animated gesticulation, which was visible to the sheriff from his outlook, though the distance was too great for him to hear what was said. At length one of them broke away from the group and rode back to the main body of the lynchers, who were restlessly awaiting orders.

"Well, boys," said the messenger, "we'll have to let it go for the present. The sheriff says he'll shoot, and he's got the drop on us this time. There ain't any of us that want to follow Cap'n Walker jest yet. Besides, the sheriff is a good fellow and we don't want to hurt 'im. But," he added, as if to reassure the crowd, which began to show signs of disappointment, "the nigger might as well say his prayers, for he ain't got long to live."

There was a murmur of dissent from the mob, and several voices insisted that an attack be made on the jail. But pacific counsels finally prevailed, and the mob sullenly withdrew.

The sheriff stood at the window until they had disappeared around the bend in the road. He did not relax his watchfulness when the last one was out of sight. Their withdrawal might be a mere feint, to be followed by a further attempt. So closely indeed was his attention drawn to the outside, that he neither saw nor heard the prisoner creep stealthily across the floor, reach out his hand and secure the revolver which lay on the bench behind the sheriff, and creep as noiselessly back to his place in the corner of the room.

A moment after the last of the lynching party had disappeared there was a shot fired from the woods across the road; a bullet whistled by the window and buried itself in the wooden casing a few inches from where the sheriff was standing. Quick as thought, with the instinct born of a semi-guerrilla army experience, he raised his gun and fired twice at the point from which a faint puff of smoke showed the hostile to have been sent. He stood a moment watching, and then rested his gun against the window and reached behind him mechanically for the other weapon. It was not on the bench. As the sheriff realized this fact, he turned his head and looked into the muzzle of the revolver.

"Stay where you are, Sheriff," said the prisoner, his eyes glistening, his face almost ruddy with excitement.

The sheriff mentally cursed his own carelessness for allowing him to be caught in such a predicament. He had not expected anything of the kind. He had relied on the Negro's cowardice and subordination in the presence of an armed white man as a matter of course. The sheriff was a brave man, but realized that the prisoner had him at an immense disadvantage. The two men stood thus for a moment, fighting a harmless duel with their eyes.

"Well, what do you mean to do?" asked the sheriff with apparent calmness.

"To get away, of course," said the prisoner in a tone which caused the sheriff to look at him more closely, and with an involuntary feeling of apprehension; if the man was not mad, he was in a state of mind akin to madness, and quite as dangerous. The sheriff felt that he must speak to the prisoner fair and watch for a chance to turn the tables on him. The keen-eyed, desperate man before him was a different being altogether from the groveling wretch who had begged so piteously for life a few minutes before.

At length the sheriff spoke:—

"Is this your gratitude to me for saving your life at the risk of my own? If I had not done so, you would now be swinging from the limb of some neighboring tree."

"True," said the prisoner, "you saved my life, but for how long? When you came in, you said court would sit next week. When the crowd went away they said I had not long to live. It is merely a choice of two ropes."

"While there's life there's hope," replied the sheriff. He uttered this commonplace mechanically, while his brain was busy in trying to think out some way of escape. "If you are innocent you can prove it."

The mulatto kept his eye upon the sheriff. "I didn't kill the old man," he replied; "but I shall never be able to clear myself. I was at his house at nine o'clock. I stole from it the coat that was on my back when I was taken. I would be convicted even with a fair trial unless the real murderer were discovered beforehand."

The sheriff knew this only too well. While he was thinking what argument next to use, the prisoner continued:—

"Throw me the keys—no, unlock the door."

The sheriff stood a moment irresolute. The mulatto's eye glittered ominously. The sheriff crossed the room and unlocked the door leading into the passage.

"Now go down and unlock the outside door."

The heart of the sheriff leaped within him. Perhaps he might make a dash for liberty and gain the outside. He descended the narrow stairs, the prisoner keeping close behind him.

The sheriff inserted the huge iron key into the lock. The rusty bolt yielded slowly. It still remained for him to pull the door open.

"Stop!" thundered the mulatto, who seemed to divine the sheriff's purpose. "Move a muscle, and I'll blow your brains out."

The sheriff obeyed; he realized that his chance had not yet come.

"Now keep on that side of the passage and go back upstairs."

Keeping the sheriff under cover of the revolver, the mulatto followed him up the stairs. The sheriff expected the prisoner to lock him into the cell and make his own escape. He had about come to the conclusion that the best thing he could do under the circumstances was to submit quietly and take his chances of recapturing the prisoner after the alarm had been given. The sheriff had faced death more than once upon the battlefield. A few minutes before, well armed, and with a brick wall between him and them, he had dared a hundred men to fight; but he felt instinctively that the desperate man confronting him was not to be trifled with, and he was too prudent a man to risk his life against such heavy odds. He had Polly to look after and there was a limit beyond which devotion to duty would be quixotic and even foolish.

"I want to get away," said the prisoner, "and I don't want to be captured; for if I am I know I will be hung on the spot. I am afraid," he added somewhat reflectively, "that in order to save myself I shall have to kill you."

"Good God!" exclaimed the sheriff in involuntary terror; "you would not kill the man to whom you owe your own life."

"You speak more truly than you know," replied the mulatto. "I indeed owe my life to you."

The sheriff started. He was capable of surprise, even in that moment of extreme peril. "Who are you?" he asked in amazement.

"Tom, Cicely's son," returned the other. He had closed the door and stood talking to the sheriff through the gated opening, "Don't you remember Cicely—Cicely whom you sold with her child to the speculator on his way to Alabama?"

The sheriff did remember. He had been sorry for it many a time since. It had been the old story of debts, mortgages, and bad crops. He had quarreled with the mother. The price offered for her and her child had been unusually large, and he had yielded to the combination of anger and pecuniary stress.

"Good God!" he gasped; "you would not murder your own father?"

"My father?" replied the mulatto. "It were well enough for me to claim the relationship, but it comes with poor grace from you to ask anything by reason of it. What father's duty have you ever performed for me? Did you give me your name, or even your protection? Other white men gave their colored sons freedom and money, and sent them to the free states. *You* sold *me* to the rice swamps."

"I at least gave you the life you cling to," murmured the sheriff.

"Life?" said the prisoner, with a sarcastic laugh. "What kind of a life? You gave me your own blood, your own feathers—no man need look at us together twice to see that—and you gave me a black mother. Poor wretch! She died under the lash, because she had enough spirit, and you made me a slave, and crushed it out."

"But you are free now," said the sheriff. He had not doubted, could not doubt, the mulatto's word. He knew whose passions coursed beneath that swarthy skin and burned in the black eyes opposite his own. He saw in this mulatto what he himself might have become had not the safeguards of parental restraint and public opinion been thrown around him.

"Free to do what?" replied the mulatto. "Free in name, but despised and scorned and set aside by the people to whose race I belong far more than to my mother's."

"There are schools," said the sheriff. "You have been to school." He had noticed that the mulatto spoke more eloquently and used better language than most Branson County people.

"I have been to school, and dreamed when I went that it would work some marvelous change in my condition. But what did I learn? I learned to feel that no degree of learning or wisdom will change the color of my skin and that I shall always wear what in my own country is a badge of degradation. When I think about it seriously I do not care particularly for such a life. It is the animal in me, not the man, that flees the gallows. I owe you nothing," he went on, "and expect nothing of you; and it would be no more than justice if I should avenge upon you my mother's wrongs and my own. But still I have to shoot you; I have never yet taken human life—for I did *not* kill the old captain. Will you promise to give no alarm and make no attempt to capture me until morning, if I do not shoot?"

So absorbed were the two men in their colloquy and their own tumultuous thoughts that neither of them had heard the door below move upon its hinges. Neither of them had heard a light step come stealthily up the stairs, nor seen a slender form creep along the darkening passage toward the mulatto.

The sheriff hesitated. The struggle between his love of life and his sense of duty was a terrific one. It may seem strange that a man who could sell his own child into slavery should hesitate at such a moment, when his life was trembling in the balance. But the baleful influence of human slavery poisoned the very fountains of life, and created new standards of right. The sheriff was conscientious; his conscience had merely been warped by his environment. Let no one ask what his answer would have been; he was spared the necessity of a decision.

"Stop," said the mulatto, "you need not promise. I could not trust you if you did. It is your life for mine; there is but one safe way for me; you must die."

He raised his arm to fire, when there was a flash—a report from the passage behind him. His arm fell heavily at his side, and the pistol dropped at his feet.

The sheriff recovered first from his surprise, and throwing open the door secured the fallen weapon. Then seizing the prisoner he thrust him into the cell and locked the door upon him; after which he turned to Polly, who leaned half-fainting against the wall, her hands clasped over her heart.

"Oh, Father, I was just in time!" she cried hysterically and, wildly sobbing, threw herself into her father's arms.

"I watched until they all went away," she said. "I heard the shot from the woods and I saw you shoot. Then when you did not come out I feared something had happened, that perhaps you had been wounded. I got out the other pistol and ran over here. When I found the door open I knew something was wrong and when I heard voices I crept upstairs, and reached the top just in time to hear him say he would kill you. Oh, it was a narrow escape!"

When she had grown somewhat calmer, the sheriff left her standing there and went back into the cell. The prisoner's arm was bleeding from a flesh wound. His bravado had given place to a stony apathy. There was no sign in his face of fear or disappointment or feeling of any kind. The sheriff sent Polly to the house for cloth, and bound up the prisoner's wound with a rude skill acquired during his army life.

"I'll have a doctor come and dress the wound in the morning," he said to the prisoner. "It will do very well until then if you will keep quiet. If the doctor asks you how the wound was caused, you can say that you were struck by the bullet fired from the woods. It would do you no good to have it known that you were shot while attempting to escape."

The prisoner uttered no word of thanks or apology, but sat in sullen silence. When the wounded arm had been bandaged, Polly and her father returned to the house.

The sheriff was in an unusually thoughtful mood that evening. He put salt in his coffee at supper, and poured vinegar over his pancakes. To many of Polly's questions he returned random answers. When he had gone to bed he lay awake for several hours.

In the silent watches of the night, when he was alone with God, there came into his mind a flood of unaccustomed

141

thoughts. An hour or two before, standing face to face with death, he had experienced a sensation similar to that which drowning men are said to feel—a kind of clarifying of the moral faculty, in which the veil of the flesh, with its obscuring passions and prejudices, is pushed aside for a moment, and all the acts of one's life stand out, in the clear light of truth, in their correct proportions and relations—a state of mind in which one sees himself as God may be supposed to see him. In the reaction following his rescue, this feeling had given place for a time to far different emotions. But now, in the silence of midnight, something of this clearness of spirit returned to the sheriff. He saw that he had owed some duty to this son of his—that neither law nor custom could destroy a responsibility inherent in the nature of mankind. He could not thus, in the eyes of God at least, shake off the consequences of his sin. Had he never sinned, this wayward spirit would never have come back from the vanished past to haunt him. As these thoughts came, his anger against the mulatto died away, and in its place there sprang up a great pity. The hand of parental authority might have restrained the passions he had seen burning in the prisoner's eyes when the desperate man spoke the words which had seemed to doom his father to death. The sheriff felt that he might have saved this fiery spirit from the sloth of slavery; that he might have sent him to the free North and given him there, or in some other land, an opportunity to turn to usefulness and honorable pursuits the talents that had run to crime, perhaps to madness; he might, still less, have given this son of his the poor simulacrum of liberty which men of his caste could possess in a slave-holding community; or least of all, but still something, he might have kept the boy on the plantation, where the burdens of slavery would have fallen lightly upon him.

The sheriff recalled his own youth. He had inherited an

honored name to keep untarnished; he had had a future to make; the picture of a fair young bride had beckoned him on to happiness. The poor wretch now stretched upon a pallet of straw between the brick walls of the jail had had none of these things, no name, no father, no mother—in the true meaning of motherhood—and until the past few years no possible future, and that one vague and shadowy in its outline, and dependent for form and substance upon the slow solution of a problem in which there were many unknown quantities.

From what he might have done to what he might yet do was an easy transition for the awakened conscience of the sheriff. It occurred to him, purely as a hypothesis, that he might permit his prisoner to escape; but his oath of office, his duty as sheriff, stood in the way of such a course, and the sheriff dismissed the idea from his mind. He could, however, investigate the circumstances of the murder and move Heaven and earth to discover the real criminal, for he no longer doubted the prisoner's innocence; he could employ counsel for the accused, and perhaps influence public opinion in his favor. Acquittal once secured, some plan could be devised by which the sheriff might in some degree atone for his crime against this son of his—against society—against God.

When the sheriff had reached this conclusion he fell into an unquiet slumber, from which he awoke late the next morning.

He went over to the jail before breakfast and found the prisoner lying on his pallet, his face turned to the wall; he did not move when the sheriff rattled the door.

"Good morning," said the latter, in a tone intended to waken the prisoner.

There was no response. The sheriff looked more keenly at the recumbent figure; there was an unnatural rigidity about its attitude.

He hastily unlocked the door and, entering the cell, bent over the prostrate form. There was no sound of breathing; he turned the body over—it was cold and stiff. The prisoner had torn the bandage from his wound and bled to death during the night. He had evidently been dead several hours.

Gary Phillips (1955–) was born in South Central Los Angeles, the son of a mechanic and a librarian, the latter inculcating a love of books to her son. As a youth and into his teenage years, he traveled regularly to France because his uncle, a soldier in Europe during World War II, became an ex-patriot in Paris after the war. Phillips attended San Francisco State University in 1972 and 1973, then received a B.A. from California State University, Los Angeles, in 1978. He has worked as a community activist, union organizer, radio talk show host, and teacher of incarcerated youth.

A mystery writing course taught by Robert Crais set Phillips on the path to a career as a professional writer. His first novel, *Violent Spring* (1996), set against the real-life L.A. riots spurred by the acquittal of the police involved in the Rodney King episode, introduced his best-known character, Ivan Monk, a private detective who also appeared in the novels *Perdition U.S.A.* (1996), *Bad Night Is Falling* (1998), and *Only the Wicked* (2000), as well as the short story collection *Monkology* (2004). He has produced two novels about a former showgirl, Martha Chainey, who works for a Las Vegas mobster: *High Hand* (2000) and *Shooter's Point* (2001), as well as stand-alone novels: *The Jook* (1999), *The Perpetrators* (2002) and *Bangers* (2003).

"House of Tears" was published in an earlier form in *Murdaland* #1 (September 2006); it appears here in its revised version for the first time.

House Of Tears

Gary Phillips

"That stuff's bad for you."

"What? You're into tofu and brown rice now?" LZ snickered and took a long pull on his Slurpee.

English Johnny turned the late '90s Astro van left off Garfield and drove slow and steady along a side street. As evening approached, kids were still out on their scooters and bikes and there was even a knot of girls jumping rope while a boom box blared a 50 Cent song.

"I'm just saying," English Johnny went on, "we ain't getting no younger and you got to take care of yourself." He scanned from one side of the street to the other as he guided the vehicle forward.

LZ scratched his armpit. "Look, man, I'm happy you ain't no longer sniffin' up your profits in crank and you're clean and sober as a Oklahoma preacher. But let me worry about my own god-damn vices."

"Uh-huh."

LZ grinned. "Fuck you." He had more of his Slurpee and

leaned out the window. "Hey, girl, what you packin' in there?" he said to a young woman in tight low rise jeans walking past on the sidewalk.

"Be cool, fool," English Johnny said. "Sit your ass back down."

"Maybe you should be on speed again," LZ cracked, "you're too wound up." He jiggled his shoulders and bobbed his head to the beat that pulsed in him. The beat that had been banging around inside him since running away from juvenile hall.

"We need to be focused. That's all I'm saying. You're head's gotta be in the moment like Iverson before a big one." English Johnny took a right and checked the rearview.

"You know I ain't nothin' but game, home," LZ replied. He pointed through the windshield. "How about that one?"

"That'll do," his partner agreed and pulled to the curb, the van idling on the lonely street.

LZ got out and trotted over to a parked Trailblazer SUV. He crouched down and quickly removed the rear license plate. Looking over his shoulder and spying no one, he got up and did the same at the front of the car, then attached them in the appropriate places on the Astro van. English Johnny then put the tranny in gear and got rolling again after LZ settled beside him.

They rode in silence, the driver taking a couple of turns until he reached Atlantic Boulevard. There he went north, the signage on stores in Chinese, Spanish and English.

Finally, LZ spoke. "Dude like this ain't got no bodyguards around? A couple of 350 pound pork chop eatin' square head bruisers all tatted up jus' praying for the opportunity to light into some sneak thieves like you and me." LZ smiled at his imagery, showing teeth he cared for daily. You couldn't get anywhere with the honeys if you had nasty teeth.

"He's a recluse. Danielle says until the stroke, he rattled

around in his castle by himself. Maybe some session dude or some arthritic used-to-be groupie dropped by from the old days."

"Man got to get his johnson waxed now and then," LZ observed. "Man go crazy if he can't have that. Get all backed up and shit."

English Johnny looked sideways at his compatriot. "That right?"

"I'm just sayin'." LZ nodded at the window. "But he was something in his day, huh? I remember moms would have her girlfriends over and after they got to drinking and get all misty-eyed about their teenage years, she'd break out the antique that played those goofy 45s. Then they'd get to finger-poppin' and tellin' more lies while they put on homeboy's hits."

LZ stared at English Johnny. "Bet you had a collection of his records, didn't you?"

"Still do, youngster. *The Slauson Shuffle, The Love You Left, Quicksand* . . . man, those were the cuts. If you didn't get a grind on a slow tune like *Heart of Fire,* you must have been one sorry chump." English Johnny looked beyond the windshield then reeled himself back to the present.

"When was that? High school?"

"Yeah." They were on the border of Monterey Park and Alhambra, and English Johnny slowed to a stop at the intersection with Emerson.

"You finish high school?" LZ asked, a tenth grade dropout.

"Sure did," the other man answered, pressing his foot to the accelerator as the signal changed to green. "Hell, I was even on the football and basketball teams."

"First string?"

English Johnny gave him a raised eyebrow. "You got to ask."

"Aw'rite, brah, cool." LZ had another long sip of his iced

soda. "So it's just Danielle up there with him, wiping his ass and chin."

"Apparently."

"And you think he keeps his shit there? In that mansion?"

"Know so."

"Danielle seen it?"

"Practically."

"Practically? What? She have a vision?" LZ chuckled at his joke.

"He's got a room and in the room is this stuffed bobcat, and—"

LZ halted in mid-sip. "A stuffed what? Like a lion?"

"Sort of," English Johnny frowned. "Well, I guess technically, it's more like a cougar."

"What the fuck, he was a hunter?"

"No, everything I've read says he's afraid of guns. When he was a kid his old man shot the old lady. The gun flashed right in front of his face, his mother's chest exploding, blood all over him. Traumatized him. In fact, that's how he got into music."

"You've studied up on him."

"Naturally." The cell phone chimed and LZ plucked it off the narrow dashboard.

"We're almost there," he said into the instrument after listening briefly. "Sure," he added, then handed the cell to his friend. "Your squeeze needs to hear your voice so she can cream."

"You need to stop." He put the phone to his ear. "Hey, baby." He listened as he drove. "Oh, yeah, we're set. Is he awake . . . I see. Okay, we follow the plan and we're gonna make out like a souvenir huntin' marine in one of Saddam's palaces." She said something else and he lowered his voice. "You know it," and clicked the device off.

"Where you guys going after this?" LZ took his bandana off

and buttoned his shirt over his breast bone. Absently, he flicked at the oval embroidered with "Steve" on the upper left side of the shirt.

"Danielle wants to go to London first because she's only seen it on TV or James Bond movies and wants to know what it's like first hand. You know, Big Ben, red phone booths, cobblestones." He shrugged. His nickname had nothing to do with the capital of England.

"Yeah," LZ said, "Go to Jimi Hendrix's grave and pay your respects."

"Hendrix is buried here."

"Here? Wasn't he from there?"

"Seattle."

"No shit."

"Nope."

"Huh." LZ reached under the seat and extracted a black Beretta.

"We're not going to need that."

"Safety first, son," LZ winked. And he tucked the gun away in his back pocket.

English Johnny weighed raising an objection but understood the piece was a security blanket for the lad and so why not. He could take care of things if LZ went off. But he didn't anticipate such a situation. No, this was going to be one sweet operation. This was the set-up he'd been on the road to since that time long ago when he stole his shop teacher's bad '67 Camaro—one of the limited Yenkos with a 427 engine. This was going to work, and nothing was going to derail his chance at a real payday.

The van took a right taking them into the hills. They traveled up an inclined street heavy with old oak trees and faint with the tantalizing scent of cooking onions and garlic.

"Hey, that was the street," LZ said, knocking the tip of his thumb against the side window.

English Johnny looked past him, straining to see the street sign in the gloom.

"That's it, I'm telling you," LZ repeated. "Where's your damn reading glasses?"

"My eyes are fine," he growled, getting the truck in reverse in a three-point turnaround. He started onto the street he'd missed, stopped, and put the automatic transmission into its lowest gear. He got going again and they lumbered up the hill, the street curving right then the other way as they neared the top. Behind them in the cargo area, canisters rattled in their harnesses.

"I've got it," LZ said, reaching around and holding on to the tanks.

The van reached the summit where an opening was partially hidden among leafy shrubs. They went through and were now on a driveway that curved and sloped downward to a metal gateway and arch done in an understated art nouveau manner. The electronic gate was open.

"I can smell it," LZ said.

"Don't start barking yet. I don't want to jinx this."

"It's ours, man." LZ gripped English Johnny on the upper arm. "You know it."

His partner's eyes widened, and he guided the van next to Danielle's dark blue '77 Grand LeMans Coupe with the Hopster aluminum rims English Johnny put on the car for her. He breathed in deep and let the air out slowly.

"Ready?" LZ asked.

"Hell yeah." He got out the driver's side and went around to where LZ had slid the side door back. They got the two oxygen tanks, heart monitor, dolly, mask and tubing and a clanking equipment bag onto the ground.

LZ was positioning one of the tanks on the dolly and glaring at some illuminated letters cut into yet another arch leading to a garden. "Fuck's that say?"

"Casa de Lágrima," English Johnny said, straightening out one of the casters on the monitor's cart. "House of Tears. It refers to his first album, which the critics liked but didn't sell."

LZ was taking in the massive Spanish-Moorish structure complete with turrets. "How many rooms in this mug?"

"Danielle said there are thirty-three."

"Damn." Together, they started up the walkway that jutted through the garden. "You sure this dude ain't Dracula?"

"You know what he's been spending his days doing? He watches reruns of *Combat, Mannix* and that goddamn *High Chaparral*."

"Those were TV shows?" LZ rolled the two oxygen tanks held in place by straps on the dolly.

"Yeah, before your time. He's got all the episodes on CDs and has them categorized so he gives her a list of what he wants played and what day."

"Does he listen to them songs he wrote and produced?"

"No, that's the funniest thing, he doesn't. According to Danielle, he never asks her to play them. And barely listens to the radio. Like he's forever shut out that part of his life." English Johnny pointed at a horizontal sliver of light that grew before them.

"There's my girl."

At the large double wooden doors, the men got the items inside while Danielle stood to one side. She was wearing a midthigh skirt and sweater blouse opened revealingly to the top of her black lace bra.

"Ain't you supposed to be in white or something?" LZ set the dolly with its load against the rough hewn wall in the circular foyer.

"Practical nurses wear what they want. And anyway, my patient likes the view." She cupped her large breasts in her hands and shook them, laughing.

"Long as he don't touch." English Johnny put an arm around her waist and pulled her close. They kissed and afterward she wiped her lipstick off his mouth with her fingers.

"He awake?"

"He was dozing," she answered. "Rough day of watching his goddamn shows."

English Johnny looked toward the staircase, visualizing what lay beyond. "Come on."

The trio proceeded and English Johnny was struck with the absence of any evidence that the house belonged to a man considered to be one of the pioneers of sixties and early seventies music, both rock & roll and R&B.

"Know what's odd?" Danielle whispered when they'd reached the mid-landing. "He started to make some notes today on a pad."

English Johnny bored in on the closed bedroom door at the end of the upper hallway. "What?"

"Looked like he was jotting down some lyrics," she said. "In all the time we've been planning this for the last month, this was the first time I've seen him do that."

"We'll give him something to sing about." LZ continued ascending backwards up the stairs with the dolly and tanks.

At the top, English Johnny gently pushed Danielle forward, his hand in the small of her back. She got ahead of LZ and opened the double wooden doors of the bedroom that, though smaller in scale, matched the main ones.

"Ian," she said sweetly, "the men are here from the medical supply." The room was spacious and made even more so by the paucity of furniture. There was a 40-inch TV atop a cart with a VCR and DVD player underneath. There was no dresser, no armoire. There was a large portrait in oils of a dark-haired woman, with a scowl and sizeable hoop earrings partially emerging from her tangle of hair. The painting was on the west wall, and to the left of that a raised oak bed atop a colorful throw rug, a sturdy night stand nearby.

In the bed reposed the former music baron. He was a thin man, bald, hawk-nosed with recessed eyes and stooping shoulders encased in blue silk pajamas. He lay propped against a thatch of pillows and was intent on the scene between Cameron Mitchell and Henry Darrow on his set. On a long, low dresser tucked under a window were a series of foam heads, each with a different style of wig.

"Gentlemen," the man in the bed said in the slightly slurred speech of one who's had a stroke.

"We'll just set this up, sir," English Johnny said, already heading toward the bed. LZ fell in step and they worked efficiently, as they'd practiced several times, putting the tank and monitor in place.

On the night stand was a pad of paper. English Johnny noted lyrics the man had been working on. Being a fan, he couldn't resist studying the words.

"I don't think it's gonna put me back on the charts," the man in bed said, looking at English Johnny. He began to chuckle hoarsely until he started to cough.

"Now, now, let's let these men do their work and you rest, dear." She came over to attend to the man, making sure not to look at English Johnny.

"Maybe you should have some oxygen," she offered. "Doctor Sawyer did suggest it would be good at this time of the evening."

"Sure, sure," he rasped, gesticulating knotted and blotched fingers more like the hinged legs of an insect's than a human's.

Danielle bent over more than necessary and slipped the oxygen mask with its elastic band around his head, the song man's eye taking in the offered view.

" 'Bout finished aren't we, boss?" LZ gave English Johnny a crooked smile.

"Sure," the other man answered, calibrating the dials on the heart monitor. He pushed the instrument toward the side of the headboard.

"The city burns at night past the windows of my four-on-the-floor," the man in the mask mumbled. "I got eight starving cylinders and a hunger to match. Something's inside me girl, and it's no lark, but in this dark my name is called . . ." His eyes closed and his lips moved slowly, but no sound came out of his mouth. Danielle slipped off the mask and shut off the valve. The tank contained a derivative of fentanyl, an opiate that induced stupor.

The three plotters exchanged grins and exited the room as one. There was a shorter hallway off the long one and they went down it past a set of tall vases with elephant stalks jutting from them. At a tee, there was a door with a hinged peep hole.

"What up with that?" LZ said.

"I think it was a study at one point, and I guess if the man of the house was into his books or brandy, he wanted to know who was knocking on the outside and disturbing him." Danielle produced a set of keys and unlocked the heavy door.

"Goddamn," English Johnny said as the trio stepped into the room and Danielle turned on the lights. The chamber was in one of the turrets, so it was circular with the ceiling high over their heads. There was even a set of stone steps built into one wall leading up to a second tiered platform. There was a low, rectangular bookcase on the platform overflowing with volumes.

On the ground level were stuffed animals, including a murder of ravens on a perch, a mandrill posed in mid-swing, a snarling wolf, and the bobcat. Another section that had bunched together, upon English Johnny's closer examination, all manner of '50s-era toy ray guns in several glass-enclosed cases.

"All this shit means something to him? Or is he just another rich boy don't know what to do with his money." LZ touched a bronze axe among a set of them grouped along one part of the curved wall.

"That's an Egyptian piercing axe," English Johnny rattled off. The other two gaped at him. "I told you, I read up on my man. There was a interview he did in *Vanity Fair* about sixteen or seventeen years ago and they had pictures to go with it."

LZ was in motion. "Well, that's really fuckin' groovy, but let's get busy."

Danielle watched English Johnny get out his torch from the equipment bag. LZ had rolled in the other tank, marked oxygen, but actually acetylene. He and Danielle pushed the bobcat, which was on its own platform made to look like a mountain path, out of the way.

"It's heavier than it looks," LZ huffed.

The woman got down on all fours to run her fingers in the grout between the pavers.

"Here we go," she said, standing up. She pushed the ball of her foot on a particular tile and depressed it. They waited.

"Ain't part of the wall supposed to open up like in an old movie?" LZ looked around.

"I didn't hear a click or anything. You sure that's how he gets to his vault?" The anticipation in English Johnny was now turning to acid and he was not a happy nor patient man. He had Danielle firm by the arm.

"Yeah, baby," she insisted, pulling her arm loose. "That time the door to the peep hole was loose and I looked in to see him stepping on that part of the floor and then he . . . oh."

"Oh what?" English Johnny said between clenched teeth.

"He walked." She turned to face the door, getting her direction right. "He went that way," she pointed, "toward the stairs. I couldn't see him then and I didn't dare stay at the door too long."

"The fuck." LZ charged close to English Johnny. "We doin' all this on your practically. This bitch never saw the money?"

"Your mama's a bitch," Danielle told him.

"Fuck you."

"Everybody relax," English Johnny advised. He was tamping it down and it was taking all his will to do so. "If he went toward the stairs, he went up the stairs." And he did so.

LZ declared. "This is bullshit."

"No, no, it can't be." Danielle looked up at English Johnny prowling about on the platform, his hands probing the bookcase. He then stared to hoot. "You were right, LZ, it's just like one of those Charlie Chan movies." English Johnny slid away a sectioned portion of the bookcase.

LZ ran up the steps, followed closely by Danielle. English Johnny was already in the exposed opening. Stepping on the paver unlocked a paneled section behind the bookcase.

Danielle asked. "Is there a light?"

"Can't tell, but there's got to be." LZ bumped into something and there was a crash. "Hey, I've got something."

"All you got is one of his framed gold records. I already saw those. This," English Johnny said, tapping metal, "is what we came for." He swung his penlight onto their smiling, sweaty faces. "Get my tools."

"Bet," LZ scrambled out.

Danielle came beside him. She had a hand on his chest,

looking at the standing safe pushed against the far wall. "How much you think is in there?"

"Enough to keep you in thongs and beamers, baby."

She put a hand on his tightening crotch. "So that's what excites you."

"You damn right." He had a hand on her breast and she kept hers where it was as they kissed ferociously . They only stopped when they heard LZ approach with the cutting tools.

English Johnny got his rig set up. "You two stay toward the front so you don't get any sparking or metal in your eyes." He flicked down his welder's mask and went to work.

When Danielle had told him what she'd seen that day peeking into this room, the idea took root. He looked up everything he could about the reclusive records legend. It was already known that he'd had tax trouble in the past and English Johnny found a couple of quotes from him attesting to his belief that the government had no right to the money he'd earned. In an article in a crumbling issue of *Teen Beat* he came across at a flea market, the first of three ex-wives was interviewed. She'd been the lead singer of the Sparrows, the girl group the legend guided to early success.

"He is one cheap, paranoid bastard," she'd said. "He grew up without and took to heart what his grandmother always told him about how the banks had ripped her folks off in the Depression. The more he got famous, the more he did lines of coke and quarts of booze, the more he felt everyone was out to get him."

The torch's concentrated flame made progress, burning a hole just above and to the left of the handle. The box was an old Mosler, and English Johnny had been weaned on safes like this one.

More digging into the record man's life had produced his last interview. Done for *Rolling Stone* in June of 1992, he'd gone on about the riots in April and May. The quote that sealed it for English Johnny was the one where he alluded to the safe.

The Idol Maker's father, a Holocaust survivor and a jeweler back when the Fairfax district was solidly Jewish, had had the safe in his shop. English Johnny learned this from a documentary he'd obtained from the library. And the impresario said that as he watched the smoke and the helicopters in the distance, he figured if the rioters should make their way up his hill, he'd roll down on them the only thing of value his shit-heel of a father had left him.

The interviewer had pressed for clarification and the man had answered, "Well, maybe I'll just take some money out of it and toss it over the wall." It was reported that he laughed uproariously at that.

"How's it going?' Danielle asked from the entrance.

"I'm almost to the pins," he said. As fine metal dust congealed on his mask, he suddenly glommed on something that had been in the back of his mind. How did a stroke victim, a man partially paralyzed on one side of his body, move that bobcat?

Then the lights went out.

"Hey," LZ yelled.

"Deal with it," English Johnny commanded. "I'm not stopping. Danielle, use my flashlight. It's in my back pocket. Shield your eyes and come get it."

"Okay." She came forward haltingly but reached him. "I've got it."

"And take this." He'd flicked up his mask and put the torch on top of the safe, cutting down its flame. Its glow cast them in wavering blues and yellows. He passed her the Glock he'd strapped to his calf. "LZ has a piece too. Maybe this is nothing, or maybe he's trying to pull something."

She didn't blink. "I can handle him."

"I know you can." She left and English Johnny went back to work. He didn't like sending her off to do what should be his job, but he couldn't have any delays in getting this box open. The hole was completed, and using the reduced flame again for light, he set about using his hammer and pointed chisel on the lock pins. Sweat gathered on his face and he had to stop and wipe the grime from his hands. The only thing he could hear was his tapping and drilling and grunting with the torch, the drill, the hammer and chisel. There was the satisfying slip of the pin from the rotor, and the auger bore through just where he wanted inside the lock mechanism. Soon. Very soon.

The Pretty Boy Floyd–era Mosler opened silently on well-oiled hinges. And just like the fairy tale this job was—the castle-like mansion on the hill, the hermit, Danielle as his princess—there was the treasure inside the safe. There were many neat stacks of hundreds the IRS would no doubt be happy to know about.

His hand jerked at the retort of a gun as he reached for one of the piles. His temples pulsing, English Johnny was still and tensed, his fist locked around his hammer. Come on, somebody say something. "Danielle," he boomed. "Danielle."

Breathing deep, he scooped the money into the equipment bag and got out of the room. Minimal light was coming through the high windows and he could make out enough to get back down the stairs leading to the hidden alcove in the turret. If LZ was up to something, wouldn't he have been there to bust a cap in him?

Once more in the larger room, every dark form was a potential enemy, every shadow a place where he could be jumped. The equipment bag banged along the side of his leg, his other hand holding on to the hammer. There were no more shots, no whispering, and no movement. English Johnny strained to discern the door they'd come though and walked purposefully to it. He was going home with the money.

Out in the passageway he stopped and listened. He started forward and bumped into a vase, toppling it. It shattered with force. Instinctively he crouched low, expecting . . . something, but there was nothing. He moved forward, feeling his way to the tee section, then stopped again. Now there was something, a presence. He put the equipment bag aside, wanting to use both hands and his hammer.

"Baby," Danielle said, the word thick with mucus. "Help me." She moaned. "Help me," she repeated. She was crawling in the long hallway that led to the master bedroom.

English Johnny frowned, trying to make sense of things. "What happened?"

"He," she started but didn't finish.

Was it a trap? Were she and LZ in on it together? She was young and fine. When the three of them had been out, working on the plan, people usually assumed she was with LZ.

"Chris," she coughed, using his real name. "I know you're there."

Fuck it. He went to her, crouching down, keyed up for anything. Through the darkness he could tell she wasn't faking. She was on her belly, doing her best to drag herself by her arms.

"What happened?" English Johnny had her face in his hands, her cheek as cold as fish flesh.

"He whacked LZ alongside his head when we turned the corner."

"He? You mean—?"

"Yeah. He wasn't knocked out by the gas. I had the light on him and was bringing my piece up when he shot, put it right into my chest. Bastard shot me right in the tit." She laughed and coughed up fluid and blood.

"Where's your gun?"

"Dropped it, back at the door. God, it hurts."

"He's in there now? The bedroom?"

"Don't know," she managed weakly. "I need a doctor, honey."

"I'm gonna get you straight, sweetie. You hold on." English Johnny wasn't going to let some gimp get the better of him. Not now, not having come this far. He rose and walked forward. "Hey, faggot. You think you're better than me?"

"Come on in and find out," the man taunted through the door. "You think because I had a stroke I can't take care of a bunch of also-rans like your F Troop crew? You know what kind of shit I've been through for forty years in the record business? What kind of suited ghouls I had to deal with? You're nothing compared to that." He coughed, then continued.

"Didn't it occur to you I might have your girl checked out? Find out about her record and known associates like you, Chris. You fuckin' loser, penitentiary bitch." He laughed. "Did you know I was a lifeguard when I was young? Still pretty good at holding my breath."

"Big man," English Johnny sneered. He positioned himself next to the door, the hammer in his hand. He felt along he door, got set, then pummeled the old-fashioned latch. Two shots went through the door but he wasn't stopping.

"Come on, motherfucker," the sick man screamed. "You aren't gonna let a cripple beat you, are you, tough guy?"

The latch gave and the door creaked open slightly. English Johnny went low against the door jamb, waiting and listening. If he were the other man, where would he be? He visualized the room as he'd remembered it, and looked to his left where the big TV was.

"Chris," Danielle called from the hallway.

English Johnny launched himself, two more shots ringing out as he dove for the bed. One of the rounds caught him right above the ankle. His momentum took him to the bed and he scrambled over to the other side, knocking the night stand and doped oxygen tank over as he got to the floor.

Another shot went wide. His wound was on fire and he grimaced in pain as he used the bed as a battering ram. He shoved the heavy frame toward the TV—and the man hiding behind it. More gunshots, wood chipping and a round pinging off a metal surface.

The bed collided with the TV, which toppled over. There was a groan, the clatter of a gun across the tiles, and English Johnny moved as best he could, the leg already cramping from effort. He reached his target beside the upset big screen. English Johnny was surprised the scrawny man still had fight in him. A hand that had more strength than he would have imagined was around his throat.

"You lousy fuck," the former record mogul said. "You think you can steal from me?"

"I earned this," English Johnny hollered, striking him. Only one side of the man's body had power and with that blow he collapsed inside his silk pajamas.

English Johnny grabbed at the man. "You shot my old lady."

"I'da shot you too if I had the chance." Pale and shaking, he was through but wasn't going to admit it.

English Johnny was about to hit him again when an approaching siren caused him to pause.

"What's a'matter, didn't think I'd call them, genius?"

As if he were a child, English Johnny shoved the squawking man aside. Straining, he got his feet under him, his leg wobbly. He started to go and there was a hand clutching at his pant leg.

He kicked the man who'd earned twenty-seven gold and platinum albums in the head and limped quickly away. Danielle had managed to sit up against the wall. She held out her arms.

"Help me up, baby."

He went past her to the equipment bag, stumbling into objects and bric-a-brac. He got the bag and turned. He'd have to pass her again on his way to the stairs.

"Chris," she wailed.

"They'll take care of you, Danielle. They'll get you an ambulance and everything."

"You backstabbing mothafuckah. Get me out, Chris," she yelled. "Get me out of here. You wouldn't have shit if it wasn't for me." She was in tears. He was at the stairs.

"No," a new voice hollered.

"LZ, wait," English Johnny began but didn't finish as the younger man tackled him and they went horizontal down the stairs to the mid-landing.

"You ain't taking that money nowhere." LZ was bleeding from his head.

English Johnny got a knee between them and leveraged his partner off him, beating at LZ's head with the stuffed equipment bag.

"No, no, you don't," LZ raged, lunging for English Johnny.

The gun punched a wicked hole in his stomach and LZ fell back against the carved banister. English Johnny had picked up the Beretta LZ had brought in against his wishes.

"Sorry," English Johnny said, getting up and stepping over the wounded man on the stairs. "I'm very sorry."

"Man, that's fucked up. That's really fucked up." LZ's warm blood leaked past the hand held to his gut.

The siren was coming up the hill and English Johnny was

barreling down it in the LeMans. The cop car, a Caprice with crash bars, was crowding the narrow incline. English Johnny drove right, like he was getting out of the way, then veered left viciously, knocking the cruiser into a parked pickup. The cop on the passenger side was aiming with his nine as the driver straightened the banged-up car. English Johnny decimated their side window with a blast from the Beretta.

As he'd hoped, the two cops had ducked, affording him the opportunity to barge past, scraping the side of his car against theirs, screeching and denting his way free. The cops put rounds in his trunk and punched holes in his rear window as he got to the bottom of the hill. Another cop car was coming. He saw another street and took that. He wasn't sure where it would take him, but it was better than where he was. Any road leading down would get him out of the hills.

Behind him the cops' radio crackled, "Black male, stocky build, approximately forty-five to fifty years of age, driving . . ."

He tore through residential streets, past high-priced houses behind high walls. He was heading into Pasadena, which meant a larger police force with more resources. His leg was bleeding into the worn mat. A chopper searched for him overhead, its spotlight cutting like a laser through the foliage. Panic and fear gurgled his stomach when he got momentarily trapped in a cul-de-sac but, miraculously, he reversed and finally reached flat land.

The hunted man got himself oriented near the Caltech campus and bore westward. He took Del Mar hoping to throw them off by not taking a major street but already two black & whites were on him. At Los Robles he got lucky and managed to beat an eighteen-wheeler heading south. The truck locked its brakes and the trailer fishtailed into a swipe through the intersection as he roared past. This momentarily delayed the pursuit and gave him breathing room. On a side street he ditched the V-8 and took off on foot.

His leg was on fire but he knew this was better than trying to escape in the moving target he was driving. In the near distance he could hear the traffic on the 110 freeway. He got to a cyclone fence, the freeway before him. Between where he was and another fence and guardrails of the freeway, was the Arroyo Seco Wash. This being the Southland, it was a concrete river, its bed dry except in the rainy season. There were access tunnels cut into its sloping walls and one was just across the wash from him.

English Johnny threw the bag over and used what reserve he had left clambering to the top of the fence. He lost his grip there and came crashing down on his back on the other side. The whoosh of the helicopter and its spotlight suddenly swung into view, trapping him in its glare. Wrenching himself up, he grabbed the bag and ran, limped, skipped his way toward the tunnel. The zipper had worked loose somehow and money began flapping from the bag. Caught in the light, the bills fluttered about with a green luminescence.

His side aching, his leg numb, English Johnny kept on. Overhead, a warning came through a bullhorn. Run, he admonished himself, run. He was on the slope, he was almost there. He was pushing fifty and he was going to live like a pharaoh.

The shot from the rifle sent a high-velocity slug clean through his hip. He went down as if struck by lightning. But he held on to the bag, he held on to the money. He would never let it go.

"It's mine," he wailed. "Goddammit, I'm way past due." He dog-walked up the sloping wall but the second shot bore between his shoulder blades, exiting his sternum and driving him back to the deck with thudding certainty.

His muscles spasmed and his body became unresponsive to his

wishes. It was all he could do to focus his eyes. Footsteps and loud voices reached him and, with nothing left but desire, he reared up, staring at the tunnel hole. It seemed then, as they put hands on him, and as a foot was slammed into the upper part of his back shoving him down again, that the slot in the wall grew. His breathing slowed, his heart beat less and less, but he couldn't look away.

That hole loomed larger, telescoping toward him, blotting out the light and pain as darkness was all about him. English Johnny could see clearly along that long dank corridor, clutching his money, never to return.

ELEANOR TAYLOR BLAND (1944–) was born in Boston and married a sailor when she was fourteen; his last station was in the Great Lakes region, where they settled. She graduated from the College of the Lake Country and Southern Illinois University with degrees in accounting and education. She has lived in Waukegan, Illinois, since 1972, working as an accountant until 1999.

With her first book, *Dead Time* (1992), Bland introduced Marti MacAlister, a smart policewoman who moved from Chicago to a suburb thirty miles away, Lincoln Prairie (a fictional town much like Waukegan), where she teams up with Matthew (Vik) Jessenovik, a decent old-fashioned Polish-American who has some problems with having a female partner, though none with the fact that she is black. In spite of being streetwise and fearless, MacAlister is softhearted, especially with children, whom she regards as among the most helpless members of society. While busy fighting crime, she also goes out of her way to lend a helping hand to other people who have a difficult time helping themselves, like the mentally ill, the homeless, and the elderly. She has had a very long romantic relationship but has not married, nor has she been intimate with her fiancé. There have been eleven novels about MacAlister. Bland also edited the anthology *Shades of Black: Crime and Mystery Stories by African-American Authors* (2004).

"The Canasta Club" was first published in *The World's Finest Mystery and Crime Stories*, edited by Edward Gorman, in 2004.

The Canasta Club

Eleanor Taylor Bland

It began snowing as Detectives Marti MacAlister and Matthew "Vik" Jessenovik drove past Springfield, Illinois. Three and a half hours later they had traveled another seventy-two miles. Visibility was close to zero and Route 55 all but impassable by the time they reached their exit. Josephina Hanson, the woman they were going to see, had been told that her eighty-seven-year-old sister Agatha was dead; what she didn't know was that the cause of death was something other than old age and natural causes. Marti pulled into a Phillips 66 and tried to get something on the radio besides static while Vik filled the tank and got directions to the address they were looking for. Over the phone, a Miss Evangeline Roberts had explained that although it could be considered an old folks' home, since elderly ladies lived there, it certainly was not a nursing home.

"We are just getting along in years," she told Marti. "We are not senile or in any way incapacitated, unless you consider being hard of hearing or visually impaired or using a cane."

Vik had not been eager to come here, but because it looked like a homicide they had no choice. The toxicology reports that came late yesterday afternoon had identified poison, and Agatha Hanson had been dead for almost a month. The case was already cold.

The car door opened. Vik said something but it was muffled by the scarf that covered everything below his eyes. He knocked snow from his boots and brushed it off of his wool cap before he got in.

"We lucked up, MacAlister. And we lucked out. The place we're looking for is only a mile and a half up that road." He pointed. "It shouldn't take us more than two hours to get there. The bad news is there's no way in hell we're going to make it back to Lincoln Prairie today. There's close to a foot of snow on the ground and another five to seven inches predicted. And guess what—the storm stayed south of Chicago. If we had waited a couple of days we wouldn't be stuck here."

"Did you remember to phone home?"

"My place, yours, and I left a message for the lieutenant. Everyone knows we made it here, so just stay on the road."

Marti hunched forward with her forehead inches from the windshield. The snow was coming down so fast that even with the wipers on high she had difficulty seeing anything, "I hope I can spot another car's headlights while I still have enough time to stop or get out of the way."

"Just worry about staying on the road," Vik advised. "Nobody but a fool would drive around in this."

"It only took half an hour," she said when she pulled into the driveway alongside a rambling two-story house with a wrap-around porch. The force of the wind slammed the car door shut and pushed her against the front fender as soon as she got out.

She fought against it, with Vik right behind her, grabbed the railing and hauled herself up the front steps.

"Oh, do come in," a stoop-shouldered woman said, opening the door before they could ring the bell. "I've been watching for you. I didn't think you would make it." The wind blew the door so hard it banged against the wall. The carpet was covered with snow before they made it inside. Vik slammed the door shut.

Vik and Marti introduced themselves and showed the woman their shields.

"I'm Evangeline Roberts; we spoke on the phone." Her breath smelled of peppermint. "I can't remember the last time we've had police officers here, not unless you count the time Claudette Colbert managed to get herself stuck in a drainage pipe. She's one of our cats."

The woman sounded more excited than concerned. She didn't reach Marti's shoulder. As Marti looked down at her blue-gray hair, teased and stiff with hair spray, she could see the scalp.

"Let me take your coats. I'd better take them to the kitchen and hang them up. They are covered with snow. And I'll have to have Elmer mop up in here before someone breaks their neck, or worse, a hip."

Vik took Marti's coat and kept his own. "Let me, ma'am."

As they followed her, she moved quickly and with far more agility than Marti expected. The kitchen wasn't as cozy as the porch had implied. The appliances were commercial and stainless steel. There were enough gadgets to stock a small store. There was just a hint of basil in the air and loaves of bread were rising on a countertop. Marti's stomach rumbled. They hadn't stopped to eat since lunch and it was well past dinner time.

"Have you eaten?" Miss Roberts asked.

"No, ma'am," Vik said.

"Well, the dining room is right over here and I'll fix you a little something right away. Josephina is playing canasta and there is no interrupting them once they cut the cards."

An elevator had been installed by the dining area. Everything was chintz and maple and meals were served at round tables seating four, with seasonal centerpieces of evergreen and holly.

"No need to rush, you won't be going back out tonight. We can put you up right here. This town is so small we don't have anything but that rinky-dink little motel, right off the highway. Route Sixty-six it used to be. They even had a TV show named for it with a song and all. Route Sixty-six it still is, as far as I'm concerned, even if they did make it much too wide and renamed it Route Fifty-five."

Marti asked for a telephone.

"The lines are down, dear, but not to worry. We've got an emergency generator if the lights go." She brought them steaming bowls of beef stew, homemade biscuits, and real butter, followed by hot coffee and apple pie.

"I told Josephina you were here. They are right in the middle of their canasta game and were more than a little annoyed by the interruption."

After they had eaten the last bit of pie crust, Miss Roberts led them to the rear of the house. From the hallway, Marti could see an older man mopping up near the front door. Elmer, she assumed. As she watched, he straightened up, put his hand to the small of his back, then continued mopping in a slow circular pattern. Marti wondered what his relationship was to the others. If he didn't live in, and wasn't the next-door neighbor, he would be spending the night here too, just as she and Vik would.

"You'll have to wait," Miss Roberts advised. "They play most evenings from right after dinner until bedtime. Once they shuffle and cut the deck, they get madder than buzzards without a carcass if you bother them. Here we are."

Windows ran the length of the porch, which had been closed in and winterized. The windows were bare except for vertical blinds, which were open. A white curtain of icy snow made tapping sounds against the glass. Marti thought of the heating bills first, then the pleasure of looking out and watching the seasons change. A log burning in a fireplace added a homey touch, but Marti doubted that the fire gave off much heat.

Everyone was in pairs. Two ladies sat at the far end of the room, watching a television with the volume turned up. Two ladies were knitting. Two who looked enough alike to be related napped in rocking chairs with their feet on hassocks and fat cats curled up in their laps.

Four women sat at a table. The one with hands crippled with arthritis had arranged her cards in some kind of cardholder. Marti studied each in turn and wondered which was Josephina Hanson. She had seen the dead woman at the morgue, as well as in photographs. None of the card players resembled her. She didn't see anyone to pair with Miss Hanson.

"Jeez," Vik whispered, shielding his mouth with his hand. "Do you think there's anyone in here under ninety? I haven't seen this many old people since my great-uncle Otto died. They had to put him in a nursing home when he was ninety-seven because he kept falling out of his wheelchair."

"I don't think any of these ladies is that old," Marti whispered back. She looked at the two in the rocking chairs and changed her mind. "Maybe those two." She nodded toward them. A walker with wheels and shelves was parked by one of the rockers.

Vik rubbed his arms, then scratched them.

"Old age isn't contagious," Marti said, under her breath. "Cut that out."

"This place is giving me the creeps. There has to be someplace else we can stay."

Marti nodded in the direction of the windows. "Got any ideas as to how we'll get there?"

Vik muttered something in Polish.

There was plenty of seating available, but nothing that looked comfortable. The chairs and sofas had straight backs and hard seats that were high off the floor. Most had pillows or an extra cushion. Marti chose a chair close enough to the card table to eavesdrop. The women played like gamblers even though there was no money on the table: all business, no small talk, certainly not any gossip. What conversation there was was mostly about melds. Canasta didn't sound anything like poker or even bid whist. Bored, Marti watched as one of the old ladies by the television stood up and steadied herself with a cane. She thought of her grandmother and how difficult getting up and down had been for her and understood the reason for the chairs and sofas.

Everything had been adapted to meet the needs of the occupants: extra space between tables and chairs; a counter that ran the length of the windows, with books and magazines and needlework and yarn all within easy reach. There were no scatter rugs, no high or low shelves or storage areas. Sweaters hung on hooks and there was a stack of afghans. This was not anything like any nursing home she had ever been in. It was an old house; remodeling it must have been expensive.

A clock chimed the half hour. Marti glanced at her watch. It was after ten. Vik leaned over and said, "I told you old people don't go to bed early. See, they don't do enough to get tired."

The conversation at the table became louder. Chairs were

pushed back. One woman detached herself from the group and walked over to them. Her movements were slow but she was not infirm.

"Miss Hanson?"

"Yes." She was short and plump with a round face and granny glasses. Her deceased sister had been much taller and three years older. There was no facial resemblance whatsoever. "Agatha has been dead for a month now, but if you had to come out in weather like this . . . What is it?"

"Is there someplace where we can talk?" Marti asked.

"Yes, right here." She pulled up a chair. "In just a few minutes."

"Here we are, ladies." Miss Roberts bustled in carrying a tray with glasses and a bottle of brandy. All of the women but two shared a nightcap. Marti and Vik declined but accepted mulled cider.

"So," Josephina Hanson said when they were alone, "what is it?"

Marti decided to be direct. "Someone poisoned your sister."

"Oh dear. But who? And how, I mean what?"

"When is the last time you saw her?"

"Oh, it's been ten years now. Not since Howie died. He was our brother."

"Had you spoken with her on the phone recently?"

"Not since June nineteenth, her birthday. We always call on birthdays and Christmas."

Marti supposed that at their age, and with this much distance between them, calls that infrequent might not be considered unusual. Neither woman had married. They had shared equally in their parents' estate. Agatha had lived alone in a small apartment. Frugal until the end, she had directed that there be no service, that her body be cremated and her ashes scattered on a bluff overlooking Lake Michigan. Josephina had inherited more from her sister than from her parents. It seemed as if they should have been closer.

"Do you have any idea of who her friends were?" The neighbors hadn't known of any.

"There was Opal, and Mary Sue, but both of them have been dead ten or twelve years now."

"Was there anyone else?"

"The mailman. She said he was a very pleasant young man and always reliable."

He was close to retirement and had worked that route for years. He found her body the day after she died. She remembered him in her will.

"Was there anyone else? A repairman? Someone trying to sell her something?"

"Agatha was not one to be taken in by strangers."

Agatha had not made any unusual withdrawals or any other bequests either. If someone had tried to swindle or otherwise pry money from her, apparently they had not been successful. If only she hadn't kept so much to herself.

As soon as Josephina Hanson excused herself to go to bed, Vik said, "That's another problem. How much can someone that old remember? And did you see how she leaned forward to listen to you and then talked too loud? Uncle Otto did that, too. He never wore a hearing aid though. One day he just couldn't hear anything at all."

"Vik, she did hear me."

"Right, but will she remember anything you said this time tomorrow? And it's been months since she talked with her sister. How do you expect her to remember any of that? We're talking about old people, Marti, real old people."

Marti leaned toward him and whispered, "What if she hired someone to kill off Agatha for her money?"

"Don't be ridiculous. At her age, how much money could she need? Living here is probably cheaper than her sister's living expenses were."

"I don't think so," Marti said. "This looks like an expensive arrangement. Greed, Vik. Think about it."

"I just did. There's got to be some other reason. You know how old people are. She trusted someone and kept money in the house. They stole from her and killed her when she found out. Or maybe she let them think they were going to get something when she died and they helped her on her way."

"How about the mailman?" Marti suggested.

"For ten thousand dollars?" He considered that. "We'll have to check him out. Did the sister's reaction surprise you?"

"Not if they've only spoken to each other three times a year for the past ten years. I'm wondering why. Something must have happened between them."

Although she would not admit it to Vik, the biggest problem she had questioning the elderly was not knowing how much of what they recalled was reliable. Then there was that ingrained habit of being respectful to her elders. She had also observed that death seldom surprised or frightened them, especially if they were old enough to have lost family members and friends.

"I can't read Josephina at all. There's something very matter-of-fact in her attitude. I don't know if it's acceptance, or indifference, or if she knows more about her sister's death than she's telling us." Tomorrow she would have to rule out two of those possibilities, even if she was disrespectful, even if Josephina did get upset.

Vik went to the window. "It's still snowing. It's drifted up to the windowsill. I bet we can't even see the car. If you tell anyone that we spent the night in an old folks' home, MacAlister, with eleven little old ladies and two cats . . ."

"Me?" If word of this got around the precinct they would both be the butt of everyone's jokes. "As far as I'm concerned, this place has vacant rooms and that makes it a motel."

"Just don't forget that. If anyone ever finds out I spent the night with a bunch of senile old women . . ."

"They are old, Jessenovik, but I don't see any indications of senility. There is a difference."

"Oh, yeah? Try telling that to an eighty-year-old man."

Miss Roberts showed Vik to a sofa in a small den. Marti got a guest room on the first floor that was a few feet bigger than a closet. "I'm afraid we've never had anyone sleep over, dear," Miss Roberts explained. "We do have the stray niece and nephew here and there. It isn't something we want to encourage." The nightgown the woman gave her was several sizes too small. Marti stretched out on the bed fully clothed and covered herself with the extra quilt. She didn't like being in a strange bed and the mattress on this one was lumpy. The bedding smelled of sachet and the springs creaked. She doubted that anyone who slept here would want to do it again.

Marti didn't think she would fall asleep. A loud scream followed by hysterical crying awakened her. She rushed into the hall just as Vik came out of the den. He let her go ahead of him.

"Elmer, my God, Elmer!" Miss Roberts sobbed. Fully dressed, she was standing in a doorway.

Marti got close enough to see Elmer lying in a small heap on the floor. The bedroom wasn't any bigger than the one she was in. There was no sign of a struggle.

"Miss Roberts . . ."

The woman turned. "He can't be dead,' she said. "He just can't be dead, not Elmer. He's only seventy-three." Her shoulders shook as she sobbed. "He just can't be dead. Nobody in our family has ever died younger than eighty."

Marti stayed with Miss Roberts while Vik knelt beside Elmer and checked for some sign of life. She wished she had asked more questions last night and knew who Elmer was.

Vik looked up and shook his head. "Miss Roberts, we need to call for an ambulance and notify the police."

"The phone lines are still out."

"Then we have to leave him here until we can get help."

"But he . . . he's just lying there . . . he . . . shouldn't we . . ."

"No."

Vik came out of the room and closed the door. "Since everyone in the house seems to be up . . ."

Marti turned to see all of the women, still in their nightclothes, standing close enough to hear what was being said but too far away to see into the room.

"Why don't we all come this way," Marti urged.

"Yes, yes," Miss Roberts agreed. "Breakfast is just about ready. I was so busy making sure those orange yeast rolls didn't burn on the bottom that I didn't even notice how late it was. Elmer always was a late sleeper, never gets up until half past six."

"Perhaps if everyone had breakfast," Marti urged.

"Yes, of course, but poor Elmer. It must have been his heart."

"Did he have heart trouble?"

"No. There was nothing wrong with his health. His eyesight wasn't what it used to be, but I never could convince him to get glasses."

"Is he a relative, ma'am?" Marti asked.

"He's my brother. My baby brother." The tears started flowing again.

"Did he live here with you?"

"Ye-e-e-s." Her shoulders heaved as she nodded.

"At least he didn't suffer," Marti said. That tended to have a calming effect for some reason. Marti wasn't sure why; like Vik said, dead was dead.

"He was always such a good boy, and handy too. He could fix just about anything. I don't know what I'm going to do without him."

"He would want you to go on."

"I know."

"We need to secure this room, ma'am," Vik said. "Just temporarily. Is there a key?"

Miss Roberts took a ring of keys from her apron pocket. "This one."

Vik slipped the key off, locked the door and pocketed the key. "Are there any other keys to this room?"

"Just Elmer's." She dabbed at her eyes and Marti expected more tears. Instead, Miss Roberts squared her shoulders and went into the dining room. "Now my dears, if you'll just give me a few minutes, breakfast will be served forthwith."

The ladies seemed subdued but otherwise okay. If it weren't for the two empty places at the table where the ladies with the cats were sitting, everything probably would have been okay. Within minutes everyone was looking there, and soon tears began trickling down their creased and wrinkled faces.

Marti shook her head when Vik motioned toward the front of the house. She was out of everyone's line of vision and curious to hear what they might say.

"How will we ever manage?" one said.

"How will Evangeline manage?" asked another. "He's been her right hand since Marjorie died. If he hadn't agreed to move in . . ."

"She'll find someone," one of the cat owners said.

"But dear," said the woman sitting beside her, "who can we trust?" That said, everyone was silent.

When the door to the kitchen opened and Miss Roberts wheeled in a two-tiered tray loaded with food, the ladies hardly noticed. Marti wanted to reach for a crisp piece of bacon, that and one of those yeast rolls.

While the ladies had breakfast, Vik checked outside.

"No change," he said. "If there were any footprints leading to the house the wind has taken care of them."

Miss Roberts brought in orange rolls and a carafe of coffee. "I tried to call Chief Harrolson. Why on earth can't they get the lines fixed? It's never taken this long. Elmer said we needed to get some kind of radio. I don't know why I didn't listen to him."

After she left, Vik reached for one of the rolls, changed his mind and rubbed his hands together. "There's over a foot and a half of snow out there and from the looks of it there hasn't been a plow within miles of here. There's no point in digging the car out and neither of us thought to bring snow shoes or skis. And, all of this stayed south of Chicago. This isn't our case, Marti. This isn't our jurisdiction."

"We're peace officers, Vik." She didn't like this any better than he did and for the same reasons. "We are the only peace officers around."

"I'd be willing to consider natural causes if it wasn't for Josephina's sister," Vik said.

"We'd better treat this one like a homicide, Jessenovik. Just in case."

"You know what that means."

"That the killer is right here in this house."

"And not a day under seventy-five unless there's someone younger hiding in the attic or basement."

"I think that's pretty unlikely, but let's get permission to take a look."

Vik agreed.

Marti found Miss Roberts in the kitchen. "Is it okay if we take a look around?"

She seemed puzzled, but the oven timer distracted her and she agreed.

"You notice anything about this setup?" Vik asked after they checked the attic and the second floor.

Marti had, but she didn't say anything.

"We've got one room with twin beds, one room with a single bed and the other four bedrooms have a double bed, one with a commode beside it."

"Umm humm."

"And, everyone seems to be in pairs."

"Umm humm."

"The two with the cats look so much alike that they have to be related, and with her sister dead, Evangeline is alone. That accounts for the twin beds and the single bed."

"Umm humm."

"But these are old ladies, Marti. Really old ladies."

"Umm humm."

"I'll be damned."

Vik paced for a moment, stopped, then said, "You know what? I'm going to pretend I didn't notice any of that. And you are not going to repeat it to anyone."

Marti didn't answer. "Lovely old house," she said as they went downstairs.

There wasn't anyone hiding in the cellar either.

They looked in on Elmer again. "Jeez," Vik said. "He's still dead."

"We'd better hope it was natural causes," Marti said, "and not something he ate."

"Ordinarily, MacAlister, when more than one death comes this close to the same person I rule out coincidence, but in this case natural causes makes sense. If the coroner hadn't run those toxicology tests, we wouldn't have known what killed the sister. It's going to take that with Elmer too."

Marti walked around the perimeter of the room. "I think Miss Roberts's permission to look around included looking around in here. Her exact words were 'Do whatever you feel is necessary to make sure we're all safe.' "

"I'm sure of it," Vik agreed. "That certainly includes anything we can do that might prevent someone killing them." He pulled open a drawer.

Twenty minutes later they concluded that Elmer wore his socks until there were holes in the toes and the heels; he owned three rifles, including one that looked like it had seen action in the Civil War; and he had probably never thrown away a piece of paper in his life.

"They're organized, though." Vik said. "Some are in alpha order, some numeric and others by type. He must have spent hours in here sorting them out. Beats the hell out of listening to women talk. He even has other people's pieces of paper. He must have filched them out of their wastebaskets. A paper fetish. That's a new one."

"Going through it will give the local force something to do while they're waiting for the toxicology reports."

"Poor man, I bet he was driven to this, living with so many old women."

"Scary, isn't it?" Marti said.

"What?"

"One of these sweet little old ladies could be a real killer."

"Maybe it's time we got to know them a little better, MacAlister. We've got to do something while we're waiting for an open telephone line or a plow."

"What I'd really like is some food that I was sure was safe to eat."

They waited until all the ladies went upstairs to get dressed, then went to the kitchen.

"Miss Roberts," Marti said, pretending surprise. "You cleaned up everything already. We thought you'd be much too upset to bother, and we haven't eaten anything yet."

"Oh, let me fix you something." She seemed to be getting over the shock of finding her brother dead. Maybe she was just keeping busy.

"Oh no," Marti said. "I'll do it myself, and clean up afterwards. Why don't you just sit and talk with us while I cook." She kept it simple, lots of eggs, plenty of bacon and a stack of toast. "We'll reimburse you, ma'am."

"Why I wouldn't hear of it. If you weren't here, with poor Elmer . . . and all . . ."

Miss Roberts hovered. Marti wasn't sure if it was because she never allowed anyone to cook in her kitchen, or if she was watching for an opportunity to slip a little something into the food. Did Miss Roberts have a reason to want her brother dead? If so, did she want Josephina's sister dead too?

"This is a lovely place you have here," Marti said. "What made you think of it? Has everyone always lived in this town?"

"It was a wonderful idea, wasn't it? We didn't want to end up alone. I'm the only one who was born here. Josephina and I met years ago at the Art Institute in Chicago. A couple of us have known each other since we took an extension course at the University in Bloomington. Then there were the cat shows. I used to raise and show Persians; when the last of them died, I didn't replace her."

"And now you're all here."

"This was my parents' home and my grandparents' before them. We've been together over fifteen years now."

Vik made a face, as if he'd just bitten into something sour.

"How do you manage financially?"

"None of us is poor. We could live on our own, at least for a while longer, but eventually we would end up in nursing homes and this is so much nicer. We have a woman who comes in and does most of the cooking, another who cleans. And, when the time comes, there's money put aside for nursing care. We can all just stay here until . . ." She put her hands to her face and cried. "Elmer was my baby brother. He was the only blood relative I had."

Marti put her arms about the old woman's shoulders and walked with her to the porch.

"Money," Vik said when she returned. "If Josephina hadn't seen her sister in years . . . we need to find out about her finances, too."

"And Elmer," Marti said.

"I don't know. He isn't our case anyway, if there is a case."

"These women aren't going to tell us anything, Vik, not unless they tell us accidentally. They are not going to do anything to jeopardize this arrangement." She thought about that. "If the deaths are related, even if they are not, that has to be the motive, something that would jeopardize their being here together."

"Right, MacAlister, and that could be damned near anything. They could all die without us ever finding out."

"Okay, okay. Let's start with what we know. Agatha died from an overdose of this stuff." She took out her notebook and read off the name of the poison. "It's tasteless, and lethal in a very small dose. The best place to find it is in antique shops. People collect the cans that it came in, sometimes there's residue inside."

"So, which one of these ladies do you think was a chemist or a pharmacist?" From the tone of his voice, Marti knew Vik was being sarcastic.

"They were born in the twentieth century. There is that possibility."

"Or it could be a relative or a friend. Then there is always the question of how the poison got from here to Lincoln Prairie. Maybe it was the one with the cane and she walked there, or took the bus. We're leaving Elmer's death up to the locals and focusing on what we came here for. Suspects, motives, and opportunity."

"We're batting zero on all three, Jessenovik, and with Elmer's death, I don't think these ladies are going to be inclined to talk with us about anything."

"Too bad we didn't have a reason to question them last night."

Marti tapped her pen against her notebook. "Antiques. Miss Roberts didn't mention anything about that."

"They've all got a bunch of old stuff in their rooms."

Marti didn't know enough about antiques to know what was valuable and what was not, but maybe that wasn't important. "The second bedroom on the right," she said.

"The one with the junky stuff?"

"Odd stuff, Vik. Things you might pick up on vacation. Nostalgia stuff. The old Log Cabin Syrup can made like a log cabin. That cracked Ovaltine cup. The kewpie doll, the Lionel train caboose, the Route 66 memorabilia."

"A cigarette roller," Vik said. "My father had one."

Everything had been arranged so decoratively about the room that she hadn't thought of it as junk at all. She would have to find out whose room it was without alerting the occupant. "There were a number of old containers. Let's see." She flipped through her notes and read off a description of the can the poison could have been packaged in.

"Oh sure, MacAlister. Didn't you notice? There was one of those right on the nightstand. Look, killing old Elmer is one thing, but Agatha lived a couple hundred miles away. Assuming that one of these ladies did do it, how did she get there?"

"I'll have to think about that," Marti admitted.

Lunch was served promptly at noon. Another check confirmed that the telephone was still out of order and not only had the street not been plowed, but it was snowing again, with another four to six inches predicted. Marti eavesdropped on the dayroom conversation, which consisted of canasta, a biography of Abigail Adams, and cat habits and behavior.

Vik looked at the tureens of soup and thick wedges of freshly baked bread and shook his head.

"You're getting paranoid, Jessenovik," Marti scolded, not that she intended to eat any of it either. Agatha's last meal had consisted of zucchini bread and preserves laced with poison.

"He has a trick stomach," she explained. "Do you mind if we just fix ourselves something?"

Miss Roberts was busy serving and just nodded.

The ladies did speak a bit loudly. With the dining room and kitchen doors open, Marti could hear most of what was said.

"Did you get the mail yet, dear?"

"What?"

"I ordered a new dish and place mat for Muffie over a week ago."

"Well, they won't come today."

"Why on earth not?"

"The blizzard, old girl. We've got snow out there."

"But why should that . . ."

"Did you see that jigsaw puzzle catalog that come in the other day? I'm ordering if anyone wants to send their order in with mine."

A lively discussion ensued on what was available in the current crop of catalogs as well as which companies misrepresented their products and who took the longest as well as the least time to ship. By the time Vik had approved lunch meat, cheese, and store-bought bread, the ladies had reached the catalog-order-from-hell stage of the conversation.

"I'm not making coffee," Marti said. "It's either what's in the pot or you can drink tap water."

Vik scowled, then relented and held out his cup.

"You'll have to decide for yourself about cream and sugar."

"Black," he said.

The discussion on catalog orders continued.

"Now you know what you have to look forward to, Jessenovik."

"I'm going fishing when I retire."

"I'm sure there's a catalog available with fishing lures if you can't make it to the hardware store in your wheelchair." She wished for the homemade bread as she bit into her sandwich. The cheese was a delicious hard cheddar.

"Delivery companies must love this place," Vik said. "With no deliveries in two days they must have a half a truckload of stuff to bring out here."

"Deliveries," Marti said. "They can pick up stuff too."

"So?"

"What if the poisoned preserves were shipped to Agatha?"

"I like that, MacAlister. I like that."

"Elmer," they both said at once.

Sandwiches and coffee in hand, they went to his room and began searching through all of his mail receipts.

"Here," Marti said, holding one up. "It's addressed to Agatha Hanson and it's dated the day before she died. It was shipped one-day service."

"The sister sent it."

"No, Jessica Perkins did."

"Which one is that?"

"I don't know, but this is as good a time as any to find out."

Jessica Perkins turned out to be a member of the canasta club, the one with severe arthritis. The scent of camphor wafted into the room as she came in. She was not Josephina's partner.

"Miss Perkins," Marti began. "What did you send to Agatha Hanson last month?"

"Why would I send her anything? I didn't even know her."

So much for being direct and catching her off guard.

"Could you explain why your name is on this receipt?"

Miss Perkins looked at it, then gazed calmly at Marti and said, "I have no idea."

Marti doubted that she could have filled out the mailing information. Elmer must have done that.

"Ma'am," Vik said. "Does it seem at all strange to you that Elmer Roberts had this in his possession and now he too is dead?"

"Why no, officer." She actually fluttered her eyelashes. "Perhaps Elmer mailed the package himself, and used my name."

As soon as Miss Perkins walked out of the room, Vik said, "Crafty old bird."

"What did I tell you about assuming senility, Jessenovik?"

Josephina Hanson was next. Marti had little hope of getting anything out of her either.

"Miss Hanson, we found this receipt among Elmer Roberts's belongings."

The woman's expression didn't change as she looked at it, but her hand trembled, unless she had tremors.

"Why are you asking me about this?"

"Did you send a package to your sister?"

"No."

"Do you know why anyone else would send her a package, express delivery, the day before she died of poisoning?"

"What kind of poison?" There was a catch in her voice.

"A poison that isn't sold over the counter anymore but is sold in containers that can be found in antique shops because they are considered collectibles."

"I see."

"Were you close to your sister, Miss Hanson?"

"We were adopted. We didn't have the same real parents. We weren't really sisters. Just legally."

Marti thought of the apartment Agatha had lived in, furnished with only the essentials. She wondered how long the woman's body would have gone undiscovered if the mailman hadn't been concerned enough to look in on her.

"Your sister didn't have any friends, Miss Hanson. She didn't have what you have. She was very much alone. Someone sent her a loaf of homemade bread and a jar of poisoned preserves. She thought it was a gift. She ate it and she died."

Tears ran down Josephina's cheeks. She dabbed at her eyes. "She didn't want any friends. She wanted to be alone. She was always like that."

"She was grateful enough for the gift to eat it."

"She was probably too cheap to buy it."

"Cheap enough to leave you quite a bit of money, Miss Hanson."

"I did not need Agatha's money."

"Didn't you, Josephina?" It was a guess, but Marti saw the woman's hand tighten around a wad of tissue.

"Is that why you sent the package to your sister?"

"I didn't," she whispered. "I couldn't hurt anyone."

Marti couldn't decide whether or not she was telling the truth.

"Who else knew you needed money?"

She shook her head.

"Someone knew. Who was it?"

There was no response. Josephina and Agatha didn't like each other. They weren't related by blood. Apparently Josephina felt little attachment or loyalty to her. But Agatha thought she was receiving a gift.

"Did you exchange birthday presents?"

"No."

"Christmas gifts?"

"No."

"Then Agatha must have been very pleased to receive a package. Even if someone else sent it, she would have believed it was your idea, your way of giving her something. Was that something that would have made her happy?"

"I don't know."

"Did you ever forget to call her?"

"Once or twice."

"What happened?"

"Nothing. I don't know."

"Would the gift have pleased her?"

"Maybe."

"Would it have pleased your parents?"

Josephina hesitated, wiped at tears again. "Very much."

"How would they feel if they knew you were responsible for her death?"

"But I didn't . . . I only told Jessica my money would run out in a few years. A few years, for God's sake, I could be dead in a few years. How did I know . . . I don't know . . . I don't know. I don't."

"You're upset, ma'am," Vik said. "Maybe you need to lie down."

"Yes," she agreed. He helped her from the room.

When they spoke with Jessica Perkins again, there was a defiant tilt to her chin.

"You knew that Josephina was having financial difficulties," Marti said.

"Nobody else here knows how to play canasta."

"Ma'am?"

"How would we play canasta without Josephina? We've played canasta for over twenty years. Just the four of us. How could we replace her?"

"Could you please tell me what happened, ma'am?"

"I couldn't write. Not the label, not anything. Elmer did it for me." She held up her hands. "I can barely eat with them."

"Why did you kill him, ma'am."

"Because he knew, damn it, because he knew. And he would have told you as soon as he found out why you were here."

"Canasta," Vik said, as Marti drove home. "Two people dead because of a card game. I suppose I've heard worse, but you'd think someone that old would know better. She's probably old enough to get away with it, too. They can just keep continuing the case until she checks out."

Marti turned on the windshield wipers. They were approaching the Chicago city limits and it was beginning to snow. This time the storm was expected to hit the city and points north.

PAULINE ELIZABETH HOPKINS (1859–1930) was born in Portland, Maine, and raised in Boston, where she graduated from the Boston Girls' High School as a stenographer, a job she held for most of the later years of her life. The precocious author wrote essays, poetry, and musical plays before the age of twenty, turning her hand to fiction when the *Colored American Magazine* was founded in 1900, providing a venue for African-American writers. Her story "The Mystery Within Us" appeared in the first issue and she became a frequent contributor under her own name and that of her mother, Sarah H. Allen, producing three serial novels (*Hagar's Daughter: A Story of Southern Caste Prejudice, Winona: A Tale of Negro Life in the South and Southwest,* and *Of One Blood, or the Hidden Self*) along with seven short stories, essays, and editorials; she became an editor of the magazine in 1902 and her name was added to the masthead in 1903.

Her fiction had been heavily influenced by the work of W.E.B. DuBois, but also owed much of its darkness to Edgar Allan Poe's short stories. None of her work owes more to Poe, the inventor of the "locked room" mystery, than "Talma Gordon," which is one of the first "impossible crime" stories to be written by an American and the very first to have been written by an African-American.

"Talma Gordon" was originally published in the October 1900 issue of the *Colored American Magazine*.

Talma Gordon

Pauline E. Hopkins

The Canterbury Club of Boston was holding its regular monthly meeting at the palatial Beacon Street residence of Dr. William Thornton, expert medical practitioner and specialist. All the members were present, because some rare opinions were to be aired by men of profound thought on a question of vital importance to the life of the Republic, and because the club celebrated its anniversary in a home usually closed to society. The Doctor's winters, since his marriage, were passed at his summer home near his celebrated sanitarium. This winter found him in town with his wife and two boys. We had heard much of the beauty of the former, who was entirely unknown to social life, and about whose life and marriage we felt sure a romantic interest attached. The Doctor himself was too bright a luminary of the professional world to remain long hidden without creating comment. We had accepted the invitation to dine with alacrity, knowing that we should be welcomed to a banquet that would feast both eye and palate; but we had not been favored by even a glimpse of the hostess. The subject for discussion was "Expansion: Its Effect Upon the Future Development of the Anglo-Saxon Throughout the World."

Dinner was over, but we still sat about the social board discussing the question of the hour. The Hon. Herbert Clapp, eminent jurist and politician, had painted in glowing colors the advantages to be gained by the increase of wealth and the exalted position which expansion would give the United States in the councils of the great governments of the world. In smoothly flowing sentences marshaled in rhetorical order, with compact ideas, and incisive argument, he drew an effective picture with all the persuasive eloquence of the trained orator.

Joseph Whitman, the theologian of worldwide fame, accepted the arguments of Mr. Clapp, but subordinated all to the great opportunity which expansion would give to the religious enthusiast. None could doubt the sincerity of this man, who looked once into the idealized face on which heaven had set the seal of consecration.

Various opinions were advanced by the twenty-five men present, but the host said nothing; he glanced from one to another with a look of amusement in his shrewd gray-blue eyes. "Wonderful eyes," said his patients who came under their magic spell. "A wonderful man and a wonderful mind," agreed his contemporaries, as they heard in amazement of some great cure of chronic or malignant disease which approached the supernatural.

"What do you think of this question, Doctor?" finally asked the president, turning to the silent host.

"Your arguments are good; they would convince almost anyone."

"But not Doctor Thornton," laughed the theologian.

"I acquiesce whichever way the result turns. Still, I like to view both sides of a question. We have considered but one tonight. Did you ever think that in spite of our prejudices against amalgamation, some of our descendants, indeed many of them, will inevitably intermarry among those far-off tribes of dark-skinned peoples, if they become a part of this great Union?"

"Among the lower classes that may occur, but not to any great extent," remarked a college president.

"My experience teaches me that it will occur among all classes, and to an appalling extent," replied the Doctor.

"You don't believe in intermarriage with other races?"

"Yes, most emphatically, when they possess decent moral development and physical perfection, for then we develop a superior being in the progeny born of the intermarriage. But if we are not ready to receive and assimilate the new material which will be brought to mingle with our pure Anglo-Saxon stream, we should call a halt in our expansion policy."

"I must confess, Doctor, that in the idea of amalgamation you present a new thought to my mind. Will you not favor us with a few of your main points?" asked the president of the club, breaking the silence which followed the Doctor's remarks.

"Yes, Doctor, give us your theories on the subject. We may not agree with you, but we are all open to conviction."

The Doctor removed the half-consumed cigar from his lips, drank what remained in his glass of the choice Burgundy, and leaning back in his chair contemplated the earnest faces before him.

We may make laws, but laws are but straws in the hands of Omnipotence.

> *There's a divinity that shapes our ends,*
> *Rough-hew them how we will.*

And no man may combat fate. Given a man, propinquity, opportunity, fascinating femininity, and there you are. Black, white,
green, yellow—nothing will prevent intermarriage. Position,
wealth, family, friends—all sink into insignificance before the
God-implanted instinct that made Adam, awakening from a deep
sleep and finding the woman beside him, accept Eve as bone of his
bone; he cared not nor questioned whence she came. So it is with
the sons of Adam ever since, through the law of heredity which
makes us all one common family. And so it will be with us in our
re-formation of this old Republic. Perhaps I can make my meaning
clearer by illustration, and with your permission I will tell you a
story which came under my observation as a practitioner.

Doubtless all of you heard of the terrible tragedy which
occurred at Gordonville, Mass., some years ago, when Capt.
Jonathan Gordon, his wife, and little son were murdered. I suppose that I am the only man on this side of the Atlantic, outside
of the police, who can tell you the true story of that crime.

I knew Captain Gordon well; it was through his persuasions
that I bought a place in Gordonville and settled down to spending
my summers in that charming rural neighborhood. I had ren-
dered the Captain what he was pleased to call valuable medical
help, and I became his family physician. Captain Gordon was a
retired sea captain, formerly engaged in the East India trade. All
his ancestors had been such; but when the bottom fell out of that
business he established the Gordonville Mills with his first wife's
money, and settled down as a money-making manufacturer of
cotton cloth. The Gordons were old New England Puritans who
had come over in the *Mayflower*; they had owned Gordon Hall for
more than a hundred years. It was a baronial-like pile of granite
with towers, standing on a hill which commanded a superb view
of Massachusetts Bay and the surrounding country. I imagine the

Gordon star was under a cloud about the time Captain Jonathan married his first wife, Miss Isabel Franklin of Boston, who brought to him the money which mended the broken fortunes of the Gordon house, and restored this old Puritan stock to its rightful position. In the person of Captain Gordon the austerity of manner and indomitable willpower that he had inherited were combined with a temper that brooked no contradiction.

The first wife died at the birth of her third child, leaving him two daughters, Jeannette and Talma. Very soon after her death the Captain married again. I have heard it rumored that the Gordon girls did not get on very well with their stepmother. She was a woman with no fortune of her own, and envied the large portion left by the first Mrs. Gordon to her daughters.

Jeannette was tall, dark, and stern like her father; Talma was like her dead mother, and possessed of great talent, so great that her father sent her to the American Academy at Rome, to develop the gift. It was the hottest of July days when her friends were bidden to an afternoon party on the lawn and a dance in the evening, to welcome Talma Gordon among them again. I watched her as she moved about among her guests, a fairylike blonde in floating white draperies, her face a study in delicate changing tints, like the heart of a flower, sparkling in smiles about the mouth to end in merry laughter in the clear blue eyes. There were all the subtle allurements of birth, wealth, and culture about the exquisite creature:

> *Smiling, frowning evermore,*
> *Thou art perfect in love-lore,*
> *Ever varying Madeline,*

quoted a celebrated writer as he stood apart with me, gazing upon the scene before us. He sighed as he looked at the girl.

Doctor, there is genius and passion in her face. Sometime our little friend will do wonderful things. But is it desirable to be singled out for special blessings by the gods? Genius always carries with it intense capacity for suffering: "Whom the gods love die young."

"Ah," I replied, "do not name death and Talma Gordon together. Cease your dismal croakings; such talk is rank heresy."

The dazzling daylight dropped slowly into summer twilight. The merriment continued; more guests arrived; the great dancing pagoda built for the occasion was lighted by myriads of Japanese lanterns. The strains from the band grew sweeter and sweeter, and "all went merry as a marriage bell." It was a rare treat to have this party at Gordon Hall, for Captain Jonathan was not given to hospitality. We broke up shortly before midnight, with expressions of delight from all the guests.

I was a bachelor then, without ties. Captain Gordon insisted upon my having a bed at the Hall. I did not fall asleep readily; there seemed to be something in the air that forbade it. I was still awake when a distant clock struck the second hour of the morning. Suddenly the heavens were lighted by a sheet of ghastly light; a terrific midsummer thunderstorm was breaking over the sleeping town. A lurid flash lit up all the landscape, painting the trees in grotesque shapes against the murky sky, and defining clearly the sullen blackness of the waters of the bay breaking in grandeur against the rocky coast. I had arisen and put back the draperies from the windows, to have an unobstructed view of the grand scene. A low muttering coming nearer and nearer, a terrific roar, and then a tremendous downpour. The storm had burst.

Now the uncanny howling of a dog mingled with the rattling volleys of thunder. I heard the opening and closing of doors; the servants were about looking after things. It was impossible to sleep. The lightning was more vivid. There was a blinding flash of a greenish-white tinge mingled with the crash of falling timbers. Then before my startled gaze arose columns of red flames reflected against the sky. "Heaven help us!" I cried; "it is the left tower; it has been struck and is on fire!"

I hurried on my clothes and stepped into the corridor; the girls were there before me. Jeannette came up to me instantly with anxious face. "Oh, Doctor Thornton, what shall we do? Papa and Mamma and little Johnny are in the old left tower. It is on fire. I have knocked and knocked, but get no answer."

"Don't be alarmed," said I soothingly. "Jenkins, ring the alarm bell," I continued, turning to the butler who was standing near; "the rest follow me. We will force the entrance to the Captain's room."

Instantly, it seemed to me, the bell boomed out upon the now silent air, for the storm had died down as quickly as it arose; and as our little procession paused before the entrance to the old left tower, we could distinguish the sound of the fire engines already on their way from the village.

The door resisted all our efforts; there seemed to be a barrier against it which nothing could move. The flames were gaining headway. Still the same deathly silence within the rooms.

"Oh, will they never get here?" cried Talma, ringing her hands in terror. Jeannette said nothing, but her face was ashen. The servants were huddled together in a panic-stricken group. I can never tell you what a relief it was when we heard the first sound of the firemen's voices, saw their quick movements, and heard the ringing of the axes with which they cut away every obstacle to our entrance to the rooms. The neighbors who had just enjoyed the hospitality of the house were now gathered around offering all the assistance in their power. In less than fifteen minutes the fire was out, and the men began to bear the unconscious inmates from the ruins. They carried them to the pagoda so lately the scene of mirth and pleasure, and I took up my station there, ready to assume my professional duties. The Captain was nearest me; and as I stooped to make the necessary examination I reeled away from the ghastly sight which confronted me—*gentlemen, across the Captain's throat was a deep gash that severed the jugular vein!*

The Doctor paused, and the hand with which he refilled his glass trembled violently.

"What is it, Doctor?" cried the men, gathering about me.

"Take the women away; this is murder!"

"Murder!" cried Jeannette, as she fell against the side of the pagoda.

"Murder!" screamed Talma, staring at me as if unable to grasp my meaning.

I continued my examination of the bodies, and found that the same thing had happened to Mrs. Gordon and to little Johnny.

The police were notified; and when the sun rose over the dripping town he found them in charge of Gordon Hall, the servants standing in excited knots talking over the crime, the friends of the family confounded, and the two girls trying to comfort each other and realize the terrible misfortune that had overtaken them.

Nothing in the rooms of the left tower seemed to have been disturbed. The door of communications between the rooms of the husband and wife was open, as they had arranged it for the night. Little Johnny's crib was placed beside his mother's bed. In it he was found as though never awakened by the storm. It was quite evident that the assassin was no common ruffian. The chief gave strict orders for a watch to be kept on all strangers or suspicious characters who were seen in the neighborhood. He made inquiries among the servants, seeing each one separately, but there was nothing gained from them. No one had heard anything suspicious; all had been awakened by the storm. The chief was puzzled. Here was a triple crime for which no motive could be assigned.

"What do you think of it?" I asked him, as we stood together on the lawn.

"It is my opinion that the deed was committed by one of the higher classes, which makes the mystery more difficult to solve. I tell you, Doctor, there are mysteries that never come to light, and this, I think, is one of them."

While we were talking Jenkins, the butler, an old and trusted servant, came up to the chief and saluted respectfully. "Want to speak with me, Jenkins?" he asked. The man nodded, and they walked away together.

The story of the inquest was short, but appalling. It was shown that Talma had been allowed to go abroad to study because she and Mrs. Gordon did not get on well together. From the testimony of Jenkins it seemed that Talma and her father had quarreled bitterly about her lover, a young artist whom she had met at Rome, who was unknown to fame, and very poor. There had been terrible things said by each, and threats even had passed, all of which now rose up in judgment against the unhappy girl. The examination of the family solicitor revealed the fact that Captain Gordon intended to leave his daughters only a small annuity, the bulk of the fortune going to his son Jonathan, junior. This was a monstrous injustice, as everyone felt. In vain Talma protested her innocence. Someone must have done it. No one would be benefited so much by these deaths as she and her sister. Moreover, the will, together with other papers, was nowhere to be found. Not the slightest clue bearing upon the disturbing elements in this family, if any there were, was to be found. As the only surviving relatives, Jeannette and Talma became joint heirs to an immense fortune, which only for the bloody tragedy just enacted would, in all probability, have passed them by. Here was the motive. The case was very black against Talma. The foreman stood up. The silence was intense: We "find that Captain Jonathan Gordon, Mary E. Gordon, and Jonathan Gordon, junior, all deceased, came to their deaths by means of a knife or other sharp instrument in the hands of Talma Gordon." The girl was like one stricken with death. The flowerlike mouth was drawn and pinched; the great sapphire-blue eyes were black with passionate anguish, terror, and despair. She was placed in jail to await her trial at the fall session of the criminal court. The excitement in the hitherto quiet town rose to fever heat. Many points in the evidence seemed incomplete to thinking men. The weapon could not be found, nor could it be divined what had become of it. No reason could be given for the murder except the quarrel between Talma and her father and the ill will which existed between the girl and her stepmother.

When the trial was called Jeannette sat beside Talma in the prisoner's dock; both were arrayed in deepest mourning. Talma was pale and careworn, but seemed uplifted, spiritualized, as it were. Upon Jeannette the full realization of her sister's peril seemed to weigh heavily. She had changed much too: hollow cheeks, tottering steps, eyes blazing with fever, all suggestive of rapid and premature decay. From far-off Italy Edward Turner, growing famous in the art world, came to stand beside his girl-love in this hour of anguish.

The trial was a memorable one. No additional evidence had been collected to strengthen the prosecution; when the attorney-general rose to open the case against Talma he knew, as everyone else did, that he could not convict solely on the evidence adduced. What was given did not always bear upon the case, and brought out strange stories of Captain Jonathan's methods. Tales were told of sailors who had sworn to take his life, in revenge for injuries inflicted upon them by his hand. One or two clues were followed, but without avail. The judge summed up the evidence impartially, giving the prisoner the benefit of the doubt. The points in hand furnished valuable collateral evidence, but were not direct proof. Although the moral presumption was against the prisoner, legal evidence was lacking to actually convict. The jury found the prisoner "Not Guilty," owing to the fact that the evidence was entirely circumstantial. The verdict was received in painful silence; then a murmur of discontent ran through the great crowd.

"She must have done it," said one; "who else has been benefited by the horrible deed?"

"A poor woman would not have fared so well at the hands of the jury, nor a homely one either, for that matter," said another.

The great Gordon trial was ended; innocent or guilty, Talma Gordon could not be tried again. She was free; but her liberty, with blasted prospects and fair fame gone forever, was valueless to her. She seemed to have but one object in her mind: to find the murderer or murderers of her parents and half brother. By her direction the shrewdest of detectives were employed and money flowed like water, but to no purpose; the Gordon tragedy remained a mystery. I had consented to act as one of the trustees of the immense Gordon estates and business interests, and by my advice the Misses Gordon went abroad. A year later I received a letter from Edward Turner, saying that Jeannette Gordon had died suddenly at Rome, and that Talma, after refusing all his entreaties for an early marriage, had disappeared, leaving no clue as to her whereabouts. I could give the poor fellow no comfort, although I had been duly notified of the death of Jeannette by

Talma, in a letter telling me where to forward her remittances, and at the same time requesting me to keep her present residence secret, especially from Edward.

I had established a sanitarium for the cure of chronic diseases at Gordonville, and absorbed in the cares of my profession I gave little thought to the Gordons. I seemed fated to be involved in mysteries.

A man claiming to be an Englishman, and fresh from the California gold fields, engaged board and professional service at my retreat. I found him suffering in the grasp of the tubercle fiend— the last stages. He called himself Simon Cameron. Seldom have I seen so fascinating and wicked a face. The lines of the mouth were cruel, the eyes cold and sharp, the smile mocking and evil. He had money in plenty but seemed to have no friends, for he had received no letters and had had no visitors in the time he had been with us. He was an enigma to me; and his nationality puzzled me, for of course I did not believe his story of being English. The peaceful influence of the house seemed to soothe him in a measure, and make his last steps to the mysterious valley as easy as possible. For a time he improved, and would sit or walk about the grounds and sing sweet songs for the pleasure of the other inmates. Strange to say, his malady only affected his voice at times. He sang quaint songs in a silvery tenor of great purity and sweetness that was delicious to the listening ear:

A wet sheet and a flowing sea,
A wind that follows fast,
And fills the white and rustling sail
And bends the gallant mast;
And bends the gallant mast, my boys;
While like the eagle free,

Away the good ship flies, and leaves
Old England on the lea.

There are few singers on the lyric stage who could surpass Simon Cameron.

One night, a few weeks after Cameron's arrival, I sat in my office making up my accounts when the door opened and closed; I glanced up, expecting to see a servant. A lady advanced toward me. She threw back her veil, and then I saw that Talma Gordon, or her ghost, stood before me. After the first excitement of our meeting was over, she told me she had come direct from Paris, to place herself in my care. I had studied her attentively during the first moments of our meeting, and I felt that she was right; unless something unforeseen happened to arouse her from the stupor into which she seemed to have fallen, the last Gordon was doomed to an early death. The next day I told her I had cabled Edward Turner to come to her.

"It will do no good; I cannot marry him," was her only comment.

"Have you no feeling of pity for that faithful fellow?" I asked her sternly, provoked by her seeming indifference. I shall never forget the varied emotions depicted on her speaking face. Fully revealed to my gaze was the sight of a human soul tortured beyond the point of endurance; suffering all things, enduring all things, in the silent agony of despair.

In a few days Edward arrived, and Talma consented to see him and explain her refusal to keep her promise to him. "You must be present, Doctor; it is due your long, tried friendship to know that I have not been fickle, but have acted from the best and strongest motives."

I shall never forget that day. It was directly after lunch that we met in the library. I was greatly excited, expecting I knew not what.

Edward was agitated, too. Talma was the only calm one. She handed me what seemed to be a letter, with the request that I would read it. Even now I think I can repeat every word of the document, so indelibly are the words engraved upon my mind:

MY DARLING SISTER TALMA: When you read these lines I shall be no more, for I shall not live to see your life blasted by the same knowledge that has blighted mine.

One evening, about a year before your expected return from Rome, I climbed into a hammock in one corner of the veranda outside the breakfast-room windows, intending to spend the twilight hours in lazy comfort, for it was very hot, enervating August weather. I fell asleep. I was awakened by voices. Because of the heat the rooms had been left in semidarkness. As I lay there, lazily enjoying the beauty of the perfect summer night, my wandering thoughts were arrested by words spoken by our father to Mrs. Gordon, for they were the occupants of the breakfast room.

Never fear, Mary; Johnny shall have it all—money, houses, land, and business.

"But if you do go first, Jonathan, what will happen if the girls contest the will? People will think that they ought to have the money as it appears to be theirs by law. I never could survive the terrible disgrace of the story."

"Don't borrow trouble; all you would need to do would be to show them papers I have drawn up, and they would be glad to take their annuity and say nothing. After all, I do not think it is so bad. Jeannette can teach; Talma can paint; six hundred dollars a year is quite enough for them."

I had been somewhat mystified by the conversation until now. This last remark solved the riddle. What could he mean? Teach, paint, six hundred a year! With my usual impetuosity I sprang from my resting place, and in a moment stood in the room confronting my father, and asking what he meant. I could see plainly that both were disconcerted by my unexpected appearance.

"Ah, wretched girl! you have been listening. But what could I expect of your mother's daughter?"

At these words I felt the indignant blood rush to my head in a torrent. So it had been all my life. Before you could remember, Talma, I had felt my little heart swell with anger at the disparaging hints and slurs concerning our mother. Now was my time. I determined that tonight I would know why she was looked upon as an outcast, and her children subjected to every humiliation. So I replied to my father in bitter anger:

I was not listening; I fell asleep in the hammock. What do you mean by a paltry six hundred a year each to Talma and to me? "My mother's daughter" demands an explanation from you, sir, of the meaning of the monstrous injustice that you have always practiced toward my sister and me.

"Speak more respectfully to your father, Jeannette," broke in Mrs. Gordon.

"How is it, madam, that you look for respect from one whom you have delighted to torment ever since you came into this most unhappy family?"

"Hush, both of you," said Captain Gordon, who seemed to have recovered from the dismay into which my sudden appearance and passionate words had plunged him. "I think I may as well tell you as to wait. Since you know so much, you may as well know the whole miserable story." He motioned me to a seat. I could see that he was deeply agitated. I seated myself in a chair he pointed out, in wonder and expectation—expectation of I knew not what. I trembled. This was a supreme moment in my life; I felt it. The air was heavy with the intense stillness that had settled over us as the common sounds of day gave place to the early quiet of the rural evening. I could see Mrs. Gordon's face as she sat within the radius of the lighted hallway. There was a smile of triumph upon it. I clinched my hands and bit my lips until the blood came, in the effort to keep from screaming. What was I about to hear? At last he spoke:

I was disappointed at your birth, and also at the birth of Talma. I wanted a male heir. When I knew that I should again be a father I was torn by hope and fear, but I comforted myself with the thought that luck would be with me in the birth of the third child. When the doctor brought me word that a son was born to the house of Gordon, I was wild with delight, and did not notice his disturbed countenance. In the midst of my joy he said to me:

"Captain Gordon, there is something strange about this birth. I want you to see this child."

Quelling my exultation I followed him to the nursery, and there, lying in the cradle, I saw a child dark as a mulatto, with the characteristic features of the Negro! I was stunned. Gradually it dawned upon

me that there was something radically wrong. I turned
to the doctor for an explanation.

"There is but one explanation, Captain Gordon;
there is Negro blood in this child."

"There is no Negro blood in my veins," I said
proudly. Then I paused—*the mother!*—I glanced at the
doctor. He was watching me intently. The same
thought was in his mind. I must have lived a thousand
years in that cursed five seconds that I stood there confronting the physician and trying to think. "Come,"
said I to him, "let us end this suspense." Without
thinking of consequences, I hurried away to your
mother and accused her of infidelity to her marriage
vows. I raved like a madman. Your mother fell into
convulsions; her life was despaired of. I sent for Mr.
and Mrs. Franklin, and then I learned the truth. They
were childless. One year while on a Southern tour,
they befriended an octoroon girl who had been abandoned by her white lover. Her child was a beautiful
girl baby. They, being Northern born, thought little of
caste distinction because the child showed no trace of
Negro blood. They determined to adopt it. They went
abroad, secretly sending back word to their friends at
a proper time of the birth of a little daughter. No one
doubted the truth of the statement. They made Isabel
their heiress, and all went well until the birth of your
brother. Your mother and the unfortunate babe died.
This is the story which, if known, would bring dire
disgrace upon the Gordon family.

"To appease my righteous wrath, Mr. Franklin left
a codicil to his will by which all the property is left at

213

my disposal save a small annuity to you and your sister."

I sat there after he had finished the story, stunned by what I had heard. I understood, now, Mrs. Gordon's half contemptuous toleration and lack of consideration for us both. As I rose from my seat to leave the room I said to Captain Gordon:

"Still, in spite of it all, sir, I am a Gordon, legally born. I will not tamely give up my birthright."

I left that room a broken-hearted girl, filled with a desire for revenge upon this man, my father, who by his manner disowned us without a regret. Not once in that remarkable interview did he speak of our mother as his wife; he quietly repudiated her and us with all the cold cruelty of relentless caste prejudice. I heard the treatment of your lover's proposal; I knew why Captain Gordon's consent to your marriage was withheld.

"The night of the reception and dance was the chance for which I had waited, planned, and watched. I crept from my window into the ivy vines, and so down, down, until I stood upon the windowsill of Captain Gordon's room in the old left tower. How did I do it, you ask? I do not know. The house was silent after the revel; the darkness of the gathering storm favored me, too. The lawyer was there that day. The will was signed and put safely away among my father's papers. I was determined to have the will and the other documents bearing upon the case, and I would have revenge, too, for the cruelties we had suffered. With the old East Indian dagger firmly grasped I entered the room and found—that my revenge had been forestalled! The horror of the discovery I made that night restored me to reason and a realization of the crime I meditated. Scarce knowing what I did, I sought and found the papers, and crept back to my room as I had come. Do you wonder that my disease is past medical aid?"

I looked at Edward as I finished. He sat, his face covered with his hands. Finally he looked up with a glance of haggard despair: "God! Doctor, but this is too much. I could stand the stigma of murder, but add to that the pollution of Negro blood! No man is brave enough to face such a situation."

"It is as I thought it would be," said Talma sadly, while the tears poured over her white face. "I do not blame you, Edward."

He rose from his chair, wrung my hand in a convulsive clasp, turned to Talma and bowed profoundly, with his eyes fixed upon the floor, hesitated, turned, paused, bowed again, and abruptly left the room. So those two who had been lovers parted. I turned to Talma, expecting her to give way. She smiled a pitiful smile, and said: "You see, Doctor, I knew best."

From that on she failed rapidly. I was restless. If only I could rouse her to an interest in life, she might live to old age. So rich, so young, so beautiful, so talented, so pure; I grew savage thinking of the injustice of the world. I had not reckoned on the power that never sleeps. Something was about to happen.

On visiting Cameron next morning I found him approaching the end. He had been sinking for a week

very rapidly. As I sat by the bedside holding his ema-
ciated hand, he fixed his bright, wicked eyes on me,
and asked: "How long have I got to live?"

"Candidly, but a few hours."

"Thank you; well, I want death; I am not afraid do
die. Doctor, Cameron is not my name."

"I never supposed it was."

"No? You are sharper than I thought. I heard all
your talk yesterday with Talma Gordon. Curse the
whole race!"

He clasped his bony fingers around my arm and
gasped: *"I murdered the Gordons!"*

Had I the pen of a Dumas I could not paint
Cameron as he told his story. It is a question with me
whether this wheedling planet, home of the suffering,
doubting, dying, may not hold worse agonies on its
smiling surface than those of the conventional hell. I
sent for Talma and a lawyer. We gave him stimulants,
and then with broken intervals of coughing and pros-
tration we got the story of the Gordon murder. I give
it to you in a few words:

"I am an East Indian, but my name does not
matter, Cameron is as good as any. There is many a
soul crying in heaven and hell for vengeance on
Jonathan Gordon. Gold was his idol; and many a
good man walked the plank, and many a gallant ship
was stripped of her treasure, to satisfy his lust for gold.
His blackest crime was the murder of my father, who
was his friend, and had sailed with him for many a
year as mate. One night these two went ashore
together to bury their treasure. My father never

returned from that expedition. His body was afterward found with a bullet through the heart on the shore where the vessel stopped that night. It was the custom then among pirates for the captain to kill the men who helped bury their treasure. Captain Gordon was no better than a pirate. An East Indian never forgets, and I swore by my mother's deathbed to hunt Captain Gordon down until I had avenged my father's murder. I had the plans of the Gordon estate, and fixed on the night of the reception in honor of Talma as the time for my vengeance. There is a secret entrance from the shore to the chambers where Captain Gordon slept; no one knew of it save the Captain and trusted members of his crew. My mother gave me the plans, and entrance and escape were easy."

"So the great mystery was solved. In a few hours Cameron was no more. We placed the confession in the hands of the police, and there the matter ended."

"But what became of Talma Gordon?" questioned the president. "Did she die?"

"Gentlemen," said the Doctor, rising to his feet and sweeping the faces of the company with his eagle gaze, "gentlemen, if you will follow me to the drawing room, I shall have much pleasure in introducing you to my wife—née Talma Gordon."

CHESTER BOMAR HIMES (1909–1984) was born in Jefferson City, Missouri, growing up in a middle-class family in Missouri and Ohio. Expelled from Ohio State University as a freshman, he was later arrested for armed robbery and, while behind bars for more than seven years, began writing the short stories that gave him respect in prison and prominence nationally.

After producing a large number of short stories, he went to Los Angeles to work briefly as a screenwriter and novelist, producing *If He Hollers Let Him Go* (1945) and *The Lonely Crusade* (1947), both of which dealt with the difficulties of the large number of southern California's black immigrants. He had greater critical and popular success in France, so Himes moved there in the 1950s, joining such fellow ex-patriots as James Baldwin and Richard Wright.

While many of his works deal with overtly political and racial themes, he is best remembered today for his hard-boiled but humorous crime novels; set in Harlem, they feature New York City police detectives Coffin Ed Johnson and Gravedigger Jones. The popular series began in 1957 with *For Love of Imabelle* (filmed as *A Rage in Harlem*, 1991) and continued with *The Real Cool Killers* (1959), *The Crazy Kill* (1959), *The Big Gold Dream* (1960), *All Shot Up* (1960), *The Heat's On* (1966, filmed in 1972), *Cotton Comes to Harlem* (1965, filmed in 1969), *Blind Man with a Pistol* (1969) and *Plan B* (1993).

"Strictly Business" was first published in the February 1942 issue of *Esquire*.

Strictly Business

Chester Himes

What his real name was, no one knew or cared. At various times, during his career of assaults, homicides, and murders, he had been booked under the names of Patterson, Hopkins, Smith, Reilly, Sanderson, and probably a dozen others.

People called him "Sure."

He was twenty-five years old, five feet, eleven inches tall, weighed one-eighty-seven, had light straw colored hair and wide, slightly hunched shoulders. His pale blue eyes were round and flat as poker chips, and his smooth, white face was wooden.

He wore loose fitting, double-breasted, drape model suits, and carried his gun in a shoulder sling.

His business was murder.

At that time he was working for Big Angelo Satulla, head of the numbers mob.

The way Big Angelo's mob operated was strictly on the muscle. They took their cut in front—forty per cent gross, win, lose, or draw—and the colored fellows operated the business on what was left.

Most of the fellows in the mob were relatives of Big Angelo's. There were about forty of them and they split a million or more a year.

Sure was there because Big Angelo didn't trust any of his relatives around the corner. He was on a straight salary of two hundred and fifty dollars a week, and got a bonus of a grand for a job.

Business was good. He could remember when at eighteen he had worked for fifty bucks a throw, and if you got caught with the body you were just S.O.L.

He and Big Angelo were at the night drawing of the B & B house, a little before midnight, when the word came about Hot Papa Shapiro. Pipe Jimmy Sciria, the stooge Big Angelo had posted in the hotel as a bellhop to keep tabs on Hot Papa, called and said it looked as if Hot Papa was going to spill because a police escort had just pulled up to the hotel to take him down to the court house where the Grand Jury was holding night sessions during the DA's racket-busting investigation.

Big Angelo had had the feeling all along that Hot Papa had rat in his blood, but now when he got the word that the spill was on the turn, he went green as summer salad.

He called Sure in the office and gasped, "Get out there and take that rat before he dumps. I shoulda let you done it a long time ago."

"Sure," Sure said, and tapped back his cater.

It was thirty minutes to the hotel where Hot Papa lived. Sure made it in twelve flat.

The red was hanging over Central and a streetcar was going East. There was an eleven foot gap between it and a following truck. He pushed that long La Salle through those eleven feet at sixty-three without even grazing, burst into Cedar at eighty-five. The light at Carnegie showed red but he was still seeing green when he turned at a dragging sixty. All the way out he rode her, sitting on the radiator cap.

Pipe Jimmy was waiting at the hotel garage entrance. "I'll take her away, Sure," he said, crawling under the wheel.

Sure gave him a glance, turned quickly through the garage, went up back stairs three at a time. When he came out on the twelfth floor, he was sucking for breath.

He fingered the knob of room 1207. The door was locked. He rapped.

"Who is it?" came a slightly accented, shaky voice.

"Calahan!" Sure rumbled, gasped another breath and added, "From headquarters."

"Oh!" The voice sounded relieved. "They told me you were here . . ." The lock clicked open.

Sure leaned against the door and rode it inward, kicked it shut. "Hello, Papa," he panted. "Those stairs got me."

Benny Hot Papa Shapiro was a big, foppish man of about thirty-five with thinning dark hair and a winged, Hollywood mustache. He had been the mouthpiece for the mob, but ever since he had seen Sure shoot Sospirato through the back, his stomach had turned sour on the job.

At sight of Sure he went putty gray and his eyes popped out like skinned bananas. "Listen—" he choked, blood spotting in his throat and neck. "For God's sake, listen—"

"Sure," Sure said and pulled out his gun. "What you got to say?"

"Don't—" Hot Papa gulped, raising his hands and half ducking as a man will from a truck about to hit him. "Don't kill me—" He had on his trousers and undershirt; the rest of his clothes lay on the bed.

"I ain't got nothing against you," Sure said and shot him in the belly. "It's business with me."

A little black hole showed in Hot Papa's undershirt where the bullet went in and his eyes began running like melting glass. He spun around slightly and hung there as if frozen.

Sure shot him in the side. He crumpled into the dresser, doubled over to the floor . . . "Don't kill me . . ." he gasped. Sure stepped closer and shot him in the back of the head.

Then he stood there, juggling the gun, debating whether to leave it there or take it with him. His flat eyes were unsmiling and his wooden face was unchanged. He decided to take the gun with him, slipped it back into the sling and stepped quickly into the corridor, pulling the door closed behind him.

A man stuck his head out of the room next door. His mouth was propped open and his eyes were stretched. But before he could speak, Sure yelled, "Where was that shooting? You shot somebody?"

The man's eyes blinked. "Who me? No sir! It came from right next door!" He pointed at the room which Sure had just left.

"Call the house detective!" Sure barked, brittle-voiced and thin-lipped, then turned as if to re-enter the room. "I'll go in and see what's happening."

The man stepped back into his room to make the phone call. Sure dashed for the stairway, made it before anyone else came out into the hall. He went down to the tenth floor and came out into the corridor. There was a woman waiting for the elevator and he said to her, "Are you having trouble with hot water, too?"

She gave him a quick, startled glance. "Why, er—er—"

"Mine's cut off again," Sure explained. "I thought maybe everybody's was cut off."

"Oh!" She smiled. "No, the water in our suite is running all right. Why don't you put in a complaint?"

"Lady, if I had a dollar for every complaint."

The elevator came and cut him off. He rode down to the mezzanine, got out and sauntered over to the writing desk, trying to cop an out. By then the stopper would be on the place, he knew. Calahan and the squad from headquarters would have every doorway blocked.

He sat down and pulled out a sheet of paper, began scratching words. Through the corner of his eye he could see activity breaking out in the lobby below. Uniformed police swarmed about like flies at a picnic, grabbing off guys right and left and shaking them down.

Sure propped his chin on his thumb as if thinking and looked about. There was a man a couple of desks away, otherwise the place was momentarily deserted.

Sure took out the gun, keeping his eyes on the guy at the second desk. He broke the gun, and discharged the bullets into his hand.

Then he took out his handkerchief and carefully wiped each bullet, wiped the gun inside and out, wrapped them together in a couple of sheets of writing paper and pushed them down to the bottom of the waste paper container.

Next he folded the sheet of paper on which he had been writing, held it in his hand and went downstairs. Two policemen, at the foot of the stairs stopped him, shook him down. Neither of them knew him by sight. Finding him clean they thumbed him on his way.

He went over to the desk and bought a stamped envelope. He addressed it to Mr. Herbie Crump, 3723 Clark Avenue, Chicago, Ill., put the folded letter paper inside, sealed it and started casually toward the outside doorway, holding the letter in his hand.

He had almost made it when someone shouted, "That's him! Going out the door!"

It was the guy he had told to call the house detective.

A policemen surged from behind a palm, tugging at his gun.

Sure broke through the doorway, pushing but not panicky, bumped over a little guy with a goatee and roughed aside a couple coming up the stairs. At the bottom step a drunk got in his way. He stiff-jabbed him across the sidewalk into the gutter and made the corner while the police were making up their minds about risking a shot.

A late show crowd filled the street, giving him a top. He wormed in and out, hurried but not hasty, casing the lay as he went.

The street was glass-fronted and solid as far as he could see, but he knew that as long as he stayed in the crowd and kept moving the police couldn't shoot.

Some fellows came out of a bar and tried to stop him, forcing him to cut left, obliquely across the street through the auto traffic.

Police whistles shrilled! People shouted! A woman screamed . . .

He ran in front of a taxi, cut behind a Buick. A curse lashed at him. He jumped across in front of a streetcar, wheeled quickly to keep from being run down by a big fast moving Packard. Rubber burnt asphalt in a splitting shriek as the driver stood on his brakes. The car behind bumped into the Packard with a crash, locking bumpers. Men began to swear.

Sure stepped on the locked bumpers, jumped across, dashed down the sidewalk, cut up an alley without looking back. Sweat filmed on his forehead like a hundred degrees in the sun.

The alley stopped dead at the back of a garage. Panic went off in him like a flare. He felt cornered and stark naked without his gun. Behind him the coppers closed in with a shower of feet.

The back of an apartment loomed to his right. He hit the back steps and scuttled upward, stiff-jointed from a growing fright. His nerves began breaking through his skin like an outcropping rash and his heart did triple taps.

On the fourth floor he spied an open kitchen window, heard the thunder of following feet. He turned, dove through the window, landed in the kitchen on his hands and knees. He came up without a loss of motion and ran into the back hallway.

There was a light and the sound of voices in the front room. He ran through the short hallway, came out into the lighted room, bumped into a man who had gotten up to investigate the commotion. The man fell backwards into the lap of a woman sitting in a chair. The woman screamed.

Sure grabbed for the door, his hand full of sweat. The knob slipped in his grasp. He kept grabbing, trying to get a hold. Behind him the woman kept screaming in high, monotonous yelps. His hair stuck straight up.

He got the door open as he heard the police piling through the kitchen window, went down the stairs in a power dive. It was quiet on the side street where he came out, but before he got halfway across the police began shooting at him from the apartment window.

He ran down the opposite alley, came out beside a night club and hailed a cruising taxi.

"Union Station," he croaked, piling in.

The driver turned around and took off.

Sure settled back, fished out a cigarette.

Then he went to pieces—just like that. He began trembling all over, his knees knocked together, even his head began to jerk as if he had d.t.'s. He couldn't get the cigarette between his lips. Mashing it, he threw it out the window.

Suddenly he began to sweat; it came off of him like showers of rain, came out of his ears, out of his mouth. All he could see was the electric chair with himself sitting in it.

The cab slowed for a red light and he opened the door and jumped out. He ran down the street with the driver yelling at him, ducked up the first dark alley. Keeping to the alleys and darkest streets, running without stopping, he finally came to an abandoned coal shed in the back yard of a broken down house on 49th Street in the Negro slums.

He crawled inside, sat down in the dirt and darkness, feeling nauseated from his terror and utterly exhausted. His heart was beating like John Henry driving steel. Then he bent over and vomited.

After that his terror began passing. He got up and walked over to Central and went into a colored bar. A boy called Blue asked, "How's business, Sure?"

He thought of the grand he had just made and got back his nerve. "Not bad, not bad at all, Blue, how's things breaking for you?"

"They ain't walking," Blue said. "They ain't walking, Sure."

"You'll get 'em," Sure said, turning toward the street. "See you, Blue, I got some ends need pulling in."

"If'n I live and nothin' doan happen," Blue said.

Sure went out to Little Brother's on 57th Street and borrowed his Studebaker. Then he drove by his downtown room on 37th Street and picked up another gun. From there he drove out to 89th where Pipe Jimmy Sciria lived.

Pipe Jimmy was getting into the La Salle. He was hopped to the gills and kept brushing imaginary specks from his clothes.

Sure got out of the Studebaker and climbed in with Pipe Jimmy. "I'm going a pieceway with you, kid," he said.

"I'm going south," Pipe Jimmy grinned. "Mexico. That way I stay clear."

"I know." Sure said.

"How'd you know?" Pipe Jimmy asked, turning to look at him.

"I'm helping you." Sure said.

They drove out the Boulevard to route 26 and followed it over to 43. "You don't have to worry about me, Sure," Pipe Jimmy said. "I'm your pal."

"I ain't," Sure said.

About twelve miles out, Sure said, "Pull up."

"Huh?"

"You heard me! Pull up!"

Pipe Jimmy wheeled over and dragged down. Sure drew his gun and stuck it against Pipe Jimmy's ribs. "Get out!"

Pipe Jimmy went a sick white and his hands shook so he could not get open the door. Sure leaned over and opened it for him.

"Look, Sure, I'm your pal," Pipe Jimmy said, standing on the pavement and licking his lips. His knees kept buckling.

"Come over on this side," Sure said, getting out into the gully.

Pipe Jimmy came around the car, walking wobbly, stepped into the gully and backed up against the running board, "Say, you ain't thinking about—"

Sure reached over and grabbed him by the collar, slung him into the gully.

"Nix, Sure, nix, pal . . ." Pipe Jimmy cried, rolling over and trying to crawl away.

"I ain't got nothing against you, kid," Sure said, shooting him in the back. "It's business with me."

Pipe Jimmy spun like a stick from the punch of the slug . . . "Nix, buddy . . ."

Sure shot him in the chest . . . "I'm your pal, Sure . . ." Sure stepped closer and shot him through the head.

He broke the gun and carefully wiped it with his handkerchief, inside and out. He wiped the bullets, scattered them over Pipe Jimmy's body, tossed the gun into the brush, got back in the car and headed toward Chicago, intending to establish an alibi and double the next week.

But a hoosier cop in Terre Haute who didn't like his looks picked him up and ran him in. Charge of *Suspicious Person*.

They made him from the "wanted" circular that had just come in and sent him back to be tried for the murder of Benny "Hot Papa" Shapiro. The state produced twenty-seven witnesses who had seen him in and about the hotel the night of the murder.

But he had a defense . . . "I didn't have nothing against the guy," he whined by way of justification. "I liked the guy, he was a friend of mine. It was just business with me."

RUDOLPH FISHER (1897–1934) was born in Washington, D.C., and grew up in Providence, Rhode Island, earning a B.A. (1919) and M.A. (1920) from Brown, then an M.D. from Howard University in 1924. He married Jane Ryder in 1925; they had a son, Hugh, in 1926.

Fisher was a major figure in the Harlem Renaissance, both as a writer and as a musician, although his full-time job was as a practicing and research physician who produced important articles for medical journals. His first published work, the short story "City of Refuge," was published in the February 1925 issue of *Atlantic Monthly*—the first mainstream publication by a member of the Harlem Renaissance.

Although frequently credited with having produced the first mystery novel by an African-American writer, *The Conjure Man Dies* (1932), he had, in fact, been preceded by John Edward Bruce, whose *The Black Sleuth* had been serialized in *McGirt's Reader* in 1907–1908, and W. Adolphe Roberts, two of whose three mystery novels were published in the 1920s.

In addition to *The Conjure Man Dies,* which was adapted as the stage play *Conjur' Man Dies* in 1936, he wrote the well-received novel *The Walls of Jericho* (1928), fifteen short stories (two of which were selected for *The Best American Short Stories*), two plays, and book reviews.

"John Archer's Nose" was first published in the January 1935 (Volume 1, #1) issue of *Metropolitan Magazine*.

John Archer's Nose

Rudolph Fisher

Whenever Detective Sergeant Perry Dart felt especially weary of the foibles and follies of his Harlem, he knew where to find stimulation; he could always count on his friend, Dr. John Archer. Spiritually the two bachelors were as opposite as the two halves of a circle —and as complementary. The detective had only to seek out the physician at the latter's office-apartment, flop into a chair, and make an observation. His tall, lean comrade in crime, sober of face but twinkling of eye, would produce a bottle, fill glasses, hold a match first to Dart's cigar then to his own, and murmur a word of disagreement. Promptly an argument would be on.

Tonight however the formula had failed to work. It was shortly after midnight, an excellent hour for profound argumentation, and the sounds from the avenue outside, still alive with the gay crowds that a warm spring night invariably calls forth, hardly penetrated into the consulting-room where they sat. But Dart's provocative remark had evoked no disagreement.

"Your folks," Dart had said, "are the most superstitious idiots on the face of the earth."

The characteristic response would have been:

"Perry, you'll have to cut out drinking. It's curdling your milk of human kindness." Or, "My folks?—Really!" Or, "Avoid unscientific generalizations, my dear Sherlock. They are ninety-one and six-thirteenths percent wrong by actual measurement."

But tonight the physician simply looked at him and said nothing. Dart prodded further:

"They can be as dark as me or as light as you, but their ignorance is the same damned color wherever you find it—black."

That should have brought some demurring comment on the leprechauns of the Irish, the totems of the Indians, or the prayer-wheels of the Tibetans. Still the doctor said nothing.

"So you won't talk, hey?"

Whereupon John Archer said quietly:

"I believe you're right."

Dart's leg came off its perch across his chair-arm. He set down his glass untasted on the doctor's desk, leaned forward, staring.

"Heresy!" he cried, incredulous. "Heresy, b'gosh!—I'll have you read out of church. What the hell? Don't you know you aren't supposed to agree with me?"

"Spare me, your grace." The twinkle which kindled for an instant in Dr. Archer's eyes flickered quickly out. "I've had a cogent example today of what you complain of."

"Superstition?"

"Of a very dark hue."

"State the case. Let's see if you can exonerate yourself."

"I lost a kid."

Dart reached for his glass. "Didn't know you had one."

"A patient, you jackass."

Dart grinned. "Didn't know you had a patient, either."

"That's not funny. Neither was this. Beautiful, plump little brown rascal—eighteen months old—perfectly developed, bright-eyed, alert—and it passes out in a convulsion, and I was standing there looking on—helpless."

"If it was so perfect, what killed it?"

"Superstition."

"Humph. Anything for an alibi, hey?"

"Superstition," repeated Archer in a tone which stilled his friend's banter. "That baby ought to be alive and well, now."

"What's the gag line?"

"Status lymphaticus."

"Hell. And I was just getting serious."

"That's as serious as anything could be. The kid had a retained thymus."

"I'll bite. What's a retained thymus?"

"A big gland here in the chest. Usually disappears after birth. Sometimes doesn't. Untreated, it produces this status lymphaticus—convulsions—death."

"Why didn't you treat it?"

"I did what I could. Been seeing it for some time. Could have cleared it up over night. What I couldn't treat was the superstition of the parents."

"Oh."

"Specially the father. The kid should have had X-ray treatments. Melt the thing away. These kids, literally choking to death in a fit, clear up and recover—zip—like that. Most spectacular thing in medicine. But the old man wouldn't hear of it. None of this new-fangled stuff for *his* only child."

"I see."

"You can't see. I haven't told you yet. I noticed today, for the first time, a small, evil-smelling packet on a string around the baby's neck. In spite of the shock immediately following death, my curiosity got the better of me. I suppose there was also a natural impulse to—well—change the subject, sort of. I asked what it was."

"You would."

"The father didn't answer. He'd gone cataleptic. He simply stood there, looking. It seemed to me he was looking rather at the packet than at the child, and if ever there was the light of madness in a man's eyes, it was in his. The mother, grief-stricken though she was, managed to pull herself together long enough to answer."

"What was it?"

"Fried hair."

"What?"

"Fried hair.—No—not just kinky hair, straightened with hot irons and grease, as the term usually implies. That packet—I examined it—contained a wad of human hair, fried, if you please, in snake oil."

Dart expelled a large volume of disgusted smoke. "The fools."

"A charm. The father had got it that morning from some conjure-woman. Guaranteed to cure the baby's fits."

"He'd try that in preference to X-rays."

"And his name," the doctor concluded with a reflective smile, "was Bright—Solomon Bright."

After a moment of silence, Dart said:

"Well—your sins are forgiven. No wonder you agreed with me."

"Did I?" Having unburdened his story, John Archer's habit of heckling, aided by a normal desire to dismiss an unpleasant memory, began now to assert itself. The twinkle returned to his eyes. "I am of course in error. A single graphic example, while impressive, does not warrant a general conclusion. Such reasoning, as pointed out by no less an authority than the great Bacon—"

"I prefer ham," cut in Dart as the phone rang. His friend, murmuring something to the effect that "like begets like," reached for the instrument.

"Hello . . . Yes . . . Yes. I can come at once. Where? 15 West 134th Street, Apartment 51 . . . Yes—right away."

Deliberately he replaced the receiver. "I'm going to post a reward," he said wearily, "for the first person who calls a doctor and says, 'Doctor, take your time.' Right away—right away—"

He rose, put away the bottle, reached for hat and bag.

"Want to come along?"

"You're not really going right away?"

"In spite of my better judgment. That girl was scared."

"O.K. All I've got to do before morning is sleep."

"Don't count on it. Got your gun?"

"Gun? Of course. But what for?"

"Just a hunch. Come on."

"Hunch?" Dart jumped up to follow. "Say—what is this? A shooting?"

"Not yet." They reached the street.

"So what?"

"Girl said her brother's been stabbed."

"Yea?—here—let's use my car!"

"Righto. But lay off that siren. It gives me the itch."

"Well, scratch," Dart said as his phaeton leaped forward. "You've got fingernails, haven't you?" And with deliberate perversity he made the siren howl.

In three minutes they reached their destination and were panting up endless stairs.

"It's a cowardly trick, that siren," breathed the doctor.

"Why?"

"Just a stunt to scare all the bad men away from the scene of the crime."

"Well, it wouldn't work up here. This high up, they couldn't hear a thing in the street."

"You're getting old. It's only five flights."

Dart's retort was cut off by the appearance of a girl's form at the head of the stairway.

"Dr. Archer?" Her voice was trembling. "This way—Please— hurry—"

They followed her into the hallway of an apartment. They caught a glimpse of a man and woman as they passed the front living-room. The girl stopped and directed them with wide, frightened eyes into a bed-chamber off the hall. They stepped past her into the chamber, Dart pausing automatically to look about before following the physician in.

An old lady sat motionless beside the bed, her distorted face a spasm of grief. She looked up at the doctor, a pitifully frantic appeal in her eyes, then looked back toward the bed without speaking.

Dr. Archer dropped his bag and bent over the patient, a lean-faced boy of perhaps twenty. He lay on his left side facing the wall, his knees slightly drawn up in a sleeping posture. But his eyes were open and fixed. The doctor grasped his thin shoulders and pulled him gently a little way, to reveal a wide stain of blood on the bedclothing below; pulled him a little farther over, bent in a moment's inspection, then summoned Dart with a movement of his head. Together they observed the black-pearl handle of a knife, protruding from the chest. The boy had been stabbed through his pajama coat, and the blade was unquestionably in his heart.

Dr. Archer released the shoulder. The body rolled softly back to its original posture. The physician stood erect.

"Are you his mother?" he asked the old lady.

Dumbly, she nodded.

"You saw the knife, of course?"

"I seen it," she said in almost a whisper, and with an effort added, "I—I didn't pull it out for fear of startin' him bleedin' ag'in."

"He won't bleed any more," Dr. Archer said gently. "He hasn't bled for an hour—maybe two."

The girl behind them gasped sharply. "You mean he's been—dead—that long?"

"At least. The blood stain beneath him is dry."

A sob escaped the old lady. "Sonny—"

"Oh Ma—!" The girl moved to the old lady's side, encircled her with compassionate arms.

"I knowed it," the old lady whispered. "I knowed it—the minute I seen him, I knowed—"

Dr. Archer terminated a long silence by addressing the girl. "It was you who called me?"

She nodded.

"When you said your brother had been stabbed, I knew the case would have to be reported to the police. Detective Sergeant Dart was with me at the time. I thought it might save embarrassment if he came along."

The girl looked at Dart and after a moment nodded again.

"I understand.—But we—we don't know who did it."

A quick glance passed between the two men.

"Then it's lucky I came," Dart said. "Perhaps I can help you."

"Yes.—Yes perhaps you can."

"Whose knife is that?"

"His own."

"His own?—Where did you last see it?"

"On the bureau by the head of the bed."

"When?"

"This afternoon, when I was cleaning up."

"Tell me how you found him."

"Just like that. I'd been out. I came in and along the hall on the way to my room, I noticed his door was closed. He hasn't been coming in till much later recently. I stopped to speak to him—he hadn't been well.—I opened the door and spoke. He didn't answer. I pushed on the light. He looked funny. I went over to him and saw the blood.—"

"Shall we go into another room?"

"Yes, please.—Come, Ma—"

Stiffly, with the girl's assistance, the mother got to her feet and permitted herself to be guided toward the door. There she paused, turned, and looked back at the still figure lying on the bed. Her eyes were dry, but the depth of her shocked grief was unmistakable. Then, almost inaudibly, she said a curious thing:

"God forgive me."

And slowly she turned again and stumbled forward.

Again Dart and Archer exchanged glances. The former's brows lifted. The latter shook his head thoughtfully as he picked up his bag. As the girl and her mother went out, he stood erect and sniffed. He went over to the room's one window, which was open, near the foot of the bed. Dart followed. Together they looked out into the darkness of an airshaft. Above, one more story and the edge of the roof. Below, an occasional lighted window and a blend of diverse sounds welling up: a baby wailing, someone coughing spasmodically, a radio rasping labored jazz, a woman's laugh, quickly stifled.

"God forgive her what?" said Dart.

The doctor sniffed again. "It didn't come from out there."

"What didn't?"

"What I smelt."

"All I smell is a rat."

"This is far more subtle."

"Smell up the answer to my question."

The physician sniffed again, said nothing, turned and started out. He and Dart overtook the others in the hallway. A moment later, they were all in the living-room.

The man and woman, whom they had seen in passing, waited there, looking toward them expectantly. The woman, clad in gold-figured black silk Chinese pajamas, was well under thirty, slender, with yellow skin which retained a decided make-up even at this hour. Her boyish bob was reddish with frequent "frying," and her eyes were cold and hard. The man, in shirtsleeves and slippers, was approximately the same age, of medium build and that complexion known as "riny"—light, sallow skin and sand-colored kinky hair. His eyes were green.

The girl got the old lady into a chair before speaking. Then, in a dull, absent sort of way, she said:

"This is the doctor. He's already turned the case over to this gentleman that came with him."

"And who," the woman inquired, "is this gentleman that came with him?"

"A policeman—a detective."

"Hmph!" commented the woman.

"Fast work," added the man unpleasantly.

"Thank you," returned Dart, eyeing him coolly. "May I know to whom I owe the compliment?"

The man matched his stare before answering.

"I am Ben Dewey. This is my wife. Petal there is my sister. Sonny was my brother." There was unnecessary insolence in the enumeration.

" 'Was' your brother?"

"Yes, was." Mr. Dewey was evidently not hard to incense. He bristled.

"Then you are already aware of his—misfortune?"

"Of course."

"In fact, you were aware of it before Dr. Archer arrived."

"What do you mean?"

"I mean that no one has stated your brother's condition since we came into this room. You were not in the bedroom when Dr. Archer did state it. Yet you know it."

Ben Dewey glared. "Certainly I know it."

"How?"

The elder brother's wife interrupted. "This is hardly the time, Mr. Detective, for a lot of questions."

Dart looked at her. "I see," he said quietly. "I have been in error. Miss Petal said, in the other room just now, 'We don't know who did it.' Naturally I assumed that her 'we' included all the members of the family. I see now that she meant only herself and her mother. So, Mrs. Dewey, if you or your husband will be kind enough to name the guilty party, we can easily avoid a 'lot of questions.' "

"That ain't what I meant!" flared the wife. "We don't know who did it either."

"Oh. And you are not anxious to find out—as quickly as possible?"

Dr. Archer mediated. "Sergeant Dart naturally felt that in performing his duty he would also be serving you all. He regrets, of course, the intrusion upon your—er—moment of sorrow."

"A sorrow which all of you do not seem to share alike," appended Dart, who believed in making people so angry that they would blurt out the truth. "May I use your phone?"

He went to the instrument, resting on a table near the hall door, called the precinct station, reported the case, asked for a medical examiner, and declined assistants.

"I'm sure the family would prefer to have me act alone for the time being."

Only Dr. Archer realized what these words meant: that within five minutes half a dozen men would be just outside the door of the apartment, ready to break in at the sergeant's first signal.

But Dart turned and smiled at the brother and his wife, "Am I right in assuming that?" he asked courteously.

"Yes—of course," Ben said, somewhat subdued.

Swiftly the courteous smile vanished. The detective's voice was incisive and hard. "Then perhaps you will tell me how you knew so well that your brother was dead."

"Why—I saw him. I saw the knife in—"

"When?"

"When Petal screamed. Letty and I had gone to bed. And when Petal screamed, naturally we jumped up and rushed into Sonny's room, where she was. She was standing there looking at him. I went over to him and looked. I guess I shook him. Anybody could see—"

"What time was that?"

"Just a few minutes ago. Just before the doctor was called. I told her to call him."

"About ten minutes ago, then?"

"Yes."

"How many times did your sister scream?"

"Only once."

"You're sure?"

"Yes."

"You had retired. You heard one scream. You jumped up and went straight to it."

"Why not?"

"Extraordinary sense of direction, that's all.—Whose knife is that?"

"Sonny's."

"How do you know?"

"I've seen him with it. Couldn't miss that black pearl handle."

"Who else was in the house at the time?"

"No one but Ma. She was already in the room when we got there. She's got an extraordinary sense of direction, too."

"Any one else here during the evening?"

"No—not that I know of. My wife and I have been in practically all evening."

"Practically?"

"I mean she was in all evening. I went out for a few minutes— down to the corner for a pack of cigarettes."

"What time?"

"About ten o'clock."

"And you've heard nothing—no suspicious sounds of any kind?"

"No. At least *I* didn't. Did you Letty?"

"All I heard was Sonny himself coming in."

"What time was that?"

" 'Bout nine o'clock. He went in his room and stayed there."

"Just what was everyone doing at that time?"

"The rest of us were in the back of the flat—except for Petal. She'd gone out. Ben and I were in the kitchen. I was washing the dishes, he was sitting at the table, smoking. We'd just finished eating supper."

"Your usual supper hour?"

"Ben doesn't get home from the Post Office till late."

"Where was Mother Dewey?"

"In the dining-room, reading the paper."

"Anyone else here now?"

"Not that I know of."

"Do you mind if we look?"

"If I minded, would that stop you?"

Dart indulged in an appraising pause, then said:

"It might. I should hate to embarrass you."

"Embarrass me!—Go ahead—I've nothing to hide."

"That's good. Doc, if you can spare the time, will you take a look around with me?"

Dr. Archer nodded with his tongue in his cheek. Dart knew very well that a cash-in-advance major operation could not have dragged the physician away.

"Before we do, though," the detective said, "let me say this: Here are four of you, all closely related to the victim, all surely more or less familiar with his habits and associates. Yet not one of you offers so much as a suggestion as to who might have done this."

"You haven't given us time," remarked Letty Dewey.

Dart looked at his watch. "I've given you five minutes."

"Who's been doing all the talking?"

"All right. Take your turn now. Who do *you* think did it?"

"I haven't the remotest idea."

"M—m—so you said before—while I was doing all the talking."—He smiled. "Strange that none of you should have the remotest idea. The shock, no doubt. I should rather expect a flood of accusations. Unless, of course, there is some very good reason to the contrary."

"What do you mean?"

"I mean—" the detective was pleasantly casual—"unless you are protecting each other. In which case, if I may remind you, you become accessory.—Come on, Doc. No doubt the family would like a little private conference."

During the next few minutes the two went through the apartment. Alert against surprise, they missed no potential hiding-place, satisfying themselves that nobody had modestly secreted himself in some out-of-the-way corner. The place possessed no apparent entrance or exit other than its one outside door, and there was nothing unusual about its arrangement of rooms—several bed-chambers off a central hallway, with the living-room at the front end and a kitchen and dining-room at the back.

Characteristically, the doctor indulged in wordy and somewhat irrelevant reflection during the tour of inspection. Exchanges of comment punctuated their progress.

"Back here," Dr. Archer said. "I don't get it. But up there where they are, I do. And in the boy's room, *I* did."

"Get what—that smell?"

"M–m. Peculiar—very. Curious thing, odors. Discernible in higher dilution than any other material stimulus. Ridiculous that we don't make greater use of them."

"I never noticed any particular restriction of 'em in Harlem."

On the dining-room table a Harlem newspaper was spread out. Dart glanced at the page, which was bordered with advertisements.

"Here it is again," he said, pointing, " 'Do you want success in love, business, a profession?' These 'ads' are all that keep this sheet going. Your folks' superstition—"

Dr. Archer's eyes traveled down the column but he seemed to ignore the interruption.

"Odors *should* be restricted," he pursued. "They should be captured, classified, and numbered like the lines of the spectrum. We let them run wild—"

"Check."

"And sacrifice a wealth of information. In a language of a quarter of a million words, we haven't a single specific direct denotation of a smell."

"On, no?

"No. Whatever you're chinking of, it is an indirect and nonspecific denotation, liking the odor in mind to something else. We are content with 'fragrant' and 'foul' or general terms of that character, or at best 'alcoholic' or 'moldy,' which are obviously indirect. We haven't even such general direct terms as apply to colors—red, green, and blue. We name what we see but don't name what we smell."

"Which is just as well."

"On the contrary. If we could designate each smell by number—"

"We'd know right off who killed Sonny."

"Perhaps. I daresay every crime has its peculiar odor."

"Old stuff. They used bloodhounds in *Uncle Tom's Cabin.*"

"We could use one here."

"Do tell?"

"This crime has a specific smell—"

"It stinks all right."

"—which I think we should find significant if we could place it."

"Rave on, Aristotle."

"Two smells, in fact. First, alcohol."

"We brought that with us."

"No. Another vintage I'm sure. Didn't you get it in the boy's bedroom?"

"Not especially."

"It's meaning was clear enough. The boy was stabbed while sleeping under the effect of alcohol."

"How'd you sneak up that answer?"

"There was no sign of struggle. He'd simply drawn up his knees a little and died."

"Don't tell me you smelt alcohol on a dead man's breath."

"No. What I smelt was the alcoholic breath he'd expelled into that room before he died. Enough to leave a discernible—er—fragrance for over an hour afterward."

"Hm—Stabbed in his sleep."

"But that simply accounts for the lack of struggle and the tranquil posture of the corpse. It does indicate, of course, that for a boy of twenty Sonny was developing bad habits—a fact corroborated by his sister's remark about late hours. But that's all. This other odor which I get from time to time I consider far more important. It might even lead to the identity of the killer—if we could trace it."

"Then keep sniffing, Fido. Y'know, I had a dog like you once. Only he didn't do a lot of talking about what he smelt."

"Too bad he couldn't talk, Sergeant. You could have learned a great deal from him."

As they approached the front door the bell rang. Dart stepped to the door and opened it. A large pink-faced man carrying a doctor's bag stood puffing on the threshold. He blinked through his glasses and grinned.

"Dr. Finkelbaum!" exclaimed the detective. "Some service! Come in. You know Dr. Archer." He looked quickly out into the corridor, noted his men, grinned, signaled silence, stepped back.

"Sure. Hello, doctor," greeted the newcomer. "Whew! Thank your stars you're not the medical examiner."

"You must have been uptown already," said Dr. Archer.

"Yea. Little love affair over on Lenox Avenue. I always phone in before leaving the neighborhood—they don't do things by halves up here. Where's the stiff?"

"In the second room," said Dart. "Come on, I'll show you."

"At least," murmured Dr. Archer, "it was in there a moment ago."

Despite his skepticism, which derived from sudden mysterious disappearances of corpses on two previous occasions in his experience, they found the contents of Sonny's bedchamber unchanged.

"Who did this?" inquired the medical examiner.

"At present," Dart said, "there are four denials—his mother, his sister, his brother, and his brother's wife."

"All in the family, eh?"

"I haven't finished talking to them yet. You and Dr. Archer carry on here. I'll go back and try some more browbeating."

"Righto."

Now Dart returned to the living-room. The four people seemed not to have moved. The brother stood in the middle of the floor, meditating. The wife sat in a chair, bristling. The girl was on the arm of another chair in which her elderly mother still slumped, staring forward with eyes that saw nothing—or perhaps everything.

The detective looked about. "Finished your conference?"

"Conference about what?" said Ben.

"The national debt. What's happened since I left here?"

"Nothing."

"No conversation at all?"

"No."

"Then who used this telephone?"

"Why—nobody."

"No? I suppose it moved itself? I left it like this, with the mouthpiece facing the door. Now the mouthpiece faces the center of the room. One of miracles of modern science or what?"

Nobody spoke.

"Now listen." There was a menacing placidity in the detective's voice. "This conspiracy of silence stuff may make it hard for me, but it's going to make it a lot harder for you. You people are going to talk. Personally, I don't care whether you talk here or around at the precinct. But whatever you're holding out for, it's no use. The circumstances warrant arresting all of you, right now."

"We've answered your questions," said Letty angrily. "Do you want us to lie and say one of *us* did it—just to make your job easier?"

"Lawd—Lawd!" whispered the old lady and Petal's arm went about her again, vainly comforting.

"Who else lives here?" Dart asked suddenly.

As if sparing them the necessity of answering, the outside door clicked and opened. Dart turned to see a young man enter the hallway. The young man looked toward them, his pale face a picture of bewilderment, closed the door behind him, mechanically put his key back into his pocket, and came into the living-room.

"What's up," he asked. "What do those guys want outside?"

"Guys outside?" Ben looked at Dart. "So the joint's pinched?"

"Not yet," returned Dart. "It's up to you people." He addressed the newcomer. "Who are you?"

"Me?—I'm Red Brown. I live here."

"Really? Odd nobody's mentioned you."

"He hasn't been here all day," said Letty.

"What's happened?" insisted Red Brown. "Who is this guy?"

"He's a policeman," Petal answered. "Somebody stabbed—Sonny."

"Stabbed Sonny—!" Dart saw the boy's wide eyes turn swiftly from Petal and fix themselves on Ben.

"A flesh wound," the detective said quickly.

"Oh," said Red, still staring with a touch of horror at Ben. His look could not have been clearer had he accused the elder brother in words.

"You and Sonny are good friends?" pursued Dart.

"Yea—buddies. We room together."

"It might make it easier for Ben if you told me why he stabbed his brother."

Red's look, still fixed, darkened.

"Why should I make it easier for him?"

There was silence, sudden and tense. Ben drew a deep, sharp breath, amazement changing to rage.

"Why—you stinking little pup!"

He charged forward. Letty yelled, "Ben!" Red, obvious child of the city, ducked low and sidewise, thrusting out one leg, over which his assailant tripped and crashed to the floor. Dart stepped forward and grabbed Ben as he struggled up. There was no breaking the detective's hold.

"Easy. What do you want to do—prove he's right?"

"Let me go and I'll prove plenty! I'll make him—"

"It's a lie!" breathed Letty. "Ben didn't kill him."

Unexpectedly Dart released Ben.

"All right," said he. "Get to proving. But don't let me have to bean you."

The impulse to assault was spent. Ben pulled himself together.

"What's the idea?" he glowered at Red. "I even call up the pool-room where you work, trying to keep you out of this. And you walk in and try to make me out a murderer."

"Murderer?" Red looked about, engaged Dart. "You—you said—flesh wound."

"Yes," the detective returned drily, "The flesh of his heart."

"Gee! Gee, Ben. I didn't know you'd killed him."

"I didn't kill him! Why do you keep saying so?"

Red looked from Ben to Letty, encountering a glare of the most intense hatred Dart had ever seen. The woman would obviously have tried to claw his eyes out had not circumstances restrained her.

"Go on," she said through her teeth. "Tell your tale."

Her menace held the boy silent for an uncertain moment. It was outweighed by the cooler threat of Dart's next words:

"Not scared to talk, are you, Red?"

"Scared? No, I ain't scared. But murder—gee!"

"You and Sonny were buddies, weren't you?"

"Yea—that's right."

"Slept in the same bed."

"Yea."

"Supposing it had been you in that bed instead of Sonny?"

"Yea—it might 'a been."

"Sonny wouldn't have let you down, would he?"

"He never did."

"All right. Speak up. What do you know?"

"I know—I mean—maybe—maybe Ben figured there was somethin' goin' on between Sonny and—" He did not look at Letty now.

"Was there?"

"Wouldn't matter whether there was or not—if Ben thought so."

"True enough. Well, Mr. Dewey, what about that?"

Ben Dewey did not have an answer—seemed not to have heard

the detective's last word. His mouth hung open as he stared dumbfounded at his wife.

His wife, however, still transfixed Red with gleaming eyes.

"It should have been you instead of Sonny," she said evenly. "You rat."

Abruptly Dart remembered the presence of the old lady and the girl. He turned toward them, somewhat contrite for not having spared them the shock of this last disclosure, but got a shock of his own which silenced his intended apology: The girl's face held precisely the expression of stunned unbelief that he had expected to find. But the old lady sat huddled in the same posture that she had held throughout the questioning. Her steadfast gaze was still far away, and apparently she had not heard or seen a single item of what had just transpired in the room.

Dart stepped into the hall to meet Dr. Archer and the medical examiner as they returned from the death room.

"I'm through," said Dr. Finkelbaum. "Immediate autopsy on this. Here's the knife." He handed Dart the instrument, wrapped in a dressing. "I don't believe—"

Dart interrupted him with a quick gesture, then said loudly enough to be heard by those in the living-room:

"You don't believe it could have been suicide, do you, doctor?"

"Suicide? I should say not." The medical examiner caught Dart's cue and matched his tone. "He wasn't left-handed, was he?"

Dart turned back, asking through the living-room doorway, "Was your brother left-handed, Mr. Dewey?"

Ben had not taken his eyes off Letty.

"Seems like he was," he said in a low voice, which included his wife in his indictment.

"Is that true, Miss Petal?"

"No, sir. He was right-handed."

"Then it wasn't suicide," said the medical examiner. "The site of the wound and the angle of the thrust rule out a right hand. The depth of it makes even a left hand unlikely."

"Thanks, doctor. We can forget the fact that it was his own knife."

"Absolutely."

"And," Dart winked as he added, "we can expect to find the killer's fingerprints on this black pearl handle, don't you think?"

"Oh, unquestionably," replied Dr. Finkelbaum. "That handle will name the guilty party even if he wore a glove. The new method, you know."

"So I thought," said Dart. "Well, on your way?"

"Yep. I'll get him downtown and let you have a report first thing in the morning. See you later, gentlemen."

"I'm afraid you will," murmured Dr. Archer.

Dr. Finkelkbaum departed. Dr. Archer and the detective conferred a brief moment in inaudible tones, then entered the living-room.

"Mr. Dewey," said Dart, "do you deny having committed this crime in the face of the circumstances?"

"What circumstances?"

"The existence of ample motive, as testified by Red Brown, here, and of ample opportunity, as testified by your wife.

"What do you mean, opportunity?"

"She corroborated your statement that at about ten o'clock you went out for a few minutes on the pretext of getting a pack of cigarettes."

"I did go out and I got the cigarettes."

"The time when you say you went out happens to correspond with the time when the doctors say the crime was committed."

"And if I was out, how could I have done it?"

"You couldn't. But suppose you weren't out? Suppose you went down the hall, opened and shut the front door, crept back silently into Sonny's room—only a few steps—did what you had to do, and, after the proper lapse of time, crept back to the front door, opened and shut it again, and walked back up the hall as if you had been out the whole time? Your wife says that you went out. But she can not swear that you actually left the apartment."

"Of course I can!" said Letty sharply.

"Yes? Then, Mrs. Dewey, you must have been in the hallway the whole time Mr. Dewey was out. You can not see the length of that hallway from any room in this house. The only way you can swear there was nobody in it throughout that time is to swear that you were in it throughout that time. Could you swear that?"

Letty hesitated only a moment before answering hotly, "Yes!"

"Careful, Mrs. Dewey. Why should you stand idle for ten minutes alone in an empty hallway?"

"I—I was measuring it for wallpaper."

"Strange. I noted that it had recently been re-papered."

"I didn't like the new paper. I was planning to have it changed."

"I see. Then you insist that you were in that hallway all that time?"

"Yes."

"And that Mr. Dewey was not?"

"Yes."

"And that no one else was?"

"No one."

"Madam, you have accused yourself."

"Wh—what?"

"You have just accused yourself of killing your brother-in-law."

"What are you talking about?"

"I'll make it plainer. The only doorway to Sonny's room is on the hall. Assuming that the doctors are right about the time of death, and assuming that the killer used the only door, which is on the hallway you so carefully kept under observation, no one but yourself was within striking distance at the time Sonny was stabbed. You follow my reasoning?"

"Why—"

"Therefore by your own statement—which you are willing to swear to—you must have killed him yourself."

"I never said any such thing!"

"You wish to retract your statement?"

"I—I—"

"And admit that your husband may have been in the hallway?"

Completely confused and dismayed, the woman burst into tears.

But disloyal or not, this was Ben Dewey's wife; he came to her rescue:

"Wait a minute, officer. At least you had a reason for accusing me. What would she want to do that for?"

"I'd rather not guess, Mr. Dewey. But it shouldn't be hard."

Only Letty's sobs broke the next moment's silence. Finally Ben said in a dull, low voice:

"She didn't do it."

"Did you?" asked Dart quickly.

"No. I didn't either. It's—it's all cockeyed."

The man's change of attitude from arrogance to humility was more touching than the woman's tears.

"Are we under arrest?"

Dart's answer was surprising. "No."

"No?"

"No. You are free to go about as usual. You will all hold yourselves ready for questioning at any time, of course. But I shall not make an arrest until this knife is examined."

Letty stopped sobbing to follow the general trend of eyes toward the gauze-wrapped knife in Dart's hand.

"Here's the answer," said the detective, looking about and raising the object. "Of course—a confession would save us a bit of time and trouble."

Nobody uttered a word.

"Well—in the morning we'll know. Dr. Archer put this in your bag, please. And do you mind keeping it for me until morning? I've got a bit of checking up to do meanwhile."

"Not at all." The doctor took the knife, placed it carefully in a side pocket of his bag. "It'll be safe there till you come for it."

"Of course. Thanks a lot. We'll be going now."

The two started out. Dart halted as his companion went on toward the outside door.

"I might say before going, Mr. Dewey," he remarked, "that anything that happens to Red Brown here will make things look even worse for you and your wife. Both of you threatened him, if I remember."

"I can take care of myself," said Red Brown coolly.

"I'm glad to know that," returned Dart. "And—oh yes. I'd like to see you all here in the morning at nine. That's all. Good night."

"From your instructions to your men," observed Dr. Archer, as he and the detective rode back toward his office, "I gather the purpose of not making an arrest."

"It's the only way," Dart said. "Let 'em go and keep an eye on 'em. Their actions will always tell more than their words. I hadn't got anywhere until Red Brown looked at brother Ben. Yet he didn't say a word."

"And," Dr. Archer continued, "I gather also that Exhibit A, which rests enshrouded in my bag, is to be a decoy."

"Sure. That was all stuff—about prints and the new method. Probably not a thing on that knife but they don't know that. Somebody's going to try and get that lethal weapon back."

"But—" the doctor's words disregarded the detective's interruptions—"what I fail to gather is the reason for dragging in me and my bag."

"You dragged me in, didn't you?"

"I see. One good murder deserves another."

"No. Look. The thing had to be planted where the guilty person figured it could be recovered. They wouldn't attempt to get it away from me. But you're different."

"Different from you?"

"Exactly."

"It's a relief to know that."

"You're no happier over it than I am."

"You'll be nearby, I trust?"

"Under your bed, if you like."

"No. The girl might come for it."

"That's just why I'll be nearby. Leave you alone and she'll get it."

"Shouldn't be at all surprised. Lovely little thing."

"But not too little."

"Nor too lovely."

"Aren't you ashamed of yourself?"

"Not at all. You see—"

"Yea, I see. Never mind the long explanation, Adam saw. too."

"Ah, but what did Adam see? An apple. Only an apple."

"Well, if it's the girl—which it won't be—she'd better bring an apple along—to keep the doctor away."

"Sergeant, how you admire me. What makes you think it won't be the girl?"

"You don't think she killed her brother, do you?"

"I hope not. But I wouldn't—er—express an opinion in cash."

"Couldn't you just say you wouldn't bet on it?"

"Never use a word of one syllable, sergeant, when you can find one of six."

"Why wouldn't you bet on it? She's just a kid. A rather nice kid."

"How did you find out?"

Dart ignored him. "She screamed. She telephoned for you."

"Nice girls of nineteen have been known to do such things."

"Kill their sweethearts, maybe—their ex-sweethearts. Not their brothers."

"True. Usually it is the brother who kills his sister's sweetheart, isn't it? Whereupon the sweetheart is known as a betrayer."

"Yea. Family honor. Course I've never seen it, but—"

"Cynic. Here we are."

But Dart drove on past the doctor's apartment.

"Whither, pray?"

"Get smart. They may recognize the detective's license-plates. Around the corner'll be better."

"And me with no roller-skates."

Shortly they returned to the apartment on foot, and soon were engaged in smooth hypotheses, well oiled.

"One of these things is going to fool us yet," meditated the physician between sips.

"They all fool us."

"Modesty ill becomes you, Perry. I mean the party who obviously did the thing from the outset sometimes does it."

"The party is always obvious from the outset—when it's all

over. What I'd like to see is a case in which the party who is obvious from the outset is obvious *at* the outset."

"The trouble is with the obviousness—the kind of obviousness. One person is obviously guilty because everything points to him. Another is obviously guilty because nothing points to him. In the present case, Ben is the one example, Red the other."

"You're drinking. How can a man be guilty because nothing points to him?"

"Because, of course, too perfect an alibi is no alibi, just as too perfect a case is no case. Perfection doesn't exist. Hence the perfect thing is false.

"This is false whiskey."

"May it continue to deceive us. Consider this: Can you imagine a lad like Red Brown living in a house with a girl like Petal and not being—er—affected?"

"So what?"

"I was thinking of the brother-sweetheart complex you suggested."

"With the brother getting the worst of it? But Letty said Red had been out all day. How could Red—?"

"Just as you said Ben could. Only he didn't slam the front door."

"Of course Letty was lying about being in the hall all that time. Maybe Red could have sneaked in and out, at that. But that's taking it pretty far. Nothing that we know indicates Red."

"Nothing except that he's altogether too un-indicated."

"Well, if you really want to get fancy, listen to this."

"Go ahead."

"Red knows that Letty is two-timing."

"Yes."

"Ben doesn't."

"No."

"If Ben finds out, it's her hips."

"Yes."

"She's rather partial to her hips."

"Naturally."

"A blab from either Sonny or Red—and bye-bye."

"Hips."

"So, tired of Sonny and afraid of Red, she decides on what is known as murder for elimination."

"Murder of Sonny?"

"No. Of Red. With Sonny implicated by his knife."

"Go on. How'd she get Sonny and Red mixed?"

"She heard Sonny come in—'way down the hall where she couldn't see. But Sonny, having developed bad habits, never comes in so early. She believes this is Red. When Ben steps out, she slips into the dark room and hurriedly acts in self-defense."

"Hip-defense."

"M—m. Only it happens to be Sonny. Well, what about it?"

"Utterly fantastic. Yet not utterly impossible."

"O.K. Your turn."

"You leave me the most fantastic possibility of all."

"The old lady?"

"No. The mother." The doctor paused a moment, then said, "There's quite a difference. Can you imagine anything that would make a mother kill her son?"

"That smell you mentioned, maybe."

"No. Seriously."

"I don't know. It's pretty hard to believe. But it could happen, I suppose. By mistake, for instance. Suppose the old lady thought it was Red—just as Letty might have. Red—leading her child down the road to hell. . . . That would explain why she said, 'God forgive me!' "

"Let's forget your 'mistake' for a while."

"Well then, look. When I was walking a beat, a woman came to me once and begged me to put her son in jail. He was a dope. She said when she saw him like that, she wanted to kill him."

"But did she?"

"No. But why can't mother-love turn to hate like any other love?"

"I guess the fact that it doesn't is what makes it mother-love."

"What about those hospital cases where unmarried girls try to smother their kids—and sometimes succeed?"

"Quite different, I should say. Those girls aren't yet mothers, emotionally. They're just parents, biologically. With a wholly unwanted and recently very painful obstruction between themselves and happiness. Mother-love must develop, like anything else. It grows as the child grows, becomes a personal bond only as the child becomes a person."

"All right. But mothers can go crazy."

"Yes. There are cases of that kind."

"That old lady acted kind o' crazy, I thought."

"Probably just grief. Or concern over the whereabouts of Sonny's soul."

"Maybe. I wouldn't press the point. But as long as we're guessing, I don't want to slight anybody."

"I did have a case once where, I believe, a fairly sane mother would have killed her son if she'd been able. He was a lad about Sonny's age, with a sarcoma of the jaw. It involved half his head—he suffered terrifically. Death was just a matter of time. She repeatedly begged me to give him an overdose of morphine."

"What prevented her from killing him?"

"I sent him to a hospital."

"Well—"

"Yes, I know. Sonny could have had a sort of moral sarcoma—eating up his soul, if you like. The sight of him going down and down might have been more than his mother could bear. But unless she was actually insane at the moment, she'd keep hoping and praying for a change—a turn for the better. That hope would prevent any drastic action. After all, sarcoma of the soul is not incurable."

"The only way it could be his mother, then, is if she went temporarily off her nut?"

"Exquisitely phrased, my friend. Have another drink."

Dr. Archer's apartment, which combined office and residence, was on the ground floor of a five-story house. Its front door was immediately within and to one side of the house entrance, off a large rectangular foyer at the rear of which a marble staircase wound upward and around an elevator-shaft. At this hour the elevator was not running.

Inside, the front rooms of the apartment constituted the physician's office—waiting-room, consultation-room, laboratory. Beyond these were a living-room, bedroom and kitchen.

It was agreed that Dart should occupy the bedroom for the rest of the night, while Dr. Archer made the best of the living-room couch. Dart could thus remain behind the scene for any forthcoming action, observe unseen, and step forward when occasion demanded.

Neither undressed, each lying down in shirt-sleeves and trousers. In the event of a caller, Dart agreed that, barring physical danger, he would not interfere unless the doctor summoned him.

"Still hoping it'll be the girl, hey?" grinned the detective.

"Nothing would amaze me more," returned Archer. "Go on—lie down. This is my party." He stretched his considerable length on the couch. Dart went into the adjacent bedroom, leaving the intervening door ajar.

As if some unseen director had awaited this moment, the apartment bell promptly rang, first briefly, timidly, then longer, with resolute determination. "I didn't want to sleep anyway," murmured the doctor. "Keep your ears open. Here goes."

He went through the office rooms to the front door, cracked the little trap-window designed against rent-collectors and other robbers, snapped it to with a gasp of astonishment, unlocked and opened the door.

His preliminary glance was corroborated. Before him stood Petal, bareheaded, with a handbag under her arm.

"I know it's late," she was saying, a little breathlessly, "but—"

"Not at all. Come in."

"Thank you." She looked behind her.

He closed the door quickly. "Someone following you?"

"I—I thought so. Just—nervousness I hope."

"Come back this way."

She followed him through the waiting-room into the consulting office. He slipped on an office coat from a rack.

"Who would be following you at this hour?" he asked, giving her a chair and seating himself at his desk.

"Detectives, maybe."

"Hardly. You're the last person suspected in this affair."

She was silent a moment. Her eyes rested on the doctor's bag, which sat conspicuously on top of his desk. Then she began still breathlessly to talk. She leaned forward in her chair, dark eyes wide and bright, gentle breasts rising and falling, small fingers moving restlessly over the flat handbag on her lap.

"Are—are we alone?"

He smiled. "Would you care to look about?"

She accepted this with a feeble reflection of his smile.

"I came here to—to warn you. About Ben."

"Ben?"

"He's—wild. He blames you. He says if you hadn't brought in that detective, he wouldn't be in a jam."

"But that's ridiculous. The thing couldn't have been covered up. The same facts would have been brought out sooner or later."

"I know. But he—he's a little crazy, I guess. Finding out about Letty and everything. He thinks he could have managed."

"Managed—what?"

"Keeping the thing quiet."

"Why should he want to keep it quiet?"

"I don't know. His job—his wife—it's all such a mess. I guess he wants to take it out on somebody and he can't—on Sonny."

"I see. What does he intend to do?"

"He's coming here and hold you up for that knife. If you refuse to give it to him—he'll take it."

"How?"

"He has a pistol. He has to have it when he's loading mail, you know. The way he is now, he'd use it."

"In which case he might be actually guilty of a crime of which he is now only suspected."

"Yes. He might kill you."

"And naturally you want to save him from that."

"Him—and you."

"Hm . . . What do you suggest?"

"Give me the knife."

He smiled. "But I've promised Sergeant Dart to turn it over in the morning."

"I know. But I'll give it back to you, I swear I will."

"My dear child, I couldn't do that. Don't you see—it would

make my position very awkward? Obstructing the due course of justice and all that?"

"Oh—I was afraid you wouldn't—Please! Don't you see? It may mean your life—and Ben's. I tell you he's crazy."

"How is it that he didn't get here first?"

"He had to stay with Ma. She passed out. I'm supposed to be out looking for medicine. As soon as I get back, he's coming."

"As soon as you get back. Well, that makes it simple."

"What do you mean?"

"Don't go back. Stay here. Sergeant Dart will come for the knife at eight o'clock in the morning. It's three now. When it has been examined, he will come back for us. It will be too late for Ben to do anything to me then."

"Stay here the rest of the night?"

"You'll be quite safe. I should hardly be—ungrateful for your effort to protect me."

"But—but—what about Ma's medicine?"

"If she simply fainted, she's in no danger."

"I couldn't stay away. If anything happened to Ma—"

The physician meditated.

"Well," he said after a moment, "strange how the simplest solution is often the last to occur to one. I can easily take care of both the danger to myself and the further implication of your brother."

"How?" Petal asked eagerly.

"By just spending the rest of the night elsewhere. Parts unknown."

"Oh."

"Come. That will settle everything. You run along now. Get your mother's medicine. When brother Ben arrives I'll be far, far away."

Reluctantly the girl arose. Suddenly she swayed, threw a hand up to her face, and slumped back down into the chair. Dr. Archer sprang forward. She was quite limp. He felt her pulse and grinned. She stirred, opened her eyes, smiled wanly.

"A little water—?" she murmured.

He filled a paper cup from the washstand faucet in the corner and brought it to her.

"It's so warm," she protested.

"I'll get a bit of ice."

He went through the next room into the kitchen, put ice in a glass, filled it and returned. She had not apparently moved, but the flap of his bag on the desk was unsecured at one end. She drank the water.

"Thank you. That's so much better. I'm sorry. I feel all right now."

Again she arose and now preceded him through the waiting-room. At the front door she turned and smiled. She was really very pretty.

"You've been swell," she said. "I guess everything will turn out all right now.

"I hope so. You've done bravely."

She looked at him, turned quickly away as if eluding some hidden meaning in his words, and stepped across the threshold. As she did so, the bang of a pistol shot shook the foyer. Archer reached out, seized the girl's arm, yanked her back, slammed the door. He secured its lock, then hustled her back into the consulting-room.

There, both drew breath.

"Somebody means business. Sit down."

She obeyed, wordless, while he went back to reassure Dart. When he returned a moment later, he found a thoroughly frightened girl.

"I—I heard it hit the side of the doorway," she breathed. "Who—who'd shoot at me?"

"I can't imagine who'd shoot at either of us. Even your brother would try to get what he came for before shooting."

"It was at me," she insisted. "You were still inside the room. It was from the stairs at the back."

"Well. Looks as if we both have to stay here a while now."

"There's no other way out?"

"Yes. The kitchen. But that door opens on the same foyer."

She gave a sign of despair. Slowly her eyes filled.

"Spoils your whole scheme, doesn't it?"

She said nothing.

"Don't feel too bad about it. It was spoiled already."

Her wet eyes lifted, questioning.

"Look in your bag," he said.

She opened the handbag, took out a gauze-wrapped object.

"Unwrap it."

She obeyed. The knife was not Sonny's pearl-handled weapon, but a shining surgeon's scalpel.

"I anticipated some such attempt as you made, of course. The real thing is already under inspection."

He felt almost ashamed at her look.

After a brief silence, she shrugged hopelessly. "Well—I tried."

He stood before her. "I wish you'd tell me the whole story."

"I can't. It's too awful."

"I'd really like to help you if I could."

"You could give me the knife."

"What could you do with it now? You don't dare leave, with somebody shooting at you."

"If Ben comes—"

"Ben has surely had time to come—come to his senses, anyway.

If Ben would go so far as to kill—as you claim—to get that knife, it can only mean one thing: He knows whom it would implicate." He paused, continued: "That might be himself."

Inspiration kindled her eyes for a brief instant. Before he was sure he saw it, the lids drooped.

"Or," he leaned a little closer, "would it be Letty? Letty, who killed Sonny for betraying her, then begged her husband to forgive her and recover the one thing that would identify her?"

She looked up at him, dropped her eyes again, and said: "Neither."

"Who then?"

"Me."

"You!"

"Me." She drew deep breath. "Don't you think I know what it means for me to come here and try to get that thing? Why make it hard? It means I killed Sonny, that's all. It means I told them tonight after you left. Ben would have come here and done anything to get the knife, to save me. But Ma passed out when I told. And I ran out while Ben was holding her, saying I'd get something for her. And then I came here . . . Why would I let Ben risk his neck for something I did?"

Dr. Archer sat down. "Petal, you're lying."

"No. It's true. I did it. I didn't know it was Sonny. I didn't go out as Letty said. I hid in the room closet. I thought it was Red that came in. When he went to sleep I came out of the closet. It was dark . . . I meant to—to hang on to the knife, but I couldn't pull it out." She halted, went on: "Then I went out, quietly. It was Ma who really discovered him as I came back in later. That's why I screamed so when—" She halted again.

"But Petal—why?"

"Can't you guess?" she said, low.

269

"Good Lord!" He sat back in his chair. "If that's a lie, it's a good one."

"It's not a lie. You said you'd help me if you could. Will you give me the knife now? Just long enough to let me clean the handle?"

He was silent.

"It's my life I'm asking for."

"No, Petal," he said gently. "The beauty of your story is that if it stands up you might get off very lightly, juries are funny about a woman's honor. It's certainly not a question of your life."

"Lightly! What good is a jailbird's life?"

"I can't believe this."

She stood up, her bag dropping to the floor.

"Look at me," she said. He looked. "I'll do anything you want me to, any time, from now till I die, if you'll give me the knife for five minutes. Anything on earth."

And, whatever her falsehood up to that moment, he had no doubt of her sincerity now.

"Sit down, Petal."

She sat down and began to cry softly.

"It's a lie. But it's a grand lie."

"Why do you keep saying that?"

"Because it's so. Don't you see how inconsistent you are?"

She stopped crying.

"Look," he went on. "You've come to me, whom you know nothing about except that I'm a doctor. Nothing personal at all. You say you've killed for the sake of your—let us say—honor. Yet the same honor, which you prize highly enough to commit murder for, you offer to sacrifice to me if I will save you from the consequences of what you've done for it. Does that make sense?"

She did not answer.

"How can you hold so cheap now a thing which you held so dear a few hours ago?"

"I'm not. It's worth all it ever was. Something else is worth more, that's all."

"How you must love your brother."

"Myself."

"No. You wouldn't do this for yourself. If you were the only one involved, you'd still be defending your honor—not trading it in."

"Please—you said you'd help me."

"I'm going to help you—though not in the way you suggest—nor at the price."

"Then—how?"

"You'll have to leave that to me, Petal."

There was complete defeat in her voice. "It certainly looks that way."

"Now call your home and say that you've been detained by the police, but will be there in the morning. Tell Ben you were detained for trying to see me. That will keep him safe at home."

She obeyed, replaced the receiver, turned to him. "Now what?"

"Now lie down on that sofa and rest till morning. I'll be in the next room, there."

With utmost dejection in every movement, she went toward the sofa. John Archer turned and went out, back through the living-room into the bedroom where Dart waited, and went into whispered close communion with the detective.

An hour later he came softly back to the consulting-room, cracked the door, looked through. Petal lay face-down on the sofa, her shoulders shaking with silent sobs.

During that hour of whispered conference, the physician

and the detective had engaged in one of their characteristic disagreements.

"You yourself said," Dart reminded the doctor, "that the party who is obviously guilty *is* guilty. That party is Ben. He is the only one with sufficient motive. This Letty and Petal stuff is hooey. Women don't kill guys that trick 'em any more. They sue 'em. But men still kill guys that trick their wives."

"You're barking up the wrong sycamore, Perry. Ben didn't know anything about Letty's two-timing—delightful phrase, 'two-timing'—till Red spilt it over two hours *after* the stabbing. The way you say he acted proves that. Why, he was still staring dumbfounded at Letty when the medical examiner and I came back on the scene. Men may kill guys that trick their wives—if I may borrow your elegant diction—but surely not till after they know the worst. It is still customary, is it not, for a cause to precede its effect?"

"You needn't get nasty. Maybe there was some other motive."

"You wouldn't abandon your motive, would you Sergeant? 'Love is all,' 'Seek the woman' and all that?"

"It's been known to play a part," said the other drily.

"I wish I could place that smell."

"I wish you could place it, too—as far away as possible."

"Let's see now. I got it in the dead boy's room when we first went in. But I didn't get it when the medical examiner and I went in."

"So?"

"So it must have been upon someone who was present the first time and absent the second."

"Yea."

"Don't growl—you're not the hound you think you are. That would mean it was on one of four people—Sonny, Petal, Ma, or you."

"Wake me when this is over."

"Then I got it in the front flat during the first period of questioning. So it couldn't have been Sonny. And I did not get it anywhere else in the flat when you and I were looking around. Hence it couldn't have been you."

"Nope. I use Life-Buoy."

"That leaves Petal and Ma. But I didn't get it when Petal greeted us at the head of the stairs, nor while I was talking to her just now. I actually leaned close to her to be sure."

"You leaned close to her—why?"

"To be sure."

"Oh. To be sure."

"That leaves Ma."

"Hmph. So Ma killed Sonny. I begin to smell something myself."

"I didn't say the bearer of the odor killed Sonny."

"No. You only said the odor would lead to the killer. You had a hunch."

"I've still got it—bigger than ever. Ma may not have killed Sonny, but I'll bet you champagne to Rochelle salts that if it hadn't been for Ma, Sonny wouldn't have been killed."

"It's a bet. And the one that wins has to drink his winnings on the spot."

"In other words, Ma is inextricably bound up in the answer to this little riddle."

"Anything besides an odor leading you on?"

"Yes. There are two things I can believe out of Petal's story: First, Petal is awfully anxious to protect somebody. Second, Ben—who was coming here also if Petal had returned home—is also very anxious to protect somebody. There was time for plenty of talk after we left, so it's unlikely that Ben and Petal are concerned over two different people. Ben and Petal, brother and sister, are trying to protect the *same* person. It wouldn't be Red, whom Ben tried to beat. It wouldn't be Letty, whom Petal has shown no special affection for. But it would be Ma, their mother, the one person in the picture whom both love."

"Are you trying to say that Ma killed her own son, and that Ben and Petal know she did?"

"Not exactly. I'm saying that Ben and Petal believe that that knife will incriminate Ma."

Dart became serious for a moment. "I get it. Ben's ignorance of Letty's two-timing eliminates him. Petal's inconsistency eliminates her. Yet each of them wants the knife, because it may incriminate Ma."

"Beautifully summarized, professor. With the aid of a smell."

"Where do you want to smell next?"

"At their apartment in the morning. Have everybody there— and a few trusty fallen arches. I'm going to locate that odor if it asphyxiates me."

"Y'know, maybe I ought to put you on a leash."

"Have the leash ready. I'll get you somebody to put on it."

In the morning about eight-thirty the two men and the girl had coffee together, Dart pretending to have just arrived. Petal exhibited a forced cheerfulness that in no wise concealed the despair in her eyes.

Even the hard habits of long police experience had not wholly stifled the detective's chivalry, and in an effort to match the girl's courageous masquerade, he said lightly:

"You know, this case is no cinch. I'm beginning to believe some of your folks must walk in their sleep."

As if struck, the girl jumped up. It was as if the tide of her terror, which had receded during the early morning hours, suddenly swung back with his remark, lifting her against her will to her feet. Controlling herself with the greatest effort, she turned from the table and disappeared into the next room.

"Gee!" said Dart. "Bull's eye—in the dark."

"M–m," murmured Archer. "Ma. But I hope I'm wrong."

"I hope so, too."

Petal reappeared.

"I'm sorry. I'm so upset."

"Better finish your coffee," said the doctor.

"My fault," Dart apologized. "I might have let you out a few more minutes."

"It's all right—about me. But there's someone I wish you would let out—as far as you can."

"Who?"

"Ma."

"I don't understand. Surely you don't mean that your mother—"

"No. Of course not. But—perhaps I should have mentioned it sooner—but it's not something we talk much about. You ought to know it though."

"I'll certainly try to protect your confidence."

"My mother is—well—not entirely—right."

"You mean she's—insane?"

"She goes off—has spells in which she doesn't know what she's saying. You saw how she was last night—she just sat there."

"But," the physician put in, "anybody—any mother, certainly—might act that way under the circumstances. The shock must have been terrific."

"Yes, but it is more than that. Ma has—I don't know—she sees things. As long as she's quiet it doesn't matter. But when she starts talking, she says the most impossible things. When you see her again, she's likely to have a complete story of all this. She's likely to say anybody did it—anybody." Her voice dropped. "Even herself."

The two men looked at her, Dart quizzically, Archer gravely.

"That's why I'm asking you to—let her out. If ever she had reason to be unresponsible for what she says, it's now."

"Quite so," the doctor said. "I'm sure Sergeant Dart will give your mother every consideration."

Dart nodded. "Don't worry, young lady. Policemen are people, too, you know."

"I just thought I'd better tell you beforehand."

"Glad you did. Now let's get around to your place and see if we can't clear up the whole thing. Some of the boys are to meet me there at nine. Perhaps something has developed that will put your mind at rest."

"Perhaps," said the girl with no trace of conviction or hope.

When, a few minutes later, they reached the Dewey apartment, they found a bluecoat in the corridor outside the door and two of Dart's subordinates already awaiting him, with the other members of the family, in the living-room.

"Isn't Red Brown here?" was the detective's first question.

"No," Ben told him. "He left right after you did last night and hasn't come back."

"The first law of nature," murmured Dr. Archer.

"Yea," Dart agreed, "but who is he protecting himself from—Mr. and Mrs. Dewey here or the law?"

"It could be both," remarked the tight-lipped Letty.

"Or neither," the doctor added. "He's probably stayed out all night before. And I doubt that I should care to occupy Sonny's bed under the circumstances."

"I told him to be here," Dart said. "This doesn't look good for him."

One of the headquarters men called Dart aside.

"Autopsy report," he said, low. "Tuberculosis both lungs. Due to go anyway, sooner or later."

"M–m."

"Here's the knife."

"Anything on it?"

"Nothing."

And the detective, knowing that every Dewey's eyes had followed where their ears could not reach, pretended a satisfaction which only valuable information could have given.

"Thanks," said he aloud. "This is all I've been waiting for."

He surveyed the four members of the household—Ma, seated in the same chair she had occupied last night, much as if she had not left it since; Petal, again protectively by her side; Letty, still disagreeably defiant, standing beside Ben, her scowling husband. But the far-away expression was no longer in Ma's eyes; she was staring now at the detective with the same fearful expectancy as the others.

After a moment of complete silence, Dart, looking meditatively at the knife which he balanced in his hand, said almost casually:

"If I were the guilty party, I think I'd speak now."

Ma Dewey drew a quick breath so sharply that all eyes turned upon her.

"Yes," she said in a dull but resolute voice. "Yes. That's right. It's time to speak."

"Ma!" cried Petal and Ben together.

"Hush, chillun. You all don' know. I got to tell it. It's got to come out."

"Yes, Mrs. Dewey?"

"Oh Ma!" the girl sobbed, while Ben shoulders dropped suddenly and Letty gave a sardonic shrug.

"I don't know," Ma said, "what you all's found on that knife. It don't matter. One thing I do know—my hand—this hand—" she extended a clenched, withered fist— "had hold o' that knife when it went into Sonny's heart."

Petal turned desperate, appealing eyes to Dart. No one else moved or spoke.

"I told the chillun las' night after you all had lef'."

Dr. Archer gave Petal a glance that at last comprehended all she had tried to accomplish in his office last night.

"You all don' know," the old lady resumed with a deliberate calmness of voice that held no hint of insanity. "You don' know what it means to a mother to see a child goin' down and down. Sonny was my youngest child, my baby. He was sick, body and soul."

She stopped a moment, went doggedly on.

"He got to runnin' around with the wrong crowd here in Harlem. Took to drinkin' and comin' in all hours o' the night— or not at all. Nothin' I say or do seem to have no effect on him. Then I see he's beginnin' to fall off—gettin' thinner by the minute. Well, I made him go 'round to the hospital and let them doctors examine him. They say he got T.B. in his lungs and if he don' go 'way to a cemetarium he'll die in a year. And I knowed it was so, 'cause his father died o' the same thing."

She was looking back over the years now, and into her eyes came last night's distant stare.

"But he wouldn' go. Jes' like his father. Say if he go'n' die he go'n die at home and have a good time befo' he go. I tried ev'y-thing—prayer, charms—God and the devil. But I'd done seen his father go and I reckon I didn' have no faith in neither one. And I begun to think how his father suffered befo' he went, and look like when I thought 'bout Sonny goin' through the same thing I couldn' stand it. Seem like sump'm kep' tellin' me, 'Don' let him suffer like that—Don' let him suffer like that.'

"It weighed on my mind. When I went to sleep nights I kep' dreamin' 'bout it. 'Bout how I could save him from goin' through all that sufferin' befo' he actually come down to it. And las' night I had sech a dream. I seen myself kneelin' by my bed, prayin' for strength to save him from what was in store for him—strength to make his death quick and easy, 'stead o' slow and mis'able. Then I seen myself get up and slip into the hall and make into Sonny's room like sump'm was leadin' me. Same sump'm say, 'If he die in his sleep he won' feel it.' Same sump'm took my hand and moved it 'long the bureau-top till it hit Sonny's knife. I felt myself pick it up and move over to the bed . . . and strike. . . ."

Her voice dwindled to a strained whisper.

"That's all. When I opened my eyes, I was in my own bed. I thought it was jes' another dream . . . Now I know better. It happened. I killed him."

She had straightened up in her chair as she spoke. Now she slumped back as if her strength was spent.

Dr. Archer went quickly to her. Dart saw him lean over her, grow abruptly rigid, then fumble at the bosom of her dress, loosening her clothing. After a moment, the doctor stood erect and turned around, and upon his face was the light of discovery.

"She's all right," he said. "Wait a minute. Don't do anything till I get back."

He went into the hallway, calling back, "Petal, just fan your mother a bit. She'll be all right"—and disappeared toward the dining-room at the rear of the apartment.

In a few moments, during which attention centered on reviving Ma Dewey, he returned with a newspaper in his hand.

"This was on the dining-room table, open at this page, last

night," he said proffering the paper to Dart. "Read it. I'll be right back."

He turned and went out again, this time leaving the apartment altogether, by way of its front door.

Dart looked after his vanished figure a moment, wondering perhaps if his friend might not also be acting in a trance. Then his eyes fell on the page which advertised columns of guaranteed charms.

Before he could find just what it was Dr. Archer had wanted him to read, a curious sound made him look up. From the hallway, in the direction of the rear, came a succession of sharp raps.

"What's that?" whispered Letty, awe-struck.

Dart stepped into the hallway, Ben, Letty, and the two officers crowding into the living-room doorway behind him. Again came the sharp succession of taps, and this time there was no mistaking their source. They came from within the closed door of Sonny's room.

Letty stifled a cry as Dart turned and asked, "Who's in that room?"

"Nobody," Ben answered, bewildered. "They took Sonny away last night—the door's locked."

Again came the taps.

"Where's the key?"

Ben produced a key, Dart seized it, quickly unlocked the door and flung it wide.

Dr. Archer stood smiling in the doorway.

"What the hell?" said Dart.

"Unquestionably," returned his friend. "May I give an order to your two men?"

He wrote something on his prescription pad and handed it to one of the two men behind Dart. The latter read it.

"O.K., Doc. Come on, Bud."

They departed.

"As I remarked before," Dart growled, "what the hell?"

The physician backed into the room. "The missing link," he said blandly.

"Red Brown?"

"You heard Ma Dewey's story?"

"Of course I heard it."

"She was quite right. She did kill Sonny. But not in the way she believes. I'm just working out the details. See you in the living-room. Lock this door again, will you?" And he shut the door between himself and the detective.

With consummate self-control Dart suppressed comment and question and obeyed.

Then he went back into the living-room with the others. The local newspaper was still in his hand, somewhat crumpled. He smoothed the pages.

"Take it easy, everybody," he advised the members of the family, with whom he was now alone. "We'll wait for Dr. Archer and Red Brown." And he began to peruse in earnest the columns of ads:

BLACK CAT LODESTONE

DRAW ANYTHING YOU WANT TO YOU.

FREE—HOT FOOT AND ATTRACTING
POWDERS WITH YOUR ORDER.

PAY THE POSTMAN ONLY $1.95 ON DELIVERY AND IT IS
ALL YOURS TO KEEP AND ENJOY FOREVER.

BURN LUCKY STARS AND SURROUND YOURSELF WITH
GOOD FORTUNE.

WIN YOUR LOVED ONE.

LET US SEND YOU OUR SACRED CONTROLLING LOVE
POWDER.

DO YOU SUFFER FROM LACK OF FRIENDS, MONEY,
HEALTH?

ORIENTAL WISHING RING

He had to read to the bottom of the right-hand column before
something caught his eye, an address which seemed somehow
familiar.

"15 West 134th Street, Apt. 51—Why, that's here!"

He re-read the advertisement:

FAITH CHARM
FAITH CAN MOVE MOUNTAINS.
DEVELOP YOUR FAITH BY USING OUR SPECIAL CHARM.
SECRET FORMULA. BOUND TO BRING HEALTH AND
HAPPINESS TO THE WEARER.

"Say!"
The front door rattled. Dart stepped out and admitted Dr.
Archer. "What kind of hide-and-seek is this?"
"It isn't," smiled the physician. "It's a practical demonstration

in entrances and exits. It shows that even if Sonny's door had been locked, his assailant could have entered and left his room, undetected."

"How."

"The next apartment is empty. Its entrance is not locked—you know how vacant apartments are hereabouts: the tenants bring their own locks and take them when they move. One room has a window on the same airshaft with Sonny's, at right angles to it, close enough to step across—if you don't look down."

"You jackass! You'd risk your hindquarters like that?"

"Sergeant—please."

"But what's the use? We've got the old lady's confession, haven't we?"

"Yes."

"And you admitted she did it—you were working out details. Good grief—would she go around to the next apartment and climb across an air-shaft—at her age? What do you want me to believe?"

"Believe in the value of an odor, old snoop. Come on."

They re-entered the living-room. Dr. Archer went to Ma Dewey.

"Tell me, Mother Dewey, where do you keep the oil?"

She looked up at him. "I don't keep it. I gets it jes' as I needs it."

"When did you last need it?"

"Yestiddy mornin'."

"After it had failed so long to help Sonny?"

"I didn' have faith. I'd done seen his father die. But somebody else might 'a' had faith."

"Curious," reflected the doctor, "but common."

Dart's patience gave out.

"Would you cut the clowning and state in plain English what this is all about?"

"I mean the mixture of Christian faith and primitive mysticism. But I suppose every religion is a confusion of superstitions."

The doorbell saved Dart from exploding. He went to the door and flung it open with unnecessary violence.

His two subordinates stood before him, holding between them a stranger—a sullen little black man whose eyes smoldered malevolence.

As they brought him into the living-room, those eyes first encountered Ben. Their malevolence kindled to a blaze. The captive writhed from the hands that held him and leaped upon the brother, and there was no mistaking his intention.

His captors got hold of him again almost before Ben realized what had happened.

"Who the devil's this?" Dart asked the physician.

"Someone for your leash. The man that killed Sonny."

"Yea—" panted the captive. "I got him. And—" indicating Petal—"I come near gettin' her las' night. And if you turn me loose, I'll get *him*." Vainly he struggled toward Ben.

"Three for one," said the doctor. "Rather unfair, isn't it, Mr. Bright?"

"She took all *we* had, didn' she? Give my wife that thing what killed *our* kid. We got to pay her back—all for all."

"Solomon Bright," breathed Dart. "The guy that lost his kid yesterday."

Dr. Archer said to the man, "What good will it do to pay Mother Dewey back?"

The little man turned red eyes on the quiet-voiced physician. "They ain' no other way to get our chile back, is they?"

Dr. Archer gave gesture of despair, then said to Dart:

"Mother Dewey made the charm yesterday."

" 'Twasn' no charm," Solomon Bright glowered. " 'Twas a curse. Cast a spell on our chile, tha's what it done."

"Its odor," John Archer went on, "was characteristic. But I couldn't place it till Mother Dewey fainted just now and I saw the cord around her neck. On the end of it hangs the same sort of packet that I saw on Mr. Bright's baby."

Dart nodded. "I get it . . . When she made that charm, she was unwittingly killing her own son. This bird's poison."

"Grief-crazed—doesn't realize what he's doing. Look at him."

"Realize or no realize, he killed Sonny."

"No," said the doctor. "Superstition killed Sonny." He sighed. "But I doubt that we'll ever capture that."

GEORGE SAMUEL SCHUYLER (1895–1977) was born in Providence, Rhode Island, and raised in Syracuse, New York. He joined the army at 17, becoming a first lieutenant. Because of a racial slight, he went AWOL, turned himself in, and served nine months of a five-year sentence before moving to New York City, where he became involved in socialism. He wrote editorials for a black magazine, *The Messenger*, before taking on the same role in 1925 for the most important African-American newspaper in America, the *Pittsburgh Courier*, which at its peak had a circulation of 200,000. His affection for socialism waned, his columns reflecting his shift of ideology, whereupon H. L. Mencken named him "the most competent editorial writer now in practice." While at the *Courier*, he began to write fiction and became a prolific contributor to the paper, producing mystery, science fiction and other popular stories under the pseudonyms Samuel I. Brooks, Verne Caldwell, Rachel Call, D. Johnson, John Kitchen, William Stockton, and Edgecombe Wright. In addition to his frequently reprinted satirical novel, *Black No More* (1931), he is remembered today primarily as a powerful voice of conservative thought, writing articles for *American Opinion*, the journal of the John Birch Society, *Slaves Today* (1931), about the reintroduction of slavery by freed slaves in Liberia, and his autobiography, *Black and Conservative* (1966).

"The Shoemaker Murder" was published under the pseudonym William Stockton in the *Pittsburgh Courier* in 1933.

The Shoemaker Murder

George S. Schuyler *writing as* William Stockton

Detective Sergeant Henry Burns knelt over the prostrate corpse in the dingy shoe shop on 126th Street in black Harlem. He looked at the gaping, fatal wound in the back of the shoemaker's skull. Brains and blood had gushed from it onto the dirty wooden floor. The tall Negro detective rose, brushed the knees of his meticulously creased trousers, and lit a cigarette. The two patrolmen, an Irishman and a brown-skin lad, waited expectantly for him to speak.

"Well, it's murder all right," he declared. "They got him with the first blow. They used that hammer. Whoever did it had a terrible wallop, all right . . . Keep that crowd away from the window, Clancy, and keep the door fastened. The inspector and the coroner will be here soon."

He flicked the ash from his cigarette and swept the little shoe shop with his keen glance.

"It's going to be a tough assignment," he observed to the colored policeman. "The door was locked from the inside. The transom was nailed down. There is no way to get from this room into the rag shop behind, opening on the little alley. Let's go around and question the old lady in the rag shop."

They went out and around the corner to the shop in the rear. The windows were covered with burlap bagging, the place was piled high with sacks of rags, bundles of old newspapers, and assorted junk. In an old broken-down chair near the door sat an aged Mrs. Ferguson, the proprietress.

"We're officers," began the detective, looking sharply at the old woman, who glanced back indifferently. "Did you hear any noise or voices in the shoe shop around noon?"

"Naw suh, Ah ain't heered nuthin'," she replied, "an' Ah bin sittin' heah since long befo' noon."

"Did you know Johnson, the shoemaker?"

"Yassah, Ah knowed him. He bin rentin' fum me foh nigh on tuh six year."

"So you own this building, eh?"

"Yassuh, my husban' left hit tuh me when he died."

"How long has that partition between your shop and the shoe shop been there?"

" 'Bout ten yeahs."

Burns worked his way through the bundles and bags back to the wooden partition. He surveyed it minutely, pressing here and there with his hand and knocking with his knuckles. There was evidently no opening.

"Is there a basement under this space?" he asked the old woman.

"Yassuh, they's ah cellar."

"How do you get down to it?"

"They's a doah outside."

The detective stood silent for a moment looking all over the room. "Have you got a furnace downstairs?"

"Yassuh."

"Who takes care of it?"

"Jerry. He's tha janitor. An' he helps me aroun' heah with mah business."

"Where is he?"

"He's downstaahs, Ah guesses."

"Stay here, Williams," commanded Burns, turning on his heel. Going outside he walked down the four steps to the basement door. Trying it, he found it fastened. He beat on it. There was no reply.

Alert now, he put his broad shoulder against the flimsy door. After a couple of lusty lunges, the door gave way. He found himself standing in the dark cellar.

Whipping out his flashlight, he lighted his way forward until he found the electric light switch. He pulled it up and flooded the place with light. He noted immediately that there was no partition in the cellar separating the two parts of the building as there was upstairs. In the center was the rusty furnace. To one side was a rickety cot with two or three dirty quilts and a filthy pillow. The rest of the cellar was filled with bags of rags, bundles of paper, and various odds and ends. Far forward was a coal bin right under the street. There was no sign of Jerry, the janitor.

Carefully the detective examined every foot of the basement floor. It had been freshly swept in the open space where there were no bags or bundles. He turned the beam of his flashlight on the ceiling. There was apparently no opening there. Burns frowned.

He was about to leave the basement when it occurred to him that there might be an opening after all. He looked again at the pile of bags against one wall reaching clear to the ceiling. He got to work immediately moving them to one side. Yes, there it was, a narrow wooden staircase leading, of all things, into the shoe shop through a trapdoor. Strange that he had not noticed the door when he was in the shoe shop. He now ascended the little stairway and examined the narrow trapdoor. It was hooked. He examined each step but there was absolutely no clue, no mark, nothing.

Then he saw two broom straws on the top step caught in a crack. He grunted, smiled grimly, and pocketed them.

He descended the stairway, stepped over the bags of rags, and was about to switch off the light when the outer doorway was darkened. Looking up quickly he saw standing there a huge elderly mulatto man in tattered overalls, scowling at him.

"Whatchu doin' here?" asked the man.

"I'm an officer," the tall Negro detective replied. "Who are you and what are you doing here?"

"I'm the janitor here," replied the man suspiciously. He looked intoxicated and the odor coming from him confirmed it.

"So you're Jerry, eh?"

"Yea, I'm Jerry. Whatchu doin' here, an' whatchu mean breakin' down that door?"

"Never mind that," snapped the detective. "You sit down there and answer my questions."

Jerry shuffled in reluctantly and sank heavily down on the cot.

"Now where have you been since before noon?" began Burns, standing over the hulking form of the man.

"Oh, I jus' bin over tuh git uh drink or two."

"So I see. What time did you leave here?"

" 'Bout eleven."

"Was Johnson the shoemaker working in his shop when you went out?"

"Yassuh. I heered him tappin' up there."

"Do you always lock that door when you go out?"

"Yassuh, allus do. Some of these boys aroun' heah might steal our rags and papers."

"Hummph. Well, how long have those bags been up against that staircase?"

" 'Bout two weeks."

"And you haven't cleaned up this place—swept it out since then?"

"Nawsuh," replied Jerry, "I don't bothah sweepin' out 'cept once in uh while."

"Where's your broom?"

"Ovah b'hind the furnace."

Burns stepped quickly behind the furnace to get the broom. It was not there. Alert now, he looked carefully everywhere. Finally he found it alongside the coal bin.

"Did you put this broom here?" he asked sharply.

"Nawsuh," replied Jerry, "I ain't had that broom in two weeks an' w'en I got through with it, then I hung it up behin' th' furnace."

Detective Burns grunted with satisfaction. Taking Jerry with him, he returned to the shoe shop. The place was crowded with high police officials and the coroner. Burns reported immediately to Inspector Sullivan.

"What have you found, Burns?" asked the inspector.

"It's a tough case, Inspector," replied the Negro. "This man Johnson has had this shop here for six years. He was found murdered at 12:30 P.M., when a woman came here to get a pair of shoes heeled. The door was locked from the inside. The transom is nailed shut. There's no door connecting this shop with the rag shop behind. However, there is a stairway leading from the basement into this shop. I found it covered up by a big pile of bags filled with rags and bundles of paper. The pile has been there two weeks. Now here's something funny. The janitor says he hasn't swept the basement for two weeks, since the last shipment of rags and papers, and yet the basement has been swept but only the space underneath this shop. I found these two broom straws caught in the top step of the stairway. There are no footprints and no fingerprints as far as I could see. The trapdoor leading from this room to the basement is hooked from the basement side. Jerry, that's the janitor, heard Johnson working at eleven o'clock when he went out to the speakeasy around the corner. The old lady who owns this dump, Mrs. Ferguson, says she has sat in her place since long before noon. And yet this fellow was murdered in here. And the murderer must have been a powerful fellow because Johnson was a big guy. But there was no way for a big man to get in the place. Everything was locked from the inside."

"It's a puzzler, all right," said the inspector, scratching his head. "Did this guy, Johnson, ever have any visitors?"

"The neighbors say not," Burns answered. "He stayed in here most of the time. Ate here, too, but whenever he did go out he hung up his little sign saying when he'd be back. It was hanging there when we broke in. Either he was planning to go right out, which was unusual this time of day, or else he had just come back. The woman looked in and saw him on the floor at twelve-thirty. He was murdered sometime between eleven and twelve-thirty."

"Did he have any money on him?"

"Yes, that's the funny thing about it, Chief. He had twenty-five bucks in his pocket. So you see, it wasn't robbery. There's quite a bit of money in the cash register."

"Well, somebody did it," declared the inspector. "Keep hunting. I'll send a couple of men to help you. There've been too many murders around here lately."

"All right, sir. I'll stay on the job."

The coroner soon departed with the body of the shoemaker. The high police officials left soon after. Patrolman Clancy kept the curious away from the door. Detective Burns sat in the shoemaker's chair near the door, smoking cigarette after cigarette and frowning in thought.

Finally, with an exclamation, he jumped up and ran out to the street. Stopping near the curb, he closely examined the coal hole in the cement sidewalk. Then, much agitated, he returned to the shop and telephoned several places. Then he rushed out, shouting back over his shoulder to Clancy to let no one into the shop.

Two hours later Detective Burns sat in the office of Inspector Sullivan with several white detectives. Before the semicircle of officers sat a Negro, very black and hunchbacked. The man sullenly watched the men as they sat silently before him.

"What's the idea of having us pick up this fellow, Burns?" asked the inspector. "He don't know nothing about it."

"Well, I think he does, Chief," insisted Burns. "I took a long chance but I'm sure I'm right."

"Where's your evidence?" asked the inspector.

"You see this little strand of cloth? Well that came off this fellow's coat. He was wearing a different coat, just this color of brown, when he murdered Johnson this noon. It caught in a nail when he went in the cellar door. It's a cinch, Chief."

"It's a dirty frame-up," yelled the hunchback, snarling at Burns. "I never had a coat like that. This is the only coat I've got. You've got nothing on me."

"He went in the cellar door, Chief," repeated Burns, ignoring the man's denial. "I've got the fingerprints."

The little man grinned but said nothing.

"You should have been smart enough to wear gloves," said

Burns, speaking directly to the accused man. "Now you'll burn for neglecting to do so."

"That's all stuff," jeered the man, "there wasn't no finger-prints."

"Oh, yes there were," accused Burns, swiftly showing a sheet with photostatted prints, "and they're yours, too."

"Well, I guess that cinches it, all right," commented the inspector, with a tone of decision, rising.

"Yes, that's all we need," commented the other officers, moving back their chairs and rising.

The little black man looked puzzled, then frightened, then panic-stricken. He swallowed a couple of times, then licked his lips.

"That was good work, Burns," said the inspector, placing his hand on the detective's shoulder. "Those fingerprints on that cellar door settle everything. We can get a conviction on that."

"Say, listen, Chief," wailed the alarmed little black man, "honest, them ain't my fingerprints. You can't put that on me. I—I—I didn't do it. I didn't kill him."

"You didn't kill who?" snapped Burns.

"Why Johnson," replied the suspect.

"How did you know he was dead?" shouted the inspector. "Who told you? We didn't. We picked you up but we didn't say what for. Why did you think we wanted you for that?"

Trapped! Tracked! The hunchback sat speechless for a minute, then alternately plied with questions and threatened, he confessed.

"That was fine work, Burns," commented the inspector after-ward, "but how did you ever conceive the idea of having us pick up the hunchback?"

"Well, Chief," explained the other. "I could see we were up

against a clever fellow. In the first place, he had almost committed a perfect crime. There were no fingerprints, no evidence of any kind. The murder had obviously been committed coolly and with premeditation, it showed the murderer was familiar not only with the building but with the habits of the occupants. Business was always slack in the shop around noon. The old lady in the rear usually read her morning papers about that time. Jerry, the janitor, generally spent his noon hour in. Johnson would be alone.

"Now it was impossible for the murderer to have got out of the cellar door, assuming he had gone down through the trapdoor after killing Johnson, because the cellar door was locked. He must have come through the coal hole. I found all the dirt around the coal hole cover had been jarred away by the cover being removed.

"Now here's the way I built up the case: the fellow had studied the layout. He knew the block was almost deserted just before school lets out at noon. He entered the coal hole, being short, and immediately placed the cover back on behind him. Then he descended the coal chute into the bin, threw the bags away from the trapdoor, unhooked it, entered Johnson's shop, and killed him. He retraced his steps, piled the bags back, but not before he had swept the steps to remove the coal dust footprints. That's also the reason why he swept the cellar floor, from the furnace to the coal bin. Unfortunately for him, he couldn't hang Jerry's broom back in its place without tracking up the cellar floor again, so he just threw it back. He left the cellar by the same way he entered, taking a chance that no one would see him. No one did. I figured that only a small fellow could get through that coal hole, and I was sure it was a man and not a boy. It had to be a small man but yet a powerful one because Johnson was a pretty big fellow. I took a chance on it being a hunchback."

"Fine!" exclaimed the inspector. "But what did he kill him for? He didn't rob him, as you know."

"Revenge. That's the answer. He confessed as much. Eight years ago Morgan, that's the hunchback, and Johnson were gold mining in British Guyana. They struck it pretty rich but they got to quarreling and in the fight that ensued, Johnson seriously injured Morgan's back, causing that hump on it. He left Morgan for dead and came here to the States. Morgan followed him here after he got well but just located him this week."

"Yes, but why didn't he just bump him off with a gun and beat it?"

"This," said Burns, displaying a piece of worn, folded paper. "It is a map showing the location of a gold mine in British Guyana. Johnson had it in his cash register. It is the only thing Morgan took. He wanted to get back to find that mine. He knew beforehand that Johnson had it."

"Smart work, Burns," smiled the inspector.

"Yes, I did some pretty good guessing," the Negro replied.

GAR ANTHONY HAYWOOD (1954–) was born in Los Angeles, where he has lived all his life and where his gritty novels and short stories have been set. He worked as a computer maintenance technician for nearly two decades and, in addition to writing fiction, has been a television script writer for more than ten years.

His best-known character, private eye Aaron Gunner, made his debut in *Fear of the Dark* (1987), which won the St. Martin's Press/Private Eye Writers of America Award. Haywood followed this highly praised novel with *Not Long for This World* (1990) and *You Can Die Trying* (1993) before taking a hiatus from his tough P. I. to start a new, lighter detective series starring Dottie and Joe Loudermilk, a pair of retirees who travel across America in their Airstream trailer. They appear in *Going Nowhere Fast* (1994) and *Bad News Travels Fast* (1995), after which Haywood returned to the more successful Gunner series with *It's Not a Pretty Sight* (1996), *When Last Seen Alive* (1997), and *All the Lucky Ones Are Dead* (2000). Haywood has also written two novels as Ray Shannon, *Man Eater* (2003) and *Firecracker* (2004), which feature a female protagonist, Ronnie Deal, a Hollywood executive.

For television, Haywood has written episodes of *New York Undercover* and *The District,* as well as the script for the movie based on Dennis Rodman's *As Bad as I Wanna Be.*

"The First Rule Is" has never previously been published.

The First Rule Is

Gar Anthony Haywood

"Why you always hatin' on the man like that?" Caprice asked, sounding like her feelings were hurt. "What'd he ever do to you?"

"He ain't done nothin' to me. But he ain't done nothin' for me, neither," C.C. said. "He ain't done nothin' for nobody, 'cept hisself."

Caprice thought about arguing with him, but she could see just from the way he was stretched out all over the couch, Seven-and-Seven held loosely in his left hand, feet dangling over the side, that her man was in one of his moods again. Say one word too many running contrary to his opinion now and your ass could wind up in the emergency room, trying to tell the doctors where it hurt through a mouth full of broken teeth.

She didn't understand C.C.'s problem with Miracle Miles and she never would. Wasn't Miracle on the television right now, four years after retiring from a decade-long, championship-studded career in professional basketball, bragging on the latest big shopping center he was helping to put up in the 'hood? Wasn't Miracle—smart, funny, and fine as a black man could ever be—what "giving back to the community" was all about?

Not in C.C.'s mind, he wasn't. C.C. could see Miracle for what he really was and had always been, just an overhyped baller with a shuck-and-jive grin white folks couldn't get enough of. From his earliest playing days in high school, they'd given him a fancy nickname and treated him like a superstar, paving the road with gold for him, first in college and then in the pros, just because he could dribble the rock between his legs and shoot a mini-mini-skyhook. But underneath all the bullshit he wasn't nothin' but a lucky punk, always in the right place at the right time to get paid. C.C. knew this for a fact because he'd seen the nigga long before all the hype set in, when Miracle was just a mediocre, sixteen-year-old point guard out of Princeton Heights High in Oakland named Stegman Miles.

He had game, yeah, but he wasn't all that. C.C. was the one who was all that. C.C. was running point for Jefferson back in those days, and there wasn't anything Stegman Miles could do that C.C. couldn't do better. C.C. could penetrate, dish, *and* shoot, from damn near anywhere on the court, and if he had to he could throw a little defense down on a fool, too. Miles got more attention because he played what the reporters liked to call a more "disciplined" game, creating fewer turnovers while hitting the boards with greater intensity, but there was no doubt in C.C.'s mind he was the better player. He made All-City three years in a row and led Jefferson to the State finals twice, and the second time around he got his chance to show folks who the real "miracle" man was. Jefferson and Princeton Heights went head-to-head and C.C. took Miles apart, outscoring him 32–18. Despite

Miles's fourteen assists and nine rebounds, Jefferson won the game, and anybody who'd watched it would have had to see that Stegman Miles wasn't half the baller C.C. Cooper was.

Which C.C. would have gone on to prove, in both college and the pros, over and over again, had he not gotten himself shot, three weeks into his senior year at Jeff. He'd made a dumb mistake, let his boys talk him into trying to jack a Mexican ice cream vendor who, it turned out, liked to keep a nine on a shelf right beneath the service window of his truck, and that was the end of C.C.'s career. The bullet hit him just below his right kneecap and blew his leg up, left just enough muscle and bone behind for the doctors to sew back together.

Becoming a pro baller was the only ambition C.C. had ever known, and once it went away, so did any effort he might have made to stay out of trouble with the law. He'd always had an appreciation for the thug life and probably would have continued down that road no matter what; some things, even money couldn't change. But it seemed to C.C. that a nigga with a limp who barely qualified for a job busing dishes had no other choice but to be a gangster. You wanted to survive, to enjoy even the smallest taste of the good life, you had to take what the world didn't give you. So that's what C.C. did, finding only fleeting relief from his constant pain and outrage in boning, getting high, and scoring a few dollars here and there by committing petty crimes.

Meanwhile, Miracle Miles was becoming an American sports icon, collecting diamond-studded championship rings and million-dollar endorsement checks the way C.C. collected court appearances. He was flashy, he was upbeat, and he was a winner, just the kind of harmless black man white folks loved to idolize. As the years went by, C.C. watched him grow bigger and bigger, fame and bank account inflating in tandem like goddamn blimps threatening to black out the sky, and smoldered with resentment. It should have been him. Everything Miracle had should have belonged to C.C.

He had hoped it would all end when Miracle's playing days were over, that in retirement the nigga would blow all his bank and dwindle down to a fat, forgotten has-been, just as so many ex-athletes had before him. But to C.C.'s amazement, only the reverse occurred. Rather than kick back and party when he quit the game, Miracle simply moved on to a new one: big business. He took the money he made in ball and invested it in real estate, showing more smarts for retail development than he had for basketball, and hell if the punk didn't become phatter than ever. Now he was getting paid not to shoot the rock and smile on billboards, but to write books and give lectures, teach Fortune 500 CEOs how to do on Wall Street what he used to do on the court.

C.C.'s mother, the crazy bitch, had even bought him one of Miracle's books as a birthday present last month, thinking it would inspire him to get a job and straighten up. "The Miracle Rule Book" the shit was called; "How to Win in Business Without Having to Foul." C.C. would have died laughing if he hadn't been so pissed. He threw the book across the living room after unwrapping it and didn't look at it again for four days. Then he picked it up, took it out to the back yard to trash it, and started reading it instead. He could read when he wanted to, he wasn't as illiterate as people thought, and now he wanted to. In spite of his hatred for the man, he was curious: Was there really anything Miracles Miles could tell him about making coin he didn't already know?

In the end, the answer was no. It was the same old shit C.C. had heard a million times before, *you gotta spend money to make money, study the market, timing is everything,* yadda-yadda-yadda. And of course, it was all delivered as one big basketball metaphor, Miracle offering the reader his own personal "rules of the game" as if putting mini-mall development deals together and makin' a no-look pass on the fast break were one and the same fucking thing. C.C. got as far as Chapter Three, then slammed the book shut and tossed it under his bed like a dirty sock, never to be thought of again.

Until moments like this one, anyway, when Miracle Miles was in the news again and there was no place on Earth a nigga could go to avoid hearin' about it. Here he was on ESPN—*ESPN!*— breaking ground at the site of his latest inner-city L.A. shopping center project, flashing teeth at the camera like a goddamn car salesman. Yeah, he was bringing name-brand retail stores to the community, but it wasn't the community he was thinkin' about. It was all the duckets he was gonna make in the process, same as always. Why was C.C. the only person in the world who could see through this fool?

"I'm gonna go over to Lottie's," Caprice said, getting up from her chair in the apartment's little dining room.

"Nah," C.C. said, still watching the television.

"What you mean, 'nah'?"

"I mean you ain't goin'. Soon as this is over, we gonna get busy."

Caprice sighed and sat back down, too experienced in the ways of her man to argue with him. "Why don't you turn it off now, then? You hate Miracle so bad, why you wanna keep watchin' it?"

" 'Cause it's givin' me an idea."

"What—"

"Shut up and get your ass to the bedroom," C.C. said, reaching for the remote to kill the TV. Behind him, Caprice stood up and left the room, sulking in well-advised silence. She didn't need to know nothin' yet, but when he was ready, C.C. would tell the bitch what he was thinkin'.

She wouldn't like it, bein' a Miracle Miles fan and all, but she was gonna help him fuck the nigga up all the same.

The first thing Jerry Dunston did upon hearing that Butterby's was about to go into business with Miracle Miles was buy a basketball. It was the first one he'd ever owned and would almost certainly be the last. Jerry hated sports in general, and basketball in particular; any game overpopulated by dope-smoking, tattoo-wearing, inarticulate black guys who made more money in an hour than Jerry made in a month was not his idea of entertainment.

Butterby's was one of the largest restaurant chains in the western United States and Jerry was their rising star, a franchise salesman only three years out of Stanford whose gift for gab seemed to be adaptable to any need. Nobody could fake interest in something he actually found thoroughly irrelevant or, worse, most suitable for morons, better than he. Jerry would walk into a conference room, chat like a giddy authority on whatever subject was most likely to be near and dear to a client's heart, and then walk out again, usually with the mesmerized client's money and misplaced affection firmly in hand. If a viper could change colors like a chameleon, his manager Lou Merrill was fond of saying, that would be Jerry.

But feigning common interests with prospective clients and business partners was not Jerry Dunston's only patented sales tactic. He also played some tricks of the trade that Lou would not have found quite so amusing, as sensitive to outdated matters of ethics as the old fool was. For one thing, Jerry liked to tweak spreadsheets to exaggerate both Butterby's sales figures and the demographic breakdown of its customer base, the latter to better meet a client's likely priorities. If, for example, a client was looking for Butterby's to appeal to a younger crowd, Jerry would fudge the numbers to lend that appearance. Further, he had learned to commit the fraud in such a way that, if caught, he could write the discrepancy off as a software glitch, an innocent mistake that could easily be corrected by pulling the offending report again. It was risky, but almost always worthwhile, and he reserved its use in any case for those clients he had judged to be either too green or too dense to catch on.

In his earliest dealings with Miracle Miles's people, Jerry had run this numbers game, confident that they wouldn't know the difference. Harvard-educated or no, they were underlings to a former jock, a man to whom Butterby's was only giving the time of day because of the incredible name recognition he'd created by doing spectacular things with a basketball over a twelve-year career. How sophisticated could they really be? And as for Miles himself, he was smart, sure; he had to be to have come this far in the dog-eat-dog commercial real estate game. But this idea some people had that he was a genius, a natural-born businessman with a mind on a par with those of all but a few Fortune 500 CEOs, was a crock. Miles was a likable college dropout with deep pockets and fortuitous instincts, nothing more and nothing less.

In any case, it was Miles's practice to let his people do all the heavy lifting, only inserting himself into negotiations when it was time to parry over the small details. Hence, following months of discussion, and weeks after a tentative agreement between Butterby's and Miraculous Enterprises, Inc., had been reached to bring Miracle Miles–branded Butterby's restaurants to various inner-city locations on the west coast, Jerry was going to meet the man himself for the first time today. His fellows at Butterby's were beside themselves with excitement, but Jerry couldn't care less;

were it his decision to make, he wouldn't be doing business with Miles at all. So what if Miles needed partnerships with franchises like Butterby's to get retail centers built in underserved urban areas? Butterby's was in business to make money, not revitalize the ghetto.

Still, a sale was a sale, and it was incumbent upon Jerry now to close this one with a bang. Asking Miles to autograph a basketball just before the meeting commenced was his idea of kissing the man's ass to maximum effect. He could have just bought a cheap rubber job at a local sporting goods store for fifteen bucks, but what he did instead was go online to drop $400 on an official game ball Miles had already signed. It wasn't enough for Jerry to appear to be a casual fan; he wanted Miles to think he was a fanatical one.

And hell if Miles didn't grin like a fool when Jerry popped the question in the Butterby's conference room, thrusting the ball and a Sharpie toward him. These jocks ate up public adulation the same way they snorted cocaine, Jerry thought; getting on their good side was as easy as teaching a smart dog to sit. Lou Merrill and Dan Kuramura, the other Butterby's execs in the room, looked on almost incredulously, having never seen Jerry exhibit the slightest interest in basketball before, but neither man said a word.

"I feel silly as hell doing this," Jerry said, gushing, "but I can't help it. If you could write something personally to me on this, Miracle, I'd really appreciate it."

Miles laughed, genuinely amused, and took the ball. "No problem. What's your name?"

"Jerry Dunston," Arvin Petrie said. A young, no-nonsense black man with the pinched, narrow face of a prosecuting attorney, Petrie was the Miraculous Enterprises exec with whom Jerry had been negotiating up to now.

Miles gave Petrie a look and raised an eyebrow. "This is our boy Jerry?"

Petrie nodded.

"Well, damn," Miles said, turning his famous megawatt smile upon Jerry again. "This will really be my pleasure."

Jerry didn't understand what he meant, but he didn't bother asking him to explain; if for some reason Petrie had been talking Jerry up earlier, that was all to the better. He watched Miles use the Sharpie to scrawl something unintelligible on the basketball, just above his signature, then took it back when it was offered.

"'Y-F-W-T-W-N'? What's that mean?" Jerry asked, curious.

But before Miles could answer, Petrie said, "I think we'd better get started," directing the comment at Lou Merrill, and Jerry's manager agreed with a nod.

They all took their seats at the conference table and got down to business. For nearly an hour, nothing seemed amiss, all the conversation following the predictable formalities of a major deal closing. But then the moment came to ink the contracts and things took an unexpected turn. Petrie intercepted the paperwork as Lou Merrill tried to pass it over to Miles, the expression on his face reaching even greater depths of solemnity, and said, "There's just one small amendment that'll need to be made here before Mr. Miles signs off."

Lou couldn't believe he was hearing right. He looked first to Miles for help, then to Jerry, but the former was unresponsive and the latter could only shrug.

"I don't understand."

Off a nod from Miles, Petrie produced a folder from his briefcase and slid it across the table toward the Butterby's V.P.

"Back in my playing days," Miles said, "I learned to do something that I've carried over to my business practice. Before every road game in the playoffs, I'd dribble a ball all around the court, looking for dead spots in the floor. 'Cause if you hit one during a crucial part of the game, if could really mess you up, create a turnover you couldn't recover from." He turned to look directly at Jerry. "Gentlemen, I'm afraid you've got a dead spot on your floor."

Lou Merrill opened the folder Petrie had passed him and began scanning the pages within, his face growing more grim by the minute.

"What's going on?" Jerry asked, annoyed.

"I'm sure you must be wondering how my people got hold of deal memos that could only have come from Mr. Dunston's computer," Miles said to Lou, ignoring Jerry's question completely. "But all I'll say in response to that is that we have our resources, and what they were in this case should be irrelevant to you. The only thing you should really care about is what those memos prove about Mr. Dunston's apparent reluctance to treat all your clients and partners equally, and what Butterby's stands to lose if you allow him to continue working for you."

"I said, what hell is going on?" Jerry asked again, leaping to his feet now. His shirt collar was soaked through with sweat.

Looking like a widower at his wife's funeral, Lou slid the folder of documents off to one side to let Dan Kuramura look them over and said to Jerry, "He's right. You've been juicing our numbers."

"What? That's crazy!"

Jerry reached across the table to snatch the documents out of Kuramura's grasp and started examining them himself. It was impossible, but he recognized them immediately, and all at once, the blood pounding through his head grew still.

"These are fakes," he said feebly. "There's no way—"

"We can't tell you who you can or cannot employ, of course," Petrie said, and Jerry looked over to see that both he and Miles were on their feet now, essentially calling the meeting to a close, "but we can take Mr. Miles's offer to partner with you off the table if Mr. Dunston is still drawing a Butterby's paycheck by the end of business day this Friday. It's entirely up to you."

And without another word, he and Miles started for the door.

On their way out, Miles peeled off to approach Jerry, who like a whipped dog involuntarily withdrew, not at all sure the man was above putting his fist through Jerry's face.

"You fucked with the wrong nigga," Miles whispered in his ear, winking. Then he flashed a particularly wicked version of his trademark smile and led Petrie out.

Hours later, sitting in a Butterby's executive office he could no longer call his own, Jerry was wondering how much of his $400 he could get back for the worthless basketball Miles had inscribed with the letters "YFWTWN" when the acronym suddenly made sense. Whether or not a "genius" lurked behind the House Negro effervescence of Miracle Miles, Jerry still couldn't say, but he knew for certain now that a killer most certainly did.

"I don't wanna do this," Caprice said again, for what had to be the ten-thousandth time, and C.C. had to give the girl props for courage, because the last time she'd said it, he'd almost taken her fool head off.

"I'm gonna tell you one last time: Ain't nobody gonna hurt 'im," C.C. said.

"If somethin' goes wrong—"

"Ain't nothin' gonna go wrong. Long as you do exactly what I tol' you, ain't nothin' gonna go wrong."

Caprice didn't say anything more, but the pitiful look on her face said it was going to take an act of God to convince her. C.C. was planning to rob Miracle Miles at gunpoint tonight outside a Hollywood bookstore, using Caprice as bait, and even a high school dropout like Caprice knew how often things like that ended up with somebody getting killed.

Still, help C.C. she would because the alternative was to get beat so bad she'd probably wish she were dead herself. Her role in the plan as C.C. described it was fairly simple. Miracle never went anywhere alone, C.C. said; a bodyguard and a driver, at least, always accompanied Miracle to such events. The bodyguard would follow Miracle inside and stay with him during the signing, but the driver would likely stay out in the parking lot with the car. Caprice's job was to distract the driver just long enough for C.C. to slip inside the car only moments before Miracle was about to return to it. C.C. would quickly relieve the surprised fool of his cash on hand and jet, neither Miracle's driver nor his bodyguard wanting to try fucking with a man with a gun in the close confines of a limo. And Caprice? By the time the police or anybody else put her and C.C. together, he said, they'd both be long gone.

During the drive out to Hollywood, spilling all out of her best black dress like a whore with a rent bill due, Caprice practiced her controlled breathing and asked God to watch over them both.

C.C. was usually late for everything but this time they were early, arriving at the store over an hour before Miles was scheduled to start signing books. Still, a crowd was already forming inside and Caprice could feel her stomach lurching around like a bouncing waterbed.

"Why we gotta get her so early?"

"'Cause I wanna see who the nigga has with 'im and where his car's gonna be."

"But what're we supposed to do 'til he's ready to leave?"

"Same thing everybody else'll be doin'. Lookin' at books."

"We're goin' *inside*?"

C.C. glared at her. "I shouldn't have'ta explain my reasonin' to you, Caprice. And if I didn't need you lookin' good tonight, I'd slap you in your mouth just for askin' me to. We're goin' inside 'cause we gotta know when he's gettin' ready to come out, remember? This thing's gotta be timed just right or it won't work. All right? You understand now?"

She did, but she didn't like it. The whole thing was beginning to sound crazier and crazier to her.

Caprice entered the store a few minutes later, alone, as C.C. stayed outside to wait for Miles to show. She had almost a half hour to kill, a packed house filling the space around her at an alarming rate, and she could only feign interest for so long in books whose titles she could barely read. She became increasingly certain that one of the staff, a middle-aged white man with the face and form of a scarecrow, was watching her intently, his right hand at the ready to grab the phone and call for security. She was about to flee, desperate for C.C.'s assurances that her fears were all in her head, when the celebrity they'd all been waiting for finally appeared.

Caprice heard a murmur from the crowd build to a dull roar and when she turned around, there he was, Miracle himself, walking through the door like a king entering his throne room. He was bigger than she could have ever imagined, towering over everyone as he slowly made his way to the table piled high with books that awaited him in the back, and his broad-shouldered, pale yellow suit fit his chiseled body with mouth-watering precision. He was smiling, of course, turning this way and that so that no one went untouched by his good cheer, and he even bumped fists with a few lucky people in the crowd.

Swooning, Caprice put a hand out to the wall beside her to keep herself from fainting.

Miracle finally reached his place at the table and sat down, and only then did Caprice notice that, just as C.C. had predicted, he wasn't alone. A brother as big and impenetrable as a cinder block wall had come in with him, his face a humorless etching in stone. Standing now at Miracle's left shoulder as Miracle chatted up the store's manager, the big man stared straight ahead and crossed his hands in front of him, waiting for a reason to defend his employer to the death.

The sight of this giant brought Caprice back to reality with a thud and, remembering why she was here, she glanced over her shoulder to find C.C. standing at the tail end of the crowd, just inside the door. He smiled as if to say all was well and then gave his head an almost imperceptible shake, warning her off any further eye contact. Caprice turned back around, heart in her throat, and pretended to listen as the impish blond book store manager introduced Miracle Miles to his audience.

When she was done, the room erupted in applause and Miles began to talk about his book, selling it the way he sold everything else, with large doses of homespun charm and self-effacing humor. Any other time, Caprice would have been enthralled, but not tonight; tonight she was busy trying to keep her dinner from climbing back up into her throat. She liked this man. She admired this man. He was a hero to her, just as he was to thousands of other people, black and white. But in less than an hour's time, if she valued her life, she was going to help C.C. jack him for all the money on his person.

Or worse.

It was the "or worse" part that Caprice ultimately couldn't stop worring over, because nothing ever came easy to Curtis "C.C." Charles and she couldn't imagine why this wack scheme of his should be any different. If it blew up in his face and Miles got killed somehow, Caprice knew she'd never be able to live with the guilt. She'd done a lot of fucked-up things in her life, to be sure, but she wasn't a bad person. Asking her to help him commit a crime that could wind up being the murder of a great man like Miracle Miles was more than C.C. had a right to do. No matter how much she loved him, and God knew she did love his pitiful ass, Caprice didn't owe C.C. as much as all this.

Emboldened by some power she didn't understand, she turned around and started to march out of the store.

Miles was still speaking but heads turned toward her all the same, so conspicuous was her desperation to depart. She didn't have to look at him to know that C.C. was staring daggers at her. Nonetheless, she kept her head down and kept moving, not stopping until the inevitable happened.

"Where the fuck you think you're goin'?" C.C. hissed at her under his breath, his right hand like a vise on her arm. Only the handful of people in their vicinity were paying them any attention so far, but if C.C. started to lose it, the star of this show would immediately cease to be Miracle Miles.

"I can't do it. Lemme go," Caprice pleaded.

"You're gonna do it or I'm gonna kill you. Understand? You're dead."

For all his past crimes against her, he had never actually threatened her life before, and the precedent caused her to groan out-loud, heartbroken. The pitiful sound again made her the central focus of the house, and this time the people eyeing her included Miles himself.

"You all right back there?"

C.C.'s hand fell away from Caprice's arm and he stepped back, leaving Caprice to answer the question for herself.

She turned and, somehow finding the will to smile, said, "Oh, yeah. I just need a little air, is all."

Before C.C. could stop her, she pushed past him to rush out the door.

He stood there for a brief moment, absorbing the singular gaze of what had to be over 150 people, Miracle Miles being the most openly analytical, and then shrugged, like this kind of innocent shit happened between he and his woman all the time.

"I better go check on her," he said, before slinking out the door like a tired old man.

C.C. thought sure Caprice was gone, but she was outside in the parking lot, shivering with fear and cold when he came around the corner to look for her.

Both of his hands were balled into fists, he didn't have enough self-control to prevent that, but he was strong enough to keep them at his sides as he closed on her.

"Please, C.C. Don't make me," she pleaded.

"You got one more chance." He gave her a brief glimpse of the revolver under the tail of his shirt, shoved down into the waistband of his pants. "I hear another word of argument out of your ass and I'll whack you right now, I ain't playin'."

"But he seen us together now! How—"

"So he seen us. So what? Don't nobody in that store know either one of us. Even if they know we're together now, it ain't gonna help 'em find us after we jet, is it? Huh?"

He'd already thought it all through, just in the short space of time between Caprice's exit from the store and this moment, and he had convinced himself it was true. It would have been better if no one had paid either one them any mind, especially Miracle Miles, but C.C. could still jack Miles as planned without getting busted because he remained as anonymous as ever. The last time he and Miles had met was sixteen years ago. So what if Miles had seen his face?

"That's the nigga's car right there," C.C. said, nodding his head at a long white Lincoln limousine sitting in the middle of the bookstore's parking lot. "His driver's inside, listenin' to music, I think. You go on over there and start workin' his ass while I go back in the store and wait for Miles to finish.

"When I come back out here, I want that ride open and that driver off in a corner somewheres, I don't care how you get 'im there. You got that?"

Caprice hesitated, riding the last of her courage to its very end, and then silently nodded her head.

Bored damn near to tears, C.C. listened to Miracle Miles read for fifteen minutes from the book C.C.'s mother had given him for his birthday, once again standing at the front of the store close to the door, and almost gave it up. What a game Miles was running on these fools. He had a rule for this and a rule for that, do's and don'ts that were supposed to turn losers into winners every time, and it was all bullshit. Every word. Miracle Miles was a 'baller, nothing more and nothing less, and what he had to teach anybody about getting ahead in life wasn't worth the paper his "expert" advice was written on.

C.C. was so disgusted by Miles and the gullibility of his enraptured audience, he hadn't noticed that Miles's bodyguard was no longer standing at his elbow until somebody behind him said, "Come on outside with me, nigga," blowing the words into his right ear like a breathless lover.

The security man was pressed up against C.C.'s back, holding a nine down low where only C.C. could see it.

"And we don't want no drama, do we?"

C.C. thought about drawing his own piece, taking his chances in an all-out shoot-out, innocent bystanders be damned, but this was a short-lived temptation. Badass gangsta that he was, C.C.

discovered with some embarrassment that he wasn't quite ready to die.

The bodyguard guided him out, no one taking notice of them, and used the nine to steer him over to the white limo idling in the parking lot. C.C. looked around for some sign of Caprice, but she was nowhere in sight. Neither was she in the car when the bodyguard opened the back door for him and said, "Get in."

C.C. did as he was told and the man with the gun eased in after him, taking a seat across from C.C. before closing the door behind them. Over the bodyguard's right shoulder, on the other side of a smoked-glass partition, C.C. could see Miles's driver sitting behind the limo's wheel. Alone.

"If you're lookin' for your girl, we sent her home," Miles's boy said, proving himself fully capable of smiling when the mood moved him. He held out an open palm, careful to keep the semi-automatic in his other hand trained on C.C.'s chest. "Let's have the piece. Careful."

C.C. gave him his revolver, too stunned and disoriented now to do anything else. What the hell was happening?

He got his answer a few minutes later when Miles joined them in the car, looking as happy and imperturbable as ever. He sat down next to his bodyguard, tapped on the glass behind his head, and the limo began to move.

"What the fuck's goin' on?" C.C. asked, unable to keep his growing sense of panic from creeping into his voice.

Miles just grinned at him. "Come on, C.C. Don't play dumb. You was getting' ready to fuck me up, same as you did in the State Finals back in '93. Ain't that right?"

C.C.'s jaw dropped. Miles knew who he was. How in the hell was that possible?

Miles took C.C.'s revolver from his bodyguard and rolled it

around in his hands, looking it over with some amusement. "You were bad news then, and you look like bad news now. Wasn't hard to guess you hadn't come out here to get a book signed."

"Look here . . ." C.C. said, trying to generate something, anything, that sounded like a fully grown man's courage in the face of certain danger.

"I know what you think. Miracle Miles ain't nothin' but a pretty face. I punked 'im once, ought'a be easy to punk again, right?" He shook his head, and suddenly the expression on the man's face was very un-Miraclelike. "Uh-uh. I grew up on the street, same as you, brother. Only worse. Princeton Heights, Oakaland, Cali, baddest fuckin' 'hood on the face of the earth. I could'a never got out'a there alive if I wasn't harder than any gangsta you'll ever know. You'd read my book, you would've understood that."

Fuck your book, C.C. thought to himself, but he didn't say it out loud because something had changed in Miles he didn't like. Something that made him genuinely afraid that the mistake he'd made tonight might cost him something more than another meaningless stretch in the pen.

"What you want me to do with him?" his bodyguard asked Miles.

"You? Nothin'," Miles said. And then he looked over at C.C. again, still flipping C.C.'s revolver around in both of his hands. "I got this one."

The following night, lying dead in a vacant field out in the wastelands of Sunland, months before his body was discovered and his murder written off as the inevitable result of a life misspent on crime, C.C. wasn't around to sit in on Miracle Miles's next book signing. And that was a shame. Because, if he had been, he might have heard something that would have explained how he had come to meet his cruel fate, and how the total sum of two pages in a book had probably made the difference between his meeting and avoiding it.

Finding it somehow fitting, Miles on this night regaled his adoring fans with a sampling from Chapter Three of "The Miracle Rule Book," unwittingly choosing to start reading less than a hundred words from the spot where C.C., too overcome by jealousy and hatred for his old high school nemesis to go on, had chosen to stop.

"'Rule number four,'" Miracle read, "is *Never forget a beatdown.*" The conventional wisdom says when you suffer a significant loss, you should put everything about it behind you and move on. But I don't agree. I think it's just as important to remember a crushing defeat as it is a huge victory, because you can use the pain of the former as motivation to succeed for the rest of your life. This is why I've always made it a point to remember everything about a major loss, including the names and faces of the people responsible for it. They may not know it, but I've had my revenge against them a thousand times over the years, even if it was only in my mind."

And to punctuate his point, Miles did what everyone here had hoped to see him do more than anything else in the world: laugh.

ALICE RUTH MOORE DUNBAR-NELSON (1875–1935) was born in New Orleans, the daughter of a seaman and a seamstress. After completing a two-year teacher-training program at Straight University, now part of Dillard University in New Orleans, she continued her studies at Cornell, the Pennsylvania School of Industrial Art, and the University of Pennsylvania. She taught at the elementary, secondary, and university levels until 1931.

When she was only 20, she published *Violets and Other Tales* (1895), a small collection of stories, poems, and essays. Three years later, she married Paul Laurence Dunbar, one of the most influential African-American writers of the nineteenth and early twentieth centuries; they separated four years later, partly because he was upset about her lesbian affairs. She published *The Goodness of St. Rocque and Other Stories* in 1899; it is generally regarded as the first short-story collection by an African-American woman.

While not regarded as one of the major figures of the Harlem Renaissance for her own work, she was a major influence on other black writers of the period because of her own very precise literary style and through her essays and prolific reviews of such significant novelists and poets as W.E.B. Du Bois and Langston Hughes. In addition to her numerous poems and short stories, she also wrote an autobiography, *Give Us Each Day*, which was not published until 1984.

"Summer Session" remained unpublished during the author's lifetime, first seeing the light of day in *The Works of Alice Dunbar-Nelson, Vol. 1*, edited by Gloria T. Hull, 1988.

Summer Session

Alice Dunbar-Nelson

"You were flirting with him!"

"I was not. I don't know how to flirt."

"So you say, but you can put up a pretty good imitation."

"You're mistaken."

"I am not. And a man you never saw before in your life. And a common taxi driver."

"He's not a common taxi driver."

"How do you know?"

"I just know."

"Strange exchange of intimacies for the first meeting."

"I tell you—"

"Shut up!"

"I won't shut up, and don't you dare tell me that again!"

There was a warning note in her usually gentle voice; an ominous tightening of her soft lips; a steely glint in her violet eyes. Logan heeded the warning and sat in grim silence, while Elise ground gears and otherwise mishandled her little car through the snarled traffic of Amsterdam Avenue.

"You told me 114th Street, and I waited for you there for a half hour, and I got jammed in the traffic and things went wrong, and this young man got out of his taxi, and straightened me out. And while I waited for you he just stayed and talked."

"To your delight."

"What was I to do? Push him away from the running board? I was standing still, and I couldn't drive away since I was waiting for you."

"I told you 115th Street, and there I stood on the corner in the broiling sun for a half hour, while you were carrying on a flirtation with a taxi driver, until I walked back, thinking you might have had an accident."

"Don't you say flirtation to me again. You said 114th Street. You never speak plain over the telephone anyhow."

"Anything else wrong with me since you've met your new friend—the Taxi Adonis?"

Elise brought the car to a grinding, screeching pause in front of the movie house which was their objective. They sat through the two hours of feature and news and cartoons and comedy and prevues in stony silence. They ate a grim meal together in the usual cafeteria, and she set him down at the men's dormitory of the university in the same polite and frigid silence. Logan glanced at her now and then just a trifle apprehensively. He had never seen just this trace of hardness in her, like the glint of unexpected steel beneath soft chiffon. But his manly dignity would not permit him to unbend. He answered her cold good night with one as cold, and for the first time in that summer session, during which they had grown to know and like one another, they parted without making a future date.

He waited for her next day at luncheon hour, as she came from her class with a half-dozen other chattering summer-school teacher-students. His manner was graciously condescending.

"Shall we have luncheon together?" Lordly and superior as usual.

She flashed her usual violet-eyed smile of delight, but he felt, rather than saw, that the smile did not quite reach the eyes; that the violets were touched as by premature frost.

"What I can't quite understand," he pursued, after he had brought her tray, deftly removed the salad, tea, and crackers, and placed the tray behind the next chair, "is, if you are skillful enough to drive from Portland, Maine, to New York alone and without disaster, how you can get mixed up in a mere traffic jam on Amsterdam Avenue, and have to have a taxi driver get you out."

Elise's brows went up at the awkward English, so at variance with his usual meticulous and precise phrasing, and a haunting query clouded her eyes. Logan quenched an embarrassed "Hem" in iced tea.

"I did not drive from Portland," was her final response. "I came from my own town, twenty-seven miles beyond Portland."

There was no particular reason for Elise's driving down Amsterdam Avenue after classes that afternoon, but she did and a friendly red light brought her to a halt at 114th Street. Adonis—Logan's sneering cognomen stuck in her mind, and she realized with a guilty start how ruggedly applicable it was—stuck his face in her car window. Poppies suffused her cheeks and dewy violets swam in a sea of flame.

"All right?" he queried.

"Quite, thank you." The light was happily green, and she meshed her gears.

"What's the hurry?" He put a protesting hand on the wheel.

"I have an engagement!" She sped away frantically. Adonis whistled at the wabbling career of her little coupe down the street.

She saw him just ahead of her in the cafeteria line next evening at dinnertime. She reached for her tray with hands that insisted upon trembling, though she shook them angrily. He smiled daringly back at her. He was even handsomer out of his taxi uniform than in it, and the absence of the cap revealed crisp auburn curls of undoubted pugnaciousness.

"You get a seat, I'll bring your dinner."

"But I—"

"Go on—"

There was a difference between Adonis' ordering of her movements and that of Logan's. A sureness of merry audacity against prim didacticism. She sat at a window table and meekly arranged silver and napkins.

"But I could never eat all that," she protested at the tray, "beef and potatoes and—and—all that food."

"I knew that's what's the trouble—diet of salads and seed tea and crackers, mentally, spiritually, physically."

Elise ate roast beef and corn on the cob and pie à la mode and laughed at Adonis' jokes, and his whimsical descriptions of man and his appetites. Over their cigarettes she chuckled at his deft characterizations of their fellow diners.

"Eat hay and think hay," he was saying, "thin diets and thin souls. You need a red-blooded chap like me to make you eat food, put flesh on your bones, and reconstruct your thinking from New England inhibitions to New York acceptance and enjoyment of life."

Elise's world rocked. School principals used muddled English. Taxi drivers talked like college professors.

Adonis paused and regarded something on his shoulder as if it were a tarantula. Logan's hand quivered in rage, and veins stood up on its pallor "like long blue whips," Elise found herself thinking.

"Aren't you taking a lot of liberties with a young lady to whom you've not been introduced?" snarled the owner of pallor and veins.

Adonis brushed off the hand and the remark with a careless gesture. He arose and bowed elaborately. "Miss Stone and I have been introduced, thank you, by ourselves—and you?"

Elise looked perilously near tears, "Oh, er—Logan—Mr. Long—this is—er—Mr. McShane."

Logan looked stonily through Adonis, "I don't accept introductions to taxi drivers, even if you do eat with them, Elise."

"Oh, please—" she began.

"That's all right." Adonis gathered up the checks. "Just let me settle this with the cashier, and then if you don't mind, we'll go outside, and settle the physical difference between a taxi driver and—" He did not finish the sentence, but the sinister drawl and contemptuous pause made Elise's scalp prickle with shame for Logan.

"You would suggest a common brawl; quite true to type. I hope, Elise, you have seen enough of such ruffianly conduct to be satisfied."

"Quite the contrary," she answered coolly, "I am going out with Mr. McShane in his taxi." It was pure spite, and she had a sinking feeling that she might not be wanted.

"Terry to you," he retorted, "and let's be going. We've got a busy evening before us."

Logan was beside them on the sidewalk, blocking the way to the taxi parked at the curb.

"Elise, don't be a fool." He grasped her arm and wrenched it, so that she gave an involuntary cry of pain. Terence McShane's next three moves were so violently consecutive as to seem simultaneous. His right hand caught Logan neatly on the point of the chin, so that he went down with amazing swiftness; his left encircled Elise's waist and lifted her into the taxi, and both hands swung the machine with a roar and sputter in the general direction of the Washington Bridge.

"But you're losing fares," Elise protested.

"Nonsense. If you can stand this bumpety-bump, what's the dif?"

"It's entrancing," she murmured at the river, the sky, the stars, the electric signs on the Jersey shore, at Terry's hatless curls.

"Police call," the radio protested, "calling all police cars. Look out for taxi license Y327D. Driver abducted summer-school student. Watch for taxi. Arrest driver. Kidnapping charge."

From their leafy shelter, where somehow the taxi had parked itself—neither could have told when or how it stopped under those particularly umbrageous trees, they stared at the radio's accusing dial.

"Well, I'll be—" Terry swore softly. "What do you think of that worm putting in such a charge at headquarters?"

"Oh, Terry, you'll be arrested and put in jail!"

"Will you go to jail with me?"

"You know I will—oh, what am I saying?"

"Words of wisdom, me darlin'. Let's go. Anyhow I'm glad we didn't cross the bridge and get into Jersey."

Through circuitous ways and dark streets, avoiding police, taxis, inquisitive small boys and reporters on the loose, they drew up in front of police headquarters.

Elise sat demurely on a bench, and began to repair damages to her hair, complexion, and neck frills. The little pocket mirror wavered ever so slightly as Logan stood accusingly in front of her, but her eyes did not leave the scrutiny of their mirrored counterpart.

"A pretty mess you've made of your life and reputation," he thundered. "Your chances for any position in my school are gone."

Elise put back a refractory curl behind her ear, then tried it out on her cheek again, surveying it critically in the mirror.

"Won't you recommend me for a job, Mr. Principal, after I've studied so hard all summer?"

Terry's gales of unrestrained mirth at the desk made them both look up in amazement. Laughter rocked the walls of the station house, rolled out into the summer street. Captain and Sergeant and Lieutenant and just plain officers roared lustily, all save one quiet plainclothes man, who laid an iron grip on Logan's arm.

"Terence McShane, you were always the best detective in the city," roared the Captain. "And you made him bring himself right into our outstretched arms."

The iron grip on Logan's arm terminated into steel bracelets.

"Okeh, Longjim Webb, alias Prof. Logan Long, the school principal, looking the summer students over for teaching material in his consolidated upstate school, we'll give you a chance in the Big House to meditate on the law against white slavery."

"Your zeal to corral this particular choice bit of femininity made you throw caution to the winds," suggested Detective Terence McShane.

Incredulity, disgust, anger swept the violet eyes. Elise flared into Terry's face.

"You—you—pretending to be a taxi driver. You just used me for a decoy," she raged.

Terry held her protesting hands tight as he whispered below the hubbub of Logan's protestations.

"Never a bit of it, my dear. I loved you the first day you stalled your car in the thick of things on 125th Street, before you even saw me, and I got in the habit of following you around while I was impersonating a taxi driver, to get a chance to know you. Then when I found this"—a wave toward the still-voluble Logan—"had marked you for another one of his prey—well you don't mind if I combined a bit of business with my pleasure?"

Elise's faint "No" was visible, rather than audible.

"It's all right then? Shall it be beefsteak for two?"

"Yes."

"And you won't take back what you promised up there on the Drive?"

"How can I," she laughed, "when my middle name is McBride?"

WALTER ELLIS MOSLEY (1952–) was born in South Central Los Angeles, the son of an African-American father and a white Jewish mother. He attended Goddard College, received his B.A. from Johnson State College (1978), then attended the writing program at the City College of New York, (1985 to 1989); the school later gave him an honorary doctorate. He worked as a computer consultant and programmer, a potter and a caterer, before becoming a full-time writer in 1986.

With the publication of *Devil in a Blue Dress* (1990), Mosley introduced Ezekiel (Easy) Rawlins to readers, breaking fresh ground in the detective fiction field as it and subsequent books incorporated the issue of race and racism into genre fiction on a regular basis. Rawlins works as a private eye, though reluctantly, in the Watts section of Los Angeles. The first book is set soon after World War II and the series moves forward in history over the next ten volumes. Tough, occasionally violent, Easy wants a normal, decent life, as well as justice, though he is willing to walk a fine line just this side of criminal behavior. His best friend, Raymond Alexander, better known as Mouse, is almost pathologically willing to commit horrifically violent acts—even on occasion threatening Easy. The series has been extremely successful, frequently hitting the best-seller list. *Devil in a Blue Dress* was filmed in 1995 with Denzel Washington starring as Easy.

"Black Dog" was first published in *Always Outnumbered, Always Outgunned* (W. W. Norton, 1997) and was selected for *Best American Mystery Stories 1998*.

Black Dog

Walter Mosley

from *Always Outnumbered, Always Outgunned*

"How does your client plead, Ms. Marsh?" the pencil-faced judge asked. He was wearing a dark sports jacket that was a size or two too big for his bony frame.

"Not guilty, your honor," the young black lawyer said, gesturing with her fingers pressed tightly together and using equally her lips, tongue, and teeth.

"Fine." The judge had been distracted by something on his desk. "Bail will be . . ."

"Your honor," spoke up the prosecutor, a chubby man who was the color of a cup of coffee with too much milk mixed in. "Before you decide on bail the people would like to have it pointed out that Mr. Fortlow is a convicted felon. He was found guilty of a double homicide in Indiana in nineteen sixty and was sentenced to life in that state; he spent almost thirty years in prison."

"Twenty-seven years, your honor," Brenda Marsh articulated.

So much respect, so much honor, Socrates Fortlow thought. A harsh laugh escaped his lips.

"And," Brenda Marsh continued. "He's been leading a respectable life here in Los Angeles for the past eight years. He's employed full-time by Bounty Supermarket and he hasn't had any other negative involvement with the law."

"Still, your honor," the bulbous Negro said, "Mr. Fortlow is being tried for a violent crime—"

"But he hasn't been convicted," said Ms. Marsh.

"Regardless," said the nameless prosecutor.

"Your honor . . ."

The Honorable Felix Fisk tore his eyes away from whatever had been distracting him. Socrates thought it was probably a picture magazine; probably about yachting, Socrates thought. He knew from his days in prison, that many judges got rich off of the blood of felons.

"All right," Judge Fisk said. "All right. Let's see."

He fumbled around with some papers and produced a pair of glasses from the top of his head. He peered closely at whatever was written and then regarded the bulky ex-con.

"My, my," the judge muttered.

Socrates felt hair growing in his windpipe.

"The people would like to see Mr. Fortlow held without bail, your honor," chubby said.

"Your honor." Ms. Marsh's pleading didn't seem to fit with her overly precise enunciation. "Eight years and there was no serious injury."

"Intent," the prosecutor said, "informs the law."

"Twenty-five thousand dollars bail," the judge intoned.

A short brown guard next to Socrates grabbed the prisoner's beefy biceps and said, "Come on."

Socrates turned around and saw Dolly Straight at the back of the small courtroom. She had red hair and freckles, and a look of shock on her face. When her eyes caught Socrates' gaze she smiled and waved.

Then she ran out of the courtroom while still holding her hand high in greeting.

2

The night before there had been no room in the West L.A. jail so they put Socrates in a secured office for lockup. But now he was at the main courthouse. They took him to a cellblock in the basement crammed with more than a dozen prisoners. Most of them were tattooed; one had scars so violent that he could have been arrested and jailed simply because of how terrible he appeared.

Mostly young men; mostly black and Latino. There were a couple of whites by themselves in a corner at the back of the cell. Socrates wondered what those white men had done to be put in jeopardy like that.

"Hey, brother," a bearded man with an empty eye socket said to Socrates.

Socrates nodded.

"Hey, niggah," said a big, black, baby-faced man who stood next to the bearded one. "Cain't you talk?"

Socrates didn't say anything. He went past the men toward an empty spot on a bench next to a stone-faced Mexican.

"Niggah!" the baby face said again.

He laid a hand, not gently, on Socrates' shoulder. But Babyface hesitated. He felt, Socrates knew, the strength in that old shoulder. And in that brief moment Socrates shot out his left hand to grab the young man's throat. The man threw a fist but Socrates caught that with his right hand while increasing the pressure in his left.

The boy's eyes bulged and he went down on his knees as

Socrates stood up. First Babyface tried to dislodge the big fist from his throat, then he tried slugging Socrates' arm and side.

While he was dying the men stood around.

Sounds like the snapping of brittle twigs came from the boy's throat.

His dying eyes flitted from one prisoner to another but no one moved to help him.

A few seconds before the boy would have lost consciousness, no more than fifteen seconds before he'd've died, Socrates let go.

The boy sucked in a breath of life so deep and so hoarse that a guard came down to see what was happening.

Some of the men were laughing.

"What's goin' on?" the guard asked.

"I was just showin' the boy a trick," the big bearded Negro with one eye said.

The guard regarded the boy.

"You okay, Peters?"

There was no voice in Peters's throat but he nodded.

"Okay," the guard said. "Now cut it out down here."

Socrates took his place on the bench. The fight was just an initiation. Now everyone in the cell knew: Socrates was not a man to be taken lightly.

"Fortlow?" the same guard called out forty-five minutes later.

"Yo."

"Socrates Fortlow?"

"That's right." It hadn't been long but the feeling of freedom had already drained from Socrates' bones and flesh.

He'd checked out every man in the holding cell; witnessed one of the white men get beaten while his buddy backed away. He'd made up his mind to go against the bearded Negro, Benny Hite, if they remained in the cell together.

Benny was a leader and naturally wanted to hold everyone else down. But Socrates wouldn't go down for anyone and so there had to be blood before there could be sleep.

"Come with me," the guard said. He had two large policemen with him.

3

"Hi, Mr. Fortlow," Dolly Straight said. Her skin was pale under thousands of orange and brown freckles. "I posted your bail."

They'd given him his street clothes back but it was too late; the body lice, crabs, from the prison garb had already begun to make him itch.

"What you doin'?" he asked the young woman in front of the courthouse.

"I'm parked illegally up the block," she said, hurrying down the concrete stairs. "I didn't know it would take so long to give them the money and get you out."

Socrates tried to ask again, *why*, but Dolly kept running ahead of him.

"I hope they haven't towed it," she said.

Her pickup was from the fifties, a Dodge. It was sky-blue with a flatbed back that had an animal cage moored in the center.

"Come on," she said, taking the parking ticket from under the windshield wiper. "Get in."

"What's this all about?" Socrates asked as they made their way from downtown.

"I put up your bail." Dolly was redheaded, plain-faced, and she had green eyes that blazed. There were fans of tiny wrinkles around her eyes but she was no more than forty.

"What for?"

"Because of Bruno," she said as if it should have been obvious.

"Who's that?"

"The dog. That's what I called him. I mean you can't take care of somebody if he doesn't even have a name. Most of your best vets always name their patients if they don't get a name from the owners."

"Oh," Socrates said. He was wondering what to do with his liberation. Some men who'd spent as many years behind bars as Socrates had wanted to go back to jail; they liked the order that they found there.

"I'd rather be dead," he said.

'Excuse me?"

"Why'd you get me outta there?"

"Because," Dolly said. "Because I know what you did you did because of Bruno. He was almost dead when you brought him in to me. And when those policemen came to arrest you I just got mad. They think that they can just walk in anywhere."

He hadn't been looking for a fight. It was an early work day because he'd had to help with inventory at the supermarket and that started at four in the morning. He'd worked twelve hours and was tired. A dog, big and black, was nosing around, begging for food and Socrates told him to *git*. The dog got himself into the street and a speeding Nissan slammed him down. The man didn't even hit the brakes until after the accident.

Socrates was already to the dog when the white man backed up and parked. The poor dog was scrabbling with his front paws, trying to rise, and whining from the pain in his crushed hind legs.

Socrates just wanted to help. As far as he was concerned the white man broke his own nose.

"How you know why I did what I did?" Socrates asked Dolly.

"Because I went back to where you told me the accident happened. I wanted to find out if the owner was somewhere nearby. I thought that I'd have to put Bruno to sleep but I didn't want to do that until I talked to the owner.

"But there wasn't an owner. Bruno didn't have a home but I met an old lady who saw what happened. That's what I told your lawyer. You know I don't know if Miss Marsh would have gone down there or not. But I told her about Bruno and Mrs. Galesky and then she told me how I could put up your bail.

"I don't know if I'd want her for a lawyer, Mr. Fortlow."

"Why's that?"

"She was trying to tell me how you were a convicted felon and that this charge against you was tough and you might run if you could. Even after I told her that I knew that you were innocent. I thought you black people helped each other out?"

"Dog gonna live?" Socrates asked.

Dolly's face got harder and Socrates found himself liking her in spite of her youth and race.

"I don't know," she said. "His legs are broken and so's his hip. I don't even think they could do a replacement on a human hip that was that bad. His organs seem fine. No bleeding inside but he'll never use those legs again."

They drove on toward Dolly's Animal Clinic on Robertson near Olympic.

4

Bruno was a biggish dog, sixty pounds or more, and little of that was fat. He was unconscious in a big cage on an examining table in Dolly's clinic.

"I gave him a tranc," she said. "I don't like to do that but he was in so much pain and his crying bothered my other patients."

In a large room connected to the examining room Socrates could see rows of cages that ran from small to large. Most of the "patients" were dogs and cats fitted with casts or bandages or attached to odd machines. But there was also a monkey, three different kinds of birds, a goat, and something that looked like a tiny albino sloth.

"Would he die if you left him alone?" Socrates asked. It was ten o'clock or later. There was only him and Dolly in the small animal clinic. He realized that he was pinching the skin through his pants pockets and stopped.

"I don't know," Dolly said. "I don't think so. His vitals are strong. You'd have to get his bones set as well as possible and then keep him immobile for a couple of weeks. All that and he'd live. But he'd have to crawl."

"Anything's better than prison or death."

"You pick that up in the jail?" Dolly asked.

Socrates realized that he was scratching again.

"My dad used to get that, all the time," she said. "He was a political activist down San Diego in the sixties. I remember they'd bust up his protests and beat him until he had black blood coming out. But the only thing he ever complained about was getting crabs in jail. He used to say that they could at least keep it clean in there." She smiled a very plain smile and said, "I got some soap'll clear that up in two days."

Bruno whimpered in his cage.

"I'ma be in a cage if they put me down for assault," he said.

"But I gave your lawyer Mrs. Galesky's number. I'm sure she'll straighten it out."

"You are, huh?"

"Yeah." Dolly's homely smile was growing on him. "I got a house right in back here," she said. "You could stay in the guest bed."

5

Dolly heated apple cider spiced with cinnamon sticks. Then she made sandwiches out of alfalfa sprouts, grilled chicken, Gruyère cheese, and avocado. Socrates had four sandwiches and over a quart of cider.

Who knew when he'd be eating again?

Dolly had fed, petted, and talked to each patient and then led Socrates out of the back door of the clinic. There was a yard in back and a large flowering tree that was dark and sweet-smelling. Past the tree was a wooden fence. The gate in the fence opened to a beautiful little house.

"Nobody can ever see my house if I don't invite them," Dolly said to Socrates as she fumbled around for her keys. "I like that."

"Where's your father?" Socrates asked after supper. It was late, past midnight, and Dolly was folding out the bed in the living room.

"He died," she said. "He was always big and strong but then he just got old one year and passed away."

"Didn't he ever tell you about people like me?"

"He never knew anybody like you, Mr. Fortlow."

"How the hell you know what I'm like?" Socrates said belligerently. "Didn't you hear what they said about me in that courtroom?"

Dolly looked up.

With a stern gaze she said, "I know what you're thinking. You're thinking why would she take a man, a convicted murderer, and take him back here in her house? A man like that could rob me, rape me, kill me." Then her serious face turned into a smile. "But I don't have a choice so I can't be worried about it."

"What you mean you ain't got no choice?"

"Because my father died when I was only twelve and my mother just left," she said. "Because the only one who ever loved me was my dog, Buster. And the only thing I ever knew was how to love him and to take care of him. If I see anyone who cares about animals they're okay with me. I treat them like human beings."

"So you mean that anybody bring a hurt animal to you can sit at your table and sleep in your guest bed?"

"No," Dolly said. She was hurt.

"Then what do you mean?"

"I mean that a dog is a living being just like you'n me. It doesn't matter if there is a God or not. Life is what's important. You're not like one of those rich bitches that shave a dog like he was some kind of fuckin' hedge and then bring him to me so I could castrate him.

"You knocked a man down and then carried that big dog over a mile. You went to jail because that dog has a right. How can I look at that and not do all I can do for you?"

6

Socrates was up late in his foldout bed. It was an old couch and the bed was more comfortable than his own. There was no sound coming through the walls in the house. There was a sweet odor. For a long time Socrates let his mind wander trying to figure out the smell. It was familiar but he couldn't place it.

Finally he realized that the scent was from the tree outside. A window must have been open. It was the thought of an open window that got Socrates to giggle uncontrollably. He hadn't slept next to an open window in over forty years.

7

Over the next three weeks Socrates dropped by Dolly's every day after work. He talked to Bruno and accepted meals in the back house.

"If Bruno live an' I don't go to jail," he promised Dolly, "I'll take him home wit' me and keep'im for my pet."

The trial came four weeks after that declaration.

8

"You're with the Public Defender's Office?" the judge, Katherine Hemp, asked Brenda Marsh.

"Yes, your honor," Brenda replied. "I've just been with them three months now."

"And how does your client plead, Ms. Marsh?" asked Judge Hemp, an older woman with gray hair and sad eyes.

"Not guilty, your honor."

"I don't want to drag this thing out, counselor. I have a full caseload and all we want to know here is if your client assaulted, um," the judge looked down at her notes, "Benheim Lunge."

"I appreciate the court's time, Judge Hemp. I have only three witnesses and each of them has less than forty-five minutes of testimony." Brenda Marsh spoke in her own fashion, as usual, pronouncing each word separately as if it had come in its own individual wrapper. Socrates wondered if Brenda thought that she sounded like a white woman talking like that.

"Benheim Lunge," said the tall young man in the witness seat.

He might have been handsome if it wasn't for the sour twist of his lips.

"... and were you then assaulted by this man?" asked Conrad MacAlister, the pudgy café-au-lait prosecutor.

"Yes sir. He hit me. I'm in good shape but he must have been boxing in that prison or something."

Socrates' eyes wandered over to the jurors' box. They were mostly women and he could see that they were appalled by Lunge's description of his broken nose and whiplash from just one swipe of the ex-convict's fist.

"Thank you, Mr. Lunge." MacAlister smiled at Brenda Marsh. "Your witness."

Brenda Marsh got up purposefully and stalked over to Lunge. "Did you, Mr. Lunge, go up to where the dog lay with a brick in your hand?"

"No."

"I see. Tell me, Mr. Lunge, what is your profession?"

"I sell sporting goods. My father owns a store on Rodeo Drive and I run it."

"So," asked Brenda. "Then you don't have a medical background?"

"No."

"But didn't you tell Mr. Fortlow that the dog was done for and that he should be put out of his suffering? And don't you think it was likely that the defendant thought that you intended to kill the dog with the brick you held?"

"Objection," said Prosecutor MacAlister. "Mr. Lunge has already stated that he didn't have a brick in his hand."

"A stone then?" asked Ms. Marsh. "Did you have a stone, Mr. Lunge?"

"No."

"Did you have anything in your hands when you approached the wounded dog and Mr. Fortlow on Olympic Boulevard?"

"Um, well, I don't remember. I, uh, I might have grabbed a, a, a, you know, a thing, a ten-pound weight I keep in the backseat."

"A ten-pound weight? What was this weight made from?"

"Iron."

"So, you approached Mr. Fortlow with ten pounds of iron in your hand?"

"How was I to know what would happen? For all I knew it was his dog. I wanted to help but I wanted to protect myself too. He looked, well, dangerous. And he was big. I knew I had to stop for hitting the dog but I wanted to protect myself too."

"And did you say that you'd kill the dog with the weight? Didn't you say that you wanted to stop his pain?"

"Absolutely not. I mean I never said that I wanted to kill the dog. I thought he was going to die, though, I mean you should have seen him. He was a mess."

9

"That man right there," said Marjorie Galesky. She was pointing at Benheim Lunge. Dolly Straight had already testified that Socrates Fortlow came to her clinic with the bleeding and crying black dog in his arms. He'd carried the sixty-two-pound dog eleven blocks to get him care.

". . . I was sitting in my front yard," seventy-nine-year-old Mrs. Galesky said, "like always when it's over seventy-two degrees. It was getting colder and I was about to go in when I see this car run over that poor dog. It hit him and then the tires ran over his legs. This man," she said, pointing at Socrates, "the black one, had gone up to help the dog when the other man, the one driving the car, comes running over with a brick in his hand. At least it looked like a brick. They say it was a weight, whatever that means, but it was big and that man came running over with it. He said something to the black man and then he tried to get at the dog. First off the black man pushed the white one and then he hauled off and hit him." The old woman was a few inches under five feet and slight. She looked like an excited child up there on the stand. There was an ancient glee at the memory of the punch. Socrates tried to keep from smiling.

10

"Socrates Fortlow," he answered when asked to identify himself.

"Yes I did," he said when asked if he struck Benheim Lunge. "He hit the dog and drove off for all I knew. I went up and was tryin' to see what I could do when he come up with a chunk'a metal in his hand. He was lookin' all over an' said that it'd be better to put the dog outta his misery. Then he said that he wanted to take the dog in his car. I said I'd go along but he told me that there wasn't room for me an' the dog too. I told him that I'd seen a animal hospital not far and that I'd carry the dog there. He said no. Then I said no. He went for the dog an' he still had the iron in his hand. I put up my hand to stop'im but he just kept comin'. So I hit him once. You know I didn't mean to do all that to him but he wasn't gonna take that dog. Uh-uh."

11

"We find the defendant guilty of assault," the foreman of the jury, a black woman, said. She seemed sorry but that was the decision and she stood with it.

12

While waiting for his sentence Socrates would go to visit Bruno every day. Dolly had made a leash with a basket woven from leather straps to hold Bruno up from behind. If Socrates could heft the dog's backside Bruno found that he could propel himself forward by walking with his front legs.

"You could put a clothesline up around your yard, Mr. Fortlow," Dolly said. "And then attach his basket to it with a pulley. That way he could walk around without you having to help him all the time."

'Yeah," Socrates answered. "Dolly, what you put up behind the ten percent for my bail?"

"The house," she said.

"Uh-huh."

Bruno was leaping from one paw to the other, yelping a little now and then because his hip still hurt, and licking the hands of the two new friends.

"If you run I don't care," Dolly said. "But you have to take Bruno with you."

13

Before the sentencing Brenda Marsh had a long meeting with Socrates. He cursed her and pounded his fist down on the table in the little room that the court let them use.

He refused to do what she asked of him.

"You wanna take ev'rything from me?" he asked her.

"I'm trying to keep you out of jail," she said in her annoying way. "Do you want to go to jail?"

"There's a lotta things I don't want. One of 'em is that I don't get down on my knees to no man, woman, or child."

Brenda Marsh did not respond. It was then that Socrates realized that she was probably a very good lawyer.

14

Three days later, after the celebration for Socrates' suspended sentence at Iula's diner, Socrates went to his house with Right Burke, the maimed WWII veteran. They sat in Socrates' poor kitchen while Bruno lay on the floor laughing and licking the air.

"I hate it, Right. I hate it."

"You free, ain't ya?"

"Yeah, but I wake up mad as shit every day."

Brenda Marsh had set up a private meeting with Judge Hemp. She'd pleaded for Socrates' freedom. But the judge said that he'd been found guilty and what could she do?

That's when Brenda revealed her plan for Socrates to apologize to the court, to Benheim Lunge, and to the community. He'd promise to write a letter to be posted on the bus stop where he'd assaulted Benheim and to go to Benheim and ask his pardon. He'd make himself available to the juvenile court to talk to young black children and tell them how he had gone wrong but that he wouldn't do it again.

He'd do an extra fifty hours of community service and for that they could suspend his sentence.

"But you free, Socco. Free, man," said Right, his best friend. "That gal did you a favor. 'Cause you know she musta begged that judge. You know after that big trial they just had the court wanna put ev'ry black man they can in the can. Shit. Guilty? Go *straight* to jail!"

"But you know it's just 'cause'a the dog, Right. It's just 'cause'a the dog I said yeah."

"How's that?"

"He needs me out here. Him and Darryl and you too, brother. I ain't gonna help nobody in that jail cell or on the run. You know

I woulda let them take that white girl's house if it wasn't that I had obligations."

The dog barked suddenly and put his nose out to be scratched.

"You just a lucky fool, Socrates Fortlow," Right said.

"You got that right, man. I'm a fool to be who I am and I'm lucky I made it this far. Me an' this black dog here. Shit. Me an this black dog."